A Touch of Deceit

Gary Ponzo

To Jennifer, Jessica, and Kyle. All that matters.

Chapter 1

There was a time when Nick Bracco would walk down Gold Street late at night and young vandals would scatter. The law was present and the guilty took cover. West Baltimore was alive with crime, but Gold Street remained quarantined, reserved for the dirtiest of the dirty. That's how Nick remembered it anyway. Before he left for the Bureau to fight terrorists. Now, the narrow corridor of row houses felt closer to him and the slender strip of buckled sidewalk echoed his footsteps like a sentry announcing his presence. It wasn't his turf anymore. He was a foreigner.

Nick scrutinized the landscape and searched for something out of place. The battered cars seemed right, the graffiti, even the shadows seemed to darken the proper corners. But something was missing. There were no lookouts on the concrete stairwells. The ubiquitous bass line of hip-hop was absent. The stillness reminded him of jungle birds falling silent in the prelude to danger. The only comfort came from the matching footsteps beside him. As usual, Matt McColm was by his side. They'd been partners for ten years and were approaching the point of finishing each other's sentences.

"You're awfully quiet," Matt said.

"Did I mention that I don't have a good feeling about this?"

"Uh huh." Matt tightened his collar against the autumn chill and worked a piece of gum with his jaw. "That's your theme song."

"Really? Don't you ever get a bad feeling about a call?"

"All the time."

"How come you never tell me?"

"I'm going to feed the flames of paranoia?"

They walked a little further in silence. It got darker with every step. The number of working streetlights dwindled.

"Did you just call me paranoid?" Nick said.

Matt looked straight ahead as he walked. His casual demeanor caused him to appear aloof, but Nick knew better. Even at halfmast, Matt's eyes were alert and aware.

"Maybe paranoid is too strong a word," Matt said.

"I would hope so."

"More like Mother-henish."

"That's better," Nick said. "By the way, did you eat your broccoli tonight?"

"Yes, Dear."

Their pace slowed as they got deeper into the projects. Low-lying clouds gave the night a claustrophobic feel.

"This guy asked for you specifically?" Matt said.

Nick nodded.

"That bother you a little?" Matt asked.

"No," Nick said. "That bothers me a lot."

Up ahead, a parked car jostled. They both stopped. Neither of them spoke. They split up. By the book. Years of working together coming into play. Matt crouched and crept into the street. Nick stayed on the sidewalk and gave the car a wide berth. In seconds Matt became invisible. The car maintained a spastic rhythm. It was subtle, but Nick understood the familiar motion even before he flashed his penlight into the backseat and saw a pair of young eyes pop up through the grimy window. They were wide open and reacted like a jewel thief caught with a handful of pearls. The kid's hair was disheveled and his shirt was half off. His panting breath had caused the inside of the window to fog up. He wasn't alone. A pair of bare legs straddled his torso.

From the other side of the vehicle, Matt emerged from the shadows and charged the car with his pistol out front. He was just a few yards away when Nick held up his hand and said, "No."

Matt stopped dead, seeing the grin on Nick's face and realizing the situation. He slowly holstered his Glock and took time to catch his breath.

Nick heard the kid's voice through the closed window. "I ain't doing nuthin', man."

Nick clicked off his penlight and slipped it back into his jacket. He smiled. "It may be nothing, but you sure worked up a sweat doing it."

When Matt fell back in step with his partner, Nick said, "You seemed a little . . . uh, paranoid?"

Matt returned to nonchalant mode. "Kids that young shouldn't be doing the nasty out in the street."

"Consider their role models," Nick said. "You can't change the tide with an oar."

"Pardon me, Professor Bracco. Who said that one — Nietzsche?"

"I just made it up."

"It sounded like it."

They slowed their pace until Nick stopped in front of an old brick building with a worn, green awning above the entrance. He gestured down a dark flight of stairs where a giant steel door stood menacingly secure. "There it is."

Matt nodded. "You bring me to all the best spots."

When he was certain of their solitude, Nick descended the stairs. Matt followed, keeping an eye on their rear. In the darkness, Nick barely made out Matt's silhouette.

"Listen," Nick said, "it'll be easier if we don't have to use our creds, but let's see how it goes. I don't want to say any more than I have to, and you say nothing at all. Just be the silent brute that you are. Capisce?"

"Understood."

"If we get lucky, I'll see a familiar face." Nick raised his fist, hovered it in front of the door, then stopped to sniff the air. "You wearing aftershave?"

"A little."

"You have a date after this?"

"Uh huh."

"When?"

"Midnight."

"Who makes a date with you at midnight?"

"Veronica Post."

"First date?"

"Yup."

"At midnight?"

"She's a waitress. She doesn't get off until then."

In the murky darkness, Nick sighed. He turned to face the door, and just like a thousand times before, he said, "Ready?"

He couldn't see the response, but he heard Matt unfasten the flap to his holster. Matt was ready.

Nick used his wedding band hand to pound on the metal door. He shifted his weight as they waited. Nick heard Matt chewing his gum.

Nick said, "Midnight, huh?"

A rectangular peephole slid open allowing just enough light through to see a dark face peering out. The face was so large the opening supported only enough room for one of his eyes.

"Yeah?" the man grunted.

Nick leaned close to the opening so the man could see his face. The opening quickly slid shut.

They stood in the silence while Nick thought of his next move.

"He seemed nice," Matt said.

The clang of locks unbolting was followed by the door squeaking open. It reminded Nick of an old horror movie.

The large black man wore a large black shirt that hung over his jeans and covered enough space to hide a rocket launcher. The man ignored Nick and gave Matt the once over.

Matt gave him the stone cold glare of a pissed-off FBI agent. No one did it better.

Then the man turned his attention to Nick. His head was round and clean-shaven. His expressionless face seemed to be set in cement.

Nick spread open his hands and raised his eyebrows. "Well?"

The man's face slowly softened, then worked its way into a full out smile. "Where the fuck you been, Bracco?" He engulfed Nick into a giant bear hug, momentarily lifting him off of his feet.

Nick patted the beast a couple of times on the back and slid down to face him. "I can't believe you still work here." He gestured to Matt, "This here is Matt McColm. Matt, this is Truth."

Truth nodded to Matt, then slapped Nick on the shoulder. "Last time I saw you, you were still with the Western."

"It's been a decade."

"Wow, seems like just yesterday you'd come in and drag Woody to G.A. meetings."

Nick grinned. He looked over the big man's shoulder to the solid green door that Truth guarded. Beyond the fireproof frame was a large, unfinished basement filled with poker tables. This time of night the tables would be surrounded by chiropractors, strippers, tax accountants, firefighters and probably even a couple of cops from Nick's old beat. A mixture of cigar and cigarette smoke would be lingering just below the fluorescents.

"How's the crowd?" Nick asked.

"Not too bad. You want a seat?"

Nick shook his head. "I'd scare them all off. You know I'm with the Feds now?"

Truth frowned. "You don't come around for ten years and the first thing you think to do is insult me?"

Nick stood silent and waited.

"We may be compulsive gamblers," Truth explained, "but we're not illiterates. I read the story. Local boy makes good."

Nick held up a hand. "Hold on. Don't believe everything you read in the rags."

"Since when is Newsweek a rag?"

Nick shrugged. "Sometimes the legend exceeds the facts."

Truth waved a thick finger back and forth between the two agents. "He's the partner. They called you two the Dynamic Duo or the A-Team or some shit."

Nick said nothing.

Truth snapped his large fingers. "Dream Team. That's it. I knew it was something like that. You two dug up some kind of terrorist cell planning to waste the Washington Monument. Isn't that right?"

He pointed to Nick. "According to the article, you the brains and he's the muscle."

Matt stood stone-faced.

"The way you say it," Nick said. "It makes my partner here sound like a bimbo with large biceps. Look at him. Does he look like he pumps iron?"

Truth examined Matt's long, thin frame and shook his head. "Nope. So he must be good with a 9."

"Precisely. He's the FBI's sharp-shooting champ three years running."

Truth smiled. "You two aren't here to raid the place, I know that much. They wouldn't send that much talent for this old joint."

"Come on, Truth." Nick said. "This is a landmark. My father used to play here. I'd rather see it turned into a museum first."

Truth's smile transformed into something approaching concern. "And you're not here to play poker either?"

Nick shook his head.

"Then it must be business."

Nick stood motionless and let the big man put it all together.

Truth looked at Nick, but nodded toward Matt. "You wouldn't bring the cowboy unless you felt a need for backup. Something I should know?"

Nick thought about how much he should tell him. He trusted Truth as much as any civilian.

"I'm not sure," Nick said. "I need to see Ray Seville. Is he still playing?"

"Seville? Yeah, he's back there making his usual donations. What do you want with a weasel like him?"

"He called the field office and left a message for me to meet him here."

Truth smiled. "The snitch strikes again."

"Maybe," Nick said.

Matt cleared his throat in a forced fashion.

"Oh yeah," Nick said. "Matt's in a bit of a hurry. He's got a date tonight."

Truth engaged Matt's hardened face again, only this time Matt threw in a wink.

Truth smiled and held out his hand, "All right then, gents. Hand them over and I'll get Ray for you."

Nick cringed.

Matt glared at his partner. "You can't be serious?"

Truth didn't budge. His palm remained open while his fingertips flexed impatiently.

"Truth," Nick said. "Is that really necessary?"

Truth looked at Matt this time. In a tone that denoted overuse, he said, "A long time ago there was a shootout in the parlor. A couple of drunks got carried away during a tight hand. The drunks were Baltimore PD. Fortunately, they were more drunk than cops that night and neither one got hurt too bad. When one of their fellow officers was called to the scene, he came down hard. Even though the two drunk cops were his senior, he was someone everyone respected and they obeyed his commands. Back then he made a rule: if Lloyd's was going to stay open it had to be firearm free. No exceptions. The mayor, the governor. No one."

Truth took his time to look back at Nick. "Do you remember who that cop was?"

Nick nodded, reluctantly. "Me."

"Bingo," Truth smiled.

Nick fished the 9mm from his holster and handed it to Truth. He looked at Matt and shrugged. "Sorry, I forgot."

Truth took Nick's gun and shoved it into the abyss under his oversized tee shirt. He looked at Matt and kept his hand out. "It's only out of respect that I don't pat you down," Truth said. "I trust Nick."

Matt moaned while removing his Glock. "Forgot, my ass."

"Relax, Truth has our back until we're done here. Right, Truth?"

"Fifteen years," Truth said. "No one's got by me yet." He gestured for them to follow and he stopped after only a few steps. He pointed to an open door and said, "Wait in there and I'll get him for you."

Before entering the room, they watched Truth walk down the hall and open the green door. As he pulled the door shut behind him, a burst of cigar smoke escaped along the ceiling and crept toward the front door. Nick followed Matt into the small sitting room and remained standing. Matt eased onto a dingy green sofa, rested his elbows on his knees and clasped his hands together.

The room was a windowless twelve-by-twelve with two corduroy sofas facing each other. Between the sofas was a carved up oak coffee table that wobbled without ever being touched. The only light came from a pair of bare fluorescent bulbs that hung from a cracked ceiling.

"I'm just glad you didn't agree to wear a blindfold," Matt said. "We would have missed this beautiful decor."

"Calm down," Nick said. "I wouldn't want you to be uptight for Valerie."

"Veronica."

"Right."

Nick paced while Matt tapped his fingertips.

Nick heard the green door open. Truth was followed by a wiry man with deep pockets under his eyes. He wore a baseball cap with the brim twisted to the side.

Nick gestured for him to sit down.

Truth said, "I'll be right outside if you need me," then pulled the door shut behind him.

Ray Seville sank into the couch across from Matt and pulled a mangled pack of cigarettes from his jeans pocket. He flipped open a pack of matches and flicked one against the striker. He sucked the cigarette to life, then shook the match and pointed the extinguished stick at Matt. "Who's he?"

Matt glared.

"He's my partner," Nick said.

"I thought I left a message for you to come alone."

"He's my partner. He goes where I go."

"Yeah, well, how do I know I can trust him?"

"How do you know you can trust me?"

Seville managed a meager grin. "Aw, come on. Me and you, we have history."

"History?" Nick said. "I arrested you half a dozen times working Gold Street."

Seville waved the back of his hand. "Yeah, but you was always straight with me. A lot of other cops were pure bullshit. Tell me one thing, then come at me from a different angle two minutes later."

Nick sighed. "Listen, Ray, I'm not with the Western anymore. You want to roll over on one of your buddies, I'll call a shoe and get him to meet you somewhere safe. Not down here in the basement of Lloyd's poker house."

Seville took another drag of his cigarette and looked past Nick at Matt still leaning forward, elbows on his knees, "What's his problem?"

"I told you, he's my partner."

"Doesn't he know how to speak?"

"He's just here to intimidate."

"Intimidate? Intimidate who?"

The guy was a pure idiot. Nick wondered how Ray survived among the predators that prowled West Baltimore on a nightly basis. Nick glanced at his watch and said, "Ray, where are we going here?"

Seville stared at the hardwood floor while the flimsy ash danced between his feet. "A couple of weeks ago I get a call from this guy asking me for a phony drivers license."

"How did he know to call you?" Nick asked.

"I dunno. Maybe somebody told him. Stop being a cop for a second and listen."

Nick folded his arms.

"Well, anyway, I meet him and get the info he wants me to use on the license. I usually ask some questions to see what I'm getting myself into, but this guy cuts me off before I can even start. I never been eye-fucked like that before."

Seville took another drag of his cigarette and pointed to Matt. "Is he like your trained monkey or what?"

Nick stretched out his arm and held Matt back as he came out of his seat, then he admonished Ray with a stare that forced his attention back to the floorboards.

Ray's cigarette slowly shrank between his index and middle finger. "Shit, the guy was talking to me like I was a moron, telling me over and over where to make the drop. How long to wait. I look like I just fell off the turnip truck?"

Nick let that one go.

"He asked me everything under the sun, except if I know how to make a good dupe. I mean shit, the guy didn't even haggle with my rate." Ray dropped the cigarette stub to the floor and twisted it with his shoe. He blew out a lungful of smoke and seemed to be looking at something off in the distance. "He's not from around here, I'd know. He's a foreigner. He's got some kind of accent, like one of those Iraqis you used to see interviewed on the news during the war. You know, one of those guys you always knew was lying just by his accent."

Nick massaged his forehead. He could feel his arteries begin to constrict. "Let me get this straight," Nick said. "You called for a meeting with the FBI because you forged a fake ID for someone with a Middle Eastern accent? Is that right?"

Ray seemed to absorb what had just happened. "When you say it like that it makes me sound like I'm wasting your time or something."

Nick waited and watched Ray shift around on the sofa. Finally, Nick said, "What are you not telling me?"

Ray looked up at Nick with a wrinkled forehead. It seemed as if he was trying to decipher the genetic code to the double helix.

"Isn't that enough?" Ray said. "I mean, I already told you he's a foreigner with an illegal drivers license. Shit, what else does a guy have to do to get arrested?"

Nick tried to figure out why someone like Ray would rat on anyone without motivation.

"You're just being a good citizen, is that it?" Nick said.

"That too hard to believe?"

"Look, Ray, do you know why you're a lousy poker player?"

"Huh?"

"Because you have a tell. Every time you're bluffing you look to your right." Nick pointed over his shoulder, "The guys inside don't know why you do it, they just know it's a tell. You look to your right, you're bluffing. Me, I know why you do it. It's because you're using the right side of your brain to think. The creative side. Like right now, you're looking over my left shoulder. You're getting creative with your memory. Don't do it, Ray. For once in your life, tell me the truth."

Ray stared blankly at Nick. "Are you shittin' me? All this time I got a tell and nobody says nothing?"

"Are you going to tell me what really happened, Ray?"

Nick waited while Ray grappled with the chore ahead of him. Possibly dealing with the truth. Ray nodded to himself. With his head still hung low, he said, "I lent my car to my buddy Skeeter yesterday. It was the last time I saw him."

"He's missing?"

Ray shook his head. "Gone."

"Gone?"

"He was blown to smithereens trying to start my car."

Nick and Matt exchanged glances.

"The guy warned me about following him and I didn't exactly listen. I was curious. I thought maybe I could scam some juice from him if I told him I knew who he was."

Nick let out a breath. "Now we're getting to it, aren't we? You tried to shakedown someone out of your league and you want us to save your greedy ass."

Ray looked bewildered. "No, no, it's not like that."

Nick slid a hand over his face and squeezed his eyelids until he saw stars, then he focused on the wiry mess sitting in front of him. "All right, Ray, who is he?"

"That's just it, I don't know exactly."

"But you were going to try and extort money from him."

"Now you got it," Ray said. "Guy like that's got to have a big identity." He looked around the room for support, back and forth between stone-faced Matt and Nick. "Doesn't he?" Ray finished.

The room was silent for a moment, allowing the slower brain cells to catch up. Finally, Nick said, "All right, Ray. Why don't we start with what he looks like."

"Pretty average I'd say."

Nick blinked. "Ray."

"All right, all right. He was a little taller than me, about five-eleven, dark hair . . . shit, what am I doing?" Ray shoved his bony fingers into his jeans pockets and yanked out a folded piece of paper and handed it to Nick. "There he is. I made a copy of the photo before I gave it back to him."

Nick slowly unfolded the paper, hoping for a lucky break. He didn't get one.

Nick tossed the paper into Matt's lap and watched his partner's eyes go dark with anger.

"Who is it?" Ray said.

Nick said nothing. He had too many neurons firing all at once. The last time he saw Rashid Baser was eight months ago in a small village just outside of Istanbul. Rashid was lying on the ground with his hand pressed to his ear to stop the bleeding. Matt had fired a remarkable shot from one hundred fifty yards, allowing them to escape one of Rashid's ambushes.

It was Nick's job to expect the unexpected, but Rashid Baser in Baltimore was pushing the limits. Even for someone as brash as Rashid.

Nick looked down at Ray and thought he saw fear in his ignorant eyes. "How did he get in touch with you?"

"I told you, he called me."

"Where? At home?"

"No, on my cell."

"How did he get the number?"

"Shit, I don't know. I couldn't get the guy to tell me nothing, man." Ray looked up at Nick again and said, "Who is he?"

Nick let out a deep breath. "His name is Rashid Baser."

Ray sank lower into the couch, getting swallowed up by the worn-out cushions. In a small voice, he said, "He dangerous?"

Nick frowned. He thought about telling Ray that Rashid was the world's greatest explosives expert. That he could turn a wristwatch into a bomb with little more than what you'd find in a typical shed. That he was an assassin. Maybe the purest human hunter on the planet. Instead, he said, "Yes, Ray, he's dangerous."

"He . . . uh . . . Al-Qaeda?" Ray asked.

Nick rolled his eyes. He wished Rashid was a mindless Al Qaeda pawn. Someone who was just smart enough to take orders and just dumb enough to follow them. No, this was a real, shrewd threat. A bonafide hands-on terrorist who would manage to slip a snake into your pants pocket and then ask you for change.

"No," Nick said. "He's Kurdish. He's not one of these guys that hides out in a cave and draws plans in the dirt. He does everything himself. And he's good at what he does. Maybe the best."

"What does he do?"

Nick was deep in thought. Rashid Baser. What would Rashid be doing here? He looked over at Matt and saw the same question going across his face.

"You think he came all the way here just for revenge?" Matt asked.

Nick shook his head. Partly because he didn't believe it. Partly because he didn't want to believe it.

"You said he's the best," Ray said. "The best what?"

"He kills people," Nick said. "He's good with a gun, but prefers to work with blades."

"Blades?"

"Yes, blades."

Ray involuntarily rubbed his neck.

"Exactly."

Nick was pacing now, gathering speed as he went. "Do you want to know the most dangerous thing about Rashid Baser? He's Kemel Kharrazi's best friend. They grew up together in Southeastern Turkey."

Ray swallowed.

"That's right, that Kemel Kharrazi. The one whose name makes serial killers sleep with the light on. So let's cut the crap, Ray. Are you positive this is the guy you saw?"

"What do you want from me?" Ray pleaded. "I swear I'm not lying to you."

Nick nodded. He grabbed the copy of the photo from Matt and examined it closely. The image was grainy, but it certainly appeared to be Rashid. Nick thought it looked to be taken about five years ago. Rashid was still wearing a mustache. He thought of something.

"Ray," Nick said, "what did he look like when you met with him? Any different than this photo?"

Ray appeared serious, as if he were adding numbers in his head. "Yeah, he wasn't wearing no mustache when I saw him."

"Is that all?"

"And . . . and . . . he was missing part of his left ear. Looked like he lost it in a fight or something. Pretty ugly."

"Great," Nick said, now certain that Rashid Baser was actually on American soil. He turned to see Matt sitting there feeling his empty holster, looking like a boy who'd left his fly open.

"We've got to get out of here," Matt said, looking at the four cement walls that contained them.

"No shit," Nick said.

Ray looked lost.

Nick crouched down and pulled up on Ray's chin until their eyes were inches apart. "What did you do, Ray? Did he pay you to set us up?"

"Huh?"

"Look, Ray, I know you're stupid, but you don't have to overdo it."

Seville's face tightened with confusion.

"Ray. He tried to kill you. He knows you made him. You don't think he's going to finish the job? You think he forgot about you?

What if he followed you here and saw two FBI agents waltz in behind you? Especially agents who specialize in counterterrorism. Faces he knows."

Seville's eyes widened with recognition, like someone who just remembered he'd left the stove on.

"You think you were tagged, Ray?"

Seville just stared.

Until the explosion broke the silence.

Chapter 2

The sound came from the outer hallway. It wasn't the searing blast of a bomb destroying the building, but the muted pop of Semtex ripping apart the hinges of a steel door. Nick knew that the next thing he'd hear would be the thump of that big piece of steel slamming into the corridor. He also knew that Truth would be hustling furiously toward his demise. Which was exactly how it happened. Nick heard a couple of coughs from a silencer, then all three hundred pounds of Truth hit the floor heavy.

By now the red light in the poker room would be flashing, signaling a breach in the entrance. Everyone would scurry out the back exit for fear of being caught in a raid.

Nick searched for a way out, but saw nothing. He knew what it felt like to be trapped inside of a coffin. Nick glanced down at his cell phone. No reception. He looked at Matt and saw him examining his phone. He shook his head. Their service was being jammed.

Matt stood up and grasped his holster as if it could grow another gun. He stared at the solitary exit from the basement room. A rickety oak door that hung there more from habit than sound construction.

There was a tap on the door. It sounded exactly what the muzzle of a gun would sound like against brittle oak. A man's voice came from the other side. It was soft, but firm, with a hint of an accent. "Raymond."

The only noise was the hum of the fluorescent lights.

"Raymond, it's not you I want. Just tell me if they're armed and I'll let you go untouched. It's the only way you'll leave here alive."

"It's him," Ray murmured.

Nick put a finger to his lips. Matt was on his knees quietly twisting off a leg of the coffee table.

"Raymond," the voice said. "Don't be a fool. These are not men worth dying for."

Nick watched Seville carefully. The guy was actually thinking about it. He saw it in his eyes. Seville blurted, "They're un—"

Matt reached him first. His uppercut smacked Ray hard under the chin. Seville's head jerked back, and his body instantly became a rag doll against the pillow of the sofa.

"Raymond?" came the voice on the other side of the door.

There was silence while Matt went back to work on the leg of the table. Nick saw him twisting the wooden dowel, but it was like watching from an out-of-body experience. A silent vacuum seemed to suck all of the oxygen from the room. Anxiety tightened its grip around Nick's neck and forced him to remain still for fear of falling down. He was slipping away again.

A vision flashed across Nick's mind. It was the image of a lipstick kiss his wife left for him on the mirror that morning. It hung there like the single digit sum to the chalkboard-crammed equation of his life. The kiss said everything that needed to be said. Suddenly, the floor seemed to be moving and he realized it was his legs wobbling beneath him.

"Nicholas," the assassin said, breaking into Nick's death dream. "I found two guns on the black man's corpse. We both know who they belong to."

Matt freed the wooden leg and motioned with his hand, encouraging Nick to engage the killer in some dialog. The lipstick kiss evaporated.

"Nicholas," Rashid said. "Is that your partner with you? Matthew?"

Rashid's voice jarred him back to consciousness. The evil seeped through the door like toxic waste.

Nick's heart felt as if it would burst through his chest. He forced himself to concentrate. He wasn't about to accommodate his assassin with any concessions.

"Nicholas, you may as well speak. They will most certainly be your last words."

Nick instantly went from resignation to anger. Fury built up inside of him like a bolt of adrenalin. He could practically see Rashid's teeth showing through his shark-like grin.

"Rashid," Nick said, "wipe that smile off your face."

A small chuckle from behind the door. "Nicholas, I should have killed you in Istanbul."

"You didn't kill me in Istanbul because you couldn't," Nick said. "Just like now."

A pop. The silenced bullet shot through the door and buzzed past Nick's ear. Both agents hit the floor, their heads only a couple of feet apart. They scurried behind the sofa across from Ray.

"He's being cautious," Matt whispered. "We got lucky once. He won't make that mistake again."

"Or he's relishing the moment," Nick said. "Prolonging the pleasure."

"Whatever he's doing, we've got thirty seconds, maybe sixty if he's in a sporting mood."

Nick nodded. He pointed to the door. "How does he come in? Heavy or slow?"

"He busts through, dives right and shoots around the room starting from his right."

"Agreed."

Another pop. This time the sound was louder. He was alternating guns. The bullet passed through the dilapidated sofa with little resistance. Rashid had them. Without return fire, he would be on top of them in a matter of moments.

Matt gripped the table leg and got to a knee. He pointed at the door. "I'll wait for him to barge through. He'll see me first and fire, but I might get one swing in. It's our only chance."

Nick shook his head. "No. It's suicide."

"Of course it's suicide. What, you think I was going to beat Rashid with a stick against his two guns?"

Nick thought a moment. Two guns. "You're right. He's got a gun in each hand."

"Now you're catching on. That's why you're the brains of the team."

"How's he going to turn the doorknob with a gun in each hand?"

Matt blinked. "What difference does that make? You see that thing? It's barely hanging on its hinges."

"Exactly," Nick said, his voice growing stronger with each cogent thought. "He rams into that door with any momentum at all and it will give way."

The both of them stared at the door.

"Nicholas," Rashid's voice sounded impatient.

"Okay," Matt whispered. "What if I remove the hinges?"

"Yes," Nick said. "He leans into it and it comes straight down. Rashid won't expect it and for a moment, he'll be exposed. Just a moment."

Again a bullet spit through the flimsy door and this one plunged into Ray Seville's chest. By the amount of blood hemorrhaging through his shirt, Nick could tell that the bullet had found his heart. The poor bastard never saw it coming.

Nick turned to Matt. "That's precisely how much time you get. One moment. Don't miss."

Matt's eyes had a glimmer of hope. As he crawled to the door with the table leg, he looked back and said, "Keep his attention toward you."

Great, Nick thought. Just what he wanted to do. He shimmied to the left and cupped his hand over his mouth, aiming his voice to the left. "Rashid, where's your friend, Kharrazi?"

As he'd hoped, the bullet missed to his left this time. It cracked through the frail sofa like it was made out of balsa wood. He rose up to see Matt working on the bolt in the top hinge of the door. He couldn't tell what he was using. A pen? It appeared to be moving.

"Nicholas," Rashid said. "Let's be reasonable men. Open the door and I will make it quick. You and your partner will never feel a thing. You have my word."

Matt had the first bolt in his hand now and was working on the middle one.

"That's a fascinating offer," Nick said. "Can I get that in writing?"

There was silence. Nick cursed his use of sarcasm. He took short, quick breaths and waited for the worst. Matt pried loose the middle hinge, applying pressure on the door to keep it upright.

An onslaught of bullets blitzed into the small room forcing Nick to cover his head and duck below the sofa. He squeezed his eyes shut as he got peppered with shards of splintered wood and fabric. The spray of debris was so dense, it actually heated up the room. He knew that the barrage was tantamount to the finale of a Fourth of July fireworks display. Rashid was simply clearing the way for his grand entrance. It would be all over very soon now.

There was a pause. In the silence, the room seemed to creak from duress. When Nick opened his eyes, it was dark. For a split second he thought he'd finally caught a fatal shot. Then he realized that one of the bullets had popped the fluorescents and left them in complete blackness. It was something Nick would have done himself had he been thinking clearly. Which he wasn't.

He couldn't see Matt, just the filtered light that outlined the doorframe and two tight circles created by the bullet holes. Nick had to make sure Rashid burst through the door with his shoulder. He couldn't afford to have the terrorist become cautious and test the doorknob. He wanted to give his partner a signal and let him know Rashid was coming, but in the darkness it had to be verbal. He prayed that Matt was finished with the hinges.

Nick took a deep breath and shouted. "Hey, Rashid. How's that ear of yours doing?"

It was the equivalent of waving a red flag in front of a snorting bull. And it worked. An instant later the door toppled straight down with a thud and the assassin stood frozen in the doorway. He was leaning backward and off-balance. It was human nature to recoil from the unexpected. But Rashid Baser was more animal than human, so when Matt came out of the dark with the table leg, he was a step too late. Rashid caught the dowel with his forearm and deflected the blow.

Rashid and Matt were clutched in a fierce embrace. Matt had done the smart thing and wrapped himself around Rashid before the assassin could fire either gun.

Nick needed to get to Rashid, but his legs were lead weights. He lurched forward and focused on the only thing his eyes could see — Rashid's silencer. It was loosely aimed at Nick, but Rashid was too busy dancing the violent shuffle with Matt. Both of them were up against the wall, head-butting each other back and forth.

Just as Nick was about to reach out for the gun, Rashid found him and aimed at his head. Nick was no more than three feet away, but he might as well have been on the moon. He wasn't going to reach the gun in time.

Rashid's lip curled upward and his face glowed with anticipation. His arm was fully extended now and marksman straight.

Nick sucked a quick breath.

Rashid pulled the trigger.

Nick's legs faltered as his entire body seemed to spasm.

Rashid pulled the trigger again and again.

The lipstick kiss flashed across Nick's mind as he waited to collapse. Only he couldn't feel the shot. Was this how it happened? Was his body protecting him from the pain and sending him into shock?

When he looked up, he realized that Rashid's silencer wasn't spitting out bullets. There was just the small click of the hammer behind an empty chamber. Rashid had committed the killer's mortal sin. He'd lost count of his rounds. Maybe he thought he didn't need to know. He'd had two guns and plenty of time to reload. Maybe Nick had infuriated him enough to hasten his entry into the room.

Either way, Nick was still breathing. While he murmured words of gratitude, his partner kneed Rashid in the groin. The terrorist grunted like a prizefighter and hunched over. Matt used his height advantage to stay on top of him. They seemed to merge into one entity as they took short, quick steps to support their upright wrestling match. Neither could afford to be the one who fell first.

Nick saw Matt's gun on the floor behind Rashid. The assassin must have dropped it in the struggle. Nick was about to scramble for it when he heard a wild shriek.

It was Matt.

Rashid had clenched Matt's ear between his teeth. He twisted and pulled on the cartilage until Matt's ear looked like silly putty. Rashid was about to pull it completely off when Nick reached down and picked up the wooden table leg. He had a clear shot at Rashid's head and he swung hard. The thick, wooden dowel reverberated in Nick's hands as he connected across the back of Rashid's head.

Rashid dropped to the floor. Nick grabbed the gun and placed his foot on Rashid's neck. He heard Matt behind him gasping and muttering curses.

Nick pointed the 9mm at Rashid's nose, only a couple of feet below him. "Just give me a reason," he said. "I misinterpret one of your blinks and it's goodnight, Rashid."

Matt came around Nick with a pair of handcuffs. He rolled Rashid on his side and yanked the handcuffs onto the assassin's wrists until Rashid's face couldn't hide the pain.

"You fight like a fucking girl," Matt huffed, bringing his blood-spotted hand down from his ear.

Rashid glared up at Nick with rattlesnake eyes. "You think this is it? You think this is the end?"

Nick didn't speak. He felt an anxiety attack tightening his chest. Shit, not another episode. Not now. He didn't dare give away his condition, though. He handed Matt his gun back and said, "Here, I'm afraid I'll shoot the bastard."

"You think he won't come after you?" Rashid spat, saliva spewing from tight lips.

"I don't know," Nick said, trying to appear nonchalant even though his entire body trembled. "I've got bigger fish to fry."

In a deliberately soft tone, Rashid said, "There is no one bigger than Kemel Kharrazi. And that is who you just brought upon yourself. You are now the target, Nicholas. No one else, just you. Are you prepared for that?"

But Nick barely heard him. He stepped around the shell casings and headed outside to slip away on his own. Maybe weather the panic attack before the place was swarming with FBI agents. Nick already knew the questions that would be asked and he was already tired of answering them.

As he approached the open doorway, Nick saw Truth's body flat on his back, eyes shocked open. There were three bullet holes in his chest directly over his heart. Nick was relieved to know he went fast. He knelt down and touched Truth's face with his fingertips. There was nothing to say. He could not have felt any more helpless than he did at that moment.

Sirens closed fast from two separate directions. The press would have a great time portraying America as a safer place because of Rashid's capture. But Nick knew better. There was something much more malicious going on. Rashid Baser didn't go through all the trouble to sneak into the United States to exact revenge on a single FBI agent. It wouldn't stop the press though. At least in the short-term. They'll raise the freedom flag high and swagger with delight. In the world of terrorism, there was no one bigger than Rashid Baser. No one.

Except Kemel Kharrazi.

Chapter 3

Nick left Dr. Alan Morgan's office on Pratt Street just after noon. It was three days since the shootout and regulation mandated a session with a professional counselor whenever bullets left a chamber. The affected had seventy-two hours to complete the session. Matt went first, then waited in the car for his partner. Nick's session took longer than Matt's. There was too much psychological damage to go over in just one visit, so Nick agreed to return when the time was right. Which meant never.

Nick got in the car and started the engine. He drove a gray Ford sedan with soot clinging so masterfully to its exterior it appeared to create a designer pattern. This was not born out of neglect as much as an attempt to blend in.

He drove west on Pennsylvania Avenue toward the Baltimore field office. Matt sat in the passenger seat with an open lunch box on his lap. He held up an apple and inspected it like he was about to dust it for prints.

"What kind of apple is this?" Matt asked.

"How am I supposed to know?" Nick said.

"You do talk to your wife at night, don't you?"

"Yeah?"

"Well, don't you tell her what I like and don't like?"

"Listen, do you know why she makes you lunch whenever I have any kind of doctors appointment?"

"Why?"

"Because, she thinks you'll sit in that waiting area eating lunch while I'm getting my teeth cleaned and you'll protect me from terrorists that might barge in and try to kill me."

"Are you serious?" Matt chuckled.

Nick nodded. "However, what she doesn't know is that you sit in the car and read Playboy, so if a terrorist ever did come in you'd have a hard-on so big you'd probably sit there with a smirk on your face and point directly to the office I was in."

Matt took a bite from the apple and chewed slowly. "Playboy has excellent interviews."

Nick rolled his eyes. He stopped the car at a light and hung his elbow out the window.

"What's this meeting about?" Nick asked.

"All I know is, it's a Red Ball special, and nothing good ever comes out of a Red Ball."

A young black kid wearing a Baltimore Orioles baseball cap approached the car holding a stack of newspapers. "Wanna paper, Mister?"

Nick reached for his wallet, pulled out a five-dollar bill and handed it to the kid. "Are you an Orioles fan?"

The kid handed him a copy of the Baltimore Sun, "You bet." He dug his hands into his pocket for change.

"That's okay, keep it," Nick said.

"Thanks, Officer," the kid smiled, then wandered toward the next car in line.

Matt laughed. "We may as well have a siren on the roof."

Nick glanced at the front page. A soldier poked his head out from a U.S. tank surrounded by a mob of angry Turkish civilians. Their faces were twisted into sinister shapes. Their mouths open, assaulting the soldier with venomous emissions, while a U.S. flag burned in the background. Nick dropped the newspaper onto Matt's lap and accelerated through the intersection. "Looks like the boys are getting a warm welcome in Turkey."

Matt gripped the paper and shook his head. "They don't belong there in the first place."

"You know that and I know that, but try telling that to the president's pollsters."

"The Kurds have every right to fight back. Just because Turkey is part of NATO, doesn't mean we should always side with them."

"It's all politics," Nick said. "The Turks slaughter thousands of innocent Kurds and when the Kurds retaliate, we show up and claim that innocent Turks are being killed. Shit, everyone's innocent." He turned to Matt, "Except you."

Matt gave him an aw-shucks grin. It reminded Nick of the night they'd met nine years earlier when Matt was still a sharpshooter with the FBI's SWAT team. Matt chose to purchase a 10mm semiautomatic pistol with his own funds and had an opportunity to use it that night while leaving a bar in West Baltimore. He saw a man in a blue FBI windbreaker crouched behind a Volkswagen, dodging shots from another man crouched three cars ahead of him. The man in the FBI windbreaker was Nick. It was his first year with the Bureau, and he'd found himself chasing down a wily gun smuggler by himself.

Across the street, Matt had acquired a perfect angle. From thirty yards away he blew out the right kneecap of the assailant, sending him to the ground, immobile and wailing with pain. Nick swiftly took advantage of his good fortune and cuffed his prisoner. When Matt approached, Nick asked him for identification. "They never asked Superman for any ID when he saved the day," Matt quipped, holding up his credentials. It was Nick's introduction to the aw-shucks grin.

A few months later Nick's partner retired and he needed a replacement. Matt was the first one he called. Now, Nick glanced over at his partner, who was slowly working his way through the newspaper. "Anything about Rashid yet?"

"That's what I'm looking for."

"If it was there, it would be on the front page."

"You would think," Matt said. He folded the paper and reached back to drop it on the backseat. "How does Walt keep that stuff locked up so well?"

"He's the best I've ever seen at controlling the flow of information."

Matt pulled a baggie of assorted cheese cubes from the lunch pail and held up a cube to Nick.

"No. Thanks."

Matt popped a cube in his mouth and began a slow chew. "So, what did Dr. Morgan have to say?"

"He said I don't see the birds and the trees."

"What?"

"He says I don't spend enough time noticing the world of nature around me." Nick shrugged. "Go figure."

"Did you tell him that staring at sparrows while doing our line of work could get you killed?"

"He wouldn't understand."

Matt ate another cheese cube. "Did you go into your dysfunctional family?"

Nick glanced at his partner. "What dysfunctional family?"

"Oh, come on. Your cousin is connected to the Capelli's and your brother is a compulsive gambler out in Vegas."

Nick frowned. "Phil's not a compulsive gambler. He's just on a prolonged losing streak."

"Yeah, a twelve-year losing streak."

Nick smiled. "That's about right. He'll spin out of it eventually."

Matt examined the contents of a power bar he took from the lunch box. He appeared dissatisfied and returned it to the box. "Too many carbs," he said.

"I'll mention it to Julie."

"So if you didn't talk about your family, what else did you discuss?"

"Well, he says I should avoid stress."

"Uh huh. Did he tell you anything of practical value?"

"I don't know. Sometimes even common sense needs to come from a different voice before you recognize it. Besides, I was thinking about taking some time off anyway. Julie deserves a vacation. We haven't been anywhere that wasn't job related in . . . shit, probably five years."

"How long have I been telling you the same thing? You're burning out. Take some time and recharge your batteries. What else did the good doctor have to say? Maybe I can offer some insight."

Nick sighed. "I'm going to get advice from you?"

"Hey, we're coming up on our ten-year anniversary together. Why wouldn't you listen to me?"

"Pardon me, sir, aren't you the guy who parked his car in the fast lane of the interstate at three in the morning to have sex with a stripper?"

"Yeah, so?"

"A stripper you'd met that night at a bachelor party?"

"Okay, so I'm a little impulsive. That doesn't mean I'm not trustworthy."

"It was your bachelor party."

"All right, so I realized I was too young to be married and I subconsciously sabotaged my engagement. I was just a kid. That was before I even met you. Besides, I only told you that story so you could see how far I've come."

Nick laughed. But when he looked back at Matt, he knew he'd exposed an old wound. Matt's fiancée was a fellow FBI agent he'd met at Quantico. They were both young, but beneath the smug veneer, Matt always lamented the loss of Jennifer Steele.

"How long did you guys date?"

"Three and a half years. She hated the city. Any city. She was a country girl at heart."

"Where did she end up?" Nick asked.

"Somewhere out west. New Mexico, something like that."

"All that time you were together she never mentioned the fact that she wanted to live in the country?"

Matt shrugged.

"I see," Nick said. "You didn't think she'd be able to resist your charm. You thought she'd be a city girl for the great Matt McColm."

When Matt didn't respond, Nick decided to let it go. They drove with the windows open, just the noise of the busy streets passing between them. After a while Matt took a bite of his apple and pointed to a cruddy white spot on Nick's windshield. "You may not see the birds, partner, but they sure see you."

Chapter 4

Just outside the Beltway, amidst the undistinguished block structures of an industrial park, a lone brick building sat quietly behind an American flag and the shade of a royal oak. The Baltimore field office afforded the FBI quick access to the highway, yet was unobtrusive enough to be mistaken for a post office. Nick parked in the lot behind the building. It wasn't a coincidence that the building itself prevented a clear view of the agents' cars. Very few things the FBI did were by chance.

Matt gripped the doorknob to the employee entrance and waited for Nick to swipe a security pass through the receptor. A small black box blinked green and Matt yanked open the steel door to the administrative wing. They entered the building and nodded to secretaries who were busy talking into headsets and tapping keyboards. They made their way down a corridor with illuminated portraits of past FBI directors surrounded by ridged wallpaper with somber geometric patterns. The corridor emptied into the center of the building; an open space whose perimeter was comprised of mismatched fabric chairs. The bullpen. A waiting area for visitors who were summoned to the office by one or more of the agents. In the center of the bullpen sat a wooden table with magazines sprawled across the top.

When Nick and Matt saw who sat in the worn-out chairs, they both stopped. Ed Tolliver, Carl Rutherford, Mel Downing, and Dave Tanner were at the far end of the bullpen in deep conversation. They were known simply as "The Team." The four of them, along with Nick and Matt, made up an elite counterterrorism squad of agents who specialized in significant foreign threats to the United States. The three two-man teams circled the globe in pursuit of foiling terrorist activity with American targets. The best of the best.

J. Edgar himself began the specialist trend in 1934 when he authorized a special squad of agents to capture John Dillinger. It was this philosophy that produced the group of specialists now gathered in the bullpen of the Baltimore field office. It also meant that each team was rarely on the same continent, never mind the same building. You didn't have to be a seasoned veteran to know that something was amiss.

As Nick and Matt approached, Dave Tanner stood and extended his arm. He tapped fists with Nick, then Matt. A tacit congratulation for capturing someone on the top-ten list. Then he got a close look at Matt's left ear.

"What happened, Deadeye?" Tanner smiled. "You finally hook a woman with too much spunk for you?"

Matt gingerly touched his taped earlobe. "Gee, Dave, that's uncanny. I'm beginning to think you're some kind of investigator or something."

Tanner didn't seem to hear him. He reexamined Matt's ear. "Rashid didn't go down without a fight, did he?"

"Would you expect him to?" Matt said, not answering the question directly, but close enough for two spies who understood the language.

"Probably not," Tanner said. "Let's just hope it sticks."

Nick picked up on Tanner's tone. Next to Nick, Tanner was the Team's senior agent and he always had his ear to the ground whenever a big prisoner was being interrogated.

"What do we know, Dave?" Nick asked.

"Nothing yet."

Nick looked at the elite group. Before he could ask the question, Matt beat him to the punch.

"What are we all doing here, Dave? I mean the last time we were all in the same room together . . ." He raised his eyebrows.

Tanner seemed to recognize the reference to a false intelligence report of a dirty bomb in Manhattan three years back. "I don't know," he said. "But Walt doesn't call us all in without good cause."

"The safe money is on Rashid," Matt said. "What else could it be? I'm sure he hasn't flipped, but I'll bet we got something. Something that nets us Kharrazi, maybe?"

Tanner nodded vacantly, but if he knew something, he wasn't giving it away.

There was an edginess to the banter now in the bullpen as the Bureau's finest minds spun their wheels in anticipation. A red ball meeting was urgent, so the hurry-up-and-wait routine added to the anxiety.

Nick nodded toward the closed door at the end of the hallway. "Who's he with?"

"No one," Tanner said. "He's on the phone. We're waiting for him to call us in."

From his chair, Ed Tolliver called out, "Hey, Matt, I hear that was the first time you were caught without your Glock since you were in the crib."

This provoked a round of laughter that caused a few secretaries to look up and smile.

Matt gave a tight-lipped scowl and saluted Tolliver with his middle finger.

Another boisterous roar lit up the room.

"Knock it off," a voice boomed from the end of the hallway. A broad-shouldered man with dark-chocolate skin leaned out of his office with the door half open.

"Bracco," Walt Jackson said. "Get in here."

Nick felt his stomach tighten as Jackson shut the door behind him. The big man disappeared and left an overt silence in his wake. Nick looked back at the team and saw something approaching compassion in their eyes. Matt seemed confused. He'd never been apart from his partner in a meeting before. Nick looked at Tanner and got an open-palmed shrug.

Finally, after a long moment, Matt said, "Better get in there and find out what's going on."

Nick moved toward Jackson's office like he was walking to the gas chamber. It had to be Rashid, he thought. Maybe some attorney found a loophole in their arrest. Shit, they were being shot at like fish in a barrel. How do you squirm out of that? Never mind the other eighteen charges that were awaiting his apprehension.

Nick opened Jackson's door and saw the immaculate desk he'd come to expect. What he didn't expect was a chair in front of his desk. A lone chair that he'd never seen before. Not even for meetings about nuclear threats or assassination attempts. Jackson always preferred people use the sofa against the wall.

Jackson gestured toward the chair. "Sit."

Walter Jackson was the Special Agent in Charge of the Baltimore field office. As SAC's go, Jackson was regarded as a prince. He was a laconic man who asked only for competence and loyalty. In return he provided unending support and sanctuary from the brass at FBI headquarters just down the road in D.C. Baltimore was far enough away to stand on its own, yet close enough to draw comparisons. It was the main reason the Team was harbored there. Besides being Baltimore's SAC, Jackson was also the Team leader and Nick was his point man.

Jackson sat behind his desk and leaned back to open a miniature refrigerator behind him. He pulled out a bottled water and tossed it to Nick.

Nick studied Jackson's solemn expression as he took his seat and twisted open the water. "What's going on, Walt?"

Jackson clicked his laser mouse and examined the flat screen computer monitor to his left. He tapped a couple of keys on his keypad and swiveled the screen around so Nick could see its content. At first the image was fuzzy, but Nick was familiar with the program. As the solid completion bar at the bottom of the screen moved to the right, the clarity sharpened. By the time it reached seventy percent, Nick could tell that the image came from a surveillance camera. Two men sat side by side at a green-felt table. At eighty percent he knew it was a black-jack table. When it was complete, Nick felt the room get warm. The man on the left side of the screen was his brother. The man on the right, he couldn't identify.

"Phil," Nick muttered.

Jackson nodded. "Yes."

Nick pointed to the man next to him. "Who — "

"Don't recognize him yet?"

Nick shook his head.

"Keep watching."

Nick studied the man's face. He wore a beard, sunglasses and a wide brim hat you might see on a tourist, yet there was something familiar about his mannerisms. The way he carried himself, full of confidence and bravado.

Jackson punched a couple of keys on his keyboard and the figures came to life.

"This is seven hours ago," Jackson said. "About two-thirty in the morning, Vegas time. It's a surveillance recording from the Rio. I understand Phil frequents the place quite a bit."

Nick's eyes narrowed as he struggled to make the man next to his brother. There was no audio, but it was obvious the two men were having fun. Phil's normally bloodshot eyes were in full bloom. The man elbowed his brother as if they were old buddies while Phil tossed back the last of his rum and coke with a flip of his wrist. The drink was so fresh it still had a full complement of ice cubes. It was his brother, all right, Nick thought. He'd never seen Phil allow a drink to linger.

Now Phil raised his hand to a cocktail waitress. The tourist pulled Phil's arm down and raised his own hand, waving a wad of folded bills. Phil made a half-hearted attempt to decline the offer, but the tourist seemed determined to buy Phil a drink. By the way Phil swayed, it wasn't the first drink he'd accepted.

Nick breathed a sigh of relief. Phil must have gotten swindled by a pro, and Walt was offering to keep it confidential. Let the FBI handle it inhouse. It was something Walt would do. It made sense now why Nick was called in alone.

Except he was wrong. Dead wrong.

"There," Jackson said, stopping the playback. In the frozen image, the tourist had lowered his sunglasses and seemed to be looking directly at the camera. His expression transformed into a sinister glare. His eyes were like black holes and his smile was pure acid.

Nick's tongue instantly dried up.

"Recognize him now?" Jackson said.

Water spewed from Nick's plastic bottle as he clenched his fists. Sitting next to his brother was the face of death. Kemel Kharrazi. Nick stared so intently at the image that he tried to will himself into the scene, or better yet, suck Kharrazi out of the image and pummel him from head to toe.

"Nick, what exactly did Rashid say to you during the arrest?"

Nick noticed that Phil was wearing his lucky shirt. The Preakness Stakes shirt that he wore the day he hit the pick-six for fifty thousand. Nick never had the heart to remind him that he wore the same damn shirt every day for the next three months until he'd relinquished every last penny back to Pimlico.

Nick looked at up at Jackson and said, "He's got four kids."

Jackson nodded. "I know."

The silence was filled with a heavy sigh from Jackson and the crumpling and uncrumpling of Nick's water bottle.

"Rashid asked me if I knew who would come after me," Nick finally answered.

"I see."

Nick stared at the image. It was the most incongruous pairing he'd ever seen. Like Hitler next to a ballerina.

Nick tried to remove emotion from the equation and mine the analytical side of his brain. He sensed Jackson watching him and he was careful not to overreact. He didn't want to give Jackson an excuse to keep him off the case. "Tell me about it, Walt. What does he want?"

"He wants to trade your brother for Rashid."

Nick kept his voice even. "We're going to trade an alcoholic gambler for a known assassin? That's the deal?"

Jackson nodded deliberately, as if he were measuring Nick's reaction before continuing the discussion.

"All right," Nick said. "Exactly how many nanoseconds did you wait before you said no?"

Jackson frowned. "He's still your brother, Nick."

"He's dead already and you know it."

Jackson squeezed the back of his neck like he was juicing a grapefruit. "Let's not get ahead of ourselves. We just received the fax an hour ago. I'm still trying to assemble a strategy."

Nick placed the deformed, half-empty water bottle on the corner of Jackson's desk, leaned forward, and stared hard at his boss. "Now tell me what's really going on here, Walt."

Jackson stood and began a slow pace. He carried his large frame smoothly, like a cougar on the prowl. Back and forth he strode. Nick's eyes followed him like match point at Wimbledon.

Jackson flipped off the overhead lights and pulled a remote control device from his pants pocket. When he clicked a button on the remote, an illuminated image was projected onto the white wall behind his desk. The faces of more than twenty Kurdish terrorists came to life. Some were grainy surveillance shots, while others were clear mug shots. Although their names were unknown to the American public, they were as familiar to Nick as Babe Ruth was to a Yankees fan. They belonged to a militant faction of the Kurdistan Workers' Party known as the Kurdish Security Force. The name was a direct response to the Turkish Security Force, which had been tormenting the Kurds for more than two decades. They were better known as Kharrazi's death squad. When President Merrick ordered troops to the area, his intention was to prevent Kharrazi and the KSF from dividing Turkey along ethnic lines.

Jackson passed a laser pointer over the medley of terrorists. "Langley has reported these soldiers missing from Kurdistan. More importantly, three of them have been sighted illegally entering the country. One was detained in a Miami airport. One was spotted departing a cruise ship in San Diego. Plus, we already know about Rashid and Kharrazi. I suspect the cockroach theory might be applicable here. For every one we know about there are probably twenty more that have evaded our intelligence."

Jackson clicked off the projector and turned on the lights. He sat down and kept a careful eye on Nick.

"I'm okay," Nick said, clenching every muscle that was undetectable. "I need to know everything. Don't skip a comma."

Jackson hesitated, then lowered his tired eyes. "The CIA had an agent infiltrate the KSF in Kurdistan a couple of months back. Ten days ago he arrived in Toronto with two groups of soldiers, including Kharrazi. He was with the lead group as they were about to enter the United States on horseback. Somewhere in the Canadian Rockies. The agent was with them up until 2 AM Tuesday morning. At that time they were five miles from the border. That's when Langley lost communications. Kharrazi had discovered the plant."

"How can you be sure?"

"Because Thursday morning the agent's family received a package. The agent's six-year-old daughter anxiously opened the box she thought was a present from her daddy in Turkey."

Nick held up his hand to prevent Jackson from finishing the story. He already knew the ending.

Jackson nodded. "That's right. The agent's severed head stared back at his little girl."

Nick covered his face with his hands and took deep breaths. He imagined the look on his niece's face as his brother's head was delivered to their home.

"I've been going to too many funerals, Walt."

"Let's not bury Phil just yet. There's still reason for hope."

Nick looked up to catch Jackson's expression. It was sincere, without pity.

"Why?"

"Because," Jackson said, "we've got explicit directions. There are timetables to be met and corroborating evidence of his health included in the demands. Kharrazi wouldn't throw those in if he were going to bluff us into believing Phil's alive."

"Okay," Nick said. "Now tell me why we're just hearing about this plant. Kemel Kharrazi is in Canada with a couple of dozen KSF soldiers—the best trained infantry in the world, and Langley waits until they've breached our border before we're notified?"

Jackson leaned back in his chair and crossed his legs. "That's the big question isn't it? Apparently, Langley felt they deserved an opportunity to bag Kharrazi as he crossed over the border. It's a gigantic political mess that I'm not willing to navigate right now.

Suffice it to say, they gambled and lost. They knew where he was with five miles to go, but Kharrazi is shrewd. He must have taken a more circuitous route. They simply waited too long. Morris admitted as much to me just before you came in. That's who I was on the phone with."

"You're kidding. That asshole actually admitted he was wrong about something?"

Jackson grinned. "You know, I thought the same thing myself." Then the smile faded and his eyes locked on Nick. "What do you want to do about Phil?"

Nick took a breath and let it out slowly. "Where are they?"

"We don't know for sure. Surveillance shows them leaving by way of a limousine. Phil seemed to be going under his own will. I'm sure Kharrazi knew just what to offer him. We've leaned on every limo company in the city and came up empty."

"Kharrazi is worth what? Ten billion? He's got plenty of hush money to spread around."

Jackson nodded. "Still, we have every runway, train station and interstate covered. The analysts say they're still in Vegas somewhere."

"What's our timetable?"

"Nine AM Eastern time. Rashid needs to be completely free. No tails. No bugs."

Nick didn't need to ask what happened if Rashid wasn't let out. He lowered his head and massaged his temple with his fingertips. It seemed like he'd been chasing terrorists forever. Now it felt different. It wasn't a job anymore. It was personal.

"You still haven't answered my question," Jackson said. "What do you want to do about Phil?"

Nick looked up. "What about regulations?"

Jackson grimaced. "I'm going to sit here and tell you the details of Phil's capture, then preclude you from getting involved because of regulations?" He leaned back and folded his arms across his large chest. "I can take the heat. It's what I do. But I need to know if you're prepared to deal with what you might find."

Nick understood. Identifying Phil's body would not be easy. He nodded. "I have to try and get him back, Walt."

Jackson reached into a desk drawer and came out with a pair of airline tickets. He slid them across the desk. "The flight leaves at seven. Take Matt with you. I have every available agent in Nevada waiting for you. Meanwhile, the rest of the Team will stay here and browbeat every informant we have. Something's happening out there. Something bigger than Phil and Rashid."

Nick reached for the tickets and stood to leave.

"Keep in mind," Jackson said. "There's a possibility that this is a—"

"Trap?" Nick said. "Yes, I know. Kharrazi's too sharp to think we'll release Rashid. He wants me. That's what the glare into the camera was all about. Phil is just bait. Kharrazi intends to honor Rashid's threat."

A modest grin tightened the corner of Jackson's mouth. He had the satisfied look of a teacher appraising his star pupil.

Nick put the tickets in his jacket pocket and turned toward the door.

"One other thing," Jackson said behind him.

Nick turned.

Jackson's grin mutated into something wicked. "Tell Matt, if he gets a clear shot at Kharrazi . . . make it a head shot."

Nick could already see the smile on Matt's face, and he hadn't even left the room.

Chapter 5

In the heavily-wooded suburb of Hampden, Maryland, Nick opened the front door of his two-story house expecting to see his wife's easy smile. Julie had a knack for seeming excited to see him even when he was precisely on schedule. That surprised expression she first showed off when he knelt down to propose and continued to shine at him every time he came home. As if the mere act of finding his way back home was an accomplishment to admire. How he loved that expression. If only he could find a way to verbalize those thoughts, those emotions that remained hidden deep inside. She had to know, yet the words somehow escaped him.

Nick circled back through the kitchen, then the den. "Honey," he called.

When he returned to the front foyer, a sound came from upstairs. He leaned over the banister and heard someone sobbing. Nick ran up the stairs two at a time. As he moved toward the master bedroom, he slid the gun from his holster. He could hear Julie whimpering now. His heart jumped as a loose thought ran through his mind. Kemel Kharrazi.

With his gun drawn, he crept up to the doorway of his bedroom and peeked inside. His heart sank. Julie sat on the floor with her back against the side of the bed. Her knees were pulled up into her chest while she wiped away tears with an overused ball of tissue. Without looking up she said, "I just got off the phone with Lynn."

Nick holstered his gun and sighed. She had just spoken with his brother's wife. She knew about Phil.

He watched her sniffle with bloodshot eyes and streaks of moisture blotching her face. Her short, brown hair was twisted into sharp angles. Yet, as distraught as she appeared, all he could think about was how striking she was. Even at her very worst, in her most awkward moment, he adored her. He couldn't imagine anyone or anything more beautiful. He wanted to tell her right there, right then. But he didn't.

He sat next to her and gathered her into his arms. He listened while Julie blurted out her sorrowful thoughts in small dosages. "Poor Lynn," she sobbed. "The kids don't know yet." More sobs. "They think he's just away on business." Her firm body wilted in his arms.

"It's okay," he whispered.

"I'm so sorry, Nick." She looked up at him with big Bambi eyes. "He's dead, isn't he?"

Nick pulled her closer and she dug her wet face into his chest. He caressed her cheek with his fingertips. It was strange to see her so distressed, she had such a strong personality and so few low points.

"Who is it?" she asked. "Who has Phil?"

Nick chewed on his lower lip. He could feel her stiffen in the silence.

"Nick?"

His reluctance was only making it worse. He whispered, "Kemel Kharrazi."

She gasped. "In America? How could that be?" She twisted in his arms and looked up at him. "Nick, what's going on? Tell me right now."

Amazing, Nick thought. She saw the big picture immediately. She was always right there with him. Never a step behind. For an investigator like Nick, it was rare to be followed so closely.

"I'm not sure, sweetie."

"You know something, though."

An open-ended question. Just like a good interrogator. She wasn't going to let him off the hook, so she sat and waited for his response.

Nick took a breath. "Kharrazi is in America with a squad of soldiers."

When he stopped there, she said, "Well he certainly didn't go through the trouble of sneaking into the country with a platoon of followers just to kidnap Phil Bracco."

Nick shrugged. "He's not your typical terrorist. He's a George-town graduate, extremely bright. Maybe too bright. You know what they say about people with skyrocket IQs," he said, looping his index finger around his right ear.

She just stared.

"All right," he said. "Kharrazi wants us to release Rashid Baser in exchange for Phil."

She pulled back and examined Nick's face. "You're serious?"

Nick nodded.

"He can't be that naive?"

"No, he isn't."

"Then what's it all about?"

Nick shook his head. "I don't know. That's what I'm going to find out."

Julie suddenly looked horrified. "You're going to Vegas?"

Nick didn't respond. He wanted to soften the blow, but she was too quick for him.

Julie wiped her eyes, then stood up and brushed off her lap, as if to wipe away her vulnerability.

"Nick," she said, "look at me. I'm thirty-six going on eighty. There's only so much I can handle before . . ." she looked away.

"Before?"

She wiped the side of her nose with the tissue ball and seemed preoccupied.

"What are you trying to say, Jule?"

She turned her back for a moment, took a step away, then turned back around to face him. "Please don't go. Please. I don't know how else to say it? It's just too much for me to handle. First Phil is taken, then you tell me about Kharrazi . . ." She pulled back the hair from her face and tried to maintain control. "I dread answering the phone because I just know one day I'm going to hear Walt Jackson's voice say, 'I'm sorry, Julie.'"

Her eyes welled up and her lower lip trembled. She leaned forward and Nick was there to collect her once again. She embraced him like he was a soldier leaving for war. He wasn't sure she would ever let go of him. He could feel her tiny frame shudder in his arms.

"Please," she pleaded. "Not Kemel Kharrazi. Not him."

Nick waited for her breathing to settle into a rhythm before he said, "He's my brother, Hon. He's the only one I've got."

"What about me?" she said with short gasping words. "What about our family? The kids?"

Nick almost said, "What kids?" but he knew what she meant. It seemed their plans for having children and a normal family life was always put on hold because of his career. With him they were always one year away before they could slow down and make time for their marriage.

She maintained her death grip around his torso. "I know it's tougher for me in the summer, Nick. I mean, without the students to look after, I have all this time to reflect. But you don't need to be chasing the most dangerous terrorists in the world. Can't you just . . ." she didn't finish and Nick didn't know if it was because she ran out of ideas, or because they'd had this discussion so often that Nick could finish it on his own.

She pulled back and locked eyes with him. "Nick, I love you. I just know you're going to be a terrific father. You don't do anything halfway, and I can already see you giving our kids horseback rides and splashing water at them in the tub."

Nick smiled. It was his dream to have children, but he never even allowed himself the privilege of imagining what it would be like to hold something that precious. To be that important to another human being.

He cupped her tiny face in his hands, "I'll tell you what . . . we won't be having this conversation a year from now. I promise."

Julie forced a meager smile and sniffled.

Nick pulled a couple of tissues from a box on top of the dresser and handed them to her.

She blew her nose and said, "I almost forgot. How did it go with Dr. Morgan?"

Nick took advantage of the shift in conversation to search for a garment bag in the walk-in closet. "Good."

Julie brushed past him and pulled the bag from a high shelf, unzipped it, and threw it open on the bed. She opened a dresser drawer and retrieved a single pair of socks and underwear and threw them into the garment bag.

"Just overnight, right?" she said, more a statement than a question.

It was no time to haggle. Nick would stay as long as it took to find his brother, but he also knew that Phil would never live past Kharrazi's deadline. "Yes," he said. "Just overnight."

Julie nodded, then began the process of putting together a shirt and pants combo that worked. As she browsed the long line of clothes in the closet, she said, "You liked him?"

"Who?"

"Dr. Morgan."

"Oh, yes. I thought he was . . . uh, insightful."

That stopped her. "What exactly did he say?"

"He thinks I should find a less stressful way to make a living."

Julie's eyes perked. "And?"

"And," he took the shirt from her hand and laid it in the garment bag, "I think he's right."

Julie followed him around the room. "Are you serious?"

"Very."

"Then what do you plan to do about it?"

"I'm not sure." He looked at her face brimming with hope. He chose his words carefully, "I'm going to continue to see him. Besides that, I'm just not sure . . ."

"Nick, you realize you're outnumbered, don't you?"

"What?"

"I know you want to save the world —"

"Stop it now. I'm not trying to save the world, I'm only trying to save this country. Maybe even just this city." His face softened. "Oh, honey, I'm just a pawn. I know that. I'd just like you to be able go to the store without the store blowing up while you're inside."

"Please try to think about us. Maybe we could find a small town in the mountains, somewhere in Wyoming, or Montana, somewhere. I don't know Nick, is that such a crazy idea?"

Nick dropped onto the bed, leaned back onto a pillow and stared up at the ceiling. "Maybe there's something to that. Maybe if I didn't know as much as I do about terrorists and all of the plots we've thwarted. Some by dumb luck." He sighed. "Maybe ignorance is bliss."

Julie curled next to him and nuzzled up to the side of his face. "Come on over to the ignorant side, Sweetie. We could use a good man like you."

His mouth grinned, but he was already thinking about his next move. Phil may have been somewhat of a drunk and loose with his lips, but he was his brother. After their parents died, Nick became almost a surrogate father to his younger sibling. Phil needed him.

"Hello in there," Julie said, knocking on Nick's forehead. "Anybody home?"

Nick pulled her down on top of him and gazed into the deep blue of her eyes. "Look here, Miss, I'm leaving town. But that doesn't mean I won't miss you every minute I'm gone."

He rolled off the bed and finished packing. He zipped the garment bag, threw it over his shoulder and bent down to kiss her. "I've got to go. See you tomorrow."

"Is Matt going with you?"

"Of course."

She smiled.

"You think he's my guardian angel, don't you?"

"I do," she said. "I always feel better when he's with you. I don't know why. Intuition maybe."

He looked at his watch. "Well, I'm meeting him at the airport at seven."

"It's only three-thirty. What's the hurry?"

"I'm stopping at Pimlico on the way."

"The horse track? You have an itch to bet a few races?"

"No," he said. "I've got to see Tommy. He hasn't missed the feature race in fifteen years."

"Tommy? Your cousin Tommy? Why, do you need him to leave a horse's head in someone's bed?"

Nick laughed. "Just because he's connected doesn't mean he's not family."

"Oh, he's family all right." She pressed her nose to the side and gave her best mobster face.

"Well, believe it or not, I need his help. We can't find any info on the limo that took Phil from the casino last night. Tommy has Vegas connections."

"With all of the favors you've used up at the DA's office getting him and Silk out of trouble, he'd better help you."

"He will."

* * *

Pimlico was the second oldest racetrack in the country. In the 1800s it was considered a nice buggy ride out of town. Since then, it had been swallowed up by growth, all one hundred forty acres entirely within Baltimore city limits, with houses visible all along the backstretch. Nick's father first brought him to Pimlico when Nick was ten. His father loved the challenge of handicapping the races. He showed Nick how to read the Racing Form and taught him the significance of pace. He'd tell him which horse would be leading going into the first turn and which horse would come with a late charge. Most importantly, he taught him how to figure out which horse fit the race best. His father was merely a two-dollar bettor, but that didn't lessen his zeal for the sport. His father's excitement was contagious and even though they went but once a month, Nick cherished each trip.

Nick pushed through the turnstile and headed for the apron in front of the finish line. After his parents' death, he used to meet his cousin Tommy there nearly every weekend, back when Nick and Phil stayed at Tommy's house. Nick's Uncle Victor was his father's brother and Tommy's dad. The house was too small for the seven inhabitants, but no one complained. Uncle Victor and Aunt Ruth always made certain Nick felt like he was at home, and for the most part, he did.

Most of Nick's youth, however, was spent with Tommy Bracco and Don Silkari. The three of them drank and pranked their way through their teenage years with reckless abandon. If someone tried to mess with one of them, the other two were always there to finish the fight. Literally. Eventually they matured and found their lives heading in different directions, but the friendship had always endured.

Nick shook his head in amazement when he saw Tommy standing in virtually the exact spot he'd stood for every feature race at the Pimlico meet for nearly twenty years. Tommy wore an Armani suit, sharkskin shoes, and a pair of large, gold cufflinks that screamed out from the bottom of his shirtsleeves. Next to him, as always, was Silk, using the same tailor as Tommy. Both had colored toothpicks dangling from their mouths.

"What's with the clothes?" Nick asked.

"Hey, Nicky, what's goin' on?" Tommy reached for Nick's extended hand and pulled him into a bear hug. "Good to see ya. How's that beautiful bride of yours?"

"She's fine. School's out, so she's taking it easy for the summer." Nick motioned to Don Silkari. "Hey, Silk."

"Hey," Silk said, his head buried deep into an open Racing Form.

"So, what's with the gear?" Nick asked.

Tommy pulled on his lapels. "Oh, this stuff, well . . . you see we're stockbrokers now."

"Stockbrokers? You two?"

Tommy shrugged. "Hey, that's where the money is these days, Nick. And we gotta be where the money is."

Nick stuck an index finger in each ear. "I'm not listening. The less I know, the less I can testify to."

Both men broke out into wide grins. Tommy handed Nick a folded Racing Form opened to the eighth race. "Nicky, look at this race. I can't understand why the four horse is going off at five-to-one. I mean he just won his last two races at the same price, he oughta be the chalk. You're the investigator. Tell me what I'm missing here."

It took Nick less than a minute to see what Tommy had missed. It wasn't something that was likely to get by his cousin. Tommy had a knack for appearing slow-witted. It went along with the way he talked and his mannerisms. He would lure you in, encouraging you to underestimate him. This was his most prized talent. Like a snake pretending to be slowed by injury, all the while waiting for the right moment to strike. Tommy had no motive to pull something on Nick, it was simply habit.

Nick slammed the form into Tommy's chest. "He's not a he, that's why. The horse is a filly, Tommy. It's her first time against the boys."

Tommy didn't bother to review his alleged oversight. He turned to Silk with pride. "See, that's why he's the law. He spots every little detail. That's why he's got the cutest wife in town."

"Hey," Nick said, "easy with the wife comments. I'm beginning the think you've got a thing for her."

Tommy held up his hands. "Hey, Nicky, don't insult me like that. I mean you're like family to me."

"Tommy, you're my cousin. We are family."

"See, you're making my point for me."

Nick's face turned serious.

Tommy said, "What's up?"

"I need your help."

"Anything," Tommy said.

"What I tell you two is confidential and —"

"That's enough," Silk interrupted. "We know the drill."

Nick paused. He was uncomfortable with what he was about to do, but there was still a slim chance he could save his brother's life. In Tommy's world, information was a currency, like cash, only more valuable. Las Vegas, limos, and kidnapping were all staples in his domain. If there was a weak link somewhere in the Nevada desert, Tommy would find it.

Nick said, "Phil's been kidnapped."

Tommy's face grew severe. His lip curled up in disgust. "Who done it?"

For the first time since Nick got there, Silk put down the Form.

"A terrorist."

"Who?" Tommy repeated, his jaw furiously working on a bright orange toothpick in the corner of his mouth.

Nick hesitated, wary of the eagerness on Tommy's face. "I can't tell you that right now, but Phil was gambling at the Rio late last night and was taken away in a limo. We're running into a wall trying to find this limo. Whoever rented it probably paid cash. Lots of cash. The kind of cash that shuts people up."

Tommy nodded.

"Do you think you could make some calls and find out something about this limo?" Nick asked.

Tommy took the toothpick from his mouth and twirled it between his fingers like a baton. "No problem. But you gotta promise me something."

Nick winced, bracing himself for the can of worms he was about to open. "What?"

Tommy pointed the orange toothpick at Nick. "When this is over, you gotta promise to tell me who done it. I want a name."

Nick tossed the idea around in his head. If Phil ended up dead, he'd gladly throw Kemel Kharrazi to the wolves. If his brother lived it would more than likely be because of Tommy's help. Either way, he could live with the trade-off. "Okay."

Nick handed him a blank business card with a handwritten name and phone number on it. "I'm flying to Vegas tonight, but I want you to call this number if you find out anything. It's the number of an FBI agent in Vegas. He won't ask questions, just tell him anything you can that might help us track down the limo."

Tommy placed the card in his pocket, "Done."

Nick saw the horses approach the starting gate. "I've got to go. I've got rush hour traffic to deal with."

"Hey, Nicky," Tommy said, pointing to the Racing Form. "What about this four horse? I got three large on her nose. You think I should change my bet?"

"Nah," Nick said, "she's the only speed in the race. She's liable to steal it."

Tommy winked. He loved asking questions he already knew the answer to.

By the time Nick reached the parking lot, he could hear the track announcer's voice rise with excitement as he described the final furlong of the race. The crowd roared as he declared the only filly in the field a wire-to-wire winner.

Nick smiled. Just like riding a bike, he thought.

Chapter 6

"Will you look at this beauty," Matt McColm said, holding up a magazine at arm's length. He sat at the window seat while Nick sat on the aisle, an empty seat between them.

Nick gave a furtive glance for spectators, then leaned toward Matt for an eyeful.

"Oh, baby, the places I could take you," Matt said, his eyes racing up and down the glossy photo.

Nick followed Matt's stare. He took a long moment examining the image, finally squinting for confirmation. "It's a gun."

"That," Matt said, "is no gun. It's a Slimline Glock 36. She's so sleek, she just begs you to wrap your fingers around her."

Nick rolled his eyes.

While Matt flipped pages of Gun Magazine, Nick sifted through files of terrorists known to have any link to the KSF. He groped for something, anything that might give him a clue why so many of them were spreading themselves across America's landscape. Why would they appear to be moving in such a diverse pattern? He found himself staring at pictures of Kurdish rebels as if the power of his glare could evoke an answer from them.

The flight was long and the closer they got to Las Vegas, the quieter the conversation became. Both agents readied themselves as the night closed around them and reduced their world to the few dozen people on board the jet. Finally, Nick broke the silence. He held up a surveillance photo of a grizzly-looking man with bad teeth and wild eyes. "They should lock this guy up just for taking a picture like this."

Matt placed his forehead up against the window. Flying west at such a rapid pace extended twilight unnaturally, suppressing nightfall as the plane chased the setting sun. Looking down at a tiny sprinkling of lights covering the Midwest, he said, "It looks so peaceful down there."

"Why can't we have that?" Nick asked.

"Have what?"

"A peaceful, uneventful life. Go to work, punch the clock, type up a few reports, and drive home. It sounds so calming."

"You mean boring."

"Yeah, boring. I like boring."

"I don't."

"That's because you've never tried it. Boring could be good for you. I hear the survival rate at AT&T is very high. A lot less stressful too."

Matt shook his head. "That's where you're wrong. There's just as much stress working for a big corporation as there is with the Bureau. Just a different type of stress, that's all."

"You're probably on to something there," Nick mused.

"Besides," Matt said, "you had it a lot worse when you were trolling West Baltimore in a cruiser five nights a week."

Nick knew he was right, of course. He wondered if he would find the world so pressing if he were a bank teller or a teacher like Julie. Her concerns must seem just as pressing to her, yet she rarely showed it. Apparently it wasn't the profession so much as the professional. He looked over at Matt, who was leaning back in his seat, eyes closed. The picture of serenity. He respected Matt's composure. He was cool, placid, skillfully poised.

As if Matt felt the weight of Nick's stare, he said, "I know what they're doing."

"Who?"

"The Kurds," Matt said, head back, hands folded on his lap.

"Tell me about it."

"Obviously they're planning a bombing. That's why it's so important for them to spring Rashid. He's the best bomb expert they have. Probably the best in the world. They're inundating us with enough riff-raff so we can't cover them all. My guess is most of them are decoys. Spread us thin so we can't possibly give them the attention they deserve. A good tactic."

Nick raised his eyebrows. "And all this time I thought you were focusing on your next trip to the shooting range."

"Hey, I'm not just another pretty face."

Nick considered the theory. "Then why take my brother? You think Jackson's right? You think it's personal?"

"I don't know. That part bothers me. There are too many other options that make more sense."

Nick continued studying files until he became weary. He lay back and rested his eyes. It seemed like only a moment had passed before he awoke abruptly to the bouncing of clear air turbulence and the whining of landing gear deployment. When he looked out the window, he saw the lights from the Vegas strip disrupting the Nevada sky like a neon bonfire.

Nick placed the documents into his portfolio and tucked it under his arm. He noticed Matt tapping his heel as he edged forward in his seat.

"Showtime," Matt said.

It was a smooth landing and as the aircraft taxied to the gate, it stopped momentarily to allow another plane to pass. As he sat there on the tarmac, Nick saw people moving inside the terminal. The gate had a bay window that jutted out toward the runway. He fixed his stare at a familiar face in the crowd. His eyes narrowed to a slit. There wasn't supposed to be anyone waiting for them. Anxiously, he shuffled through photos from the files he'd been reviewing. He pulled one from a file marked "classified" and examined it closely. When he peered back into the gate crowd, the man was gone.

Matt saw the grim expression on his partner's face. "What is it?" he asked.

"Probably nothing," Nick said.

* * *

Abdullah Amin Shah waited impatiently for the plane to arrive. He had purchased a ticket for a departing flight to have access to the gate. The flinty plastic knife, razor sharp, jabbed him from under his coat, reminding him just how lethal his assignment was. He leaned against the wall where the passengers deplaned. He only needed a moment to recognize the FBI agent. His face was burned into his memory, Kemel Kharrazi had made certain of that. He would surprise the FBI agent from behind and slit his throat to the bone. After that, it didn't matter if he were caught. He would have accomplished his mission.

The agent, Nick Bracco, posed a problem for Kharrazi. It was not good to have an American law officer with strong convictions in Kharrazi's path. Especially an extremely clever one. Especially now.

Kharrazi spoke of revenge, eye for an eye. He claimed that Bracco had to pay for what he did to Rashid, but Abdullah knew better. For the first time in all the years he'd known Kharrazi, he sensed fear. Something about the American bothered Kharrazi. That's why Abdullah was at the airport with an undetectable knife waiting to slit Bracco's throat.

Abdullah saw the first passengers exit the jetway. He blended into the wall so well, they never saw him. Their eyes focused forward, searching for a sign pointing them toward the baggage claim.

Abdullah knew there were seventy-five passengers aboard the direct flight. Eighty, including the crew. There would be no mistakes. No mishaps. Abdullah began counting heads: nine, ten, eleven. A man similar, but no, too short. Thirty-seven, thirty-eight. A businessman in a dark suit—too heavy. Fifty-nine, sixty, sixty-one. His hand trembled as he clenched the knife firmly under his coat. Sixty-nine, seventy. Where was he? It was confirmed he had boarded the plane in Baltimore. Seventy-three, seventy-four. One more passenger. He nearly jumped at the next man who walked through the ramp, but it was a pilot. The man wore sunglasses and he strode almost to the corridor before he turned, sat down, and began tying his shoelaces. Strange, Abdullah thought, why would he be wearing sunglasses at night? He had no time to ponder the American psyche.

Abdullah stood motionless, as if his stillness could lull everyone into believing he was harmless. There was one passenger left and it could be only one person. Escape was impossible. His eyes roamed the terminal casually. See Americans, I am just like you. Just another citizen waiting to board the next plane. He sensed the pilot watching him from across the room. Abdullah quickly looked away, but when his eyes returned, the pilot was smiling at him, curiously moving his fingers into a friendly gesture, as if he was waving. Why was the pilot acting so peculiar? While Abdullah tried to make sense of things, a man passed by briskly. It was Bracco!

Nick Bracco was getting away. Abdullah ran up behind him, swung the knife from his coat and with one great lunge he made his move. Abdullah was in midstep when he heard the thunderous clap and instantly dropped to the floor. What happened? He felt a sharp pain run up his right leg. When he looked down he could see a hole in his pants just above his knee, with a dark-brown stain spreading across his pant leg. He poked a finger into the warm hole up to his knuckle. When he retracted the finger, it was covered with blood.

Abdullah looked up to see the pilot holding a gun. How could the pilot of the airplane shoot him? He was disoriented and becoming lightheaded. As he lay his head down he began to pant. His eyes stared straight up in disbelief and saw a figure kneel over him. It was the pilot and he was talking to Abdullah, yelling at him. What did the pilot want from him? Someone was pushing on his leg, but he couldn't tell whom? The room was getting dark. The pain began to fade.

* * *

Matt applied pressure to the wounded limb as he shouted down at Abdullah. "Don't you dare bleed out on me, you son of a bitch."

Nick unfastened his tie and quickly wrapped it around the terrorist's leg, high up on the thigh, above the wound. He stretched the silk into a tight knot, trying to stop the flow of blood. He slapped Abdullah's face, which was losing color rapidly. "Where's my brother?" he demanded.

Abdullah was unresponsive. A growing pool of blood gathered under his leg.

Matt pressed down hard on the wound site. "I hit the damn femoral. Of all the rotten luck. If he weren't jumping so fast—"

"Cut it out," Nick said. "You did exactly what you had to do. Anyone else would have gone for the torso." He trusted Matt with his life and Matt hadn't let him down. Nick groped for better words, but settled on a simple, "Thanks."

Matt ignored the comment. He was busy keeping Abdullah alive.

Nick looked at his watch, then at Abdullah; his chance of gleaning information was draining from the man's body in dark-red streaks.

Matt looked down at the terrorist who had tried to take his partner's life. "I'm not finished with you, Abdullah."

Chapter 7

"You don't look so good," Matt said.

The two men sat on the bright, geometrically patterned carpet, between a row of slot machines inside the Vegas airport. It was nearly midnight and they had just finished a futile attempt to extract information from the Kurdish assassin while he drifted in and out of consciousness. Finally, they let the paramedics take him away with a police escort.

"Ask me what kind of day I'm having?" Nick said.

Matt ignored the rhetorical question.

"Go ahead," Nick urged. "Ask me what kind of day I'm having."

"Okay," Matt said. "What kind of day are you having?"

"Don't ask."

Matt shoved him, toppling him over. Nick lay there staring up at the ceiling, welcoming the respite. He wouldn't tell Matt about his headaches, or the anxiety attack he was about to have. He thought about what Dr. Morgan told him about the effect stress could have on him. His breathing became quick and short. His head throbbed with an unfamiliar condition that probably only existed in some esoteric textbook with a picture of a German psychologist on the cover. His miserable descent into the abyss was interrupted by an authoritative voice.

"You two wouldn't be Bracco and McColm, would you?"

Nick remained supine and rubbed his temples. He let Matt do the introductions while he regained what little composure he had left. He heard a man suggest that they'd had an eventful trip to the desert. Matt sounded casual until Nick heard a second man say, "Looks like your partner here might need a little help. You want us to make a call?"

Matt said, "No, no, he's fine. He just needed a little rest, that's all."

Nick felt Matt tugging his arm upward. He got to his feet and shook hands with four men wearing blue FBI windbreakers. They looked at him carefully, like they were in the produce aisle inspecting fruit for damages.

They looked relieved when Nick said, "We're working on East Coast time, so it's practically time for breakfast."

* * *

The six men exited the airport in a heavily tinted van. Nick and Matt sat in the middle bench seat of the van with two Vegas agents in front of them, two in back. The driver, Jim Evans, held the seniority of the group. "I got a call a couple of hours ago from that informant of yours," Evans gave Nick a quick glance. "He gave us the license plate of the limo that took your brother. Turns out the limo was supposed to go home with the driver last night, only the driver lent it to a friend. A friend that the driver doesn't know all that well, but he gets an envelope with twenty hundred-dollar bills inside, so he hands over the keys. I mean the regular driver's only a kid, maybe twenty-one tops. So we paid him a visit."

An agent in the backseat said, "You should have seen the look on the kid's face when we show up waving FBI badges. He nearly vomited on us."

"Yeah, well, he's still living with his mother," Evans continued. "So we sit down and the kid told us everything."

"Except maybe which side of the mattress he hides his Playboy magazines," the voice from the backseat again.

Nick leaned toward Evans, "What did you find out?"

"That's some informant you've got there back in Baltimore," Evans said. "With extremely long-range connections. Who is he?"

"He's an old informant from my days with the Baltimore PD."

"What about the kid?" Matt shifted the conversation back into focus.

"Long story short, we found the limo," Evans said.

Matt slapped his knee, "Finally, something goes right."

"It's parked in front of a house in a residential area," Evans said.

"It's in front of a house?" Matt said.

"We've got a SWAT team and a couple of sharpshooters already in position."

A new voice behind Nick said, "Do you really believe that Kemel Kharrazi is, uh . . ."

Nick turned to see a young man, clean-cut, no more than twenty-three, with wide, inquisitive eyes.

"What's your name?" Nick asked.

"Jake Henson."

"How long you been with the Bureau, Jake?"

"Six months," Jake answered, sitting painfully upright.

"What do you know about Kemel Kharrazi?"

There was a pause, then Jake said, "Well, I know that he's forty-two and received a journalism degree from Georgetown. His father owns the largest construction company in Turkey. He has two teenage sons, Isal and Shaquir. He's had his hand in the bombing of the US Embassy in Jordan and American Airlines flight 650, to mention just a couple. And there's a twenty-million-dollar reward for any information leading to his arrest."

Nick was impressed until he saw the blue-green glow across Jake's face and realized he was holding a small handheld computer.

Matt twisted in his seat, stuck a piece of gum in his mouth, and pointed at the young man. "That's pretty good. You get that Dr. Skin website on there? You know the one with all of the naked celebrities."

Jake's face became grave. "This is official FBI merchandise. I can't use it for personal use."

Matt looked at the older agent sitting next to Jake. "Is he for real?"

"Are you kidding me?" the agent said. "He thinks watching a woman eat a banana is considered cheating on your wife."

"Jake," Matt said, "you ever meet a fugitive on the List?"

"No, sir, this would be my first."

Evans pointed his thumb over his shoulder at Jake and said, "The kid's done a good job. He digs into that tiny machine and finds out that there's only been one house sold in the nearby vicinity in the past six months. Guess which house?"

Jake beamed.

"That's right," Evans said. "The very house that limo sits in front of was sold to a businessman just four months ago. His name is Kalil Reed."

Nick and Matt exchanged glances.

"Anyway, Jake runs the name into the computer and comes up with an alias for Mr. Reed. Anyone care to guess whose name comes up?"

Evans looked into his rearview mirror at the two agents, anxious for one of them to respond.

Jake couldn't hold it. "Abdullah Amin Shah!" he exclaimed. "He owns the house."

Nick could see Matt about to get sarcastic, so he grabbed Matt's arm and gave him a look.

"Come on," Jake said. "Surely you know who Abdullah Amin Shah is? He works for Kemel Kharrazi."

"We know," Matt said. "I think you'll find some of his blood on my pant leg."

Nick turned to Jake. "Without the mechanical cheat sheet, how much do you really know about Kharrazi?"

Jake shrugged, "I've heard all the stories. You know, the CIA agent's head sent to his home, the story about him slaughtering children in the streets of Ankara because they didn't know his name. He killed his own mother for betraying him. After a while, you wonder whether they're just urban legends."

Nick rubbed the stubble growing on the side of his face. "I used to wonder the same thing myself."

"But you know it's all real, don't you, Agent Bracco?"

Nick sighed. "You don't have to worry. You won't be setting eyes on Kemel Kharrazi tonight."

"Why do you say that?"

Nick took a breath. He was tired, he needed a shave, he was hungry, and most of all, he wished he could turn off his brain. Just long enough to relax and make believe it was going to be all right. His brother was alive—he had to hang on to that thought.

"Sir?" Jake said. "Why won't we see him?"

"Because," Nick said, "when you're dealing with terrorists, coincidences are dangerous."

Nick could tell by the silence that his message had fallen short of its target. He added, "When you find a square peg on the ground and a few feet away you find a perfectly square hole to put it in, it's time to look over your shoulder. Nothing is ever that easy, especially when you're dealing with someone like Kharrazi."

Jim Evans peered through the rearview mirror and said, "You think this is a wild goose chase?"

Nick could sense a schism developing between the two branches. Vegas dealt mostly with racketeering and organized crime. The majority of their criminals engaged in murder, extortion, bribery—spontaneous acts that lacked the planning required to escape detection. An evidence-collector's dream world, Las Vegas. But Nick and Matt's world revolved around one thing—terrorists. A type of criminal who planned attacks eons before they were enacted. There were many cases where a terrorist would spend years infiltrating a community. They'd teach in schools, run grocery stores, repair cars. Then one day the word comes and it's time to act. Few could prepare for that kind of operative. Nick knew he needed everyone on the same page if he was going to find Phil.

Nick said, "Never interrupt your enemy when he is making a mistake."

This brought more silence. He could hear Matt sigh.

"Napoleon," Matt said.

"Exactly," Nick said. "Let's hope this limo thing is their mistake."

It was nearly 2 AM when the van rolled to a stop behind a second nondescript van. The agents exited into the cool night air and followed Evans to the forward van. The door slid open and exposed a man and a woman wearing headphones. The woman held an index finger to her lips. "They're on the phone," she whispered. "My Kurdish is a little rusty."

Nick asked Evans where the house was. Evans pointed down the narrow street. "It's around the corner. They can't see us from here, but we own the perimeter." He tapped the radio clipped to his shirt. "We're in contact with Hostage Rescue. Twenty of them. When the time comes, we'll be ready."

The woman lowered her headphones. "I keep hearing the same casual conversation."

A faint ringing sound caused Nick to walk away from the van and push a button on his secure phone. "Bracco," he answered.

"I just got word about the airport incident," Walt Jackson said in a half-yawn. "I caught a nap here in the office, but the coffee's flowing now. You two okay?"

"We're fine. We found the limo in a residential area and we're intercepting phone messages from the house. The conversations are in Kurdish. The deed is under the name of Kalil Reed." Nick looked back at the two vans. Even in the dark, Matt stuck out among the Vegas agents. And not just because of his height. "I don't like it, Walt."

"Too much good luck, huh?"

"Exactly."

"All right, Kharrazi's giving us until 9 AM Eastern time to release Rashid, which gives you about four hours. We're pretty sure they're still in Nevada. We're able to trace the calls to somewhere in the state, that's all." Jackson paused, as if searching for the proper words. "Nick, I spoke with Phil. He sounded worn down. In exchange for the conversation, I'm having Rashid moved to a less secure site for the time being. You know we can't release him, but the minute Kharrazi knows, Phil will be expendable. I'm buying as much time as I can."

"Thanks."

"One other thing. I'm adding a new security system to your house and I'm having Julie tagged. We have to be prepared. At least until this is over."

"I knew you would. Appreciate it. We'll be in touch."

Nick made eye contact with his partner and Matt hustled over to him.

"What's up?" Matt said.

"What do you make of all this?" Nick asked.

"It's a setup," Matt said, like he was answering a simple third grade math equation.

Nick nodded. "If you were Kharrazi, would you set up a decoy on the other side of town, as far away as possible? Or would you want to keep the law within viewing distance?"

Matt thought about the question. "This wasn't done on a whim. I'd say he's on the opposite end of town, as far away as possible."

"You're probably right," Nick said. He looked over Matt's shoulder at a neighbor approaching the van. An older man wearing blue jeans and a robe. "We could have every law enforcement officer in the state canvass the city and come up empty. What would we look for? They're not going to have a neon sign out front saying, 'terrorists inside.'"

The neighbor was nodding as Jim Evans explained the nature of the impromptu command post. The neighbor seemed satisfied with the answers he was getting.

The man passed Nick and Matt as he headed back to his front door.

"Excuse me, sir," Nick said. "You're wondering what's going on?"

"Yeah, the guy over there explained everything," the man said. "You're searching for some kind of kidnapper. You think he might be in our neighborhood."

"That's right," Matt said. "Have you noticed anything suspicious lately, even mildly peculiar?"

"I can't say that I have," the man said.

Nick was about to let him go when he thought of something. "There hasn't been many houses sold in the area, has there?

"Not really."

"What about visitors? Are there any homeowners in the neighborhood who leave during the summer and rent the place out?"

The man's eyes perked up. He began to point at a house directly across the street and Nick slapped his arm down before he could get it halfway up. The man looked perplexed.

"Please don't point," Nick said. "Just tell me."

"The Johnsons have a son who lives in Montana," the man was straining not to look at the house. "They go up there every summer and don't usually get home until after Thanksgiving. This is the first year I remember them ever renting the place out. I understand they got paid handsomely. Ol' Norm couldn't keep from grinning when he told me about how they were approached to rent it. And how the guy told him he'd pay him cash up front, because he was so excited about moving to Las Vegas and needed a place to stay until his home was built. Nice guy, too. I don't see him very often, but he always smiles and waves to everyone. They seem like a nice family."

"Family?" Nick asked.

"Yeah, well, I guess I haven't actually met his wife, but he's shown me pictures. She's back in Jersey with the kids."

"Does he have dark hair, dark complexion?"

"Sure. I can't remember his name, though."

"He ever have any company? Other men visiting?"

The man shook his head. "Not that I've ever noticed."

Nick patted the man on his upper arm, dismissing him. "You've been a great help. Thanks."

"You think that guy renting the Johnson's place is a criminal?" the man asked.

"No," Matt said. "He doesn't fit the description. The guy we're looking for is fair-skinned and blond."

"Oh," the man said. Then he smiled and wagged his finger at the agents, "You guys are good. Asking me if he was dark-haired, when all along your man is blond. You guys know all the angles."

The man shook his head and mumbled with short bursts of laughter all the way back to his house.

Instinctively, the two agents turned their backs to the Johnson house. Nick pointed down the block toward the limo house for effect.

"We can't tell Evans and the crew about the rental," Nick said. "We keep everyone focused down the street, the way it's supposed to look."

Matt agreed. They returned to the van where the female agent was screwing her face into a knot trying to decipher the phone calls she'd been tapping.

Matt tugged on Jake's arm. "You have a parabolic with you?" he asked.

"Sure," Jake said, "but they've got one aimed at the place already. You need another one?"

"Yeah," Matt said, "Nick and I are going to take a stroll around the neighborhood and see what we can pick up."

Jake shrugged, entered the second van and returned with the small, funnel-shaped parabolic microphone. "Here you go."

Nick told Evans not to move until he and Matt returned, no matter what they heard in the house. Nick and Matt walked toward the limo house, then after they were out of range, they turned right and away from the house, down a side street. They doubled back toward the Johnson rental using a parallel street behind the house. Under the bright moon of the desert sky, they were careful to work within the shadows of shrubs and palm trees. When Matt peeked past a property line wall, he pulled his head back like a frightened turtle.

"It's right there," he said. "Give me the mike."

Without exposing anything but his left hand, Nick crouched, pointed the cone toward the house and placed the miniature headset over his ears. At first he heard loud static, the rustling of trees, the sound of a car's engine in the distance. He twisted a knob on top of the cone, adjusting its focus, narrowing its beam to the Johnsons' house. He heard a man's voice speaking a foreign language. Nick was fluent in Kurdish, Russian, and Spanish, and got along all right with several other Latin-based languages. His eyes widened when he heard an authoritative voice speaking Kurdish say, "Where is Bracco? I lost him."

"Forget him," another voice said. "He went to the other house."

Nick went rigid when he heard, "Kill the brother and get out of here."

Chapter 8

Hasan Bozlak peeled away the rug and yanked up on the trap door. He peered down into the dark tunnel. A simple string of lights illuminated the passageway. Working behind drawn curtains, Hasan was assigned four workers, mechanical drilling devices, and instructions on how to build the escape route. Twice a week the dirt was hauled from the backyard by a truck with a pool logo on its doors. A gate in the tall fence slid open and closed abruptly with each departure.

The American government had its law officers surrounding the decoy house while Hasan prepared to lead his team of Kurdish workers through the tunnel to a house on a street directly behind them. It was only sixty feet to the garage where a car was waiting to take them to Kharrazi.

He directed two of the men into the tunnel and was waiting for the final member of the team to execute the prisoner when he heard the strangest sound. The doorbell rang.

The two men in the tunnel also heard the doorbell. The three of them swung their automatic weapons from the strap on their shoulders and assumed an attack position. Hasan held an index finger to his lips and motioned for the men to spread out. He peeked out from the side of a curtain. Standing at the front door as casual as if he were delivering flowers, was Nick Bracco. Bracco didn't appear to be expecting trouble. His hands were empty and loose at his side. Maybe the FBI was canvassing the area?

Hasan's first instinct was to shoot. Kill the FBI agent and his brother. But too many years of following orders prevented him. The shooting would attract attention and cause the house to be invaded by FBI agents. There was a plan for the situation, which was just as deadly and allowed them more time to escape. In fact, Hasan had secretly hoped for an opportunity to use the alternate escape plan. It would send a necessary message to the Americans. The end of their cozy little lives was near. No one was safe in his homeland, why should America be immune from the danger?

Hasan stepped silently into the kitchen where a bearded man examined a syringe full of noxious liquid, flicking the syringe to remove excess air bubbles.

Phil Bracco sat motionless in a wooden chair in the middle of the room. His arms were tied behind him, his legs bound to the chair's legs, and his mouth taped shut. His sleeve was rolled up in preparation for his silent death. As the man bent over to inject Phil's arm, Hasan grabbed the man's wrist.

"Leave him. We need him alive," Hasan said.

The man gave a perfunctory shrug.

Hasan reached down and unfastened one of Phil Bracco's legs from the chair. He leaned close to the prisoner's ear and whispered, "Count to thirty, then make all the noise you wish."

* * *

Nick Bracco trembled while he waited at the front door. There wasn't a plan. There wasn't time for one. He had to interrupt his brother's execution. He banked on the fact that the terrorists inside might be concerned about gunshots causing attention. Matt was sent to get help while Nick shifted his weight from foot to foot, acting as innocent as possible. He caught himself wiping his sweaty palms on his pants and quickly placed his hands behind his back. Unarmed and harmless. Just checking with the neighbors, that's all.

Suddenly, a light came to life from behind closed curtains. Then another blinked on from an upstairs window. To his left another slit of light escaped from a closed drape. The entire house was being lit up. Did he have the wrong house? He considered that for a moment, yet the door remained closed. He rang the bell again. Still no answer.

He heard the hushed tones of FBI agents and Hostage Rescue experts closing in from a distance. He didn't dare turn and acknowledge their presence. He rang again, this time hearing a noise. A faint thumping, not rhythmic or in any cadence. Carefully, he held his ear to the door. Again the thumping from inside the house.

He slowly walked away from the house and headed for a clump of bushes where he knew Matt would be waiting. Once behind the cover of the foliage he asked Matt for the cone.

"I hear something inside," Nick said. He slipped on the headphones and listened to the amplified sound through the cone. "Someone's banging . . . I can't make it out. It's not hard like steel, more like someone banging their fist on a wall."

"We've got the place surrounded," Evan's said. "Let's crash this party." He looked at Matt, "How many do you think?"

"Five, maybe six," Matt estimated.

Evans lowered his head and spoke into the miniature radio attached to his collar, "When I give the signal, you take the rear. We have the front."

The team began their inspection from a window on the side of the house where the noise seemed to originate. Others were doing the same thing to each wall of the house. Jake positioned a slender black tube to the side of the window, where only a crease of light showed. The tube was attached to a video device that relayed the image to a handheld screen. With one hand holding the screen, Jake used his free hand to twist the fiber-optic tube into position. It allowed Jake to scan the brightly lit kitchen. He maneuvered the tiny screen so Nick could see the image. The camera showed a man tied to a chair, swinging his leg wildly against the floor and the stove and anything else he could kick.

"Recognize him?" Jake asked.

Nick examined the image. It was definitely Phil. He was tied to a chair and swinging a free leg against the wall, thumping for attention. Nick realized that Phil was left alive for tactical reasons, and it almost worried him more than seeing him dead. His brother's survival was no oversight. He nodded to Jake. "It's him."

Quietly Evans spoke into his radio, "What do you see on the east side, Cliff?"

"Nothing," a voice came back. "I don't see a thing in either room."

"What about the south side?" Evans said.

"It's empty over here," a different voice responded.

"North?" Evans asked.

"Zippo," a third voice said.

Evans looked at Nick. "The bottom floor is clear. We're going in."

Nick couldn't put it together, but he knew they were in danger.

Evans waved for his men to fall in behind him. They moved toward the back door. Nick followed. Everyone had guns drawn except for two of Evans' men who stood facing each other, gripping a large door ram between them. They rocked the steel pole, preparing to smash in the door. Evans pressed the button on his radio and was about give the order when Nick held up his hand.

"Wait," Nick said.

Evans seemed confused. "Wait for what?"

Nick thought for a moment. "The lights," he said. "There's a reason all the lights are on."

"You think they're upstairs with night-vision goggles?" Matt said. "We go charging in there and they shut off the electricity and ambush us with night gear."

Evans radioed everyone to have their infrared gear ready.

Again Evans wanted to move and again Nick interrupted him.

"This is what they want," Nick said. "There's a reason my brother is allowed to move around in there. They're using him as bait."

This time Evans' voice had an edge to it. "Listen, Bracco, we've got them surrounded and outnumbered. The longer we wait, the less chance we have of saving your brother."

"Believe me, I want him out of there more than you know," Nick said. "There's something very wrong here. Just give me a minute."

Evans' eyes narrowed. For the first time since arriving in Las Vegas, Nick considered who had rank. He could see that Evans was pondering the same question. Evans pushed the button on his radio while looking into Nick's eyes. "Stand down," he radioed. "We move in three minutes."

Nick returned to the side of the house with Matt alongside. Jake was still playing with his fiber-optic toy when Nick asked him to step aside. Without ceremony, Nick took the butt of his gun and busted a hole in the kitchen window. The soprano pitch from the glass shattering sprung a couple garage lights to life. Evans looked thoroughly disgusted as he radioed his team a play-by-play description so they understood the noises being made.

Nick slid the shade aside with the muzzle of his gun and caught a glimpse of his brother kicking his heel into the oven door.

"Phil," Nick called.

Phil sat still, swinging his head from side to side, searching for the owner of the voice.

Nick said, "Phil, don't move."

Phil's eyes frantically delivered the screams that he couldn't get from his taped mouth.

"Do you want me to come get you?" Nick asked.

Phil closed his eyes and shook his head violently.

"No?"

Again Phil shook his head. This time he arched his head toward the backdoor entrance to the kitchen.

"What?" Nick asked. "You want me to go through that door?"

Clearly frustrated, Phil glared at the door, desperately trying to draw Nick's attention.

From Nick's angle he couldn't see the entire door. He asked Jake for the video device and Jake allowed him to slip the black tube into the opening of the window. Nick scrutinized the back door, but couldn't see anything unusual. He looked back at Phil. "I don't see a thing," he said.

This time Phil motioned with his free leg. He seemed to sweep a straight line with his foot. An idea grew in Nick's head.

"Matt," he said, pointing to the fluorescent light hanging in the center of the kitchen. "Shoot out the light."

This caused some curious looks, but no one ever had to ask Matt McColm twice to fire his weapon. Before a word was spoken, Matt lined up his pistol and fired two shots, knocking out both bulbs without wasting a bullet. The blasts caused shards of glass to rain over Phil's head. Up and down the quiet neighborhood houses began to light up like an excited pinball machine. Evans feverishly broadcasted every move with the same tone used to announce the Hindenburg disaster. Once again Nick slipped the fiber-optic tube into the darkened room and steered its gaze toward the kitchen door.

"There you are, you bastard," Nick said.

Matt glanced down at the tiny screen and saw a thin stream of red light across the base of the door. "It's booby-trapped," he declared. "Call the Bomb Squad, this baby's wired to blow."

Evans saw the laser beam and immediately gave orders not to touch any doors or windows.

"Do you see anything around this window?" Nick asked Phil.

Phil's shoulders hung low, his head moved side to side slowly, full of relief.

Nick curled his hand through the jagged opening in the glass and unlocked the latch. He slid open the window and with eight sets of hands training their weapons on the inside of the kitchen, Nick climbed into the house and quickly pulled the tape from his brother's mouth.

"I'm sorry, Nick," Phil pleaded.

Nick untied him. "Are they all upstairs?"

"I couldn't tell, but it sounded as if they left. I heard a door slam shut."

Nick hustled Phil back through the open window into Matt's welcome arms, then followed him out of the house. "Nice to see you breathing," Matt said with a wide grin.

Phil collapsed onto the lawn, which was moist from the

morning dew. He took shallow breaths and hugged himself tightly, shivering from more than just the night air.

Nick crouched down over his brother. "You okay?"

Phil nodded. "They've been keeping me pretty doped up, but I think I'm all right." He grabbed Nick's arm. "I'm worried, Nicky. I kept hearing them talk about what you did to someone named Rashid. Did you arrest him or something?"

"Something like that."

"Well, I think they're holding a grudge against you."

Evans barked out a name and instantly a young man in a blue FBI windbreaker emerged from the darkness. "Take this man over to Desert Springs, get him checked out."

Nick tenderly slapped his brother's face. "I'll see you over there in a little while."

While waiting for the Bomb Squad to show, Nick found a tree to sit under and leaned up against the trunk for support. Wiping his clammy hand on his pants, he forced himself to subdue the throbbing in his head. Two episodes in one night, not good. Worse yet, his stomach wanted to join the party. First a slight seasick sensation, then a full-out race for his throat. A couple of hard swallows later, Matt began running interference for him. He shuffled away anyone coming too close, citing flu-like symptoms to anyone who asked about Nick's condition.

The bomb squad showed up wrapped in Kevlar and drew attention away from Nick. Matt, a veteran of bomb threats, knew that once the explosive experts arrived, they immediately gained custody of the crisis. Everyone else followed their lead except Matt, who had grown allergic to taking orders from strangers. Without ever taking his eyes off the bomb squad's antics, he squatted next to Nick and said, "You want to tell me about it?"

"What's to tell? I'm sick."

"That's obvious, but sick from what? You seemed perfectly fine a few minutes ago."

Nick hesitated. "Well . . . if you ask Dr. Morgan he'll suggest Post-Traumatic-Stress-Disorder."

Matt rubbed the side of his face. "That's just great."

"Don't give up on me," Nick said, wanting to give hope. Wanting to believe it himself. "I could beat this thing."

Nick's phone rang. Walt Jackson was on the line. "I'm afraid I've got some bad news," Jackson said.

"Well, I've got some good news," Nick said.

"I'm all ears."

"We've got Phil."

There was a long pause. Nick could hear Jackson's exhale turn into a faint whistle. Jackson's voice suddenly contained a smile that could be heard over the thousands of miles and three satellites used to transmit the highly secure conversation. "You have no idea how glad I am to hear that," Jackson said. "I underestimated the significance of transferring Rashid Baser to a minimum security site. Thirty minutes ago he escaped from Poplar Hill Pre-Release Unit. No guard tower. No razor wire fences. A real country club atmosphere and Rashid took advantage of the situation."

"It wasn't a fluke?"

"Oh no. They've had this set up all along. They never once thought we would release Baser, all they wanted was the opportunity to spring him. Anyway, Phil's safe and that's all that really matters."

"That's right." Nick could see the first wave of bomb experts enter the house from the kitchen window. Matt stood next to Evans with his arms crossed, nodding at the occasional comment. "I've got to go, Walt. Bomb Squad just showed up. Matt's over there right now telling anyone who'll listen how arrogant those guys are."

"Any casualties?"

"No," Nick said. "I'll keep you posted."

Nick felt queasy standing up, but by the time he reached the house, the tunnel had already been discovered. The primary team was moving cautiously and Evans let everyone hear his radio transmissions from the team. When the lead group made it to the garage, the house search was over and the area search began.

An aggressive search of the Vegas area commenced. The airport and bus terminal were staked out and highway roadblocks ensued, but none of Kharrazi's men were found.

At the hospital, Phil pointed out three Kurdish Security Force members out of a stack of eight-by-ten glossies from Nick's files, including Kemel Kharrazi. For Kharrazi, it was a remarkably bold appearance in the United States, which caused consternation among all law enforcement agencies, including America's most interested citizen — the President of the United States.

By the time Nick and Matt flew back to Baltimore, the reward for any information leading to the arrest of Kemel Kharrazi was upped to forty million dollars. To the discerning eye, it would appear like an act of desperation.

It was.

Chapter 9

Lamar Kensington was suffering from insomnia at three thirty in the morning, when he decided to inspect the fridge for a snack. With just the dim light of the moon to guide him, he salted a piece of leftover pizza, stood over the sink, and stared out the window. As he chewed groggily, he fixed his gaze on the neighbors' house across the street. A majestic Victorian stood on the crest of a hill, overlooking tightly mowed grass that meandered through the manicured landscape like a poet's version of a putting green. He marveled at the tiny spotlights that accented trees at precise angles, causing a warm, dreamy effect that Lamar longed for in his own yard. He had neither the fervor nor the funds that Senator Williams possessed, yet he could never view the yard without the urge to grab his putter.

He was imagining himself lobbing a wedge shot into the middle of the senator's yard when the detonation occurred. A flash of bright fire erupted from the Williams' house, instantly illuminating the quiet neighborhood and engulfing the home. A thunderous blast shook the ground and Lamar braced himself as he watched the house explode into a huge fireball. The deafening crash propelled misshapen debris with such velocity that a fragment of the front door screamed through Lamar's kitchen window, hitting him square in the chest and knocking him to the floor. He gasped for air while flicking off shards of glass. Almost as an afterthought, he pulled up his tee-shirt to inspect the wound. A flap of skin hung open and exposed a raw sliver of his ribcage. Blood seeped from the opening like an undercooked steak. Just before he passed out, he heard sirens wailing in the distance.

* * *

Julie Bracco stared at the ringing phone with contempt. She had just spent two quiet weeks with her husband following his return from Las Vegas. Two weeks uninterrupted by stakeouts, overnight flights, or middle of the night phone calls. Two weeks of therapy with Dr. Morgan and a prescribed break from action. It was difficult, but Nick managed to get by on just a couple of phone calls a day to the office, always hanging up shaking his head.

Nick was in the shower and couldn't hear his tiny phone bleating for attention on the bedroom dresser. She was hugging a load of

laundry and hesitated for a moment before tapping the shower door
with her foot. "Phone," she called.

Nick shut off the water and sprang from the bathroom with a
towel wrapped around his waist. Julie stepped into the hall and lingered for a moment to eavesdrop.

"Shit," was the only thing she heard. She leaned against the wall
and closed her eyes. Nick turned on the television. The urgent tone of
a tremulous female voice caused her to reenter the bedroom.

In bold letters across the bottom of the screen were the words,
"Breaking News." A blonde reporter with a hint of mascara trickling down her cheek stood in front of the charred skeleton of a large
house. The morning sun unveiled ripples of smoke drifting across
the enormous ruin. Wooden frames leaned awkwardly in unnatural
positions. A stubborn portion of a smoldering wall wavered in the
slight morning breeze. Two men in yellow raincoats huddled over a
pile of ashes.

Nick turned up the volume. The reporter held a hand to her chest
and spoke to the camera like a mother gasping out the horrors of her
murdered child. "The Senator and his family were all at home," she
panted. "Senator Williams was forty-seven." She shifted sideways to
give the camera a fuller view of the wreckage. "As you can see, there
is very little left of the –" she choked.

Nick switched the channel. Through the miracle of a satellite dish,
another reporter in a different city stood in front of a house in a similar condition. Nick switched the channel again and saw that all across
the country reporters with somber faces stood in front of the premeditated destruction of different households. Random assaults had devastated individual homes in each of the fifty states.

"What's happening?" Julie cried.

"It's begun."

"What's begun?"

Nick stood in front of the television, tight-lipped, his jaw clenched,
his eyes distant. He turned and seemed to look through her as if she
was invisible. Not the same man she had just made passionate love
with twenty minutes earlier.

"I've got to go," he said and disappeared into the closet.

* * *

The Baltimore field office housed the largest War Room in the country. It was built during the cold war era and was bunkered in the basement, where the only access was through an elevator fronted by an iris-scan entry. The room itself was more like an auditorium. It had an elevated podium, which stood above rows of wooden booths that resembled church pews. Surrounding the seats were four stark white walls with assorted maps and diagrams tacked to them. An occasional poster of Marilyn Monroe or Mickey Mantle remained behind, mementos from the patriotic souls who first used the bunker during the Cuban missile crisis.

Walt Jackson stood at the podium, his massive frame looming over the seventy-five FBI agents seated in front of him. Behind him stood the Director of the CIA and next to him, drawing the attention of every man and woman in the room, sat a telephone with one line conspicuously blinking. Nick sat in the front row next to Matt.

Jackson pushed the blinking button activating the speaker-phone. "Mr. President?"

The unmistakable voice of President John Merrick said, "Yes, Walt, I'm here."

"Mr. President," Jackson turned to make eye contact with the Director of the CIA, "I have Ken Morris with me. We're all assembled, Sir."

"Good," said President Merrick. "Gentlemen, and, of course, ladies—Senator Williams was a close personal friend of mine. Some of you may know he was the best man at my wedding." He sighed. Everyone sat at attention and listened as if the principal was addressing his students.

"Unfortunately, he was only one of fifty families that are grieving this morning as a result of the brutal attack on our nation.

"We received an e-mail from the Kurdish Security Force. Walt, I know your people follow this stuff closely, so the message won't come as a shock. They will bomb one home in each of the fifty states every week that we don't withdraw our troops from Turkey. The same message was sent to the Washington Post. The American people are going to know of their demands. It's a shrewd tactic, folks. The occupation of Turkey wasn't popular to begin with. Now it appears as if it will cost innocent citizens their lives if we don't cave in."

The President's voice grew harsh, "Walt, you know damn well I can't withdraw our troops under these conditions. Our presence was mandated once the Kurds began slaughtering hundreds of Turkish civilians. I know I don't have to sell you on my decision, but now every time an American is killed, it's my fault. I'll accept the responsibility, but I need answers and I need plausible options and I need them quick."

President Merrick stopped abruptly and it seemed to take Jackson by surprise, as if he expected the longwinded political statement that usually came from a White House conference call.

"Walt?"

"Yes, Sir, Mr. President."

"Walt, how many KSF do we have in custody now?"

"As of thirty minutes ago, we have nine, Sir."

"Nine KSF members—how many do you suspect are directly or indirectly related to the bombings?

"All of them."

"That's good. What have we learned from them?"

The assemblage of agents knew the answer before it ever left Jackson's mouth.

"Nothing, Sir."

"Nothing?"

"No, Sir. They'd rather die first. As a matter of fact two of them have attempted suicide."

"I see." In the silence, a deep breath could be heard.

Ken Morris stepped closer to the speakerphone. "Mr. President, this is Ken."

"Yes, Ken," the frustrated voice said.

"Sir, this is similar to stomping on roaches as they crawl across the floor. We can't protect every citizen in the country. We have to find the source. That's the only way we'll put an end to it. The scheme is too elaborate not to have a leader dictating the details of the mission."

"And you're sure who that leader is?"

"Yes, Sir. It's Kemel Kharrazi. We find him and we can end the terrorist acts."

"You're positive?"

"Yes."

"Then why haven't we found him yet?"

"Sir . . . uh, there are some leads, but—"

"Ken, we have satellites circling the Earth that could read the date on a dime sitting in the road between two parked cars. Are you telling me we can't find the most infamous terrorist in the world, in our own backyard?"

Ken opened his mouth but only to take a large breath.

The President exploded. "Gentlemen, I want Kemel Kharrazi's picture on every television, every newspaper, every magazine cover. I want you to burn up every favor you have with every informant you've ever used. Offer immunity, offer pardons, offer money, whatever you want, I'll approve it. Bottom line—I want Kharrazi! Do you understand?"

"Yes, Sir," came the collective answer.

President Merrick hung up.

Walt Jackson stood tall, his long arms leaning on the podium in front of him. In one slow sweep of the congregation, he seemed to make eye contact with every individual in the bunker. "Well then," he said, "let's get started."

* * *

In the aftermath of the two-hour briefing that followed the President's call, Walt Jackson lumbered into his office, walked behind his desk, and dropped onto his leather chair. He rubbed his eyes, feeling the stubble on the side of his unshaven face. When he looked up, Nick and Matt were seated across from him.

Jackson's finger tapped a staccato cadence on his desk. "The President thinks we dropped the ball," he said.

"Don't beat yourself up, Walt," Matt said. "You made all the right moves. Don't second guess yourself now."

"Fact is," Walt grimaced, "we can protect our national monuments. We can make provisions for all of our federal buildings, our courts. But we simply can't cover every single household in the United States. It's just not possible."

"Kharrazi is shrewd," Nick said. "He knows America doesn't have the stomach for this type of warfare. Not here at home. Not with the media flashing the faces of our dead neighbors on every news channel. This isn't some distant operation in the jungles of Asia. The political pressure will eventually become so great, we won't have a choice but to retreat from Turkey."

Jackson nodded. He smiled at the two agents, coming to support him. He sat upright and pointed a finger at Nick, who was already glancing down at digital pictures he pulled from a stack on Jackson's desk. "What do you make of those photos?"

"These bombs have Rashid's signature all over them," Nick said, scrutinizing the closeups of bomb parts already partially reassembled. "The design of the circuitry is identical to the White House bomb. No matter how sophisticated he gets, he always uses the same configuration."

"Yes, but where does he get the material?" Matt said. "Find the place he gets the parts and you'll find Rashid."

"And if you find Rashid," Nick added. "You find Kharrazi."

Jackson leaned back in his chair, enjoying the rhythm of the banter between his two agents. "All right," he said. "I want you two to follow the bomb trail. All of the bombs were Semtex, therefore massive amounts of RDX were made for the explosions. Stop by the Explosives Unit on your way out and talk with Norm Boyd. He knows more about RDX than anyone we have. Find an ingredient, a chemical, a blast cap, anything you can that might be hard to find in normal retail stores and zone in on that item. Since RDX is a fairly stable compound, my guess is that Rashid is making the stuff in quantity, then transporting the devices to the appropriate city. It makes more sense than risking fifty different chemical labs."

Jackson looked at his watch. "I suggest you gentlemen get going. I have to decide whether to rewrite my will or my resume."

* * *

Nick was bent on getting home that evening, even if it was just for a nap and a change of clothes. Julie would be worried about him and he'd try to disarm her concern with a smile and a hug. He would show her no visible signs of stress. She wouldn't see the neurons firing back and forth across his brain, pressing for the answers that would lead him to Kharrazi and, ultimately, refuge for his overactive mind.

When he turned on his car radio, he heard the Washington Post story about the KSF demands leading every newsbreak. As he drove home, talk radio was having a field day with the subject. A paranoid America tuned in to hear the news, rumors, or anything else that could keep them even the tiniest bit safer than their next-door neighbor. The President was getting hammered from both sides of the political aisle. One right-wing commentator even suggested impeachment. A poll had already been taken, and sixty-two percent of the American public wanted troops out of Turkey immediately. That number skyrocketed to eighty-seven percent when they polled anyone who lived within twenty miles of a bombed house.

The Associated Press reported that most of the bombs had been planted for some time before they were detonated. In a few cases they were fired from passing cars. A delivery method that was harder to defend, yet easier to track down. Out of the nine KSF members in custody, eight had been involved with the drive-by method of bombing. Nick marveled at the accuracy of the information. It was almost as if AP had a reporter inside the War Room that afternoon.

* * *

Nick arrived home late and hugged Julie so tightly, he felt the breath surge from her diaphragm.

When he finally released her, she delicately swept a tuft of hair from his forehead with the back of her index finger. "Rough day at the office, Sweetie?"

Nick smiled for the first time since he'd left her arms that morning. "I can't slip anything by you, can I?" They both laughed and released whatever pressure their tense bodies would allow.

"Do you have time for a meal? I've got sauce warming on the stove. I could boil some pasta real quick."

"Sure," he said, jogging up the stairs to their bedroom.

"Oh, I almost forgot," Julie said. "Tommy's been calling all day. He said he needs you to call him on his cell right away."

Nick grimaced. "Like I needed to hear that."

* * *

Tommy picked up on the first ring. "Yo."

"It's me," Nick said.

"I think you owe me a favor," Tommy said.

"Of course. You want the name of the person who kidnapped Phil— right?"

"It's a little more complicated than that. You see, I know the name you're gonna give me, and that's not quite enough."

"What do you mean?"

"Nicky, I know you've been busy today, but did you happen to catch the name of the family that was killed this morning in Baltimore? You know, the terrorist's pick for the state of Maryland."

"I saw the list."

"The name was Capelli. Joseph and Mary Capelli. Ring a bell?"

"Aw shit, Tommy. I had no idea."

"Yeah, well . . . now I need a favor from you."

Nick flinched. "I'm listening."

"The Capellis have given me the responsibility of finding the monster who killed their family. I'm talking three gorgeous little kids, Nicky. I need your help and I need information. Don't let me down."

Nick was about to react by rote. Normally, he would dismiss Tommy with the standard policy and be done with it. But this was different. The President had said as much that afternoon. Technically, Tommy was an informant. Informants exchange information with the government and almost always receive more information than they give. It was the quality of the information that counted, not the quantity.

Tommy waited patiently while Nick sorted things out. He could sense Tommy's rebuttal about to commence.

Finally, Nick said, "How much do you know about Semtex?"

Chapter 10

Rashid Baser stepped into the pawnshop, flipped over the open sign to read "closed" and locked the door. Behind the counter, Fred Wilson offered him a sheepish smile while running a cloth over the barrel of a gun. When he glimpsed the manila envelope in Rashid's left hand, he set the gun on the glass counter in front of him and nodded toward a doorway. Rashid followed him into a dark room, where guns and cameras mingled together on the warped wooden shelves that covered all four walls. To one side of the room a large mound was covered conspicuously with a canvas tarp. Fred sidestepped his way to the mound, mumbling apologies about the condition of his storage room. Rashid understood the maneuver very well. He recognized it from his native Turkey. It was the dance of the intimidated. Back home his reputation had grown to such proportions, he could move through the crowded streets of an entire village without ever viewing the back of a head. The Red Sea of fear would part before him. But not in America. At first he was disturbed by the absence of respect, but he grew to revel in the anonymity. Blending in made his missions that much easier. That's why Fred's demeanor was so troubling. He didn't even know Rashid's name.

As if he was trying not to wake a sleeping baby, Fred carefully lifted the corner of the tarp revealing a load of large silver tubes. "Here they are," he said.

Rashid lifted one of the tubes. He was unprepared for its weight and accidentally clanked it slightly on the side of another canister.

Fred jumped back, "Careful," he said. "Those are mighty powerful blasting caps, the primer alone could blow the roof off a hou . . ." he dropped his eyes. In the tension of the moment, Fred Wilson had made a mistake.

Rashid seemed to let the comment go, as if he didn't hear it. He busied himself with the detonators, counting the stacks.

Fred removed his baseball cap, leaving its imprint in his hair. He fondled the hat, reluctant to look at Rashid directly. After an uncomfortable silence, Fred got the words to his mouth. "Well, Sir . . . how about the money?"

Suddenly, Rashid thought, he'd become Sir. Two weeks ago he

was foreign trash. Now he was Sir. He was certain the fifty thousand dollars was only part of the reason.

"Aren't you curious why I needed such a large cylinder?" he asked.

"I . . . uh never get involved with the details."

"But surely you must wonder."

Fred refused to engage him. He picked lint from the bill of his cap. "Sir, I haven't the slightest idea what you might be using it for. I'm just the middleman. I don't make judgments."

"Do you watch the news?" Rashid asked.

Fred hesitated a moment too long. "Sometimes. I'm pretty busy with work and all."

"You're a liar," Rashid said.

Fred stepped back, rigid with fear, his eyes searching for something over Rashid's shoulder. Rashid heard a familiar click from behind him.

"Don't turn around," a man's voice said. "Just take the money out of the envelope and give it to Fred."

Rashid's blood raced through his body. "You expect me to trust you."

"I don't see that you have much of a choice," the voice said.

Rashid listened carefully to the voice. Years of training aligned his thoughts. He ran an index of moves through his mind, then waited to hear the voice and determine whether it was moving or stationary.

"This ain't no pistol I'm holding here."

That sentence offered Rashid everything he needed to know. He slid his hand into the manila envelope and gripped the knife inside. Judging the position of the voice, he dove straight back onto the floor, rolled, and heard the shotgun blast whistle over his head. Rashid heard Fred Wilson scream in agony as he jumped up, caught the barrel of the shotgun with his shoulder, and thrust the blade under the man's ribcage. Standing inches from the man's shocked face, Rashid twisted the knife, skewering the life-sustaining organs and draining his mortality until the only thing that held up his lifeless form was Rashid's hand holding the knife.

Rashid turned to see a streak of red on the floor where Fred Wilson had dragged his wounded leg. Fred frantically crawled toward a rifle that leaned against the wall. Rashid grabbed a fistful of Fred's hair, pulled his head back and lashed his steel blade across his neck so deep it nearly decapitated him. The head hit the floor with a thump.

* * *

Nick Bracco sat at the kitchen table surrounded by heaps of files and photographs. With his secure phone planted to his left ear, he scribbled notes on a yellow legal pad. Working from home was his meager attempt at spending more time with Julie.

Julie stood at the counter flipping through pages of a magazine while she waited for the coffee to finish brewing.

"I'm pregnant," she said.

Nick glanced at her, half listening to a diplomat from the Turkish embassy reciting a verse from a propaganda textbook. He cupped his hand over the phone. "What did you say?"

"I'm pregnant."

Nick dropped his pen on the table and hung up the phone. His jaw was slack and his eyes drooped, as if she'd announced that she'd been diagnosed with cancer. No elation. No "I'm-going-to-be-a-father" glow on his face. Just surprise and confusion.

"But how?" was all he could manage.

She shook her head, "I was just seeing if you were listening. I guess I'll know what to expect from you, should I ever really be pregnant."

Nick stepped behind her and rubbed her back, "I'm sorry, honey. It's just—"

"You don't have to explain. Your job will always take precedence over our marriage. I knew that going in and I guess I just like to test the theory every now and again."

"Aw, come on, Jule, do you really believe that?"

"Nick, there's always a reason why we can't go on a long vacation, or plan a party, or raise children. That reason is your job. I know it seems like more than a job to you, but in the grand scheme of the universe, that's all it really is. A job."

Nick walked to the bay window overlooking the backyard. The grass needed mowing and the hammock he'd bought over the summer swayed unoccupied between two large oaks. It occurred to him that he'd never even sat in the hammock. She was right, of course. Even after the therapy sessions, Nick was still compelled to police the country. Single-handedly, if necessary.

He wondered what Julie had seen in him that kept her so close. Even when they were dating she must've been aware of his preoccupation with his work. He wished he could give her more. More time. More emotion. More . . . life. Julie was thirty-five, and if they didn't do something soon, time would sweep past them and deny her what she deserved. She loved kids so much she chose a profession that surrounded her with children all day long.

"Okay," he said, staring out the window. "I'll quit."

"Don't be sarcastic."

"I'm not. I'll get out of terrorism and find a resident agency in some small town and work nine to five. I'll come home at night and eat dinner and read books to our children and push them on the swing set I'll build in our backyard."

She wrapped her arms around him from behind and pressed her head into the nape of his neck. "Oh, honey, I'm sorry," she whispered. "You don't know how it kills me to talk about this stuff, but every time you go on a mission, Nick, part of you doesn't return. I shouldn't be adding any more stress to your life, but I just want us to be happy, that's all."

Once again it was time to say it. Let those three words out and watch her eyes sparkle with delight. He leaned back into her hug, letting the moment pass as it had a thousand times before.

"Just let me handle the KSF attacks," he said. "Once they're resolved, I'll get out."

She sighed, rocking back and forth with Nick to an imaginary song. "However long it takes, Mr. Bracco, I'll be there."

* * *

Tommy Bracco knocked and when the door opened he was hit with the aroma of homemade marinara sauce. Don Silkari swatted him on the back and led him into the kitchen. Three men in white, starched shirts shoveled spaghetti into their mouths, a paper napkin tucked into their collars. The burly one in the middle pointed his fork at an open seat.

"Sit down, Thomas," the man said.

Tommy sat down while Silk stood over his shoulder.

The two bookends eating next to the husky man timed their bites to coincide with their boss. They wouldn't be caught with a mouthful if a quick, respectful response was needed.

The boss wiped his mouth and Tommy couldn't help feel like he was watching a silent film. The three men were practically breathing in unison.

"Thomas," the boss said. "How's your father doing?"

"He's good, Sal." Always the family questions first. That was Sal Demenci's style. He could be about to whack someone and he'd ask how the guy's sister was doing in school.

Sal dove into his mound of pasta. When he came up for air, he said, "Ever been to Payston, or Patetown?"

"Payson," one of his men clarified.

"That's it, Payson," Sal said. "It's in Arizona. You familiar with this place?"

Tommy shook his head.

"Well," Sal said, "it's supposed to be beautiful. Up in the mountains a couple of hours from Phoenix. Anyway, there's a guy up there, he likes to book with a friend of ours. One day last week, the guy lays down ten large on a football game . . . I forget who he bet—it doesn't matter. The thing is—this guy's a twenty-dollar bettor. He never dropped more than a small one, not even on the Super Bowl. The guy's name is Fred Wilson. One day he started blabbing to our friend about how he's gonna make a killing selling some Arab a bunch of giant blasting caps. Our friend doesn't think anything of it until Fred loses his head."

The bookends chuckled while Sal drew a finger across his throat, "I mean literally."

Sal twirled long strands of pasta into a spoon, the image of headless Fred Wilson unable to slow his appetite. "Anyhow, our friend gets to thinking maybe this Arab has something to do with the bombings. You know, that whole one-house-in-every-state thing."

Sal looked Tommy in the eye, as if to say, "You see what I'm getting at here?"

Tommy nodded.

Sal waved his fork between Tommy and Silk. "You two get down there and find out what our friend knows. I want this rat bastard to pay for what he did to the Capelli's. Capisce?"

Tommy stood and waited for his final instructions. Sal wiped his mouth. "I trust you, Thomas. I don't need nothing from you but your word. Don't come home until the Arab is dead."

Tommy winked at Sal, then followed Silk out the door. It was standard procedure for Sal to request a finger or an ear as evidence that the hit was completed. But Sal had awarded Tommy with the ultimate show of respect. Trust.

Chapter 11

Rashid's patience was reaching its limit. Both the hardware store and Target were out of the batteries he needed and he was on his way to Wal-Mart to continue the search. Something about the stores made him uneasy. They both had plenty of AA and D batteries, but no C batteries. They were conspicuous in their absence. Rashid became suspicious of everyone he saw. Every movement in the corner of his eye became a concern. There was no way anyone could recognize him in a place like Payson, Arizona, even if they knew what to look for. He'd shaved his mustache and changed the color of his hair from dark to blond. Besides, if the government knew where to look, he'd be back in custody already. He had to control his emotions and get through this last chore before the next series of bombs could be transported. He'd hoped to avoid attention by spreading out the purchases among several stores, but he was running out of options. He parked the van in an empty row of parking spaces and decided to buy only twenty batteries this trip. He would come back tonight after the employees changed shifts and purchase the remaining thirty.

He was relieved to see a full shelf of C batteries and got up the nerve to purchase twenty-five of them. When he exited the store he spotted a thin, dark-haired man wearing a navy-blue blazer, brand new blue jeans, and shiny black boots. The man was just three or four steps behind him and he made no pretense to be ignoring Rashid. The man smiled at him as if he was about to begin a conversation. Rashid picked up his pace and when he reached the van he noticed the man had stopped in the middle of the parking lot and was scanning the grounds for onlookers. Rashid was so mesmerized by the man's actions he didn't notice the second man approaching from his blind spot. The man waited for Rashid to open the door and sit down before he jabbed him in his side with the long barrel of a silencer and said, "Get in the back."

Rashid froze. He knew time was critical in these situations. The element of surprise was with his attacker for a few moments, but any sudden reversal of aggression would be just as surprising to the attacker. Something in the way the man held the pistol made him hesitate. The man was maneuvering a purple toothpick from one side of his mouth to the other. While Rashid contemplated his counterattack, the man glanced around the near-empty parking lot, raised the gun an inch and said, "Goodbye, Rashid. Nice knowing you."

"Okay," Rashid blurted. He jumped off the driver's seat and scuttled into the windowless rear of the van. There were no seats, just a loose-fitting carpet that slid under the quick moves of the two men entering the space. Rashid sat with his back to one wall and the man sat directly across from him, pointing the gun at him as if it were part of his hand. The passenger door opened and the other man sat in the passenger seat and began reading a newspaper like he was alone.

Rashid's knife was taped to his back and he began to creep his right hand toward the weapon.

The man across from him inspected the austere interior of the van and said, "I like what you've done to the place, Rashid."

The man reached into his pocket with his free hand, unfolded an eight-by-ten photo and held it in front of him. He switched his gaze between Rashid and the photo a few times then stuffed it back into his pocket.

"It looks like you a little, but you must've got fancy with the hair, eh?" the man said.

Rashid had no intention of speaking. The man could guess all he wanted, but Rashid wasn't about to give him any answers. His mind raced, working out the escape plan. His knife would take too long to retrieve, he needed another option.

The man said, "Hey, relax. My name's Tommy and that's Silk." Silk waved the back of his hand without ever looking up from his newspaper.

"I'm not going to hurt you," Tommy said. "I'm just here to give you a message. If I kill you, then the message doesn't get sent and I've wasted a lot of my time. Shit, a five-hour flight with headwinds and all. Just don't give me a reason to put you down."

Something about Tommy's mannerism had Rashid believing him, but it didn't prevent Rashid from running through a plan of attack. The man in the front seat wasn't even an issue, it was down to one on one, and Rashid liked those odds, even without a weapon.

Tommy removed the purple toothpick from his mouth and pointed it at Rashid. "You Middle-Easterners think you're real bad, don't ya? Well, I'm not here to judge your methods. Shit, I don't even give a crap what you're all pissed off about. All I know is you guys killed a family in Maryland who was very dear to me and my friends. The name was Capelli and you morons killed them while they were sleeping. Cowardly, really. Anyway, I'm here to tell ya— don't let it happen again. Don't let any of those missile thingy's find their way into any more Sicilian homes. Capisce?"

Rashid had read about the Capelli family and how they were considered one of the largest crime families on the East Coast. It had been a random pick, but Rashid had no regrets. Maybe that's how these Sicilians operated? Maybe they sent messengers to protect their interests. He definitely wasn't with the police or FBI, or Rashid would be on his way back to prison. And if he was there to kill him, why would he wait?

Something gnawed at Rashid. If these guys could find him, then someone else could too, and that would be devastating. As if Tommy could read his mind, he said, "Want to know how I found you?"

Rashid's curiosity got the best of him, but he resisted the urge to nod. Even though Tommy kept calling him by his name, the man might still be guessing.

"Ever hear of something called tendencies?"

Rashid stayed motionless.

Tommy appeared amused. "Didn't think so. You see my cousin is in law enforcement and recently I had a conversation with him about this situation. At first he gave me this long speech and told me not to be a vigilante and all that jazz, but he did tell me a lot about these things called tendencies. You won't believe this, but you know when you go to the can when you first enter the joint, the FBI actually gets a fucking stool sample from you without you even knowing it. Wanna know why? They find out what kind of eating tendencies you have. Wanna know what they discovered?" Tommy waved a finger at him. "You have a sweet tooth, my friend. Chocolate to be exact. With nuts."

Rashid winced as if Tommy had revealed some deep, dark secret. He noticed the gangster lower the gun into a more casual position in his lap. It was almost as if Tommy was daring him to make a move.

"Anyway," Tommy continued, "another, more important tendency you have is your pattern for making bombs. Apparently you have a habit of using C batteries for your detonator devices. This isn't that uncommon except you tend to purchase them shortly before you set the bombs. Maybe you like using fresh batteries, maybe you're superstitious. I don't know. So Silk here got the idea—see, Silk, I'm giving you credit for that one."

Tommy grinned at Rashid. "He thinks I don't give him enough credit for his creative thoughts. He thinks I'm a little selfish. I probably am. Anyhow, where was I? Oh yeah, Silk got the idea to buy up every C battery here in Payson, except for Wal-Mart. This way all we had to do was wait for someone to show up and purchase a large quantity of them here. Pretty clever, huh?"

Rashid shrugged. Still, Tommy didn't answer his question. How did he find out Rashid was in Payson to begin with? It was killing Rashid not to ask, but he knew to keep his mouth shut and not engage this guy in dialogue. He was so intrigued by Tommy's informal demeanor, he'd almost forgotten about his knife, or any other method of counterattack. Rashid was not used to this form of warfare. Why talk with your enemy? When you're assigned to kill someone, you kill them quickly and leave. You don't stay and chat like this American gangster. Was he really just there to give him a warning? Was that possible?

Tommy was making sucking sounds while jabbing his toothpick into various creases between his teeth. "You know, Rashid, you and I aren't so different. I mean both of us operate on the wrong side of the law. Right? So why can't we agree to keep it simple. I mean, I could've followed you to your little hideout up here in the woods and ratted you out to the Feds, but no, I came peacefully. Just me and Silk delivering a little message to you and your Arab friends. You're an Arab, right? I mean I know you're from Turkey, but does that make you Arabic?"

Rashid blinked and nothing else.

Tommy got to his feet. He said, "Well, we gotta go, Rashid. It's been a pleasure talking to ya. You're a regular fucking chatterbox. Just tell me one thing. Who issued the bomb in Maryland? Was that you, or that Kemel Kharrazi guy?"

Tommy said it so casually, like he was asking for the time of day. He was leaving now and practically out the door. Rashid couldn't believe it. These Americans were completely irrational. Tommy closed the door behind him, then stuck his head back in through the open window. "C'mon Rashid. I just wanna know who's in charge of the bombings so I can tell my boss I spoke to the right guy. It's you right?"

Rashid's nod was imperceptible, but it was enough to forge a smile on Tommy's face.

Even before the barrel of the silencer reappeared through the window, he knew he'd been duped. Tommy probably wasn't sure he even had the right guy until Rashid had raised his head an inch.

Rashid knew it would be the last mistake he would ever make.

Chapter 12

Hasan Bozlak clutched the steering wheel with both hands. Rashid had been gone for three hours and it was getting dark. Hasan's concern was for the mission, not Rashid. Rashid was a brash megalomaniac who had grown up as childhood friends with Kemel Kharrazi. No matter how dutiful Hasan was to Kharrazi, he would never reach the status that thirty years of friendship had shaped. While Rashid was busy getting himself arrested for attempting to blow up the White House, Hasan was constructing the blueprint for gutting America's democratic resolve. The week Rashid's mug shot was on the cover of Time Magazine with the words "The Face of Terrorism" below it, Hasan was busy planning the nationwide bombing of the United States. Hasan was the one with the foresight to calculate the pressure President Merrick would receive from the American people should they all be put in harm's way. No one would be immune from the danger. Not even senators.

Hasan's prognosis appeared sound. From everything he was hearing and seeing on CNN, America was not willing to risk their lives over some country most civilians couldn't even pick out on a map.

Rashid had insisted on purchasing the batteries himself. Another bold move that lacked the prudence required at such a critical time in the operation.

Hasan had just as much talent with explosives as Rashid did, but without the swagger. It was almost as if Rashid wanted to get caught so he could receive credit for his genius with a remote detonator.

Hasan pulled into the Wal-Mart shopping center and groaned when he saw the van at the far end of the parking lot. He crept the vehicle through the lanes as if he was searching for a good parking spot, all the while observing the van. He became alarmed when he saw a strange man sitting in the front seat shifting his glances over an open newspaper. Hasan parked the car two aisles away facing the van. The man folded his newspaper and opened the door to leave. Suddenly, there were two of them. The other man must have exited from the side door. He saw the second man lean into the passenger window and reach for something inside. Hasan thought he heard a distant clap of thunder, but when he looked up he saw nothing but blue sky. By the time he returned his attention to the van, the two men were striding away and entering a car. The tall one was driving. Hasan recognized the car as a rental. He wrote down the license plate on a scrap piece of paper from the glove compartment and waited a few minutes, carefully watching the rental car drive away. He wanted to run to the van, but knew to remain patient. What had Rashid gotten himself into? Did his temper finally get the best of him?

Finally, when Hasan was convinced there was nobody interested in the van, he walked over to the vehicle. He peeked his head through the open passenger window and saw Rashid slumped over in the back of the van, a round circle above the bridge of his nose. Both eyes were open and they stared at Hasan as if they had a story to tell.

"You stupid, arrogant man," Hasan murmured. He looked down and saw the bag with twenty-five C batteries, then noticed the keys were still in the ignition. He knew it wouldn't be long before the sheriff's office found Rashid's body, and soon after that, the town would be flooded with federal agents. He had to get the van away from any spectators. He got in and started the engine. He would send someone for his car later.

* * *

The cabin was set deep in the woods, forty miles from downtown Payson and five from the nearest paved road. It was chosen with painstaking care. There was no way to approach the building except down a narrow dirt road that even the skilled Kurdish drivers struggled with after twenty trips. Although it was a small A-frame, it contained almost forty KSF soldiers. This included the twenty-five who worked in the five-thousand-square-foot basement, building bombs and dispatching them to the appropriate locations. The site was cleverly chosen—the canopies of the surrounding trees obscured the roof from view, making it almost impossible to detect the cabin from the sky.

The surrounding thirty acres were wired with enough miniature cameras and microphones to detect an ant colony shifting locations. Hasan drove down the tortuous dirt road, his mind searching for answers. He knew the police hadn't shot Rashid, but he struggled for an explanation. Hasan would inherit the top spot under Kharrazi's regime, and he needed to assume his post with answers, not problems.

A hundred yards before he reached the cabin, he could feel the eyes of the armed sentries concealed in the treetops lining the road.

He parked the van behind the cabin under a clump of overgrown shrubs and tugged on his left ear. A signal to the invisible eyes that he was alone and not followed.

The back door opened and Hasan entered the kitchen where Kemel Kharrazi stood at the head of a large oak table, leaning over a map of the United States. Two personal guards stood stoically behind Kharrazi, while a dozen soldiers surrounded the table, listening to his instructions.

Kharrazi was clad in his usual khakis. His skin was pale from lack of sun and his full eyebrows protruded from his forehead like antennae. His eyes were cold and as dark as tunnels. He was barely five foot nine and maybe one hundred and sixty pounds, but just by the way he carried himself, everyone looked busy when he entered a room.

When Hasan approached the table, the room became quiet. Kharrazi raised his eyebrows as if to say, "Well?"

The first few words out of Hasan's mouth were in Kurdish, then he caught himself and spoke in the practiced English that Kharrazi ordered everyone to use while in America. "I bring bad news, Sarock. I found Rashid in the Wal-Mart parking lot . . . dead. He was shot in the head. I saw two Americans leaving the van when I approached. I waited for them to leave the area before I risked a look."

Kharrazi's lips pursed. "Where is he?"

"He is in the back of the van where I found him. I drove it back here as soon as I was certain I was not being followed."

Kharrazi rose and the soldiers backed away, opening a path for their leader. He motioned for Hasan to follow and he walked out the kitchen door. The two of them were alone when they reached the van. Kharrazi opened the back door and saw Rashid. He was lying on his stomach, his head turned away. Kharrazi grabbed a fistful of hair and twisted the dead man's face toward him. He inspected the wound for a long minute. Hasan felt as though Kharrazi was praying, but soon realized he was reflecting. Maybe considering the actions that took place in order for Rashid to wind up this way.

Suddenly, Kharrazi spun around, a Beretta magically appearing in his hand. He pressed the muzzle of the Beretta to Hasan's temple and pulled the slide, chambering the first round.

Hasan stood motionless, eyes wide. He made no attempt to protect himself. He was going to die and instantly accepted his fate.

Kharrazi withdrew the gun and returned it to his holster.

Hasan let out a breath.

"You had nothing to do with Rashid's death," Kharrazi stated.

"Of course not."

"I know now. If you had a guilty mind you would have been prepared for my attack."

"Sarock?"

While staring into his eyes, Kharrazi placed both hands on Hasan's shoulders and gripped down firmly. A rare smile creased his face. "Hasan, you do not think I know how you felt about Rashid?"

Hasan was taller than Kharrazi by four inches, yet he met his leader's gaze as if he was an overgrown child listening to his parent. "I'm not sure I understand."

Kharrazi reached an arm around Hasan's shoulder and led him down a path with twilight simmering around them. Hasan heard the kitchen door open and knew Kharrazi's bodyguards were trailing them.

Kharrazi sat on a fallen tree at the side of the path and nodded for Hasan to join him. From his wallet, Kharrazi removed a folded piece of paper and handed it to Hasan. Once unfolded, the paper revealed a photograph so old the back was peeling off. The picture showed two young boys standing with their arms around each other. They had huge smiles and leaned into each other with complete ease.

"We were only twelve when that was taken," Kharrazi said.

"Rashid?"

"Yes. The day before that picture was taken, Rashid taught me the most valuable lesson of my life. We were eating fish in an alley that afternoon when a group of older boys gathered around us. I was nervously watching the boys while Rashid ignored them. They wanted our fish. At least that's what they said they wanted, I'm sure it didn't matter what we had, they would have wanted it. I was just about to hand one of the boys my food when Rashid grabbed my hand and shook his head.

"Well, I have to tell you, Hasan, I was terrified. One of the boys produced a pipe as long as my arm and began slapping it against his thigh. But all through this Rashid kept eating his meal. Just as the group was about to launch into us, Rashid jumped toward the largest boy and jammed his fork into his testicles. The boy howled like a cat while the others gawked at the blood spreading from his crotch. Rashid grabbed the pipe from the boy and waved it over his head like a wild animal. He kept screaming, 'Who's next?'"

Hasan watched his leader reminisce. It seemed Kharrazi was speaking to the trees and the air around him, only occasionally making eye contact with Hasan. Kharrazi stood up and snapped a branch from a low-lying limb. He withdrew a knife from a skintight holster attached to his chest and began working on the branch.

"Of course the group fled," Kharrazi said. "And Rashid returned to his meal as if he'd just swatted away a fly. I'll never forget that day. He taught me the efficiency of going after the biggest bully."

Kharrazi slashed at the wood while pacing up and down the narrow path, working the stick with incredible dexterity. Hasan couldn't tell if he was whittling anything in particular or just flicking off tiny fragments of anguish.

"America is the biggest bully," Kharrazi said. "For decades we've endured prolonged attacks from the Turkish government while the world turned their back."

Kharrazi pointed his knife at Hasan. "Where was America when the Turkish Security Force sent warplanes to bombard our villages with cyanide gas? Ten thousand Kurds massacred in one Friday afternoon. Your own sister fallen at the threshold of her front door, never to rise again. Where were the American zols then? Now that we finally exact some deserved revenge, America sends troops into our homeland to interfere. Our homeland, where we have yet to gain our own sovereignty."

Kharrazi kicked up dirt while Hasan sat in silence, allowing his leader to vent, busily carving up the branch. He knew Kharrazi was mixing rationalization with grief. It was Kharrazi's idea to come to America and now it had cost him his best friend's life. Explaining his motive to Hasan was entirely unnecessary but perhaps just what he needed.

Kharrazi glanced at the group of soldiers carrying Rashid's body from the back of the van. Shovels could be heard plunging into the earth one after another, rhythmically excavating a final resting place for Rashid. Kharrazi was not a religious zealot. He ruled from the strength of his devoted Kurdish following. Thirty million people searching for a state to call their own. This is what drove Kharrazi — what was here on earth, not up in the sky. He would allow his soldiers to mourn however they saw fit, but he would not participate in any formal ceremony. Hasan knew that Kharrazi was unique in this manner and it seemed to allow him a freedom that a more spiritual person couldn't afford without inviting contradictions.

Kharrazi looked away from the scene. "I allowed Rashid to act foolishly at times and I know it cost me a certain amount of respect from my men. But not you. You kept your mouth shut when I allowed such blunders. You were loyal and loyalty is what I need from someone in your position. When I return to the cabin I will announce you as the new captain of the American mission. You are now my eyes and my ears. I may allow you to make mistakes also, like Rashid, because you are loyal and deserve that right."

Hasan felt his body quiver. Was he just now getting over the gun to his head, or was he absorbing the importance of Kharrazi's words? "Sarock," he said, "Rashid was killed, but not by an officer of the law."

Without looking up from his whittling, Kharrazi said, "You make me proud, Hasan. I test the strength of your integrity with the notion of death, and yet you present me with the issue we need to discuss at once." Kharrazi looked around the facility they'd been working on for almost a year. "We are safe here. Whatever Rashid did to deserve his fate, it will have no affect on our plans."

Hasan nodded.

Kharrazi closed his eyes and said, "Did you get the license plate of the vehicle the Americans traveled in?"

"Yes. It was a rental."

Kharrazi smiled. "Good. Speak with our local contact and get the name of the person who rented the car. I will give Rashid the only thing he would have asked me for."

"What is that, Sarock?"

Defiantly, Kharrazi gripped the stick with his right hand and held it up to the deepening purple sky. It had taken the shape of a razor-sharp fork. "Revenge."

Chapter 13

"**I**'m getting worse," Nick said.

Dr. Morgan sat across from him in a tall, leather chair. He had no paper or notebook, no pencils to write with. Nick felt more comfortable knowing the psychiatrist wasn't documenting his fall from mental stability.

Dr. Morgan folded his hands across his stomach. "Nick, your brother was kidnapped, there's been an attempt on your life, and terrorists have decided to bomb the country until we withdraw our troops from Turkey." He leaned forward. "Do you think it's possible that these things have something to do with your worsening condition?"

Nick gave a reluctant shrug. He didn't like hearing the events stated out loud; they sounded more dangerous that way.

Dr. Morgan continued, "Remember when we first spoke and I told you stressful situations could cause consequences? These headaches you're suffering, the dizzy spells, these are all symptoms caused by stress. I promise that if you spent a month in Hawaii or, I don't know, a cabin up in the mountains somewhere, you would find your headaches would subside. How are the breathing exercises going?"

"They work better on days that I'm not stepping over dead bodies."

"My point exactly."

Nick pointed out the window. "Doc, you don't know what's going on out there. How can you expect me to relax when terrorists are prowling the streets at night with missile launchers and canisters of plastic explosives?"

Dr. Morgan sighed. "If it wasn't terrorists blowing up houses, it would be someone threatening to poison our water supply, or someone using chemical weapons. You're looking at this situation as if it's the final threat to our society that we will ever face. Long after you and I are gone, someone will be performing dastardly deeds on our culture. That will never end, and the sooner you realize that the better."

Nick smiled. He could see the frustration on his shrink's face and was beginning to wonder who was affecting whom the most.

He imaged Dr. Morgan fixing a drink and lighting up a cigarette the moment Nick left his office. Maybe glancing out the window for anyone suspicious.

"Doc, I see all of this deception played out by terrorists and generally we've come to expect it. It's like playing a game of chess with an opponent who's allowed to move any piece on the board in any direction they want, yet the FBI is restricted by law to move its pieces in only the direction the game allows."

"It doesn't seem fair, does it?"

"No, it doesn't."

"And what do you intend to do about that?" Dr. Morgan asked.

Nick looked out the window at nothing in particular. "I don't know."

"But it's not going to be fair for terrorists, is it?"

Nick shook his head. He was working on something, but nothing solid. Sometimes he just needed to let his mind float. That's when his best ideas seemed to surface. "Whatever I do," he said, "it'll sure beat breathing exercises."

Nick didn't need to look over to know that Morgan was rolling his eyes.

"You're still working toward getting out, aren't you?" Morgan asked.

Nick knew precisely what he meant. He nodded. "Soon."

* * *

Tommy Bracco woke to the low growl of his dog and instinctively rolled onto his stomach and reached under the pillow for his Glock. It was three thirty in the morning, and the German Shepherd stood still, glaring at an invisible sound from the front of the house, teeth exposed.

"Sheba," Tommy whispered. "What is it?"

Sheba lifted her nose and sniffed in the direction of the open bedroom door. Tommy had won Sheba in a card game three years earlier and she proved to be a great asset. She was so protective of her owner that Tommy couldn't play basketball in Sheba's presence without her assaulting anyone trying to defend him. Unlike other dogs who would yelp at the first sign of an intruder, Sheba would lie in wait, a soft growl her only warning. She'd rather sink her teeth into the prowler than chase him away with a vicious bark — another quality Tommy loved about her.

Tommy eased out of bed wearing only a pair of boxer shorts and a fierce stare. He crouched down next to Sheba and felt the hairs bristled on the back of her neck. He gave her a quick pat, then crept down the dark corridor with the Glock hanging by his side. Tommy didn't have an alarm system, but his house sat strategically in the middle of a cul-de-sac — a built-in barrier for anyone who might try casing the place. The neighbors in the bedroom community all knew each other and any unfamiliar vehicles were immediately conspicuous. Tommy was the single guy who made it a point to know everyone and even help build a fence or pitch in with the yard work when he could. One Christmas Eve, Tommy dressed up as Santa and made a special trek through the neighborhood, treating all the kids to presents he'd purchased himself. To his neighbors, Tommy was golden, and that's just the way he wanted it.

Now he heard the sound of a car engine idling. It seemed close, definitely within the cul-de-sac. He saw the dim shadow of headlights moving across his living room wall. He decided to slip through the kitchen and sneak out the back door. Sheba was at his side, anxiously lifting her legs in a mock trot. She wanted a piece of the action, but Tommy wasn't sure he could control her. "Stay put, sweetheart," he said, squeezing through the narrowly opened door. She gave a slight whine as the door clicked shut behind him.

Tommy crept along the side of the house, the wet grass cool on his bare feet. He wondered what the neighbors might think if they saw him sneaking around in his underwear carrying a gun. A noise from the bushes beyond his pool startled him. He aimed the silenced gun at the bush and was about to squeeze off a quick round when a cat leapt out and ran across his lawn, jumping up and over his block fence before he could even put the weapon down.

He continued his slow advance to the front of the house. He peeked out from the corner of his one-story home and saw a black sedan with the passenger window open and a hand tossing a newspaper into the neighbor's driveway. It rolled gradually past his house and another newspaper was flung into his driveway. Tommy grinned. Sheba was usually pretty accurate when it came to sensing danger. But even she was allowed an error every now and again, he thought.

As he turned to go back, he heard a faint clang, a metal on metal sound that seemed out of place. When he glanced back he saw the sedan still lingering in front of his house. Tommy looked down at his attire, as if maybe he'd grown a pair of pants since leaving the back door. When he looked up he caught a flash from the open window of the sedan and realized he had only a moment to react. He dove to the ground just before the blast ignited the house, propelling debris and waves of flames that rushed over his body as he covered his head for protection. He wasn't sure if the blast had physically moved him or if he was simply disoriented. He thought he began on his stomach, but now he was on his back, his legs kicking in the air.

The explosion deafened him so he couldn't know how loud he was cursing as he frantically brushed live embers from his bare skin. He also couldn't hear his wooden-framed home teetering like a house of cards. When he finally managed to extinguish himself, he braved a peek back just in time to see his roof collapsing. A segment of exterior wall began to drop and before Tommy could scramble away from the structure, it toppled towards him and landed flush across his back. His head was jolted down into the earth. The last thing he remembered thinking was, "Sheba."

Chapter 14

"It's happening," Matt McColm said. "See you at the office." Nick hung up the phone and noticed it was four-thirty in the morning.

Julie rolled over, rubbing her eyes. "Who was that?"

Nick didn't answer. Instead, he flipped on the TV. He and Julie watched a split-screen image of two different CNN reporters in two separate states. One talked over the commotion of fire trucks and police evidence-collectors' vans. The other reporter waited his turn with the details of another grizzly terrorist attack. The camera showed the incongruous picture of neatly manicured lawns and gardens with the devastated ruins of houses abruptly destroyed by the KSF. One home in each of the fifty states.

Julie held her hand over her open mouth. "Oh my gosh. Nick, this can't be happening."

Nick flipped channels. A woman in South Carolina was screaming, "My baby! They killed my baby!"

The camera followed the woman as she was led away from her smoldering home by a couple of firemen. The distraught woman fought with the two men who were trying to pry something from her grasp. In the dim light of early morning, the camera operator maintained the woman's battle as she was twisted and maneuvered away from the two men. The camera zoomed in on the focal point. The woman held her hand up high playing keep-away with the firefighters. In her hand was the mangled remains of a child's arm. "It's mine!" she shouted. "You can't take my baby, it's all I have left."

Nick felt queasy while Julie dashed into the bathroom and slammed the door behind her.

He sat on the edge of the bed and mindlessly flipped up one channel at a time, barely noting where the carnage had taken place. Virginia, Kentucky, Texas. His grip on the remote tightened until his hand began to cramp.

Finally, a still image of Kemel Kharrazi was displayed on NBC, while commentators spoke about the terrorist's history. It was a photo of Kharrazi that Nick himself had picked out. He felt it was the clearest shot of the killer's eyes. Kharrazi could change his appearance by altering the shape of his face, or even manipulating his facial hair, but he couldn't disguise the lifeless depth of his eyes.

Nick had studied those eyes for hours, trying to understand what lurked beneath the surface. Kharrazi must have had a personal investment in this mission. He wouldn't have come all the way to America to hide behind the scenes and watch the music play before him like an orchestral conductor. That wasn't his style.

Julie opened the bathroom door, wiping a small towel across her face. "Isn't there anything you can do? Certainly there's a way to stop them, isn't there?"

Nick turned off the TV and flung the remote against the headboard. "Shit, Jule, we need help, I can tell you that. We need lots of help."

Julie moved to Nick. She stood next to him and caressed the hair over his ear. "Please be safe, Sweetie."

Nick grabbed her around the waist and tugged her closer. "I'm going to find an answer. It may not be pretty, but one way or another I'll put an end to it."

* * *

The basement of the KSF cabin had three rooms. One was used strictly for manufacturing bombs. Twenty soldiers kept the Semtex, blasting caps, and detonators all separated. In the corner, a sturdy wooden shelf cradled the finished product. There were already enough explosives stockpiled for the next three bombings. A van tucked away out back would be loaded and driven west on a dirt road, over the mountain that shielded the cabin from any discernable population. It would then meet up with a series of vehicles that would carry the devices to their ultimate destinations. Each state had a hideout where instructions were given as to when to detonate the bomb. The timing was precise and thanks to the Internet and wireless connections, the coded messages were easily attained, and untraceable.

The main room held the communications center. This was the brain trust of the operation. Hasan oversaw all aspects of this room, including a section dedicated to monitoring all news media broadcasts. He was amazed at the information that America freely dispersed among its civilians. It was as if they didn't care who retrieved the information as long as it was readily available. The competition between media agencies was such that each one spent tireless energy trying to outdo the other. If one broadcaster claimed that a KSF member was arrested, another would profile the soldier's career, and yet another would indicate how the terrorist was captured and by whom. If one of their men was captured, a replacement would be sent out immediately to a new hideout in the same state that lost its soldier.

Hasan monitored the media coverage of the bombings carefully. So far NBC had the most accurate assessment of the explosions. Their experts closely matched the damage of a home in Vermont with the precise amount of Semtex used in the pre-set planting. Hasan couldn't keep the grin from his face as he watched a dozen TV monitors display the domination of interest with the nationwide bombings. America was in a frenzy and President Merrick was receiving full responsibility for the calamity.

The third room in the basement, adjacent to the main room, was Kemel Kharrazi's private quarters. The suite contained a bedroom, a bathroom, an office with a large desk, and several chairs along the perimeter, ready to be aligned in front of Kharrazi's desk for continuing instructions.

The door to Kharrazi's quarters opened and a strange man emerged from the private residence. The man was bald and wore dark sunglasses. He had large, puffy cheeks that matched his oversized waistline. Several soldiers reached for their weapons, ready for the stranger to make a move. The man stood still, then a grin spread across his face as he removed his sunglasses. There was no mistaking the eyes.

"Sarock?" Hasan said. "What is it you are doing?"

"My name is Walter Henning," Kharrazi said, holding up a phony driver's license from his wallet. "I'm going to Baltimore on business."

Hasan's mouth became dry. "Business? Please tell me this business."

"Don't be alarmed, I am not recognizable. I will bring extra hairpieces and makeup. You forget how easy it is to move about in America."

"This business you speak of—what could it possibly be at this particular time?"

Kharrazi's face grew severe. "The American who shot Rashid, he is still alive. Those fools allowed him to live, at least for a little while longer. I am going to personally defend Rashid's honor. This is something I must do myself."

Hasan was concerned with Kharrazi's passion for revenge. He

feared the minute they discovered the last name of Rashid's assassin, Kharrazi's thoughts would become distorted. It was as if the entire mission was secondary to acquiring retribution. "The man who shot Rashid," Hasan said, "he is definitely related—"

"Yes, he is the cousin of the government agent. The one who arrested Rashid. He will also be eliminated. Do not worry Hasan, I will be back in less than forty-eight hours. The private jet is waiting for me. It is effortless to move about this country through chartered airplanes. There are no checkpoints to avoid. Simply have money and the nation is yours to travel unbridled. Capitalism at its finest. You have all my instructions and if you need me . . ." Kharrazi held up a small mobile phone. Months ahead of time, a series of cell phones were purchased with cash, along with pre-paid calling minutes. Each one was purchased in a different state with phony names. In case the FBI had tapping abilities that the KSF wasn't aware of, each phone was disposed of after every call.

Kharrazi placed a hand on Hasan's shoulder. "Do not worry, Hasan, I am not Rashid. I will be discreet. Deadly, but discreet."

* * *

It was barely daybreak when Nick pulled into the parking lot of the Baltimore field office. A black limousine idled in front of the employee entrance. An American flag hung limp from the antenna. Nick glanced into the open door as he passed by.

"Nick," a voice came out of the back of the limo. Matt poked his head out and waved him inside.

Crammed into the long bench seating were ten agents from domestic terrorism on their way to a field trip. Nick sidled onto a seat next to Matt.

"We're going to the White House," Matt said. "Shit's going to hit the fan."

"I'd imagine so."

Walt Jackson eased into the back of the limo and shut the door. The silence was funereal as he signaled for the driver to go. Walt closed his eyes and rubbed his neck. When he opened them, he realized he was the center of attention. "What are you looking at?" he said. "You've never seen a man have a nervous breakdown before?"

It was classic Walt—deflecting the fear and absorbing the blame. It was never anyone else's fault but his own, and only the most self-conscious agent would feel an ounce of responsibility for anything that went wrong under Jackson's regime.

A gray sky threatened to conceal the sun's affect for the duration of the day. Nick didn't think the Bureau deserved the sunshine and wondered if he was the only one who felt that way. The silence lingered as the limo rolled towards Pennsylvania Avenue. America was waking to a new world. A world where no one was safe: not the affluent, the privileged, the famous. The prosperous shared vulnerability with their penurious counterparts. For the first time that Nick could remember, America was becoming a community. A very frightened community.

The limo slowed and entered a gated driveway just west of the White House. In the distance Nick could see a podium set up on a grassy area near the front of the building. There were bright, reflective lights hanging from booms and a crowd of journalists huddled in front of the podium, waiting for an official response from the president on the bombings.

From the guard station, a uniformed attendant approached the limo and made a thorough examination of its contents. After an exchange with the driver where code words and signals were exchanged, he waved the limo through the opening gates. Once around back, the limo stopped in front of a burgundy awning and a group of secret service officers in suits and headsets ushered the agents into the secured entrance.

Once inside, the pack of terrorist specialists was led into a conference room on the first floor. It was a large room with bare, white walls and a long table in the middle. At the head of the table with his arms folded was President Merrick. To his right was CIA Director Ken Morris, to his left, FBI Director Louis Dutton. Dutton had an exhausted look on his face as he motioned Walt Jackson to take the seat next to him. The assemblage of agents filled in the remaining seats.

Nick recognized a couple of members of the Joint-Chiefs-of-Staff, the Vice President and Secretary of State, but he didn't recognize the elderly man who stood next to President Merrick with an expectant look on his face. He wore a suit like everyone else in the room, but his was an older style, as if he'd been forced to dig deep into his closet earlier that morning and came up with that solitary option.

President Merrick stood and placed an arm around the man. "Thank you for coming on such short notice," he said. He addressed the group around the table. "This is Malik Bandor. He is a retired professor of Middle-Eastern studies from Georgetown University. He has a wealth of knowledge on the plight of Kurds in Turkey. He is also my personal guru on the subject and has been for years, therefore, he is privy to information that most civilians are not." President Merrick swept his hand toward the professor in an introductory fashion and sat back down.

"Thank you, Mr. President." The old man in the old suit smiled. He seemed to assess the gathering of minds assembled before him. "It's kind of early in the morning to be giving a history lesson, so I'll present you with only the information that we feel is vital to your mission. And please, feel free to ask any questions as I go along. I've always thought that was the best way to distribute intelligence."

A few older heads nodded, giving Nick the impression that Professor Bandor had orated more than a few White House meetings over the years.

"Since the end of the cold war," he began, "the United States has no more important ally in NATO than Turkey. This year, Turkey will receive three hundred and twenty million dollars in military loans from the United States. That's three hundred and twenty million U.S. taxpayer dollars going directly to the Turkish government for the unequivocal purpose of killing their own citizens. Of course these citizens I speak of are Turkish Kurds. There are twenty million Kurds in the region of Turkey, Iraq, and Iran, making them the largest ethnic group in the world without a country.

"In the past ten years, the U.S. has provided Turkey with no less than six billion dollars worth of military firepower— F-4 fighter jets, M-60 tanks, and Cobra helicopters. It's unfortunate, but every time a Kurd is killed, it's with an American weapon."

President Merrick had become visibly uncomfortable with this portion of the dissertation and when he made eye contact with Bandor, the old man said, "Of course, these funds were all allocated two administrations ago. However, it doesn't alleviate us from the dilemma we now face as a consequence of those past decisions. In southeastern Turkey there were an estimated twenty-five hundred Kurdish villages destroyed by the Turkish Security Force, the military muscle of the Turkish government. It stands to reason that the Kurds would feel obligated to fight back and they have—firing at government troops at every opportunity. The numbers of the Kurdish Security Force is much lower than that of the Turkish Security Force, but their atrocities are no less brutal. The KSF was caught retaliating, and the world became outraged. And since Turkey is such an important ally, we had no choice but to send our troops over there to try and settle things down."

"And therein lies the dilemma," President Merrick added. "Since the Kurds have no country, they have no voice. They have no diplomats or embassies for us to appeal to. We can't threaten them with anything, because they have nothing for us to threaten. We can't deny them resources because the Turkish government has already milked them dry."

President Merrick leaned forward. "Walt, this is our war. We have to fight it here in the States. The Kurds have overreacted and if we're going to stop them, it'd better be soon. Public outcry has become so loud that our airwaves are flooded with nothing but impeachment and withdrawal discussions. And we all know what happens if we back down from the KSF and withdraw our troops from Turkey. Every two-bit terrorist organization on the planet will be on the next flight to America, threatening to blow up our schools unless we serve free ice cream with every meal at McDonald's. There will be no end to it."

Jackson asked, "If the KSF has a substantial amount of soldiers here in the U.S., what's happening over in Kurdistan?"

"That's a good question," Professor Bandor said, then pointed to CIA Director Ken Morris.

"As you would suspect," Morris stated. "They're vulnerable. However, our troops are instructed to prevent violence from both sides and it seems to have tempered the bloodshed." He turned to Jackson, "Now if we could only find Kharrazi . . ."

The President looked at Jackson.

Jackson pushed his chair back and crossed his legs. He nodded, as if he was agreeing with something that someone had said. But nobody spoke.

Finally, Jackson said, "I could tell you that we have fresh leads and we're only hours away from capture, but I'd be lying. The fact is, I have every warm body with a badge scouring the landscape for this guy, and so far, every lead has led to a dead end. I haven't slept for more than a couple of hours a night in weeks, and if I thought it would help our situation, I'd hand in my resignation right now."

The President held up his hand, "Hold on, Walt. There'll be plenty of time for scapegoats after this is over. You're taking this the wrong way."

"No, he's not," Louis Dutton said, teeth clenched. "He's taking it exactly the right way." The FBI Director pointed at Morris. "You're the one who kept all of this tucked safely in a Top Secret file. Only when one of my agent's brothers was kidnapped did we even find out there's been KSF movement out of Turkey. If anyone deserves to be the scapegoat, it's you."

The President slammed his fist on the hardwood table. "That's enough!"

The room became still. Some thirty professional government employees sat in total silence as the President admonished them with his eyes.

Professor Bandor stood with his hand covering his face. It was only when President Merrick asked him to continue that the professor's reticence became conspicuous.

"Professor?" Merrick said.

"You don't deserve to be fighting like this," Bandor mumbled.

Nick wondered what he'd missed. He looked at his partner and Matt simply shrugged.

Dutton stood and approached the old man. "Professor, we fight like this all the time. This is what our forefathers did when they were faced with matters of national concern. It may seem ugly, but it works."

He helped the old man to a seat at the table. When Dutton returned to his seat, President Merrick stood. He walked away from the gathering to an oversized map of Turkey. With his arms folded he said, "Professor Bandor is upset because he feels a sense a responsibility with this entire KSF mess."

Bandor nodded with his head down.

"Tell them," President Merrick said.

Bandor pulled at a loose piece of cuticle from his left thumb. "I believe Kemel Kharrazi has killed my sister. I've suspected for some time, and now I am certain of it."

He seemed reluctant to continue until the president said, "Go on, Malik."

"My sister told me in confidence that Kharrazi was coming to America to exact revenge on the United States for interfering with their defense against the Turkish Security Force. This was months ago. I don't know how, but I suspect Kharrazi found out about our conversation and killed her."

"How can you be sure?" Dutton asked.

The professor continued his fascination with his cuticles. "She was allowed to leave a note saying goodbye to my brother-in-law and her other children."

"Her other children?"

"Yes . . . you see, Kemel . . . well, he's my nephew. And my sister is his mother."

A collective gasp seemed to fill the room.

"Kharrazi killed his own mother?" Vice President Hearns asked. It became evident that he was the lone person in the room who didn't know the Kharrazi legend and he immediately sank back in his chair.

The professor nodded. "You have no idea how sick I am about this. He is not what you think. He is much, much worse. His only loyalty is to the Kurdish people and their struggle for a separate nation of their own. Other than that, everyone and anyone is expendable. Even me."

"Which brings us to the real reason the professor came to me with his dilemma," President Merrick said. "He knows what a hothead Kharrazi is and he feels there's a good chance we can use the professor as bait to lure Kharrazi out of hiding."

"You can't be serious?" Dutton said.

But the remainder of the room hoped he was. They were desperate for Kharrazi's shoe size, never mind a trap that could actually help capture him.

"Tell us about it," Jackson said.

President Merrick stood behind the professor and placed a hand on his shoulder. "In a few minutes I'll leave the White House and address the media and the nation about the latest series of bombings. As I'm leaving the White House, I'll be seen shaking the professor's hand and thanking him. The camera set up insures that every television station with a news department will see us. Later, there will be a leak to the Washington Post about intelligence we've received from a Kurdish relative of Kharrazi's. Our office will confirm the allegation and add that the information is extremely helpful in our pursuit of the madman known as Kemel Kharrazi. We will not name any names, but that will be a moot point. Kharrazi will know who we're talking about."

"Kemel is a news junkie," Bandor added. "He monitors cable news stations all day long. He will come after me without question."

Dutton rubbed the side of his face. "It's risky. And there's no guarantee that Kharrazi will make the attempt himself. He could send one of his soldiers to do the job."

The President nodded. "Professor Bandor feels strongly that Kharrazi would be compelled to bring him down personally. There's been bad blood between them for some time."

"I can only apologize for not coming forward sooner," Bandor said.

Nick said, "You realize if we keep close tabs on you, he'll spot us. And if we leave even the slightest gap . . ."

"He's right," Dutton said. "Kharrazi will be disguised. An old woman, a homeless person, you'll never be able to walk down the street without wondering who's around you."

There was no reaction from Bandor. Dutton lowered his head to meet the professor's eyes. "What Nick is suggesting is . . ." Still no recognition of fear showed in Professor Bandor's face. "It's a suicide mission."

President Merrick patted the professor's back as he stared down at the old man.

"He knows, Louis. He knows."

Chapter 15

Kemel Kharrazi exited the private jet and waddled across the tarmac toward a small brick building just south of the runway. His padding had come loose during the flight and was beginning to bunch up inside of his jacket. A suspicious eye might've noticed his unbalanced appearance, so he decided to adjust himself in the men's room. But the second he opened the glass door to the building, an overzealous young woman standing behind an abbreviated counter accosted him.

"You must be Mr. Henning," she said cheerfully.

By instinct Kharrazi headed directly toward the woman. His training commanded the response. Growing up on the streets of Istanbul, he'd learned to never allow a possible threat catch you avoiding their attention. A sure sign of weakness.

Kharrazi dropped his leather suitcase, leaned over the counter and smiled. "Yes, that would be me."

The woman tapped her long, purple fingernails onto a keyboard and said, "Well, let's see what the computer says, Mr. Henning."

For a brief moment Kharrazi was startled. What was this woman going to find on the computer? He was about to feel for his Beretta when she said, "It looks like everything's all set. I'm just checking on your rental car now."

Kharrazi's nerves were frayed and he chastised himself for being so jumpy. "Yes, of course," he said. "Take your time."

Kharrazi noticed a stack of USA Today newspapers on the counter next to him. On the cover was the headline, "America Under Siege." Below the headline was a surveillance photo of Kharrazi taken last year. He had a snarl on his face and it reminded him how important it was for him to smile. With puffy cheeks and a bald head, Kharrazi was certain he was unrecognizable, but the smile made him practically invisible.

He scanned the parking lot. It was vacant. A couple of men stood in front of a hangar across the runway, sipping coffee from Styrofoam cups, engaged in conversation. The airfield had been chosen carefully. Even though it was scarcely used, it was only forty minutes from Ronald Reagan airport, which was certain to be infested with federal agents.

"So, Mr. Henning, what brings you to Maryland?" the woman asked, still scanning her computer screen.

"Business," Kharrazi said.

"Business? How come so far away from the metropolitan area?"

Kharrazi grew irritable at the line of questioning, but he could see that she was making the silence between them go away. This was something that Americans were known for—their trivial conversations. The weather, sports, traffic, all harmless topics that Americans were compelled to whittle away their lives talking about.

He smiled. "I sell custom boats. Most of my customers live here at the south end of the bay."

This seemed to satisfy the woman's curiosity, which coincided with the end of her search. "Here you go, Mr. Henning." She handed Kharrazi a folded pamphlet and a set of keys. "Just go through that door and hang a left. Your rental car is the third one in, the green Taurus. Just bring it back tomorrow with a full tank and leave the keys in the ignition."

Kharrazi thanked the woman and hurried towards the men's room, where he adjusted his padding. After he was rearranged, he found his car and left the complex. There was no need for a map since Kharrazi had the route committed to memory. Once he reached the D.C. area, he would call upon his college days at Georgetown to assist his recollection of the district.

He switched the radio to an all-news station, where he heard an aggressive dialog between a journalist and a civilian caller. The caller wanted the President impeached and the journalist countered with talk of rounding up all non-American civilians from the Middle East. Kharrazi was fascinated with the grouping of all Middle-Eastern countries into one giant alliance. As if Iraq, Israel, Lebanon and Turkey all shared the same doctrine.

At the top of the hour, a newscaster spoke of late-breaking news from the White House. Apparently President Merrick had addressed the nation earlier that morning and made reference to an informer who'd volunteered valuable information about the terrorist behind the bombings. Kharrazi turned up the volume and listened as the announcer confirmed a Washington Post report that the informer was a relative of Kharrazi who lived in the Washington, D.C. area.

Kharrazi slammed his fist against the steering wheel. Malik, the old fool! He tried to recall how much information his uncle could have known. How much did his mother know about his mission?

He saw a sign directing Washington D.C. traffic to the left lane. He was disgusted with his meddling family and was determined to tie up any loose ends. Just then a large SUV passed his Taurus on the passenger side and he caught the driver spying on him. Kharrazi realized that the driver was reacting to his temper tantrum and he forced a benevolent smile. The driver became uninterested and quickly moved ahead.

Kharrazi steered the car into the left lane and drove toward the nation's capital with an entirely new agenda.

* * *

Nick sat at his desk at the Baltimore Field Office clicking the mouse on different files on his computer screen. He'd been navigating through the maze of information in a slow methodical manner for the past two hours. In the top left hand corner of the screen were the names of every Kurd who had applied for a visa over the past year. The right side ran a program called Linksgate. It cross-referenced every possible connection between the names on his computer screen and any KSF sympathizers. As the individual names were linked to a possible association, they were highlighted. Once highlighted, Nick would click on the name and instantly identify the connection. Some were weak, like Assad Jihed, who went to school with a KSF member fifteen years earlier. Yet other connections made him feel that the CIA had dropped the ball. There were twelve eavesdropping and surveillance satellites continuously inundating the CIA with information without the proper manpower to keep up. They routinely intercepted two million phone calls, e-mails, and faxes daily, only to decipher the information months and sometimes years later.

He was sifting through Rashid Baser's file when the intercom beeped on his phone.

"Nick?" a woman's voice said.

"Yes, Muriel."

"Fourteen thirty-two is for you. It's Julie."

"Thanks," he said, then pushed a button and picked up the receiver. "Hi, Sweetie."

"Nick I'm down here at Johns Hopkins. I think you'd better come."

Nick jumped from his seat. "Are you okay?"

"I'm fine. It's Tommy, he's . . . well, he's in intensive care."

"What happened?"

"He was a victim of the bombings. He's not doing very well. There might not be much time."

"I'm on my way." Nick hung up the phone and found Matt slapping the side of a printer trying to get it to print. "Let's go," Nick said.

"Where to?"

"The hospital. They got Tommy."

* * *

Johns Hopkins contained Maryland's only regional burn center. Nick could sense the competence of its professionals the moment he entered the hundred-year-old building. He approached the information desk and introduced himself to an older woman. The woman pointed to a room with a narrow slit of a window in the door. "They're all in there."

The room appeared to be a waiting area. "You don't understand, I'm family," Nick flipped open his FBI credentials as if this would be the magic pass to his cousin.

The woman had a peculiar expression that held concern and curiosity. "Exactly how many family members—" she stopped herself. "I'm sorry, sir," the woman frowned. "The staff is doing the best they can. I've already notified the doctor and as soon as he is available he promised to meet with you and all of your family." Again she pointed to the room.

"All of my family? How many family members are we talking about?"

The woman took an exasperating breath. "A lot."

Nick opened the door slowly to avoid hitting anyone in the crowded room. The small room was intended for intimate conversations between doctors and family members of patients undergoing surgery. The architect didn't have Tommy Bracco's family in mind when he drew up the blueprints. Nick found Julie sitting in a corner with his Uncle Victor and Aunt Ruth, who was openly sobbing. Julie rubbed Ruth's back while Victor carried on a conversation with Don Silkari.

Nick crouched down to his aunt's eye level, "I'm sorry, Ruth," he said, taking her hand into his. He looked at Julie, "What do you know?"

Julie shrugged. "Nothing. The doctors are still working on him."

Nick said, "Ruth, there couldn't be a better place for Tommy to be right now. These guys are the best in the world at this kind of stuff. Have hope."

"Hope?" His Uncle Victor flicked the back of his hand from under his chin. "There's your stinking hope. They better not take these terrorists to trial, because I'll be outside with my Remington. They'll never see the inside of a courthouse. I'm telling you right now, Nicky, it ain't ever happening in a courtroom."

Nick allowed his uncle to vent. There was no sense trying to calm him down, especially when Nick felt exactly the same as Victor.

Silk made eye contact with Nick and anger flashed across their eyes like lightening bouncing between two mirrors.

"Victor," Nick said, "I'll make this right."

"How are you going to do that? You gonna bring my boy back to me? Cause if you can't do that, then you can't make it right." Victor's lips twitched. His mouth acted like it wanted to continue, but his heart seemed too damaged for the job.

Silk gently tugged on Nick's coat jacket and gestured to the opposite corner of the room. Nick saw his partner having an animated conversation with husky Sal Demenci. Sal was surrounded by five of his men, who regarded Matt with dubious expressions. Nick heard Matt say something about justice and this brought Sal to his feet. He pointed a finger at Matt, "You have the audacity to come in here and talk about justice? Do you have any idea what the fuck you're talking about?"

Nick immediately wedged himself between the two men and patted Sal's shoulders with baby taps. "Come on, Sal, settle down." He looked into Sal's eyes with compassion. "This isn't a contest to see who cares about Tommy the most. Everyone in this room is hurting—including Matt. You know that, Sal. You know that."

Sal took a breath and sat down, muttering obscenities.

"Did they give you any indication how bad he was?" Nick asked.

Sal shook his head. "I got a glimpse of him when they were moving him around. He's burned all over. They're keeping their mouths shut, so they don't hedge any bets." He looked up at Nick as if he'd forgotten something. "Hey, by the way, how's Phil?"

"He's good, Sal."

"Good. Listen, I think maybe we need to talk."

"What about?"

Sal stood and examined the crowd. He gestured toward the door and Nick followed. Sal's men fell into step behind them until Sal turned and said, "It's okay. Me and Nick are going to have a little chat." He looked at Matt and said, "We'll be right outside."

Nick nodded to his partner and Matt grimaced.

Sal walked out of the hospital and led Nick to a bench under the canopy of the entrance. Nick sat next to him at arm's length.

Sal stared at Nick like he was waiting for him to say something. Nick shrugged. "What?"

An Army Jeep rolled by, patrolling the street next to the hospital. It was full of soldiers with M-16's strapped to their shoulders. They scrutinized the terrain with stern expressions.

"This country's in bad shape," Sal lamented.

Nick saw something in Sal's eyes he wasn't familiar with. Sincerity. He'd known Sal back when Sal was merely a Captain with the Capelli family. Nick avoided any law enforcement that involved family business, an easy chore from within the counterterrorism division of the Bureau. Besides, Nick was Sicilian and something deep inside always held a certain understanding for the Sicilian ways, as perverted as they were.

"You're right," Nick said. "The country is hurting right now."

Sal moved his hands in a circular motion. "Your boss, I'll bet he would love to know where this Kharrazi guy is, wouldn't he?"

The smile vanished from Nick's face. "Is there something you want to tell me, Sal?"

Sal leaned back into the bench and crossed his legs. "What if I told you a story? A story about a friend of mine who happened to figure out where they're making these bombs. I mean we're talking strictly fiction here, you understand?"

Nick nodded, knowing that nothing was further from the truth. "Go on."

"Well, these terrorists have to get their supplies from somewhere—I mean, hey, they didn't just check it in with their luggage on the plane, right?"

"Right."

"So this friend of mine gets wind of a large underground purchase of blasting caps, big enough to blow up, oh, say, a house or something. Capisce?"

"Capisce."

"Anyway, my friend finds the guy who makes these bombs

and he confronts him. Well, of course, the bomb maker, he's not so happy to see my friend and my friend—in self-defense, mind you—shoots the bomb maker and kills him."

Sal stopped talking when two men wearing blue scrubs and stethoscopes draped around their necks walked past them into the hospital. Nick wanted to slap the story out of Sal, but he remained calm. When the traffic around them quieted, Nick couldn't resist any longer, "Sal, are you going to finish?"

Sal appeared to be taking in the sights from the park bench, as if the sun and the clouds were a new experience for him. He waved at a group of birds fluttering around the crown of an oak in the median of the parking lot. "You know what kind of birds those are?"

Nick lowered his forehead into his hand and used his thumb and middle finger on either side of his face to massage his temples. "Tell me, Sal. What kind of birds are they?"

"Those are what you call Orchard Orioles. They're rare this time of year. Very pretty coloring, but very fragile. They don't do well in cold weather."

Nick wasn't sure whether Sal was speaking metaphorically. "Are you a bird lover, Sal?"

Sal seemed content listening to the birds chirping. He nodded to the question as if in a trance. "I'm a charter member of the Chesapeake Audubon Society."

Nick couldn't help but follow Sal's gaze to the large oak tree. He tried for a moment to focus on the birds, their musical cadence, and their sense of community. The country was slowly being destroyed, house by house, and these creatures didn't seem to notice. Apparently none of them read USA Today or they'd be starting a block-watch program like everyone else in the nation. Neighborhoods were taking shifts sleeping and yet the birds kept singing. Nick realized that Dr. Morgan was right. If Sal hadn't brought the loud chirping to Nick's attention, he never would have noticed. Still, he couldn't last thirty seconds on the birds without shifting his thoughts back to the KSF and Kemel Kharrazi.

Nick watched Sal withdraw a plastic bag of breadcrumbs from his pants pocket, dip his hand into the mix and toss it onto a patch of grass next to the bench. A moment later, a black bird with a sliver of purple on its chest landed on the far edge of the newly-discovered banquet and pecked at a couple of breadcrumbs. After another moment, two more birds braved the trip down to the buffet line. Sal's eyes gleamed with delight.

"Mangia," he said, losing himself in the ceremony. "Mangia."

"Sal," Nick said, "if you know something that would help us find these terrorists, we would be very grateful. Maybe even rewardingly grateful."

This seemed to get Sal's attention. He quickly dispensed the remainder of his baggie and turned to Nick with a somber expression. He smoothed Nick's arm with his hand, as if he were ironing out imaginary wrinkles from the sleeve of his jacket. "I have a proposition for you."

Nick knew right away it wasn't anything he was going to like.

Chapter 16

The Oval Office sat on the southeast corner of the White House, overlooking the Rose Garden. During their tenure, each President got to choose the décor inside of the office. President John Merrick decided to use the Oval Office to memorialize his brother. Paul Merrick was killed on September 11th, 2001, when a suicide terrorist crashed a commercial jet into the office where he worked in the Pentagon.

Directly across from the rosewood desk hung a large framed photo of Paul Merrick in his lieutenant's uniform, taken just a week before the attack. Other photos of his brother, his wife, and their two daughters intermingled with portraits of Harry Truman and JFK. Paul's favorite putter leaned against the wall next to a couple of golf balls. Whenever Merrick got the nerve, he gripped the club and felt the indentations where his younger brother's hands had worn down the leather. His fingers wound around the grip and rekindled the warmth that his brother's hands left behind. Merrick would lean over, aim a golf ball at the leg of his desk and stroke the putter. Like a magic wand, it conjured up teenage memories of Saturday afternoons sneaking over to the local public course and playing golf with his brother deep into the darkness. In more recent years, with the finances to back him, Paul would constantly tinker with new equipment. Somehow the latest technology always ended up in his golf bag, but the putter was the only club that Paul would never replace no matter how old and worn.

Now Merrick stood over a golf ball, his hands duplicating his brother's position on the putter. With memories of his brother resurfacing, he stared intently at the ball as if he might see his brother's face when his head came up. He didn't. Instead he saw the stern expression of Chief of Staff William Hatfield, who was sitting on a leather chair, scrolling down the screen on his laptop.

Situated in various chairs and sofas fronting Merrick's desk were five of Merrick's aides, who'd pulled an all-nighter with him collecting data and discussing options. A tray of cut fruit and vegetables sat on a coffee table in the middle of the room. Secretary of State Samuel Fisk interrupted his pacing to take a celery stick and nervously chew it down to his fingertips. Fisk had the longest running relationship with Merrick, going back to eighth grade, and he always had the last word on serious issues. Everyone in the room knew this, so Merrick would sometimes catch his staff addressing Fisk instead of him. This was of no concern to him. Merrick was as no-nonsense as they came, and everyone who worked for him understood his loyalties. The Presidency was one of the few occupations where cronyism was not only allowed, but practically a necessity. Merrick surrounded himself with people he trusted and in return, his people trusted him.

Standing behind Hatfield and looking over his shoulder, Press Secretary Fredrick Himes, who craned his neck to get a better glimpse of the overnight polls.

Hatfield scrolled down the computer screen with his index finger. "Do you want the bad news, John, or the worse news?"

"Just give it to me, Bill." Merrick hunched over the putter, eyeing the golf ball.

"Your approval rating has dropped again. It's down from forty-three to thirty-nine percent."

Merrick felt the room tighten up. A lame-duck president not only lost the support of his political constituents, but could indelibly tarnish a staff member's career. The captain might go down with the ship, but the crew didn't escape unscathed.

Hatfield scrolled further until he found what he was looking for. "When asked whether the President was handling the KSF attacks properly, sixty-five percent said no. Only twenty-five percent said yes. Ten percent were undecided."

Merrick looked up at the faces before him. They were long, tired and confused. They'd spent the past week performing masterful acts of damage control and it seemed to be paying little dividends.

Hatfield said, "Then there's the people who were asked whether—"

"That's enough," Merrick announced. He didn't need to hear any more, especially from his Chief of Staff, who was the White House's version of Chicken Little. Hatfield was a good, loyal man, but the pressure associated with the everyday dealings of a sitting president was becoming too much for the man. Nobody wanted to hear bad news from the panic-stricken voice of Bill Hatfield.

Merrick leaned the putter against the wall and walked to the front of his desk. "I want to remind all of you, this is not a permanent condition. We will ultimately succeed in finding Kharrazi and we will put a stop to the bombings, and our approval rating will go up."

This inspired a few nods of sympathetic agreement. Merrick could sense the disingenuous consent to his appraisal and wondered how long he had before he would lose even his own staff.

"Sir," Press Secretary Himes said, "if you don't mind me asking—how close are we to accomplishing our goals?"

This, of course, was the real question. Merrick could tell a story and buy an extra day or two, but eventually it would come back to bite him. He knew better than to fabricate scenarios that didn't exist. He received confidential information from the FBI three or four times a day, and each briefing was more frustrating than the last. Apparently, Kharrazi had cultivated a team of Kurds whose only purpose was to act suspicious enough to be brought in for questioning. Hundreds of decoys were sent out into the streets of America asking hardware storeowners for large amounts of fuses and other curious materials. They would linger long enough for the clerk to contact the FBI and get themselves dragged into custody without any possibility of furnishing information about Kharrazi. It cost the Bureau precious man-hours of investigative time, which they desperately needed.

"Fredrick, I'll have a full report available to you for the three o'clock press conference. I'll know more when I get my briefing from the Bureau this morning." He gave Himes a trust me look, but his clout was wearing thin and he knew it.

Merrick pointed to Defense Secretary Martin Riggs. "Marty, what about that other option?"

This drew some flinches in the room. It was the option that no one wanted to consider. The eight-hundred-pound gorilla that sat on Merrick's desk in the form of an order to withdraw troops from Turkey.

Riggs was an ex-marine, ex-CIA, and exceptional at finding a middle ground in almost every situation. He knew the terrors of war intimately and Merrick took him on as Defense Secretary for that very reason. Merrick wanted someone who understood the consequences of combat, and therefore would be more agreeable to alternatives. Riggs wasn't afraid of confrontation, just aware of the costs.

"Sir," Riggs said, dropping a clipboard onto the coffee table and leaning over, elbows on his knees. "We're prepared to release military footage from Turkey showing Turkish Security Forces in Kalar raising the Turkish Flag and shouting cheers as they pump their guns into the air. Kalar was the Kurds' last stronghold and this should be enough evidence to show that the United States is no longer needed. It could allow us the dignity to leave on our own terms, without pressure from the KSF."

"Bullshit," came a voice from the back of the room.

Merrick saw Samuel Fisk shaking his head, looking down at the wood floor. "Sam," Merrick said, "you think the public will buy it?"

"Fuck no — would you?" Fisk snorted.

Merrick laughed for the first time in so long that his cheeks hurt from the unused muscles. "You shouldn't pull any punches, Sam."

Fisk muttered a few words under his breath and returned to a contemplative posture.

Merrick tugged down on his tie and pulled a melon ball out of a crystal bowl with a frilled toothpick. Before he finished chewing, he said, "Marty, thanks for the report."

The intercom buzzed to life and Merrick's secretary said, "Sorry to interrupt, Mr. President. Nick Bracco is on the line. He says it's urgent that he speak with Mr. Fisk right away."

"Put him through on the speaker phone, Hanna," Merrick said.

There was a pause. "Uh . . . Mr. President, Mr. Bracco insists that it is for Mr. Fisk's ears only."

Merrick raised an eyebrow at Fisk. They both understood the move. Bracco obviously had information that flirted with unethical, immoral, or illegal operations, and he wanted to allow the president deniability. Merrick waved a hand at Fisk and watched him hurry out of the room.

Riggs stood, retrieved his charcoal gray jacket from the brass coat rack and slipped it on. "Mr. President, I have a meeting with the Joint Chiefs in twenty minutes. Which of these options do you prefer we discuss?"

Any large-scale military action attempting to wipe out the KSF within the United States would end badly, and Merrick knew it. He felt as if his body was crawling with poisonous ants and he needed to suppress the urge to stab them with a knife.

Merrick frowned. "Marty, I want you to tell the Chiefs we're not leaving Turkey. Not today, not tomorrow, not as long as we're being blackmailed by Kharrazi. Tell them I want more options. I don't like the corner we're in, and I want out."

Riggs nodded, "Yes, Sir."

Attorney General Mitchell Reeves also reached for his jacket. "I'd better be going too," he said. "I've got a dozen defense attorneys screaming that I can't keep their clients locked up for over a week without formally charging them."

Merrick pointed an accusing finger at Reeves. The Attorney General held up his hand, "Don't worry, we're not releasing anyone. I've just got to juggle with the Bill of Rights a little."

Merrick watched the two men leave. He circled around behind his desk and sank into his high-back leather chair. He tugged even further on his tie, loosening it to the point of separation. One piece of silk now looped around his collar and hung down in two separate strands. He unbuttoned the top button of his starched, white shirt, placed his feet up on the desk and closed his eyes. Even with two people left in the room and another seventy-five currently roaming the corridors of his residence, he'd never felt more alone.

* * *

Outside of the Oval Office, perched on a drooping tree branch, an oriole scrutinized the White House lawn for an easy meal. Three blocks west of the Oval Office, a construction worker peeled back the cellophane wrapper from his tuna fish sandwich and sighed at the long day still ahead of him. Less than a mile northwest of the Oval Office, a short, chubby, bald man waddled through the pedestrian traffic on the perimeter of Georgetown University. A Welsh Terrier pulled on the leash in front of him as he gleefully made his way down L Street NW, drinking in the worried faces of students and businesspeople as they passed him by. He wasn't enjoying the anxious expressions because of some prurient thrill, but because he knew that his plan was working. The president was just blocks away, receiving pressure from every imaginable sector of the public. He had virtually no other political choice but to withdraw U.S. troops from Turkey and Kemel Kharrazi beamed with satisfaction.

Kharrazi made his way down a residential neighborhood with the innocent stroll of an old man walking his dog. He knew precisely which streets to turn down, so his moves lacked any unfamiliarity. The street where his uncle lived was tree-lined. The houses were mostly 19th century Victorian with sprawling mounds of grass and sidewalks that buckled from maturity. The terrier was a sturdy animal with a thick, wiry coat, and when he pulled Kharrazi in a serpentine path, Kharrazi's Beretta pinched the skin along his waist.

Kharrazi casually inspected every parked car, every conspicuous individual who looked like he didn't belong. He hadn't gone more than thirty yards when he noticed a heavily-gabled house across from Professor Bandor's with an upstairs window open. He continued his journey unabated when he discovered a windowless, black van parked a few doors down. Behind his benevolent smile, Kharrazi fumed. He kept walking, occasionally giving gentle tugs on the leash of the terrier he'd just purchased thirty minutes earlier. With his peripheral vision, he caught a glimpse of something metallic peeking out from the window across from his uncle's.

He couldn't fathom his uncle's betrayal. As a boy, the professor would drape his arm around young Kharrazi and tell him of the social immorality of the United States. Then he persuaded Kharrazi to attend Georgetown, where he headed the program for Middle-Eastern studies. What kind of person does that? If not for Professor Bandor, Kharrazi would have never come to see the corruptness firsthand. He would have dismissed it as the professor's own personal issue. Now, the immorality surrounded him at every turn, and it was disgusting.

Kharrazi left the neighborhood at a leisurely pace, taking side streets for about a quarter mile before he unleashed the dog and set him free. He found his rental car and with a stranglehold on the steering wheel, he merged into the midday traffic. So much adrenalin pumped through his veins, he almost ran a red light. He steered toward the safe house, where he would find seven KSF soldiers who were prepared to die for whichever order he gave them. And Kharrazi had a whopper for them.

Chapter 17

President Merrick woke up startled. He found himself leaning back in his chair in the Oval Office and was halfway through rubbing his eyes when he realized he wasn't alone. Sitting on a sofa, reading the Washington Post, was Samuel Fisk.

"Sam," Merrick said, "how long have I been out?"

"About an hour and a half," Fisk said, turning a page.

"You should have gotten me up."

"I canceled your noon appointment with Stanton. He'd just waste more time pinching you for a withdrawal. Besides, you needed the sleep."

Merrick opened a side door to a small bathroom, where he splashed water on his face, wiped dry, and began running an electric razor over the stubble. "I should be getting my briefing from the Bureau any time," Merrick said over the noise of the razor. "Has Walt called yet?"

"Not exactly," Fisk answered.

Merrick clicked the razor off and faced Fisk from the bathroom doorway. Fisk continued as if he was reading the Sunday paper at his kitchen table. Merrick suddenly remembered Nick Bracco's phone call. "Sam?"

"Yeah."

"You have something you want to tell me?"

Fisk folded the paper neatly and placed it on the coffee table in front of him. He motioned to the sofa across the table from him. "Why don't you have a seat?"

Merrick replaced the razor and began looping his tie into a knot as he approached the couch. Sitting down, he said, "Talk to me."

"John, how long have we been friends?"

Merrick froze. "Oh shit, Sam. I don't like the sound of this one bit."

"There is an option that just became available to us and I can't tell you very much about it."

Merrick finished knotting his tie and secured it snugly around his neck. "Does it entail anything unethical?"

Sam looked at Merrick stone-faced. As the seconds passed and the silence grew conspicuous, Merrick nodded his head. "I see."

"John," Fisk said, "I'm going to do you the biggest favor anyone has ever done. I'm going to get rid of these bastards, and it's not going to be pretty, and it's not going to be fair, but we've been hog-tied by the law for too long."

Merrick gave his friend a sideward look. "Have we been hogtied by the Constitution as well?"

Fisk stood and turned to study the large photo of Paul Merrick on the south wall. He nodded his head toward the picture. "Do you think the terrorists that killed him cared about the Constitution?"

"Don't, Sam."

"Why not?"

"It's too personal. I can't carry that kind of baggage into a decision that involves our nation's policy on . . . on . . ."

"On what?" Fisk said, turning to face Merrick. "Exactly which policy are you referring to? Is it our policy allowing foreigners to kill our civilians for political purposes? Or is it our policy involving innocent lives destroyed because we have to wait until there's enough evidence to guarantee a conviction? I am sick and tired of surveilling terrorists who we know are plotting violent acts inside of our borders. Borders that are open to a myriad of criminals to play in our backyard, with our tools, and with our personal rights guaranteed by the Constitution. By the time we have the legal right to make an arrest, blood's been spilled and alibis have been perfected for a jury of their peers." Fisk pointed at the large picture. "I'm not only doing this for you, I'm doing this for him. He doesn't have a voice anymore and I'm speaking for him."

Merrick sighed. He approached the Secretary of State and placed a hand on his shoulder. "Sam, don't risk your career over this."

"I'd gladly give up my career for this cause. It's time you took this personally too. Otherwise, just have those pollsters run the damn country. What the heck do we need you for?"

Merrick and Fisk faced Paul Merrick's image together. Lieutenant Merrick seemed to be looking down smiling eerily at them. The president began to reach for his brother, then pulled back. He took a deep breath. "Sometimes, Sam, I look up at this thing and think, 'There he is.' It's so lifelike, so real. I can't believe he's not here anymore."

Fisk looked squarely into Merrick's eyes. "All you need to do is say 'go.' One word and I'll set this thing in motion."

Merrick considered what his friend was protecting him from. The CIA? Covert operations?

"John?"

Merrick stared up at the soldier framed on the wall above him and became lost in his brother's gaze. "Let me think about it, Sam."

Fisk nodded. "Okay, but don't take too long."

"Sam, I don't even know what—"

"Stop," Fisk interrupted. "You're going to have to trust me. It's all on me, not you. I just need a command. I won't do it without one."

When Merrick finally wrestled his gaze away from his brother, Fisk was already leaving, closing the door behind him.

Merrick found his brother's putter and returned his hands to the proper position on the grip, his fingers melding into the grooves his brother left behind. He stood over a golf ball with his brother's face in his mind. "I don't know, Paul," he said out loud. "What would you do?"

He stroked the golf ball and watched it hit the leg of his desk square-on with a tiny thud. "Bull's eye."

* * *

Nick Bracco was parked over a quarter of a mile away from a suspected KSF hideout. The building was in an area of the city that featured crowded residential streets and row houses that lined the narrow passages like giant dominos. Nick had been holding binoculars to his eyes for so long his arms ached. The afternoon was beginning to wane and so were his hopes of discovering anything of value from the stakeout.

Matt sat next to him fingering a stack of documents on his lap. "So, do you think the president knows about Sal's little proposition?"

"What do you think?" Nick said, his left eye beginning to tear up.

"He'll make the call, but the trail will end at Fisk's desk."

"That's about right."

"What did Fisk think about it?"

"I'm sure he thought I was more than a little goofy."

"Oh, so then he's spoken with Dr. Morgan."

"Very funny." Nick put the binoculars on his lap and rubbed his eyes. "Give me those files again."

Matt handed him four manila folders with the word "classified" stamped across the top. Nick examined the files for the third time in the past three hours. "It's incredible. How could all four of these guys get student visas? For crying out loud, Nihad Tansu is pushing forty."

"Can't blame Homeland Security; most of these guys had never been outside of Turkey before. They're not your traditional international terrorists."

Nick flipped the files back to Matt and began another stint with the binoculars. "One more hour. That's all I'm giving this lead."

"It could be worse. We could be digging through KSF garbage cans like Tolliver."

Nick saw a red sedan slowly making its way down the street toward him. Nick didn't recognize the male driver. The man seemed to be searching for an address.

Matt said, "All of this overtime is putting a real crimp in my social life."

"Crimp?"

"Yeah, you know, it's crimping my style."

"You mean cramp. It's cramping your style."

"That too."

Nick watched as the sedan stopped in front of the KSF safe house. He was clutching the binoculars with a death grip and Matt must have noticed the tension.

"What do you see?" Matt asked.

"A car stopped in the street in front of the house and the driver seems to be looking for spectators."

Matt squinted with futility. "What's he look like?"

"Male, dark hair, mustache, blue collared shirt."

"Anyone we know?"

"No."

Nick noticed the driver staring intently toward the house. Nick switched his view to the front door and saw four dark-haired men exit the house and head toward the car. The last one hesitated and looked around before he got in.

"They're leaving. Get down," Nick said as the sedan began to move.

The two men slumped below the dashboard. As soon as Nick heard the car pass, he peeked into his side-view mirror and nabbed the license plate. He recited the number out loud and Matt called it in.

When Matt finished the call to the office, he stared at Nick, who had a sudden urge to examine the magazine of his pistol.

"What are you doing?" Matt asked.

"Just checking out the equipment."

"I mean, why aren't you following those guys?"

Nick snapped his holster shut and opened his car door. "Let's go see what we can find out."

Matt beamed, as he jumped out of the car and fell into step next to Nick. "Finally my partner has moved to the dark side."

"Relax, all we're going to do is talk with some neighbors."

"Maybe we could knock on the door and see if anyone's home?"

"And lose the element of surprise?"

"The element of surprise is overrated. It pales in comparison to old-fashioned bullying and intimidation. Maybe they'll think twice before they get bomb-happy."

Nick found himself following Matt up the steps to the KSF safe house. Before he could object, Matt rang the doorbell. Nick winced, placing a hand on his holster for comfort.

They waited for a few minutes and several more rings before Matt played with the doorknob.

"What are you doing?" Nick asked.

"I'm seeing if they need a carpet cleaning."

To Nick's surprise, the doorknob turned enough to hear a click and they looked at each other. "Don't," Nick said.

"Why not."

"First of all, it's against the law."

"C'mon, Nick, do you think there's any way we're going to get these guys without bending the rules a bit?"

Nick shook his head. "Don't do it, Matt. Besides, anything you find in there will be inadmissible in court and permanently protected from any further searches."

"Not if we leave unnoticed."

Nick folded his arms. "I am not breaking and entering."

"You don't have to. Wait here and I'll be right back."

Matt opened the door and Nick grabbed his arm. "I can't let you."

Matt shook off his partner's grip. "This is my choice. You had nothing to do with it."

Nick unholstered his pistol and chambered a round.

Matt froze.

Nick said, "You're an asshole for doing this, but I can't let you go in there by yourself."

"Good." Matt smiled, took a step inside the house, then pulled back and faced Nick. "Listen, should something go wrong, we need a play."

"A play?"

"Yeah, remember the Hartford raid?"

"Yes."

"We'll use that one."

"If I'm not mistaken, we almost got killed in that bust."

Matt nodded, "Yeah, that's why I like it—it worked."

Guns drawn, Nick followed Matt into the tiny foyer and surveyed the unremarkable interior. The fake wood-paneled walls gave the place a dark, dreary atmosphere. The living room had an old tan couch, a mid-sized TV with rabbit ears, and a wooden coffee table with a TV guide in the middle of it.

"Looks like Ozzie and Harriet's place," Matt whispered. He pointed toward an archway leading down a hallway. "Go check out the bedrooms and I'll visit the kitchen."

Nick felt uncomfortable on so many levels. He placed one foot in front of the other and balanced his step like a cat burglar. The first door on the right was closed and he opened it slowly, gun first. The room was just as banal as the rest of the house. A small bed was neatly made and the dresser showed off a display of swimming trophies. Nick suspected the place was inhabited by KSF soldiers and the décor disturbed him.

He opened a dresser drawer and saw children's clothes, Batman underwear, and Snoopy tee-shirts. He thought he heard a noise, but when he peeked out of the room, there was nothing.

He silently crept down the corridor to the next bedroom. This time the door was already open and he saw a much larger room with a big bed. The room had the clinical feel of a hotel room right after the maid's visit.

Nick was beginning to think they had bad information, when he opened the closet door and froze. Stacked up past eye level was a row of surveillance monitors. Each one captured a different section of the exterior of the house. When he examined the monitor that was aimed in the direction of his car, he realized that it was parked too far away to tell if it was occupied. His mind raced with all kinds of wishful thoughts. Maybe they'd gotten lucky and went unnoticed.

Nick moved closer to the monitor and saw a green button with the symbol of a magnifying glass stamped in the middle of it. He pushed the button and was startled to see his car zoom into view. It became so large so quickly that Nick withdrew his finger before it had even reached its maximum capability. Nick blinked. He stared at the closeup and was able to distinguish a crevice in the headrest of the passenger seat. What bothered him the most was that his car seemed to be centered in the camera lens.

Suddenly, he felt it get warmer in the house. He'd seen enough, and he wanted out. Before he could turn to leave, a male voice said, "Drop the weapon."

Nick didn't move. He wondered how many there were, when a second voice said, "So nice of you to join us, Mr. Bracco."

Nick turned to see a young man pointing an automatic machine gun at him. The second man was older and a bit plump. He didn't fit the description of a KSF soldier, yet the way he stood, weaponless, casual, Nick could tell he was in charge. Nick dropped his pistol on the bed. A rush of adrenalin shot up the back of his neck. He knew then that not only was he dead, but there was a good chance his death might be preceded by a considerable amount of pain. Nick wanted to tell him that the place was surrounded, that the FBI had an entire battalion of agents training their weapons on the hideout. He couldn't say a word.

"It's just the two of you isn't it, Mr. Bracco?" the man asked.

Nick stood motionless. His heart pounded fiercely, every labored breath a miserable prelude to death. The blood left his brain and he wobbled on numb legs.

Two more soldiers appeared in the doorway. One of them said, "The other one must've ran out the back door. The coward."

The old man seemed skeptical. "Did you see him leave?"

"No," the man said, "but the door was left open."

The old man looked at Nick. "Is your partner still in the house?"

Nick heard the question, just barely. He nodded. There was something about the man's eyes that caught Nick's attention. Could it be?

The man with the machine gun scoffed at the response. "I wouldn't believe him. He is just trying to save his life."

The old man looked at his watch. "We don't have time to play games, Mr. Bracco. Tell us where your partner is and I'll promise you a quick death."

Nick gasped for air, wondering how many seconds he had left. A surge of blood hit his brain and he remembered something important. "He's in the kitchen."

"Good," the old man said.

"We've searched the kitchen," one of the soldiers said. "He is not there."

Again the old man peeked at his wrist. He pointed to one of the soldiers in the doorway and said, "You go with Nhikad here and take Mr. Bracco to the kitchen. You will find his partner there. Use Mr. Bracco to lure him out and kill both of them. Then get out of here quickly and meet us at the other location."

The old man gestured to the other soldier and said, "Let's go, we must leave now."

As Nick began his death march to the kitchen, he heard a door close behind him, then a car start up and leave. When he glanced over his shoulder, he saw both of the soldiers with their weapons pointed at him. The lead one still held the machine gun tight to his chest and he shoved Nick with it.

Nick realized that the second soldier was merely a kid. In just a flash of eye contact, the kid seemed to stiffen. He appeared more afraid of Nick, who was weaponless and outnumbered.

Somehow this awareness gave Nick a glimmer of hope and it made him even more nervous. He actually had a slim chance of surviving and began to tremble.

When they entered the kitchen, Machine Gun grabbed Nick around the neck and jabbed the weapon into the base of his skull, using Nick as a shield. "Now where is he?"

Nick searched the small room and found what he was looking for. Two metal racks were standing between the refrigerator and the adjoining cabinet. He knew he couldn't afford to hesitate. He pointed to the refrigerator, "He's in there."

Machine Gun sneered. "You're a bad liar."

Nick stretched his eyes to the right and noticed something peculiar about the second soldier. He was backpedaling, frantically searching the room, as if he expected Matt to come flying out of a cabinet.

Speaking to the skittish soldier, Nick said, "If you two don't believe me, open it and find out."

The kid simply shook his head.

Machine Gun gave Nick a shove and crouched into a combat position. "You open it."

Nick deliberately stepped in front of the refrigerator, keeping his eyes trained on Machine Gun. But his peripheral view was on the more important component. The retreating accomplice.

"I'm losing my patience," Machine Gun said. "Open the refrigerator."

Nick knew he had stretched his luck to the limit. He placed his hand on the refrigerator door and gave it a concise tug, allowing it to open no more than an inch. The interior light did not come on and Nick anxiously searched for a sign. Machine Gun was directly behind him now and he heard him say, "All the way."

Finally, Nick could barely make out the tip of a blue piece of metal about naval high. Without opening the door any further, he stepped to the side as if he needed the room to pull open the door the rest of the way. Machine Gun was a second too late. Nick watched in amazement as the bullet penetrated directly into the center of the soldier's forehead. For a disgustingly awkward moment, Machine Gun appeared to develop a third eye, then he dropped hard onto the linoleum floor. Nick was diving and rolling across the floor as a defensive maneuver, but it was unnecessary. The second soldier had already fled the kitchen and was on his way out the door.

Nick chased after the man for a couple of steps, then remembered that he was weaponless. He turned to see Matt McColm sitting in the open refrigerator in a curled position, knees to his chest, and a small light bulb clenched between his teeth. Matt delicately stretched one arm out of the confined space, then the other. He rolled forward and made a controlled fall onto the floor, his legs still wound into a tight knot. He spit out the light bulb and began the process of stretching his legs. "Just like Hartford," Matt said.

Nick's hands were shaking uncontrollably. "How did you know?" he asked.

"I heard the voices. I figured I'd use the element of surprise."

"I thought the element of surprise was overrated."

Matt smiled. "It's making a comeback."

Chapter 18

Necmetin Ciller had been the Turkish Ambassador for only six weeks when he was summoned to the White House for the first time. Ciller was a thin man with short, black hair and displayed a nervous tic that was common among first time visitors to the Oval Office — he tapped his fingers on the arm of his chair.

President Merrick listened to Ciller, a consummate diplomat, and was growing weary of the political courtship. It was late afternoon, though, and that meant nightfall was just around the corner. The U.S. was about to face another round of random bombings and the intelligence agencies weren't capable of stopping every one of them. Innocent citizens were going to lose their lives tonight and Merrick was finding it hard to get past that fact.

Merrick looked across his desk at the ambassador. "Mr. Ciller, I've been listening to you for the better part of an hour now, and I have yet to hear one reason why the Kurds can't live peacefully in Turkey."

Ambassador Ciller gave a frustrated shake of his head. "Mr. President, these people are ruthless killers. Our country has endured devastating losses due to these creatures. I think your country is now seeing the true nature of their malevolence."

Merrick nodded, his eyes glazing over with disinterest. He wasn't going to create a diplomatic solution to the Hatfields and the McCoys in the short time he had.

"Sir," Ambassador Ciller explained, "we are in complete sympathy with your situation and we'll do anything in our power to help rid the Kurds from your peaceful nation."

Merrick rubbed his eyes. "I'm sure you would, Mr. Ambassador."

"Mr. President, if I may say, you look very tired."

"No, you may not say," Merrick snapped.

The door to the Oval Office opened and Press Secretary Fredrick Himes hustled to Merrick's side without a glance at the ambassador.

"What is it, Fredrick?" Merrick asked.

Himes grabbed the remote control sitting on Merrick's desk and clicked on the widescreen television. It was tuned to CNN, as usual.

"You need to see this, Sir," Himes said.

The camera showed a dark, wild-eyed man using a young woman as a shield. He had his arm around her neck and a knife pressed firmly under the tender skin of her jaw. The man stood in the middle of a crowd that was frantically dispersing around him. "Breaking News" was displayed at the bottom of the screen.

"Oh no," Merrick muttered. The camera was zoomed onto the man's face. Merrick couldn't tell where the scene was, but they appeared to be at some sort of outdoor festival.

"Where is this?" Merrick asked.

"Right here," Himes answered. "Washington Square."

Policemen could be heard yelling orders to the man, but the angry face spat out foreign words. He kept moving the young woman to position her between him and the nearest threat. It took a moment for Merrick to recognize the woman's terrified face. It was Professor Bandor's daughter, Isabel.

Merrick's stomach cramped into a tight ball. "Dear Lord," Merrick uttered. He remembered something that wasn't obvious from the blown-up images on the screen. Isabel was four months pregnant.

It was all his fault. He was the one who rubber-stamped the idea of using Professor Bandor as bait. He had taken every precaution. A team of professionals shadowed the professor around the clock, yet his worst fears were being realized right in front of his eyes. Khemel Kharrazi was exposing every weakness available to him. He was picking indefensible targets that were small in quantity, but enticing enough for the media to eagerly display every treacherous episode. Kharrazi was one step ahead of him, beating him with the one weapon that garnered more value than any nuclear device. The power of public opinion.

Merrick heard other staff members enter the Oval Office, but his eyes remained focused on the monitor. His thoughts ran wild with retaliatory actions that went far beyond the limits of the law. Rage mounted inside of him as he watched the man shout in plain English, "This is the President's burden. If he didn't insist on meddling in other country's affairs, we would never need to resort to such tactics."

The staff that crammed into the Oval Office clamored with outrage at the accusation. Merrick held a hand up to quiet the chatter.

"Do you see what monsters these people are?" the Turkish Ambassador declared.

Merrick took a moment to glare at the Ambassador. Without a word spoken, Ciller sank back in his chair.

Merrick returned his attention to the TV. Police sirens screamed while SWAT team, military, and local authorities cornered the man.

His head swiveled from side to side, taking in the sheer number of law enforcement that he was up against. He dragged Isabel backward with the knife snug under her chin.

"Get him," Merrick murmured.

As if the man could hear the President's words, he took his knife and slashed it ruthlessly across Isabel's throat, twisting her head to the left as he tore the knife to the right. The screen showed the disgusting image of a wide-open neck and blood gushing from the gash. Isabel dropped to the ground.

The screams inside the Oval Office drowned out the audio, but Merrick clearly heard the shots fired. The man's exposed body jerked spastically from all of the incoming shots he'd received. At first he fell to his knees, but the barrage of bullets relentlessly sustained their assault on the man's limp frame until he collapsed face down onto the asphalt.

An officer approached the corpse with his weapon pointed at the back of the man's head. He bent over the man and blasted two more rounds from close range. A soldier in camouflage grabbed the officer around the waist and pulled him away from the dead man.

A rush of police and soldiers surrounded the bodies and shooed the cameraman away from the scene. As the camera retreated, an ambulance skidded to a stop next to the crowd of uniforms. From off-camera, a newscaster began a running commentary on the tragedy that America had just witnessed live on CNN.

Merrick's hand closed into a fist. "Shut it off," he ordered.

Himes clicked the remote. The crowded room fell into a vacuum of silence.

Merrick knew he needed to react quickly. He examined his staff thoughtfully. "Fredrick, schedule a 6 PM press conference."

The Press Secretary looked at his watch. "Sir, that's only forty minutes from now."

The President looked up with weary eyes, dark circles like the rings inside of an old tree. "I know what time it is, Fred."

"Should I announce the subject matter?"

Merrick shook his head. "I don't think that will be necessary."

National Security Advisor Bob Rankin spoke up, "Mr. President, I recommend a cooling off period. I suggest you take a few hours to consider your thoughts. Under the circumstances, I'd hate to see you do or say anything rash."

Merrick leaned over his desk. He knew what Rankin was afraid of. He'd recognized the anger brewing in his gut and it was hard to ignore its affect. He took a deep breath and said, "I appreciate your concern, Bob. You don't have to worry about my temper." He pointed to his secretary. "Hanna, find Marty. We've got a statement to compose."

His staff lingered, waiting for direction. Merrick grimaced, "Folks," he said, as serenely as possible, "I need some time alone here, please."

The room emptied, but as Secretary of State Fisk reached the doorway, Merrick called, "Sam."

Fisk stopped and allowed the remaining staffers to exit. Merrick motioned for him to close the door, and he did. He stood in front of Merrick's desk with raised eyebrows.

President Merrick came to his feet and leaned over his desk, palms flat on the polished wood, every muscle in his face straining to maintain control. His voice was low and powerful. "All right, Sam, I want these guys eradicated. I don't care how. I'm willing to sacrifice my eternal soul for this. Just make it happen."

Fisk stood across from the President, studying Merrick's face as if to determine his state of mind. Finally, after an uncomfortable moment of consideration, Fisk's expression appeared to show satisfaction with his inquiry. He gave one nod and said, "Done."

* * *

Julie Bracco tenderly wiped her husband's forehead with a damp washcloth. He'd bumped his head when he hit the floor in the KSF safe house and it was throbbing. She was doting over him as always, picking away loose strands of hair from his face.

Nick had made it home in time for Julie to prepare dinner for him and Matt. Even though he appreciated her reticence, her silence concerned Nick. He didn't want their conversations to grow so economical that it affected their marriage. Sure he needed to keep most of his work confidential, but at what cost?

They were both sitting on the couch now, while Matt leaned back in the recliner and drank a beer.

"I've gotta get me one of these things," Matt said, playing with the handle that lifted the footrest.

"How can you be so glib after what just happened?" Julie asked. Her anger finally surfaced. Nick realized he'd done the right thing by bringing Matt home with him. Matt was the antidote to fear and trepidation. It was as if he'd become so acquainted with death that he could sit in its lap and ask it to tell him bedtime stories.

"We're fine," Matt shrugged. "I've had scarier moments on a first date."

Nick was grateful for Matt's euphemisms. Something he couldn't imagine grappling with in his current state of mind.

"You're not going to give me any details are you?" she asked. "Just that you were involved with a shooting."

Nick took a moment to touch her face, unabated by Matt's presence. "It was scary, Jule. It was very scary. But no one fired a shot in my direction. I promise."

Nick could feel his left eye twitch with the word promise. He placed his finger across her lips, and she took the tip of it into her mouth and kissed it gently.

Matt conspicuously turned his attention to the muted television. He turned up the volume and said, "It looks like the President is finally about to speak."

President Merrick stood behind a podium fronted with the Presidential Seal. He wore a dark blue suit and his makeup was so thick that even the bright television lights couldn't penetrate its shell. Instead of shadowy eyes, he appeared whitewashed. His expression was somber as he stood hunched over the podium as if he needed the platform to remain upright.

"Good evening," President Merrick began. "A short while ago, an innocent young woman was killed by a Kurdish terrorist. Any time terrorists murder an American citizen, I mourn their passing. In this case," he paused for a breath, "I knew the woman personally."

He stopped and sipped water from a crystal glass. A bead of sweat trickled down the side of his face. It was apparent that he was attempting to compose himself before speaking further. He studied the glass as if it contained plutonium. After what seemed like hours, he replaced the glass and continued. "The Kurds are a very misunderstood and oppressed people. The average Kurd is a peace-loving and considerate citizen. Unfortunately, a minority belong to the KSF, a bunch of thugs who will stop at nothing to get their way. They are willing to kill women and children in cold blood as witnessed earlier today.

"So far the authorities have apprehended over thirty KSF terrorists and the overnight bombings have been thwarted in all but twenty-two states. This does not mean we are satisfied with the results, it simply means that we are gaining control of the situation."

Merrick took another deep breath, then leaned over the podium, his hands clenching the sides of the wooden structure in a vice-like grip. He stared straight into the camera, "Folks, there has never been a time in U.S. history when a terrorist group has forced us to relinquish our freedom as a nation and we will not do so now. The young men and woman of our military were sent to Turkey because of the brutalities acted out by the KSF. They are there to protect the innocent citizens of Turkey and they will remain there until the KSF is dismantled. And be assured, they will be dismantled. Every last one of them will be brought to justice, including their ring-leader, Kemel Kharrazi. Never before has a President guaranteed the capture of a criminal. But today I am here to tell you that Kemel Kharrazi will be apprehended, and it will happen very soon."

Nick and Matt looked at each other. If anyone knew how close Kharrazi was to being apprehended, it was them. The President was writing checks he couldn't cash. This didn't prevent Matt from grinning widely.

"I love that guy," Matt beamed.

Julie examined her husband's face. "Is that true?" she asked. "Are you close to getting Kharrazi?"

Nick winced. "Well," he began. Then his eyes met hers and he saw the hope that lingered there.

Julie pointed a finger at him. "You remember your promise?"

"What promise?" Matt asked, watching the president leave the podium.

"Nick is going to quit being a field agent after the KSF is through terrorizing the country," Julie said.

"Really?"

"Really," Nick answered firmly.

"You mean I'm going to have to find a new partner?" Matt asked.

"It looks that way," Nick said.

Matt crushed his empty beer can and frowned. "I'm not so sure I want to stick around without you."

"What are you talking about?" Nick scoffed. "You love your job. You couldn't do anything more gratifying."

"That's true, but the reason I love it so much is because we work so well together. I don't want to have to go through that whole breaking in process again. I could find investigative work in the private sector and probably double my salary."

"See?" Julie said. "Everybody wins."

Nick decided to change the subject. "How's Tommy?"

"When I left the hospital this afternoon, the doctors felt like he was out of the woods," she said.

"Good." Nick checked his watch. "We'd better get going."

"Now where?" Julie said.

"We have a meeting downtown."

"At the office?"

Nick glanced at Matt. "Not exactly."

Julie tossed the washcloth playfully at her husband. "I swear Nick Bracco, living with you is like living with a — "

"A spy?" Nick finished for her.

"That's right, a spy. I can't wait until you get a regular job and come home and tell me every boring detail about your day."

Matt went over and gave Julie a peck on the forehead. "Thanks for the chow, Jule."

She smiled at Matt. "All I ask is that you take care of him. He hasn't far to go."

"Don't worry," Matt said heading for the door, "I can see his pot belly growing already."

Chapter 19

Huseyn Yildiri was surrounded by thirty of the KSF's most powerful soldiers. They stood around him sharpening their knives and cleaning the barrels of their rifles. A conference table was wedged into the corner of the room where a computer and three small televisions continuously displayed news and information. He was the only one seated at the folding table in the middle of the room. He sipped his cup of water with shaky hands while they all waited for Kemel Kharrazi to speak.

Kharrazi paced opposite the table with his hands behind his back. His face screwed up into a tight, pained expression.

Huseyn prayed for Kharrazi to say something, but his leader simply stalked the cellar where they assembled and listened to Huseyn explain his ordeal. Huseyn didn't dare delve too deeply into the explanation of his exit from their safe house. It was one thing to run from bullets, yet another to leave a fellow KSF soldier behind, dead. He tried to paint his escape as necessary. "I knew that you must learn of this situation. That is why I came here immediately, Sarock."

Huseyn wiped his brow and studied the smooth, cement floor. He thought about the look the FBI agent had given him. The man was walking to his death when he glanced over his shoulder and gave Huseyn a deliberate warning. It was as if the agent knew something and he was trying to caution Huseyn. He was trying to get Huseyn to run off. It had worked.

Kharrazi stopped in front of Huseyn and crouched down, so he was looking up at the man. He spoke to the young soldier as if he were speaking to one of his children, soft and calm. "He told you that his partner was in the refrigerator and somehow you were surprised when he turned up there?"

Huseyn's body was shuddering so powerfully that he simply willed his torso to remain still and allowed his head to bobble itself into a nod. "Yes, Sarock. The door blinded me from viewing the inside of the machine, but I barely escaped when the shots were fired."

Kharrazi looked skeptical as he stood and made another pass by the table. "So then, Mr. Bracco is still alive?"

Huseyn remained paralyzed with fear. He could think of nothing to say.

A roomful of muttering soldiers echoed off of the bare concrete walls. Kharrazi shook his head like a disappointed principal and knelt next to Huseyn. His fingers caressed the young boy's face and sent icy streaks of panic down Huseyn's neck. He knew that Kharrazi had the quickness of a leopard with hands capable of tearing his face apart before he could flinch.

"Tell me something," Kharrazi whispered. The room became still. At first Huseyn thought that fear had caused him to become deaf. He couldn't hear anything but Kharrazi's voice. He suddenly realized that even the televisions had been turned down so that every soldier could eavesdrop on the proceedings. "How many rounds did you fire at the agents?"

Huseyn wasn't prepared for such a refined interrogation. He hadn't thought through all of the details. How many shots? Why did he want to know? Wasn't it enough that he was shot at?

"Uh, I think two," Huseyn hesitated. "It happened so fast, I can't remember exactly."

Kharrazi held out his hand. "May I have your gun?"

Crazy thoughts ran through Huseyn's mind. He couldn't possibly shoot his way out of the cellar. He considered turning the gun on himself. It would be quick and ease his tension. But a glimmer of hope lingered in his mind. The way Kharrazi was touching him, gently, and speaking so softly. Maybe the leader had pity for his soldier?

Huseyn removed the gun from his belt strap and with trembling fingers, he handed Kharrazi the fully loaded weapon.

Kharrazi didn't examine the gun. He looked straight into Huseyn's eyes and seemed to be measuring his reaction while his hands roamed over the exterior of the weapon, searching for any evidence of a recent firing.

A voice from behind them urgently said, "Sarock, the American President is speaking on television."

Kharrazi didn't turn right away. He lightly patted Huseyn's cheek. A momentary reprieve.

The KSF soldiers fell in around their leader and watched as President Merrick announced the imminent capture of Kemel Kharrazi. The raucous crowd of soldiers hollered their disapproval at the TV screen, but Kharrazi gestured for them to stop. He listened as the president made false promises to the American people. When the president left the podium, Kharrazi switched off the TV and turned to address his followers.

"This is exactly what I had hoped for," he said. His words stunned the group.

Nihad Tansu elbowed his way to the front and said, "Sarock, they must know something. Maybe we should change our location."

Kharrazi stared out over the heads of his soldiers, deep in thought. "No, that is what he wants. He's desperate. He is trying to force us into a mistake."

"What about the White House?" Tansu asked. "Are we still going to follow the original plan?"

Kharrazi nodded slowly. "Yes, tomorrow night, as planned."

He pointed to a short, bearded soldier to his right, "Jihite, send a fax to the President. Tell them about the bombing of the White House tomorrow night. Also send the same information to the Washington Post, the same reporter as last time. He will have credibility."

The man's eyes widened. "Tell them about our plan ahead of time? Is that wise, Sarock?"

Kharrazi seemed amused at his own idea, as if struck by how brilliant it was. "Yes, it's perfect. It will force the President to remain in the White House. If he leaves now, he will appear as a coward. Besides, it's too late. They can't stop the bombing. Especially with our detonator in a bunker three thousand miles away. It's the perfect plan."

Nihad Tansu stepped forward, directly into Kharrazi's path. Kharrazi had to look up at the much taller man. "Yes, Nihad?"

Tansu stood firm, his muscular frame seemed anxious to flex its muscles. "Sarock, allow me to take the White House."

Kharrazi regarded his soldier with a partial smile. He placed a hand on Tansu's shoulder, "You make me proud, Nihad. However, I have another chore for you. A more important chore."

"Sarock, what could be more important?"

Kharrazi folded his arms.

Tansu's face fell.

"Good," Kharrazi grinned. "Would you like to know what I have for you?"

Tansu nodded.

"You must kill the wife of this FBI agent. She is very important to him. I want him to lose something as important as our independence is to us. I want him to feel our pain as no one else could."

Huseyn observed the conversation with eager eyes. He was grateful for the distraction and wondered if his mishap might be forgotten altogether. He watched as the KSF soldiers listened intently to their leader. It was apparent that Kharrazi's objectives seemed to have become much more personal. He wondered if Kharrazi was simply losing perspective of their overall goals, or just blind with revenge. Either way Huseyn was going to stay quiet and pray for the continued lapse of attention.

Kharrazi met Tansu's eyes. "This is no trivial task, I assure you. If you succeed, this will take one of the FBI's finest brains out of commission. Bracco will never be the same man. Once again, one of our small targets will become a significant factor to our success."

Kharrazi regarded his soldier with an air of wariness. "You will not fail me, will you, Nihad?"

Nihad Tansu appeared to stand taller now. He looked around at the other soldiers, the center of attention. "This woman is already a corpse, Sarock. That much is certain."

"Good," Kharrazi smiled. Then the smile faded as he turned and pointed to Huseyn, alone, still sitting at the folding table. "First, get rid of this coward."

Huseyn became lightheaded and his body lost its ability to hold itself upright. He saw the wicked expression on Tansu's face and he surrendered to a wave of nausea. There was nothing in his stomach to purge, so he bent his head down and shuddered with his mouth open, gagging on pure fear itself. When he looked up, he saw Tansu over him with his knife gleaming in his hand. "Please," he begged. "Make it quick."

* * *

Just north of Little Italy in Baltimore on a narrow, dead end street, sat a group of abandoned warehouses. To the naked eye they appeared as innocuous as negligent businesses harboring a tax write-off. To a select few in the FBI, they were known as ten acres of training ground for new recruits. On select occasions, it became a perfect meeting place for the seedier activities of the Bureau. Whenever an informant had information to exchange and couldn't afford to be seen strolling through the front door of the FBI building, or sharing a booth in a local restaurant with a man in a blue suit, the warehouse district was used.

The warehouses were topped with six-foot walls around their

perimeter. Stingy slits in the walls allowed just enough room for snipers. It was dusk and a group of dark clouds threatened overhead. Nick thought he saw a shadow cross one of the slits on the roof as he maneuvered his car through the minefield of potholes. He was comforted to know it was one of his own up there. Someone almost as good as the guy sitting next to him, and that would have been plenty good enough. Nick turned into what looked like a dead end alley. At the end of the alley, a steel door yawned open as they approached.

"I guess they know we're here," Matt said.

Nick drove into the warehouse and found a huge parking lot taking up the bottom floor. There were already several cars there. He parked next to the familiar sedan of Walt Jackson.

Their shoes echoed on the cement floor as they made their way to the elevators. Matt pushed the third-floor button and waved at the undetectable miniature camera above the doors.

When they got out on the third floor, they found themselves before the only room in the entire building with a padlock and silent alarm. Now, however, the door was open and Nick could smell the coffee brewing before he saw the strange inhabitants.

Along the left wall, sitting on an odd array of army cots and folded chairs were Jimmy Ferraro, better known as Jimmy Fingers, Don Silkari, and several other Italian Americans. At the end of the row, sitting in the only leather chair in the building, Sal Demenci picked lint from the sleeve of his jacket.

Across the room from them sat Walt Jackson and FBI Director Louis Dutton. The room was noiseless, save for the humming of a second hand refrigerator, copy machine, and computer that occupied the far wall. The only things the two sides of the room had in common were the Styrofoam cups of coffee they drank.

Nick and Matt grabbed a couple of folded chairs and diplomatically sat in the middle of the congregation.

Nick nodded to Sal, "I hear Tommy's going to make it."

Sal smiled faintly. "He's a fighter, that kid."

Louis Dutton sat behind a worn wooden desk and scribbled notes on a legal pad, while Jackson sat next to the desk, elbows on his knees, foot tapping the linoleum floor.

Just as Dutton glanced at his wristwatch, the elevator dinged and a slow-moving pair of footsteps grew louder. The large angular frame of Samuel Fisk filled the doorway. He stopped for a dramatic moment and looked over the incongruous crowd, his hands by his side like he was there for a high noon shootout.

The long, awkward silence continued as Fisk made his way to the desk and withdrew a bottle of scotch from the bottom drawer. As if by sleight of hand, a shot glass appeared, and he filled it to the brim. Fisk managed to appear professional while downing the booze with one quick gulp.

He wiped one side of his mouth with his fist and looked over the Italian Americans without judgment. He sat at the edge of the desk, his back to Dutton, and acknowledged Nick and Matt with a look.

The Italian Americans sat with their legs crossed, checking their nails, the usual look of boredom fixed on their faces whenever in the presence of the law.

Fisk pointed the empty shot glass at Sal Demenci. "Sal, how much prison time have you done in your life?"

The opening line didn't amuse the left side. They watched Sal frown. "I don't remember," Sal said. "Is it important I know the answer?"

Fisk grinned. "Now I know why they call you all wise guys. No it's not important. What is important is how much evidence we have against you to send you back."

"You threatening me?" Sal bristled.

Fisk shook his head. "Not at all." He turned to Walt and the SAC handed him a manila file. Fisk opened the file and read silently. He looked up at Sal and said, "Hmm, racketeering, extortion, pretty impressive."

"That why we're here?" Sal snapped. "You gonna make me come all the way down here just to bust my chops? I thought we had a deal?"

Fisk's face lightened. He leaned over and handed Sal the file. Sal took it from the Secretary of State warily, as if it were flammable. He perused the file with Silk hanging on his shoulder, and they both raised their eyebrows at what they saw.

"Pretty interesting stuff, huh?" Fisk said.

Sal closed the file and left it on his lap. "Why are you showing me this?"

A loud clap of thunder boomed overhead and Fisk went over and peeked through a slat in the horizontal blinds. The sky was dark now and rain pellets began to dance off of the bulletproof glass window.

Fisk turned and stuffed his hands in his pockets. He said to Nick, "Do you know what Sal here is?"

Nick gave Fisk an are-you-kidding-me expression. He knew that there was no right answer, so he looked at Sal and said the first thing that popped into his head. "Italian."

This got the room chuckling.

"That's close," Fisk said. "He's Italian, but he's also American. Like me, like you, like everyone in this room."

Sal nodded. Silk nodded. Tony the Butcher nodded. They seemed to understand where Fisk was going and they liked it.

Fisk splashed another pinch of scotch and downed it with a flip of his wrist. He pointed the empty shot glass, "You see, Sal, if you and your men help us out here," he shrugged, "maybe these files get lost. I don't know, maybe they go away permanently."

"Maybe?" Sal asked.

"Definitely," Fisk said. He looked back at Dutton and Jackson, who reluctantly made agreeable expressions.

Now Fisk took a different stance. He seemed to be addressing the government employees in the room, while looking at Sal and the gang. "I'm not going to debate the constitutionality of this meeting. There's no question that we're . . . uh . . . I am trampling on certain amendments. And I am here to tell you that I am taking full responsibility for this arrangement. No one outside of this room is aware of any of this. Personally, I don't think Thomas Jefferson wrote the Constitution with foreigners in mind. He was declaring an official document to protect the citizens of the United States against their own government. Assuring them their right to bear arms and speak freely against what could be a totalitarian regime in the future.

"There was no way these rights would have been afforded to the Redcoats, should they have needed them, and they will not be used to protect the invasion of Kurdish rebels in our country, killing our innocent population."

Fisk sold the idea like an umpire selling a close third strike with an aggressive fist pump. No one seemed ready to challenge. Nick wondered how deep this mess was going to get.

Fisk turned to make eye contact with him and Matt. The only two men in the room who spent their days in the field tracking terrorists for a living. "We have data that suggests seven hundred Kurds have entered this country legally over the past eighteen months. They've got visas and they're protected by our civil rights policies. As law enforcers you guys are forced to stand on the sidelines and wait for them to do something illegal before we can act. In most cases, after they kill Americans." Fisk worked his hand into a fist, selling it again. "The time for waiting is over. I'm not going to ask you two to cross the line yourselves. It's not fair. But these guys make a living on the other side of that line. I want you two to assist them with your knowledge of these terrorists and their behavior patterns. You know where they congregate, where they shop. We've run out of surveillance time. It's time to get rough."

Fisk paused a moment, letting the idea settle in on the men. Both of them knew what was coming so they weren't surprised at the concept. Fisk addressed Sal while pointing a thumb over his shoulder at Dutton and Jackson. "These two gentleman are going to furnish you with confidential files, intelligence that is known to us about these Kurdish intruders. Most of them are ignorant boys instructed to buy material that is suspicious, yet perfectly legal, so we waste our manpower on the wrong guys, while the real terrorists go to work. In the end, every one of them is culpable. No one gets a free pass."

Fisk made his way to the doorway and turned to Dutton. "I want you to give them everything. Even if it compromises our intelligence-gathering devices. They need to know it all. The President has received a fax demanding the withdrawal of troops from Turkey or the KSF threatened to blow up the White House. It sounds incredible, but we're in no position to call their bluff. We have twenty-four hours to find Kharrazi and cut the head off of the snake." He made a sweeping glance at everyone in the room. "Let's get it done, gentleman."

For the first time all day, Nick's headache went away.

Chapter 20

Julie Bracco had just finished loading the dinner plates into the dishwasher when she heard the doorbell. It startled her. She looked up to see that it was nearly nine o'clock, then turned on her TV on the kitchen counter and switched to channel 777. The security system displayed the image of a man standing at her front door in a dark blue suit with his hands in his pockets. His face was down, trying to elude the brunt of the wind-strewn rain. She didn't recognize the man, so she clicked a button on her remote and spoke into the tiny speaker at the bottom of the device. "Who is it?"

The man's voice came back through the television. "Agent Ford, Ma'am." He held up FBI credentials above his head and waved it with the nonchalant gesture of daily routine. "There's been intelligence gathered that leads us to believe you are in danger. I've been instructed to escort you to a local safe house."

Julie had never heard of the agent, but she knew there were several hundred inside the beltway who she wasn't familiar with. She'd felt safer since Nick had installed extra security devices. There were twelve cameras, double-bolted locks, and alarm triggers throughout the house. One push of a button and she would have help inside of three minutes. Nick never took chances when it came to her safety, and it was one of the many ways he showed her how much he loved her.

Still, it bothered her that she wasn't told ahead of time about the move. She said, "Hang on a minute," and dialed Nick's secure phone.

* * *

The strange crowd that congregated in the abandoned warehouse was now divided into four groups. Each FBI staff member took five Italian Americans into a separate corner of the room and gave them detailed information about the KSF. Walt Jackson spoke about how to determine a KSF soldier by his gait, the way they didn't make eye contact and how they all wore the same ten-dollar haircut. He also gave them a declaration of immunity. He spoke of their need to flee the scene and not to be concerned about leaving evidence behind. The FBI would be the lead investigator in any domestic terrorist activity

and whatever evidence remained would never resurface in any sub-
sequent investigations.

Louis Dutton touted the significant advantage of working
undercover. He explained the Bureau's policies to the men and their
responsibilities. He also highlighted the expensive surveillance toys
they had access to, which brought smiles to the faces of more than
one gangster.

Appropriately, Matt discussed high-tech weaponry. He demon-
strated laser sights and new silencers that required a keen ear just to
hear the shot fired. The silenced machine guns drew excited expressions as eager hands passed around the new weapons like starving
pilgrims at Thanksgiving dinner.

Nick trained the men how to avoid the traps that were certain to
be waiting for them. He updated them on the latest leads they had
developed and passed out surveillance photos of the major players known to be on American soil. He was directing their attention
toward the changing of facial hair, when his phone vibrated in his
pocket.

Nick held up a finger to the group and pushed a button on his
phone, "Bracco."

Julie sounded winded. "Nick, did you send over an agent to take
me to a safe house?"

Nick squeezed his eyes shut. "Sorry, Sweetie, I forgot to call you."
He didn't want to worry her any more than he had to, but they had
received intelligence warning him to protect his wife. "Julie, we're
just being extra cautious. Maybe for a day or two. Things are going
to come to a head here pretty quick."

"What's the agent's name?" Julie asked.

"Agent Ford," Nick said. "William is his first name. He's a rookie,
but he's a good man. He'll take good care of you."

Julie seemed satisfied and asked when she would see Nick again.

"I'll make it to the safe house for breakfast," he said. "I'll bring
some bagels and fresh coffee."

Julie was quiet.

"Jule? Are you okay with this?"

"No, Nick, I'm not. But if you tell me this is almost over, I trust
you."

Nick hung up wondering how long his wife could put up with
all the stress. He tried to remember the last quiet moment they'd
had together without the threat of interruption. He sincerely felt he

was the luckiest man on the planet to have found someone as compassionate and patient as Julie. He didn't have time for these sentimental thoughts right now, yet there they were, hanging around the fringes of his mind like bees buzzing around honeysuckle.

Walt shouted, "Time," signaling the groups to switch corners. The announcement snapped Nick back to his task — training gangsters to eliminate terrorists. The ultimate exterminators.

* * *

Julie packed an overnight bag while Agent Ford remained in the rain, pacing on the porch. She trusted no one, even if his credentials were valid, and Nick had vouched for him, she wasn't allowing any margin for error.

There was a knock on the door and the strained voice of Agent Ford came through the solid oak slab. "Mrs. Bracco. How much longer?"

"I'm just about packed," she shouted from the bedroom.

Julie pulled a large suitcase on its casters across the tiled foyer to the front door. She set the alarm before quickly exiting the house. She locked the deadbolt behind her and hustled through the rain to Agent Ford's sedan.

The FBI agent followed her to the car and opened the back door for her. "Throw your stuff in here," he said. "The trunk's lock is jammed."

Julie hesitated, sensitive to every deviation from the norm.

Agent Ford looked puzzled, his shoulders hunched over in the downpour. "What?" he asked.

"The trunk is jammed?" Julie asked, gripping the handle of her suitcase tighter than necessary.

Agent Ford opened his palms. "Mrs. Bracco, is there a reason you're acting this way?" He showed her an embarrassed smile. "I could give you the phone number of my kindergarten teacher, she'd vouch for me."

Julie realized she was overdoing it. Too many years married to a cynical FBI agent. She managed a tight grin. "I'm sorry, Agent Ford. I'm a little tense, that's all."

She tossed her suitcase in the backseat and slid in beside it. Agent Ford shut the door and hurried into the driver's seat. Pulling his hands over his scalp, he squeezed the moisture from his hair. Looking over his shoulder he said, "Ready?"

Julie nodded. She looked back at her home, getting smaller as the car drove away, and wondered what kind of world she occupied. Her own residence was no longer considered safe.

* * *

It was almost ten o'clock and Nick was working his last group of mobsters. They stood with their arms folded, taking in the information with nods and smiles. A hit man's dream come true, Nick thought. The government was not only sanctioning their occupation, but they were actually getting targets to choose from.

The fax machine rang to life and Walt pulled out the first page. Everyone stopped to see his reaction. Walt scanned the sheet and looked up. "Ohio," he said, leaving out the emotion. "They left a garbage can full of Semtex in front of an apartment building in Cleveland. No one noticed it. It killed twelve, including three kids." He crumpled the paper into a tight ball and tossed it into the trash.

The room remained silent for a few dreary moments. Grown men looking at each other with sorrowful eyes. Suddenly, the unethical cloud that hung over the assortment of criminals and policemen seemed to lift. Opposite sides of the law began to merge like in-laws for a family crisis. Nick made eye contact with Don Silkari and the both of them shook their heads at each other in disbelief of what was happening to them. To their country. Their homes.

Finally, Sal broke the silence. He cemented the accord with a sentiment that connected every man in the room. "Kids," he said, with a mouthful of disdain. "The bastards are killing our kids."

Dutton's cell phone chirped. He answered, spoke a couple of brief words and hung up. "We've got a lead," he said. He looked at Sal with something approaching a grin and said, "Let's go do something with it."

* * *

Julie looked at her watch. It was ten thirty and the rain was slapping the windshield so hard visibility was a chore. She'd made little conversation with Agent Ford. This seemed to suit the man since he made no attempt at small talk. Julie spent her time gazing out of her window as residential streets turned into tree-lined corridors. She'd lived in Maryland all of her life, but wasn't familiar with the roads she'd seen tonight.

"Just out of curiosity," she said, "where exactly are we going?"

Agent Ford kept his attention on the obscure dashes in the middle of the road. "Someplace where you will be safe."

"How far away is it?"

Agent Ford sighed. "Not much longer."

He was evasive, which was typical for an FBI agent, but he seemed to get edgier with every question she asked. The deeper into the wilderness they got, the less cordial he became.

There was a faint knock from under her seat. It sounded like a tire had flung a rock into the undercarriage of the car. She listened intently for a few minutes, but there was nothing more.

There were very few cars on the road and it disquieted her, although she wasn't sure why. The car slowed as Agent Ford appeared to be searching for a marker of some sort, peering back and forth as if he'd become lost.

"Can I help you find something?" she asked.

Agent Ford ignored her, maintaining a hyperactive inspection of his surroundings.

Then, the knock again. This time it seemed to come from behind her.

"Did you hear that noise?" she asked.

Agent Ford sounded annoyed. "No, I don't hear anything."

Again a thump sounded, only louder this time. "That noise," she said. "You can't hear it?"

Agent Ford made eye contact with her through the rearview mirror. It was a look that forced her into a quick breath.

Another loud thump sent her nerves into overdrive. It wasn't the thump that unnerved her as much as the reaction from the FBI Agent driving the car. He seemed annoyed, as if Julie was causing the noise.

"Certainly you heard that," she insisted.

"Yes," he said with a perfunctory nod.

"What do you think it is?"

"I know what it is," he said. But he stopped there.

Why was he being so coy?

It dawned on her that she was locked in the backseat of an FBI vehicle. Which meant she was locked inside the car without any means of escape. The man was leering at her now through the mirror. This was not the way an agent treated another agent's wife. Something was very wrong.

There was one way to find out if her worst fears were being realized. "Listen," she said, "I . . . uh, what was your first name again?"

A hesitation, then, "Wesley."

"Wesley," she continued casually, as if she hadn't caught the misnomer, "is there something wrong with the car?"

He mumbled something about a wheel bearing, but she didn't hear a word. Instead, she heard her husband's voice telling her the Agent's real first name. William. Her world seemed to stop. She thought about Nick, about how they would never get to have a child together. How she'd never be a mother and watch her husband push their kids on the swing in the backyard, as promised. Nick was going to leave the Bureau and they would be safe, and everything was going to be all right. But not anymore and she knew it.

When her eyes met the stranger's again in the rearview mirror, she thought she saw uncertainty. He wasn't sure whether she had made him or not. She remembered something that Nick had told her years ago, when they were still dating. He was worried about her teaching in a public school in a rough section of the city. If she was ever in a situation where she was about to become a victim, strike the first blow. An attacker is never prepared for a woman to be aggressive. It sets them back. She thought it was peculiar advice from a law enforcer. She'd always read the best method of survival was to acquiesce.

But Nick was used to dealing with a different type of criminal, and she had a feeling it was exactly the sort of assailant she was dealing with now.

She stealthily removed her belt and re-looped it in front of her, low and out of sight. She slid her cell phone from her purse and glimpsed down at it just long enough to see where the redial button was, then quickly returned her attention to her driver. She knew Nick was the last person she had called and she was sufficiently frightened enough to call him back.

When her thumb pressed down on the redial button, the tiniest of beeps sounded. The man swiveled his head, saw the device in her hand, and snatched it from her with adroit swiftness. He rolled down the window, tossed it out, and shut the window.

"You're not supposed to be using that thing. It could be traced," the man said, searching her face for a reaction.

The banging became louder. Before she could think about what she was saying, she asked, "What in the world is that noise, really?"

He heaved a reluctant sigh. She thought she saw relief on his face. "It's Agent Ford. He's locked in the trunk." The man shrugged, "I guess he's no longer unconscious."

Julie tensed. Her stomach began to cramp up. The thumping was constant and had developed a desperate cadence. The car was on the shoulder now, spitting up gravel. The man masquerading as Agent Ford searched for an opening in the trees. With the rain pounding the hood, Julie couldn't tell if there was a dirt road ahead, or just a path in the woods.

The man's eyes briefly smiled back at her through the narrow slit of the reflection. This time she could detect a slight accent. "You're going to be our hostage, Mrs. Bracco. Stay calm and you won't be hurt. Do something stupid, and I'll cause you pain that you couldn't imagine in your wildest nightmare."

Julie knew she had to act now or become a casualty. His threat was meant to buy him time. He expected her to be paralyzed with fear and she knew the minute the car was away from the road, she was a casualty.

"Who are you?" she demanded.

The man paid no attention. She could see the opening he was searching for a mere fifty yards in front of them. A pair of headlights peeked over the horizon, blurring the view of the road ahead of them. Julie took a deep breath, slipped the belt over the man's head and pulled it tight around his neck. One hand held it taut to his skin, the other pulled the excess strap with every ounce her hundred-twenty-pound frame could muster. The car skidded sideways while the man dug his fingers at the restraint around his neck. They found themselves fishtailing in the middle of the road, the man frantically turning into the skid with his knees.

The approaching car swerved dramatically to miss them, the horn wailing as it passed the out-of-control vehicle. Julie didn't relent. The car made a full circle and she hung onto the belt as the momentum flung her back and forth between the headrests.

The man desperately rummaged through his jacket. Looking down over his shoulder, she saw him pull a gun from his inside pocket. She could feel the car slowing.

The man tried to get a shot off without hitting himself. Julie felt the bullet whiz by her head and heard the blast of glass shatter behind her. A second bullet immediately followed. This time she felt it burn into her shoulder. She let go of her grip to see and feel the gravity of the wound. She touched the opening with her finger and felt the warm moisture escaping the site. Her blouse absorbed the oozing fluid like a tissue soaking up spilled tomato juice. She turned away, unable to deal with the reality of the hole in her body.

The man gasped a critical breath of air. He snatched the belt from his head and leaned back against the headrest, rubbing his neck.

The car had stopped in the middle of the road and Julie found herself crouched in the backseat, an easy target. When she looked up, she noticed the broken back window behind her. Jagged triangles of glass framed the opening like a menacing jack-o-lantern. She didn't hesitate. She flung her body through the aperture, scraping her torso with razor-like tears as she shimmied her way out of the car.

She slid across the trunk, hit the slick asphalt with open palms and rolled onto her back with a thud. In her peripheral vision, she could sense the brightness of headlights approaching. She turned and crawled for a couple of yards until she could get to her feet. She ran toward the light. Her legs felt weighted down as she waved her arms. She was only upright for a couple of wobbly steps when she heard the shot and felt the bullet hit her in the back of her head. Then the lights disappeared, and so did Julie Bracco's world.

Chapter 21

Don Silkari, Jimmy "Fingers" Ferraro, Tony "the Butcher" Florio, and Sal Demenci sat on a bench in the back of the FBI's high-tech van in amazement. Across from the awe-struck Italians was a wall of flat-screen video monitors, radar screens, dials, and blinking lights. So many that even Nick Bracco had to strain his memory to recall the purpose of all of them.

Three FBI Agents sat on bolted stools in front of the screens wearing headphones and playing with knobs and switches. Nick and Matt sat in the front portion of the van familiarizing themselves with a detailed map of the surrounding streets. Nick looked up from the diagram and watched as Don Silkari stretched his neck to see the young FBI technicians at work. They were the new breed of agent. In the old days they would have been analysts, looked down upon as nerds who didn't have the nerve to make it in the field. Nowadays, they were revered as sophisticated agents. The ones who used technology in the field to outmaneuver the enemy, making it safer for field agents to go places where they had previously avoided. In the past, the FBI went in heavy with SWAT teams and snipers. Now they surprised their opponents with small groups of prepared agents who were already informed about the obstacles they would face. Preserving evidence and saving lives.

Silk pointed to a blue screen with four straight lines flowing across it. "What's that one for?" he asked.

Paul Hartwick pulled his headphones down around his neck and tapped the screen. "These are the lines that represent the voices inside of the house." He looked over at Nick tentatively and Nick gave him a reassuring nod.

"Well," Hartwick continued, "we have an acoustic laser pointed at a window of the home and it gives us readings on the noises inside. These lines indicate vocal tones. There are four flat lines, representing four different human voices detected inside the house at one time or another." One of the lines began to wiggle. "See, right now this voice is talking. When the lines move it represents vocal changes. If a new voice should speak, the computer recognizes the different inflection and adds a new line to the screen. So far it looks like there are only four men inside of the house."

Silk shook his head in amazement. He was like a kid watching Santa land reindeer on his rooftop. "You can hear what they're saying?" Silk asked.

"Every word," Hartwick assured him.

Nick leaned over and grabbed an available headset. He stuck one earpiece over his right ear.

Hartwick looked at him. "You know Kurdish?"

"Somewhat."

After a few minutes Nick said, "What's that word mean?"

Hartwick was listening to the same conversation on his headset. "Which one?"

"Sarock."

"It's a very respectful term, usually reserved for patriarchs of a family."

"Could it mean . . . leader?"

Hartwick thought for a moment. "It could."

Nick pulled his headset off. "Who's in charge of Satellite Patrol?"

Hartwick was adjusting a dial on the panel in front of him. "I think it's still Stevie Gilpin."

"Can you get him on the line for me?"

Before Nick could finish his thought, Hartwick was handing him a smaller, thinner headset and dialing a number into a keypad to his left. "He usually answers on the first ring, twenty-four hours a day."

Nick heard half of a ring, then, "Gilpin."

"Stevie?"

"That's me."

"Listen, this is Nick Bracco. Could you add a key word to our scavenger hunt?"

Gilpin laughed. "One word, Nick. You're kidding, right?"

"No, I'm not. I just need the word Sarock added to the list."

"Do you know which language so I can route it to the proper interpreter?"

"Kurdish."

"Nick, for you, it will be done inside of thirty seconds. That fast enough?"

"You're beautiful, Stevie."

"That's what everyone tells me."

Nick hung up with a smile. Between the NSA, CIA, and FBI, there were twenty-two satellites circling the earth. Half of them were video surveillance recorders, the other half audio. The audio satellites were listening to every conversation sent through the air-waves around the world, and were programmed to record every conversation in every language that included any one of hundreds of key words: kill, bomb, nuclear, destroy, murder, etc. Once they were recorded, they were sent directly to FBI headquarters, where a translator would determine whether the conversation warranted any further investigation. Most of the time it was housewives talking about killing time, but every now and then something good happened. Adding Sarock to the list of words probably added a boatload of work for the Kurdish translator and nothing more. But it was worth a shot.

Sal Demenci looked over at the FBI crew with an expression of amazement, "If you guys can hear all of our conversations through windows and doors, then how come we're all walking around freely?"

Paul again deferred to Nick with raised eyebrows.

Nick shrugged. "Because a lot of this stuff is illegal and inadmissible in a court of law. Believe it or not, Sal, even you guys have rights."

"How did you guys find out about this house anyway?" Sal asked.

Matt didn't look up as he responded to Sal's inquiry. "The INS picked up a young Kurd and brought him in for questioning. His visa was in order, so they let him go. Fortunately, we've got a team working over there undercover. They tagged his coat with a tracking device and we followed the signal to this house."

Sal looked at Nick. "Is that legal?"

"Not always," Nick said. "This time, however, we had the proper paperwork in place." The lines of legality were getting blurrier every minute. It was ironic that Nick wound up explaining the law to one of the most lawless men he knew. They were using lions to track down a wild bear running loose in the neighborhood. Not only that, but they were training the lions how to kill a predator more efficiently. This could not turn out well.

Matt placed a finger on the map. "There," he said. "That's where we plant him."

Nick nodded. He gestured to get Paul Hartwick's attention and the agent pulled one of the headphones away from an ear.

"You still think one of them is leaving?" Nick asked.

Paul held up a finger while listening to the conversation inside the house. "They're still arguing about it. Apparently this is a

bombing crew and they're supposed to commence their mission at
1:30 AM."

Nick glanced at his watch. "That's less than two hours from now.
Where does the guy want to go?"

Hartwick didn't respond. He held his gaze on one of the screens
in front of him while concentrating on the voices in his ear. "He
wants to get a drink."

Nick squinted. "What?"

Hartwick nodded. "Yes. That's it." He pointed to a line on the
blue screen. "Number three wants to get a drink. He wants to go to
a bar. Number two is telling him that it's too dangerous. They can't
afford any attention."

"You're kidding," Matt said, scrambling with the map to find a
bar nearby. "Is he mentioning any names?"

"Something about blues." He smiled at Nick. "Number three
wants to hear some blues music."

"Shit," Matt said, fumbling with his diagram. "Blues, blues,
who's got blues music?"

"The horse you came in on," Silk uttered.

Matt and Nick both stopped to look at him.

"That's the name of the place," Silk explained. "The Horse You
Came in On. It's a dive, but they've got the best blues in the city. It's
down on Thames, shit, walking distance from here."

"He's right," Matt said. "That was my fiancée's favorite club."

"Your fiancée?" Silk said. "You have a fiancée?"

Matt shrugged. "A long time ago."

Nick leaned back behind Matt's shoulder and shook his head at
Silk. He needed to sublimate any thoughts of Jennifer Steele.

Hartwick jumped up from his chair. "He's leaving." He stood
over the agent's shoulder next to him and punched a button on the
panel. On the screen in front of him a man was seen opening a door,
then scouring the street for anything suspicious.

"Can he see us?" asked Sal.

"No," Hartwick said. "We're too far away."

Nick looked at Silk. "You ready?"

Silk stood up and checked the inside pockets of his denim jacket.
"Guess it's time to have some fun."

Sal grabbed his arm. "You be careful out there. These guys aren't
going to be there to back you up." Sal looked at Nick for confirmation.

"He's right," Nick said. "We can't be seen escorting you in and
out of trouble. Place this in your ear." He handed a tiny rubber

earpiece to Silk, who placed it in his right ear. It was flesh-colored and practically invisible unless you had an otoscope handy.

"We can hear you and you'll be able to hear us. If we see something that concerns us, we'll warn you. Other than that, you're on your own."

Jimmy Fingers shook his head. "I don't like this setup. It stinks. We're not allowed to back up our own people?"

"Hey," Matt snapped, "we can scrap this entire project right now if you don't like the terms."

Sal held up his hands. "Okay, okay, cut it out. Silk goes out alone, but if we hear trouble, you gotta let us go after him—give him some kind of protection."

Matt pursed his lips. "If we see it falling apart, we'll drop you off. But then we disappear. There can't be any evidence of collaboration."

"Guys," Hartwick said, tapping the monitor in front of him. "He's moving."

Silk slid open the panel door and looked at Nick.

"Careful," Nick said.

Silk flashed a thumbs up, then looked back at Sal with a glint in his eye. "This one's for Tommy."

They sat there wordless, just the hum of the computers breaking the midnight stillness. Nick looked out the front window and recognized a figure approaching the van. There was a soft knock on the passenger window and Nick opened it. Agent Dave Tanner stood in the night air with a concerned expression.

"What's up, Dave? Why are you out of position?"

"Walt called," he said, staring at Nick with such a mournful expression that Nick could only think of one thing that could cause such a look.

"Julie?" Nick breathed.

Tanner nodded. "You'd better come with—"

Nick was out of the van before Tanner could finish the sentence.

* * *

Mustafa Derka sat at a small round table against the brick wall. Besides the candles flickering on the tabletops, the only light in the bar came from the stage twenty feet away. Four young men with messed-up hair and ripped blue jeans swayed rhythmically to the grinding wail of a Muddy Waters song. The guitarist hunched over and slid his fingers up and down the neck of his guitar until he reached a high note, where he bent the bottom string with precise timing to the beat of the drums. Derka sipped vodka from a short, ice-cubed glass and smiled. Being the boss had its privileges. While his crew was gearing up for tonight's bombing, he was enjoying the final moments of a set of American blues.

He'd been in America for six months and the one redeeming value he saw with the place was their music. Back in Kurdistan, in his youth, Derka's ambition to play a musical instrument was ignored. After all, there were so many hardships. Derka's parents were killed in Saddam Hussein's mustard gas raid of 1988. In the streets and alleys of his village, Halabja, corpses piled up while Derka played in the hills with his friends. They were fortunate in their ignorance. They remained playing as Iraqi helicopters dropped the chemical bombs on his village. While his Kurdish relatives scrambled into their cellars for protection from another routine round of artillery from the air, Hussein surprised them with the deadly poison. The invisible gas settled down to the lowest point on the ground. The basement.

No, Derka wouldn't get the chance to play any guitars or drums, but it didn't lessen his enthusiasm for the sounds they could make. Especially when they stirred the emotions that the blues seemed to bring.

He chewed on an ice cube and sat back in his seat with a gratifying smile. The singer, sweat dripping from his chin, poured his heart out to the dwindling crowd.

Derka became aware of a presence near him and it sent him into attack mode. His hand stretched for his knife. It wasn't there.

"You looking for this?" A dark-haired man with a purple toothpick dangling from his lip sat next to him. The man was playing drums on the tabletop with Derka's knife. A drunken smile etched on his face.

Derka assessed the room. Besides the stranger, there were only twenty or so people left. Every one of them was there when he sat down and gave no appearance of association with the stranger. "Who are you?" he demanded.

The man was using his free hand to tap the table opposite the knife-beat to resemble drumsticks. He ignored Derka, lowering his head and moving it to the beat, his eyes closed. He bumped into Derka's shoulder when he swayed too far left. Derka was pretty sure the man was intoxicated; he knew he was crazy.

"Why are you sitting here?" Derka asked.

"Just enjoying the blues, man."

Derka glanced at his wrist. It was almost time for him to get back to the safe house. There wasn't time to deal with the drunk just now. He needed to do the smart thing and leave. But he wanted to be certain this nut sat next to him by chance. He didn't believe much in coincidences.

Derka turned in his seat and faced the man. He was forceful now, letting the man know he was in charge. "Why did you choose this seat?"

The man leaned into Derka and whispered, "I know who you are."

Derka cursed to himself. He was going to have to kill this man and it didn't matter how much attention he drew. He could straight-hand the man's throat, then work his eyes until they became useless. Permanently. This could be done in less than five seconds. Derka understood his abilities and he knew that Kemel Kharrazi himself wasn't quick enough to stop Derka's attack from such a close distance. This man was already dead, but he didn't know it yet.

"Who am I?" Derka seethed.

The stranger stood up and dropped the knife on the wooden table. "I've gotta go to the men's. Be here when I get back."

Derka found himself with his mouth open. He watched the stranger strut in between empty tables, snapping his fingers to the bass line of an old Willie Dixon tune. He was beginning to wonder who the man could be. A drunkard pickpocket maybe. He certainly wasn't a police officer. And what in the world was 'the men's'?

Derka picked up his knife, discreetly pulled up his pant leg and slid it back into his leg strap. He watched the man enter a hallway that he knew only contained the men's and women's bathrooms. The men's, he thought.

When Derka entered the men's room, the stranger was swaying in front of a urinal, his head resting forward against the cold tiled wall, his free hand grasping the flushing device for leverage. Derka felt that without the metal handle, the man would be making an awful mess.

The bathroom was larger than expected for such a small bar. Double sinks hung below a single stretch of mirror that ran across both basins. It had two urinals and two stalls. Derka crouched to check the stalls and confirm their solitude. The drunk seemed oblivious. He was murmuring the lyrics to the song that could be heard bleeding through the thin walls.

Derka twisted the deadbolt lock to the room. He bent over to withdraw his knife and decided to make it quick. He'd taken two steps toward the man, when he heard, "I wouldn't do that if I were you."

The drunk had his head turned slightly in Derka's direction. At first Derka thought the man was standing in an awkward position because he'd lost his balance. After a moment he realized that the man had his arm across his body in front of him. His hand peeked out under his armpit holding a gun. The man pointed the weapon at Derka as if it were part of his body. Something told Derka that the man wasn't just a pickpocket.

The stranger flushed and zipped without taking his eye from Derka. "Surprised, Mustafa?" he said, dangling an open wallet from between his thumb and index finger.

It took a second, then Derka felt his back pocket and found it empty.

"What kind of name is Mustafa, anyway?" The man appeared sober now, and Derka wondered if he would have acted differently had the man appeared sober from the start.

Derka was still going to kill the man, he only needed one small lapse, a hesitation. "What is it you want?" Derka asked.

The man gestured with his hand. "First, gimee the knife."

Derka considered doing just that, but the gun deterred him. He bent over and slid the knife across the tiled floor to the man.

"Good boy." The man took the knife and tossed it into a stall. Derka heard it splash into a toilet.

"What did you mean when you said you knew who I was?"

The man switched hands with the gun while removing his jacket. He draped the jacket over the partition of the stall and unbuttoned the top button of his collared shirt. "You guys killed some friends of mine and I'm here to settle the score."

"I have no idea what you're talking about. You must have me confused with someone else." Derka couldn't help himself, the man was removing his clothes. If he were going to shoot him, he would have done it already. "Why are you removing your coat?"

"Because as much as I want to nail you, I'm going to do it with my bare hands. I want you to have hope and I want to see that hope evaporate as I beat the ever living crap out of you."

Derka watched as the man crouched and placed his gun on the floor under the sink, then sidestep back to the middle of the floor. He couldn't believe his luck. It was the opening he needed.

While rolling up his sleeves, the man seemed to examine Derka. "I understand you guys are going to bomb the White House tomorrow night. How do you go about doing something like that?"

Derka shook his head. The idiot actually expected an answer. He was looking at the man, but in the corner of his eye he measured the distance to the gun. It was even closer to him than the man was. He decided he wouldn't need it. He leapt toward the stranger and sprung his foot into the man's chest, sending him backward against the wall. The man caught Derka's ankle with his hand and pulled him down on his back.

The man jumped on Derka and squeezed one hand around his neck, the other smacked jabs into his face. Derka was impressed with the man's abilities. Unlike most Americans, who were used to fighting with high-tech equipment, this one seemed to be familiar with hand-to-hand combat. Still, he was no match for Derka.

Derka jammed his thumb into the man's eye and applied the necessary pressure to force the man's hand from his throat. For a moment the man rolled to his side and tended to the pained eye. Mustafa looked over his shoulder and realized that the gun was now within arm's reach. He grabbed the gun and straddled the man's chest, digging the barrel into the loose skin under his chin.

"Who are you?" Derka demanded.

The man choked on the pressure the gun caused on his larynx. "Please," the man said, looking up with his one good eye. "I was supposed to find out how you were going to blow up the White House, then get the information back to the FBI," the man gasped while Derka enjoyed cramming the pistol deeper into the man's throat, trying to prevent him from talking any further. "Before you shoot . . . at least tell me how you were going to do that."

A sly grin spread across Derka's face. Why not, he thought, the secret's going to die on the floor of this bathroom. He leaned over the man and whispered, "With a missile, from underwater. It cannot be stopped and it cannot be found. Kemmel Kharrazi himself is on his way to our headquarters thousands of miles from here, where he will detonate the device himself."

"Where's that?" the man urged.

"You are very curious for a dead man," Derka sneered. He spat down on the man's face. Slowly, and with great satisfaction, he pulled the trigger. Nothing happened. He pulled it again. Nothing, just a faint snap. He removed the magazine and saw that the gun wasn't loaded. Sitting on the man's chest, he cocked his head, "You threatened me with an unloaded weapon?"

The man looked up at him, the fear in his face replaced by a broad smile. One that Derka had remembered seeing on his cousin Ledlee's face after he had just fooled Derka with a card trick.

The man reached down and pulled a small Colt revolver from his ankle holster. Derka felt the muzzle of the gun tickling his temple. The stranger, who went from drunk to sober, from weaponless to armed, looked up at Derka with a dirty grin. "You fucked with the wrong people, Mustafa."

Derka never had the time to consider the comment.

Chapter 22

Dave Tanner explained what he knew about Julie Bracco's capture, then narrow escape from a KSF soldier. There were plenty of witnesses to fill in the blanks for the team of FBI investigators who rushed to the scene. Nick sat stiff in the front seat while he listened to the fate of FBI Agent William Ford, found dead on the side of the road. Nick stared into the night as the car's headlights cut through the darkness that surrounded him. He closed his eyes. The combination of stress and weariness forced his mind to wander. He saw his wife's face, smiling, encouraging him to come closer, see what she had for him. His heart pounded fiercely as he approached. She's holding something in her cupped hands, but he can't see it. He moves closer. She holds it up to his face and he realizes that it's a human heart. It's bloody and dripping from her hands, but it's beating. He returns his gaze to her face and he blinks. It's not Julie. It's Kemel Kharrazi and he's squeezing the heart, squashing the organ like a ball of clay. "You know it's personal, Nick." Kharrazi says.

Nick sees Kharrazi in front of him as clear as day. The voice next to him says, "I said it's personal."

Nick turned and saw Dave Tanner. He narrowed his eyes at Nick. "You look washed out."

Nick sat back and realized his heart was pounding in his chest. A trickle of sweat snaked down the side of his face. "Just hang with me, Dave. I'll fight through it."

"That's all right," Tanner said. "I'm on your side, remember?"

Nick slumped his head against the car window. "I know."

Dave Tanner was driving too fast when he skidded to a stop in the half-circle drive that fronted the Emergency room. Nick jumped from the car and ran inside. Breathlessly, he scanned the waiting room for a familiar face. Between the fatigue and the short, quick breaths, he was forced to see through a maze of floating spots across his field of view. Without knowing where he was going for certain, he leaned his head forward and his body followed. Nick almost knocked himself out when his momentum drove him into a closed steel door.

"You can't go back there, Sir," a woman's voice came from behind him. He turned to see a heavyset woman sitting behind a stark white desk.

Nick yanked his credentials from his pocket and shoved them to within an inch in front of the woman's nose. "FBI. Where's Julie Bracco?"

The woman was startled for a moment, then searched her computer screen. "She's in OR number three. She's being operated on right now." The woman looked at Nick as if she wasn't sure how far she had to go to appease him.

Nick shook his credentials, which were still accosting her face. "Let's go."

"Sir, I . . . uh—"

"If you want to see my gun, I'll be glad to show it to you."

That got her picking up the phone. "OR nurse to reception desk please," she said, her eyes never leaving Nick's face. "Stat!"

The steel door swung open and Nick rushed past a girl in blue scrubs, who was pulling down her mask. "Sir," she started, but Nick's mind was too occupied for her trivial objections. He was going to find his wife and make certain she lived, even if he had to hold his 9mm to a surgeon's head to get his best effort.

Nick frantically scanned the labels above each door as he scurried down the long corridor: storage, scrub room, OR #1, OR #2—there it was, OR #3. Nick thrust open the heavy door and rushed inside.

The room was vacant. There wasn't even a table sitting under the enormous round light that hung from the ceiling. Nick stepped outside the room and quickly double-checked the number. When he returned, he heard water running. A man dressed in green from head to toe was scrubbing his hands in a metal sink, his back to Nick. Nick was so frenzied, he'd missed him the first time around. He quickly glanced under the surgery light again to see if the table had returned. It hadn't.

The man seemed to sense Nick's presence and looked over his shoulder. "Can I help you?" he said, pulling off his green surgeon's cap.

"Julie Bracco?" Nick stammered.

The man hastily worked his hands between a couple of paper towels. He stepped on a lever at the bottom of a white waste receptacle and discarded the towels when the lid opened. He strode toward Nick with an open hand. "I'm Doctor Williams," he said, shaking Nick's hand. "Are you Julie's husband?"

"She was here?" Nick breathed, pointing to the empty spot where a table belonged.

Dr. Williams didn't bother to look. He appeared to understand what Nick was suggesting. "She's alive."

Nick felt the color return to his face. "She is?"

Dr. Williams coaxed Nick to an empty stool that sat next to a dormant ECG monitor. "Sit down," he said. "You are Julie's husband, right?"

Nick nodded.

The doctor removed a cone-shaped cup from a dispenser and filled it with cold water from a water cooler. He handed the cup to Nick. "Here, drink this."

Nick poured the water down his throat in a gulp and crushed the cup into a tiny ball. "Tell me, Doctor. I want to know everything."

Dr. Williams pulled a rolling stool in front of Nick and sat facing him. "Mr. Bracco, your wife was shot in the back of the head at pretty close range." He pointed to the back of his own head with an index finger. "The bullet entered her scalp here, in the occipital, at such an angle that it deflected off of her skull, remained inside her scalp, then traveled around the exterior of her skull—" He traced a line from the back of his head around to the middle of his forehead. "Then it exited here, at the frontal hairline, never entering her skull, and never compromising the integrity of her cranium." He smiled, exposing a mouthful of perfectly straight teeth. "Mr. Bracco, your wife is a very lucky woman."

Nick's jaw trembled. "She's not going to die?"

The doctor shook his head. "She has a few contusions from her head hitting the ground and a clean gunshot wound in her shoulder, but that's all." Dr. Williams slapped the side of Nick's thigh. "She's going to be fine, Mr. Bracco. Now you on the other hand?"

Nick felt a smile crease his face.

"She's down in recovery," the doctor said. "Go ahead and grab a seat in the waiting room, and a nurse will take you back to her when the anesthesia wears off. Should be another hour or so."

He must have seen a suspicious look on Nick's face, because he held up his right hand as if being sworn in to testify in court. "I promise, Mr. Bracco, she's in the best of hands here. Let her rest up and you'll be able to see her."

Nick slowly traced his steps back to the waiting room. He ignored the stares from the few employees that milled around the reception desk and found a hard plastic seat at the far end of the room.

Dave Tanner appeared in the seat next to him. "How is she?"

"She's going to be all right," he said. "Apparently, she's got a hard head."

Dave didn't ask any more questions and Nick leaned back in his chair, closed his eyes and dreamed of open fields of grass, swaying in the breeze. A mountain full of trees loomed over a valley with a cool stillness. Somewhere in the distance a child giggled.

* * *

Walt Jackson and Louis Dutton were never the closest of associates. Dutton always tolerated Jackson's defense of his Baltimore Field Agents and Jackson merely endured Dutton's arrogance as FBI Director. But ever since the KSF began their bombing spree, the two men seemed to unite in an unspoken bond.

In a gesture of great deference, Dutton declared the Baltimore FBI field office as the command center for the KSF operation. This gave Jackson the show of confidence that not only FBI agents took notice of, but the White House as well. Louis Dutton was throwing his support behind Walt Jackson and if there were going to be any political scapegoats, they were going to have to indict the entire agency, not just Walt.

Inside of the War Room, Jackson paced in front of the computer-generated images projected onto the white walls. There were twelve separate images of varying sizes. Some showed a constant satellite image of suspected KSF safe houses, while others displayed radar screens. At the end of the wall, sentences scrolled downward in a continuous display of real-time Associated Press releases. The image getting most of the attention was the illustration of North America.

Jackson wore a sophisticated headset with a wireless transmission that contained seventy-five separate frequencies. In his left hand was a tiny control panel that he used to direct the traffic of information that he was constantly receiving. Feeding him the data were ten FBI analysts, twenty-two FBI terrorist specialists, three CIA operatives, and two NSA analysts who were furiously feeding information into the multi-million-dollar computer linkup between all three agencies' database. A merging of information the intelligence agencies had never seen before.

The analysts wore headsets of their own and sat in cubicles set up in the War Room, each one with his or her own assignment. Once their information became significant, they buzzed Jackson and updated him on any modifications.

Jackson strolled across the front of the room, a maestro conducting a symphony of data. Dutton caught up to Jackson, both of them with unbuttoned collars and loosened ties. Dutton scanned a printout of the latest KSF arrests while Jackson stared at the immense visual of the United States.

"According to our best estimates," Dutton said, peering down at his information, "we've been able to capture sixty percent of their force."

Jackson nodded. "That leaves three hundred or so still on the loose."

"And the names that aren't on this list include the top twenty soldiers in their arsenal. So we've gotten their pawns, but their upper echelon remains intact."

Jackson pushed a button on his remote. "Janice, exactly how many KSF remain unaccounted for?"

He turned to Dutton, "Two hundred and ninety four to be precise."

Dutton's focus remained on the data sheet. "You know, Walt, this kid in Colorado was talking way too much to—" He looked up at Jackson and saw him holding up his finger, requesting silence while he listened intently to an analyst talking in his earpiece.

"Okay," Jackson said, nodding, agreeing with the analyst who sat in front of a computer screen less than twenty feet away. "I understand."

Jackson clicked a button on his control panel, then slid half of his headset down so he could converse with his boss. "The Navy has five subs scouring the shoreline. The Army is scoping every lake, stream and pond within fifty miles of the White House."

"This KSF guy could've been blowing smoke."

"I think it's the best juice we have to go on. He had no reason to fabricate a story like that. Especially when he believed the man he's talking to was going to be dead in a few seconds. If he wanted the guy to leave this world with a dire outlook for the future, he could've said they were going to detonate a nuclear weapon and destroy the eastern seaboard. But no, he specifically said a missile would hit the White House from underwater. That's too precise to be made up."

A young analyst handed Jackson a sheet of paper. "The computer confirms our hypothesis."

Jackson scanned the sheet, then examined the map with narrowed eyes.

Dutton looked over his shoulder. "Makes sense," he said.

Jackson took a swig of cold coffee. "I believe the info our friend ascertained in the restroom was genuine. I think Kharrazi probably is thousands of miles from here, and if you figure how much scrutiny the borders are receiving, well . . . it's only logical."

Jackson placed his mug down. "Tolliver, Downing," he barked.

A moment later, two disheveled men with droopy eyelids lumbered up to their boss.

"You guys look like crap," Jackson said. He got a perfunctory shrug from Tolliver while Downing just stared back.

Looking past them, over their shoulders, Jackson said, "I want you to take Farnworth, Curtin and Chambers with you to Las Vegas."

"Vegas? Where they kidnapped Nick's brother?"

"That's right. We suspect that's where their headquarters is stationed. We'll get the National Guard and local authorities to assist you."

"Las Vegas is a big town, Walt. You want us to go door to door?"

Dutton stuck his nose in the circle. "You're right," he sneered. "Let's just call it a day and grab some donuts."

Jackson regarded his men with raised eyebrows, the Director of the FBI next to him with his hands on his hips. Power like that money couldn't buy.

"Yeah, yeah, we got the message," Tolliver responded wearily. Both men shuffled off like they were being sent to the gas chamber.

A light flashed on Jackson's remote designating an incoming call. He pushed the appropriate button and said, "Jackson."

"I just read the paper," Samuel Fisk's voice was somber.

Jackson looked at his watch. Was it almost 6 AM already? "You're working early this morning, Mr. Secretary."

"Actually, I'm working late. I took a break to read the Post and found an interesting story about a homicide in a nightclub down on Thames. Supposedly the victim was Kurdish. Anything I should know?"

"Nothing you should know, Sir."

"Is this for my own good?"

"Nothing you should know, Sir," Jackson repeated.

A pause. "I see. Well, I hope this nothing afforded us some valuable information."

"You're an insightful man, Mr. Secretary."

"Walt?"

"Yes, Sir."

"The President refuses to vacate the White House. We're going to stash him down in the bunker. He'll be safe there unless there's reason to suspect this thing could be nuclear."

"There is not a shred of evidence that suggests that. However, I would still do everything I could to get him out of there."

A frustrated voice came back, "Shit, Walt, is the White House going to be ground zero tonight, or not?"

Jackson hesitated. If he waffled about his ability to prevent the White House bombing, he may as well hand in his resignation right then. "Not on my watch, Mr. Secretary."

There was silence. When Fisk finally spoke, his voice seemed to contain a smile. "Exactly what I wanted to hear. How'd you know that?"

"Because it's the truth," Jackson said. "And I know you always want the truth."

Chapter 23

"Nick."

Nick woke up startled. Matt stood in front of him, holding a Styrofoam cup with steam escaping from the lid. The waiting room was bright with sunlight and beginning to buzz with activity.

Nick wiped his mouth dry. He was slumped back in an uncomfortable position for how long? He looked at his watch. Almost 8 AM.

"There's a woman who'd like to speak with you." Matt said, slipping Nick's cup of coffee into the beverage holder at the end of the armrest.

"How long have you been here?" Nick said, rubbing his eyes.

"A couple of hours. Julie's been sleeping, so I told the nurse to let you snore for a while. But she's up now and for some strange reason she wants to see your ugly mug."

Nick massaged a cramp from his neck. "Where is she?"

"Room 406. She may not look too good, but she's going to be fine."

Nick got to his feet and lagged a half-step behind Matt, following his lead. He opened the lid of coffee and took a sip. "What happened to Ford?"

Matt pushed the button in the middle of two shiny, stainless steel elevators. He looked at Nick and shook his head. "Nihad Tansu was waiting for him at your house. He got the jump on him."

They stepped into the elevator with a couple of nurses who were carrying on their own conversation. Nick spoke softly. "Tansu was at my house?"

"We think it was a coincidence that Ford happened to show up to take her to the safe house. Probably saved her life."

Nick shook his head. Matt kept talking, and Nick nodded at seemingly appropriate moments, but his mind was already two career changes ahead. He couldn't possibly put his family at risk any longer. His obsession to rid every terrorist from the nation had gotten his brother kidnapped and his wife hospitalized. He was prepared to hand over his badge and gun to Walt Jackson and flee for the serenity of a simpler life. He looked forward to seeing Julie's face when he finally told her of his decision.

"Anyway," Matt continued, as they exited the elevator and headed down a busy corridor, "Walt's turned the War Room into a computer geek's wet dream. They've got the NSA, CIA, and FBI's mainframes all linked together. Every tech who can type is down there banging keyboards and scrambling for info on KSF members in the U.S."

Standing at attention in front of room 406 was a stocky police officer. His eyes caught Nick and Matt heading in his direction and he slid his wide body in front of the door. He ignored Matt, but he held up a hand to Nick. "He's been cleared, but I need to see some identification from you, Sir."

Nick showed the officer his credentials and the uniformed policeman examined a clipboard with a list of names written across it. He saw what he was looking for and stepped aside. "Sorry, Agent Bracco, I've got my orders."

"Don't apologize, Officer. That's my wife in there you're protecting."

"Yes, Sir."

Nick opened the door with the precarious manner of a tipped-off recipient to a surprise party. Nick saw Dave Tanner and Carl Rutherford milling around Julie's bed. They blocked Nick's view of a couple of other people behind them. He thought one of them was Sal Demenci sitting on the only chair in the room.

The room was small and seemed eerily dark. A vital signs monitor sat next to Julie with one wire going to a probe attached to her fingertip, and black tubing extending down to a blood pressure cuff around her left arm. Julie was sitting upright with the aid of several pillows. Her head was wrapped with white gauze and a clear tube hung from an IV bag, which gravity fed sodium chloride to the vein in the crook of her elbow. Her left eye was dark and it looked like someone with long nails had scratched the side of her face.

Through it all there was a smile on Julie Bracco's swollen face. With her good eye she managed a wink, and Nick nearly wept. He was next to her instantly, holding her hand, mining her body with his eyes. "How are you?" he whispered.

When she spoke, her words were muffled, as if she had a mouth full of cotton. "I've been better."

"Have you seen the doctor?"

"He just left. He said the surgery went well, and that I should make a full recovery." She spoke evenly, but her eyes were distant.

"Nick?" she said.

"Yes."

"He said I was shot in the back of the head."

"You don't remember?"

She shook her head slowly, as if she might grab a piece of the incident before she finished her answer. "No."

Nick felt a rush of sorrow hit his nervous system and he had to look away from Julie to gather himself.

She clutched his hand. "Don't be sad, Nick. I'm going to be all right. All I remember is running from the car."

He wanted to run himself. Right out the door to rip Kemel Kharrazi's heart from his chest with his bare hands. But he'd already decided. He hung his head in resignation. "I'm handing in my credentials, Jule. Enough is enough."

"Don't you dare," she uttered in a clear, forceful tone.

Nick looked up. "Isn't that what you want?"

"I did, but now it's different. I'm not going to be able to sleep knowing someone like Kharrazi is out there, maybe sending someone back to finish the job. No, Nick, now is not the time for you to quit."

It was a peculiar attitude for her to acquire and it alarmed him. "Are you sure?"

Julie licked her lips. "Nick, I want you to do something for me."

Nick quickly glanced down and found the nurses button. "Of course. Anything."

She pulled Nick tight to her chest and stretched forward until her lips delicately nestled up to his ear. She whispered, "Kill him."

Nick lurched back and examined his wife, as if to be certain that it was her who'd spoken those words.

Julie's bandaged head nodded confirmation. Her hands were wound into fists and her jaw seemed to lock her face into a maddening scowl.

Nick sighed. He wasn't sure which was worse, the attempted murder of his wife or the pilfering of her benevolent heart. He looked down at the woman who'd taken in stray cats and fed them organic milk. Julie, the kindhearted wife who would find a cricket in the corner of the closet and cup it in her hands until she could free it outside onto the lawn. The same woman who was now ordering hits on fellow human beings like she was Don Corleone.

Julie's wounds were much deeper than could be seen on an MRI. Kharrazi had damaged the one thing that Nick loved more than her shiny, happy eyes or her contagious smile. He'd broken her spirit.

He unraveled her fist and gently stroked her hand. "Get some rest."

"I've never been more serious, Nick." Her eyes blazed into him like a laser beam.

He realized that for the first time in their marriage they were on the exact same page when it came to his career. He nodded. "After that, we walk away. Buy that house in the mountains."

She grinned briefly, then pain jolted her back into submission. But the smile lasted just long enough for Nick to see the relaxation return to her face. Just long enough for Nick to grasp the depth of his responsibilities. His new mission would be more important than ridding terrorists from America or saving the White House from destruction. Nick could restore the love to his wife's soul.

Nick felt a hand on his shoulder. He turned, expecting to see Matt, but was surprised to see a man hunched over an aluminum cane, his arm strapped tightly into a sling against his chest. A tan adhesive bandage covered the entire left side of his face.

"Tommy?" Nick asked.

"At your service."

Nick gingerly tapped his cousin's arm. "How are you doing?"

Tommy hobbled past Nick to Julie's side and said, "Question is — how is she doing?"

Tommy wiped a tear from Julie's cheek and patted her hand. Nick always suspected that his cousin had a thing for Julie, but now, watching him bend over her and listening to the soft exchange of words between them, Nick realized that he was wrong. Tommy never really wanted any more than to include Julie into the family. He coddled her like a little sister. Tommy said something to her that widened her eyes, then just as quickly returned with a wicked smile. She stretched out her hand and gently stroked the side of Tommy's face, where the bandage covered up the scars.

Nick almost felt voyeuristic watching them. He turned and greeted his fellow agents who were there for support. He knew they were overloaded with assignments, so the gesture meant even more. A hand patted his back and he saw Dr. Morgan.

"Doc, thanks for coming. I know it means a lot to Julie." Nick shook Dr. Morgan's hand.

"I'm not just here for her, Nick. I'm here because I know you're in trouble."

Nick looked over his shoulder and caught Dave Tanner avoiding eye contact with him.

"I see," Nick said.

"You must realize that I can't help you, Nick, unless you want to be helped. And part of that desire for help requires a healthy aversion to stress."

Nick nodded. "I'm closer than you think, Doc. I've only got one more obligation to fulfill."

Dr. Morgan frowned. "I feel like you're staring at the Grand Canyon and telling me that you only need one more day of practice before you can jump it."

Nick smiled. "I'll prove you wrong, Doc. I promise."

Julie closed her eyes and it appeared to be the cue for Tanner and Rutherford to get back to work. They said their goodbyes to Nick, seemingly unsure whether it was for a day or a lifetime. Matt and Tommy followed them out. Dr. Morgan implored Nick to see him soon, and Nick agreed.

Sal Demenci lagged behind and Nick realized that the room's evacuation was more a direct order than an act of politeness. Sal, flexing his muscle with a simple nod of his head. Once they were alone, Sal led Nick into a corner away from Julie's deep breaths. They stood by a window that overlooked a grassy knoll in front of the hospital.

Sal looked Nick in the eye. "I have to tell you something, maybe it's important to you."

"Shoot."

Sal looked over Nick's shoulder, back at Julie. He spoke softly. "There's something I haven't never told you guys. Something I was saving in my back pocket, in case Fisk didn't want to play ball."

Nick suddenly remembered. He pointed to a park bench in front of the hospital. "Down there," Nick said. "You never told Walt the entire story about the blasting caps. Someone in your crew shot a KSF soldier."

Sal was shaking his head. "It don't matter who shot who. What matters is where the shooting took place. I'd say that it's important because this guy was buying a shitload of batteries. Like the kind they use in making time bombs. You know what I'm saying?"

"Give it to me, Sal. All of it."

Sal held up his hand like a traffic cop. "Hold it right there. I want something for this information. I ain't just givin' it away for nothin.'"

Nick took a breath, "What do you want this time, Sal?"

"Hey, wait a minute. I'm offended by the attitude. I'm being all patriotic and everything and you treat me like I'm a schnook. Forget I said anything." Sal began to walk away.

"Sal."

Sal turned, "What?"

Nick swallowed. "I'm sorry. I didn't mean to insult you. Tell me what you want from me."

Sal smiled. "That's better." He looked over his shoulder, then pulled Nick even farther away from Julie's bed. "All I'm asking for is an opportunity for revenge. That's all. If I tell you where this shooting took place, I want a guarantee that I can send a few of my men to this place to sort of . . . you know —" He pointed his index finger and cocked his thumb. "Take care of some business."

Nick placed his hand over Sal's protruding fingers. "Please, don't point that thing at me."

Sal laughed. "What are you worried about — it ain't loaded." Then his expression changed. His eyes narrowed to slits. "We're talking about what they did to your cousin. Are you forgetting about that? And what about this?" He pointed to Julie, her head tilted to the side, in the midst of an exhaustive sleep.

"I'm not forgetting anything, Sal. That's why it's important that you tell me where the shooting took place."

"Not until I get your word."

"You know I need to get this approved."

"Listen, Nick, your word is gold. You tell me what I want to hear, and I tell you what you want to hear."

Nick stared at his wife. "All right. I promise I'll take one of your men. Just one. But it has to be Silk."

"You gotta let him stay with you. What you know, he knows. And he gets the whole immunity thing like we've been getting."

Suddenly, the door opened. Matt walked up to Nick. "Walt called. He needs me. Take care of your sweetie over there."

"Where are you going?" Nick asked.

Matt furrowed his brow, sneaking a sideways nod toward Sal.

"It's all right," Nick said. "You're not going there anyway."

"Why not?"

"Because you're going with me to . . ." he looked at Sal and held out an open palm.

"Payson, Arizona," Sal relented.

"Arizona? Why there?"

"Because," Sal said, proudly, "that's where we got rid of Rashid Baser."

"What do you mean? Rashid Baser is dead?" Matt asked.

"Apparently," Nick said. "And if it's true. That's where we'll find the bomb-making facility."

Matt glanced over at Julie. "What about her?"

Nick looked at the woman he loved, mangled in bandages and tubing. He still felt the chill that ran down his neck when she'd used the word kill in a sentence with only one other word in it. It was the subject of the sentence that bothered Nick, not the verb. If she wanted to kill time, or kill a volleyball, he didn't have a problem. But 'kill him?' She was sleeping now, but he hoped that he would be able to pull her out of her trauma, just like she did for him every day of their lives together. "The quicker I find Kharrazi," he said, "the quicker she'll begin the healing process."

Matt nodded.

Sal said, "While you're gone, you want maybe we give your wife a little . . . you know . . ." the finger gun returned, "protection?"

"What, you going to poke someone in the eye?" Matt deadpanned.

"Very funny, Mr. G-man. You notice over in Sicily this kind of stuff doesn't happen."

"Don't get me started, Sal."

Nick stepped between the two men. "That's enough. C'mon Matt, we've got to get going."

"Don't forget about Silk," Sal said, reminding Nick of their agreement.

Matt followed Nick to the door. "Silk?"

As he passed Julie's bed, Nick stopped for a moment to give her a peck on the bridge of her nose; the only bare spot between the tube in her nose and the bandage on her forehead.

She surprised him by whispering with her eyes shut, "Get him."

Bending over her, he said, "Just try and stop me."

Chapter 24

As Kemel Kharrazi pulled up in his rental car, he could see the gravel parking area that stretched all the way to the bottom of the brick building that housed the airfield's office. There were only two cars in the lot and they were parked an abnormal distance from the front door. Kharrazi assumed these were employees' vehicles. He parked his car along a chain link fence in between the only two rental cars remaining.

It was a small complex with little security, yet he still scrutinized the facility for any sign of irregularity. There was none. Past the brick building, sitting on the solitary runway, was his chartered jet with the engine running and the door open. The airfield was so small that the diminutive jet was only thirty yards from the front door to the office.

While making his way on the cracked cement path toward the building, he reminded himself to hobble. He was a plump, old businessman and he had to walk the part. His right shoulder developed an exaggerated sag from the weight of his suitcase. As he approached the glass door to the office, he could see that it appeared vacant. He stopped. Why did he even have to bother going in? He'd prepaid for the return trip already. All he had to do was board the plane.

He walked the short distance to the idling plane and lumbered up the steps. He felt a presence as he got halfway and looked up to see a uniformed pilot reaching out to get his suitcase. The man said something to Kharrazi, but the loud drone of the jet engines drowned out his voice. Once inside, he plopped himself down onto a wide, leather chair and huffed from exertion. The pilot secured his suitcase in an upright closet and returned to his seat in the cockpit. He took the copilot's seat on the right, while the pilot on the left was busy with a pencil and a clipboard. He seemed to be marking off a preflight checklist and paid no attention to Kharrazi, which soothed any concern Kharrazi had about his identity being discovered.

Settling back in his seat, he found a copy of the Baltimore Sun laying open on the secure tray next to him. It was nearly 9AM and he hadn't had the time to scour the newspapers as he normally would. The front page displayed pictures of burning buildings from several states still suffering from the nightly bombings. A story about President Merrick's approval ratings spiraling downward was below the fold. He flipped the pages impatiently until he saw the story about a Turkish National who was shot to death in the bathroom of a downtown bar. Kharrazi scrutinized every word searching for anything that could suggest the man was Kurdish, but there was nothing. The fake identification seemed to have satisfied the authorities and once the victim was dead they probably had no motivation to investigate further.

Kharrazi knew that Mustafa was a hot head, so it didn't surprise him when his Baltimore crew was arrested last night and that Mustafa was the only one who ended up dead. He realized that an officer of the law must have gotten to Mustafa, and shot him after he became an unproductive suspect.

Satisfied, Kharrazi browsed further and tingled with excitement when he came to the story of Tansu's deadly visit to the Bracco residence. The story confirmed the death of an FBI agent, but fell short of declaring Julie Bracco dead. It simply stated that she was at Johns Hopkins in critical condition. His grip on the paper tightened as he considered the possibility of Nick Bracco's wife surviving an encounter with one of his best soldiers. He read the story again and began to fume.

He stood, hunched over, and shuffled to the back of the plane, where he pushed a button on one of the four cell phones that he would use just once, then dispose of after the flight.

"Yes," a voice said.

"You told me that you were successful," Kharrazi seethed in a low boil of a voice.

"I was."

"Then why am I not reading about it this morning? I am leaving now, I have to ignite our operation, or I would deal with you personally."

"Sarock . . . uh . . . we are being tricked. There is no other explanation. I am certain of the shot . . . I hit her directly in the back of her—"

"Enough already. I want you to check and make sure there is no doubt. Do you understand me?"

"Yes, Sarock."

Kharrazi clicked off the phone and returned to his seat. The pilot was holding a hand to his headset as if he was receiving an incoming transmission. He turned to Kharrazi and said, "Mr. Henning?"

Kharrazi leaned forward. "Yes."

"Airport security needs to speak with you."

Kharrazi mentally became aware of his hidden weapons, tucked inside of his padded torso. "What is the problem?"

The pilot continued touching dials and flicking switches on the instrument panel in a practiced manner. "Just routine, they're required to ask you a couple of standard questions before we take off. It will only take a few minutes and we'll be on our way."

Kharrazi looked at his watch. "But I have a very important meeting to make. That is why I chose to charter, rather than fly commercially. I was guaranteed to be on time."

Now the pilot took a moment to look at Kharrazi. In his reluctance to speak with security, Kharrazi could see a spark of suspicion flicker in the pilot's eye. "Mr. Henning, it will only take a few minutes and I promise I can make it up in the air."

Kharrazi slowly came to his feet. "Of course, of course," he said, hobbling toward the exit. He kept his peripheral vision on the pilot and noticed him return his attention to his clipboard.

When he entered the small building, a man in a blue uniform was waiting for him. He wore patches that reminded Kharrazi of Boy Scout accomplishments and he showed no signs of possessing a gun. The only other person visible was the same young woman who checked him in the day before. She stood behind the counter and looked busy. The only thing sitting on the counter was a single computer terminal, and there was a metal file cabinet with just two drawers behind her. The place was so sparse, it looked like they were moving out in a couple of hours.

"Mr. Henning?" the slightly graying man asked.

Kharrazi shuffled toward the man with an outstretched hand. "Walter Henning. How can I help you?"

"Max Reynolds," the man said, clasping hands with Kharrazi. "I just have a few routine questions to ask. You know we're all at a heightened state of security ever since those KSF cowards began bombing our citizens. Those spineless bastards." He looked at the girl behind the counter. "Sorry, Tina. Pardon my French."

Reynolds couldn't see Kharrazi clench his teeth; he was busy writing on a notepad.

"Mr. Henning—"

"Please, call me Walter."

"Of course, Walter." He wrote Kharrazi's fake name at the top of the form. "Where exactly are you traveling to today?"

"Payson, Arizona."

"Payson? What a coincidence, I'm from Phoenix myself."

Kharrazi forced a smile. "Small world."

Reynolds took his pen and pointed to the plane idling outside. "Does Payson have an airfield long enough for a small jet like that?"

"Just barely."

Reynolds nodded, thoughtfully. "Anyway, how long was your stay in Maryland?"

"Just overnight. I had a quick sales call."

Reynolds wrote on his pad as he spoke. "What kind of sales?"

"I work for a custom boat builder."

"Really?" Reynolds looked up with a smile. "Which company?"

"A small firm out of Payson."

Reynolds held his eyebrows up and Kharrazi realized that he was expecting a name.

"Klein Brothers," Kharrazi came up with.

"Never heard of them."

"It's a small family company," Kharrazi said with an understanding lilt to his voice.

"I see," Reynolds had his head down, scribbling on his form. Kharrazi used every muscle in his face to read what Reynolds was writing, but either the man was being deliberately discreet, or Kharrazi was trying too hard at the art of subtlety.

Reynolds broke off the writing and acted like he'd forgotten something important. "Do you have any children?"

"Yes, two. Twelve and fourteen."

Reynolds shook his head. "Teenagers. I don't envy you."

Kharrazi had forgotten about his disguise. He must have looked a bit old for teenagers. He knew that the more questions asked, the more chance there was for a mistake.

"Are we almost done?" Kharrazi asked, turning his body toward the door.

"Almost, Mr. Hen—" he stopped himself, then gave an overly thick smile. "I mean, Walter."

The man was either trying to be smooth or he was genuinely a nice person. Kharrazi couldn't tell which, but either way he was running short on patience.

Reynolds placed the tip of his pencil on top of a row of boxes to the left of some sentences on his form, ready to check them off. "Did you pack your own luggage today?"

"Yes."

"Has anyone had possession of your luggage after being packed?"

"No."

"Has anyone asked you to transport any items for them?"

"No."

Each time Kharrazi answered a question, Reynolds checked a box with his pencil.

"Have you come in contact with anyone who's asked peculiar questions about airline security?"

Kharrazi scowled. "You mean besides you?"

Reynolds looked up. "That's good, Walter." Then pointing the pencil at Kharrazi, he said, "I'll have to remember that one."

The security guard peeked down at his form and said, "Last question. Are you carrying anything on board the plane that could be construed as dangerous?"

Reynolds stared at Kharrazi like a biological lie detector. Kharrazi did his best not to flinch, but the question took him off guard.

"No," Kharrazi's voice jumped at the word. "Don't be ridiculous."

Reynold's stare lingered a moment before he looked down at his form and checked off the last question. But it wasn't the usual check mark. This time the man circled the box instead of checking it. It was the only time he'd done that. Finally, after an uncomfortable gap in the conversation, Reynolds placed the pad behind his back and said. "That's all, Walter. You're free to go. Have a safe trip."

Kharrazi hesitated a moment, wondering what had just happened there. He turned to leave and when he placed his hand on the handle to the glass door, he heard Reynolds over his shoulder. "Oh, by the way, Walter, has that new high school on Ponderosa been built yet?"

Kharrazi stopped. He looked down, thoughtfully. Which way to go here? "I'm not sure. I thought I heard something about that, but now, my recollection is foggy."

"Of course," Reynolds said, appearing satisfied with the response.

Kharrazi left the building and took a couple of steps before looking over his shoulder. Through the glass door, he locked eyes with Reynolds. Kharrazi couldn't read the old guy. If Reynolds had asked that last question to trick him, then he would be trapped once he entered the plane. It could have been an innocuous attempt at small talk, but Kharrazi was almost out the door.

Kharrazi decided he couldn't afford to risk it. He turned back. His mind was flooded with ideas, but only one made the best sense. When he reentered the building, Reynolds was standing in exactly the same spot.

"Can I ask you a question?" Kharrazi said.

Reynold's shrugged. "Of course."

"If I did hear something suspicious here at the airport — how would it be handled?"

"It depends on what you heard and how serious it was."

"Well, I don't know how to put this," Kharrazi looked over at the girl behind the counter, then back to Reynolds. "Can she be trusted?"

Reynolds laughed. "Tina? She's family. Her dad actually owns Apex Field."

Tina had short, dark hair with a hint of spike to it. She was busy working the mouse on her computer and barely acknowledged the mention of her name.

"All right, then," Kharrazi said. He looked around, suspiciously. "Are you two the only employees working today?"

"Walter, if you have something to say — say it. Tina and I are the only employees here, period. I'm the janitor, the maintenance man and head of security. Tina does all of the operational stuff: flight plans, billing, just about everything else. If there's something I should know, come out with it."

Suddenly, Kharrazi knew what he had to do. He looked at Tina. "Can you radio the pilots and ask them to hold up for five minutes?"

With a bored expression, Tina picked up a small wireless transmitter and communicated the delay. Kharrazi heard the pilot mutter back an acknowledgement.

"Good," Kharrazi said, walking away from the glass door and deeper into the small waiting area. There was a row of hard plastic chairs against the wall. Kharrazi dropped his weighted-down body on a seat farthest from the door and virtually undetectable from the outdoors. He leaned forward with his elbows on his knees, his head down. He heard Reynolds sit down two seats away to his right.

"What is it, Walter?" Reynolds asked with sincere concern.

Kharrazi looked up. "Do you know anything about Kurds?"

Reynolds shrugged. "Just what I read in the paper."

"What if I told you that the Kurds were the only ethnic group in the world without a nation of their own? And that they've been persecuted by the Iraqi and Turkish government for more than twenty years, with nowhere to run and call home. Can you imagine not having a place to call home?"

Reynolds looked confused.

"Then," Kharrazi continued, "when the Kurds finally have enough financial backing to fight back, the United States sends its soldiers to Kurdistan to prevent them from defending themselves. Could you understand how frustrating that must have been for these poor people?"

Reynolds was nodding, but with a vacant stare. "Why are you telling me this?"

Kharrazi leaned close to Reynolds as if he was going to whisper the answer. His hand was already grasping the handle of his knife under his jacket. Reynolds turned his head to allow Kharrazi to get to his ear. Kharrazi said softly, "Because I want you to understand us before you die."

Reynolds jumped back, but it was too late. The long blade had already punctured his heart as Kharrazi shoved and twisted the knife under his ribcage. Kharrazi pressed his face up against Reynold's face and watched closely as his eyes went from shocked to lifeless. Reynolds slumped to the floor and Kharrazi called to Tina. "Come here, quick."

Tina looked startled. She rushed from behind her counter until she was close enough to see the blood saturate Reynold's shirt. She stopped ten feet from Kharrazi, who already had his Beretta aimed at the girl. "If you scream or move, I'll kill you."

The girl anxiously stepped in place, her long, purple fingernails fluttering in the air. "Don't hurt me, please."

"I won't, if you do exactly what I tell you."

The girl was shaking. Her arms and elbows flapped like a chicken attempting flight. "Please," she begged, "please, please. I'll do anything."

"You're going to have to get a hold of yourself," Kharrazi demanded. "You're no good to me unless you calm down." He yanked the knife from Reynold's chest and swiped it clean on the dead man's sleeve. He replaced his knife and gun to their holsters hidden under his jacket. Standing up he held out both hands. "Now, I want you to write a note on a blank sheet of paper."

She started toward her counter.

"Stop," Kharrazi said.

She turned to face him.

"If you make even the slightest gesture to signal anyone, I can remove my gun from its holster and have a fresh bullet inside of your body in less than three seconds. Do you understand me?"

She nodded.

"Good. Now, I want you to write in large letters, 'Gone until 4 o'clock', then tape it to the inside of the glass door."

She pulled a sheet of paper from the copy machine and began to write the message. She stopped halfway through and looked at Kharrazi.

"What is it?" he asked.

"Well, there's a charter flight due to leave here at 3:45. They may wonder—" she hesitated. As if she might be giving more information than she should have. Then, with a nervous wince, she said, "What are you going to do to me?"

"I'm going to tie you up and place you in the women's room."

"But I could be there for days. I'm the only one left with a key."

"Relax. Once I get where I'm going, I'll make an anonymous call and tell them to get you. I'm not as bad a person as you think, Tina." He gave her a fatherly smile, then nodded toward the note. "Let's put this on the door, as it is."

She stretched a piece of scotch tape from her dispenser and taped the note to the glass door.

"Now, tell me about flight plans."

"What do you need to know?"

Kharrazi heard the jet engines rev and knew his time was running short. "Where do you keep them?"

"In the computer."

"Show me."

She walked behind her counter and tapped a few keys on her computer. Kharrazi stood behind her. A moment later a screen displayed that day's schedule. There were only two flights scheduled. "We only do flight plans for charters, the locals come and go with their props whenever they want."

Kharrazi pointed to the screen. "Can you delete the flight plan for my charter?"

She looked at him skeptically. "Why?"

"Please, just do as I say."

Her fingers worked tentatively, as if there was an internal struggle going on in her brain. Kharrazi hoped that she wouldn't recognize her fate until she was finished with her task.

"There," she said, "It's done."

"Good. Now, do you have to signal the pilots before they take off?"

"Yes."

"What do you tell them?"

"I let them know they're cleared for takeoff. But it's mostly ceremonial. We don't have any control tower or anything."

"Tell them that you have to leave—you have to go home. Do you have any kids?"

She shook her head.

"A sister or a brother?"

"Two sisters."

"Do the pilots know them?"

"I don't think so."

"Good. Tell them that you're leaving. Your sister was in an accident and you have to go to the hospital, but that they're clear for takeoff. Understand?"

She nodded. Her voice cracked when she spoke to the pilots; she seemed noticeably upset. The pilots certainly must have thought her sister's accident was the cause of her behavior.

"Go on, Tina. We'll take it from here. I hope your sister's going to be okay," came back the pilot.

Kharrazi smiled. "Do you have a key to the door?"

She handed him a key ring with a set of wings attached. "It's this one."

"You've been a good girl, Tina. Just do me a favor and sit down right here."

She stared at him warily as she crouched down below the counter.

"Turn toward the wall please," Kharrazi said.

Slowly, she shifted her body away from Kharrazi, facing the wall, but her head strained to keep Kharrazi in her sights.

"Tina, it's okay. I'm just going to tie you up. Turn around."

The girl listened to her assassin just long enough for Kharrazi to draw his knife over her head and grab a handful of hair with his free hand. He pulled the sharp blade across her exposed neck with a quick, forceful jerk. Her hands scratched at his arms for a few desperate seconds, breaking every last nail until finally they fell to her side. When the weight of her dead body gave way, Kharrazi was struck with how light her head felt without her torso dragging it down.

"You must understand, Tina," he whispered. "No one person should stop the persecution of thousands of innocent Kurds. Not even you."

He peered over the counter and saw nothing to alarm him. He stood all the way and examined himself for any blood. A few spots, but his clothes were dark enough that they could be mistaken for a sloppy cup of coffee. He didn't have time to do anything with the bodies. They were out of viewing distance from the front door and once the office was eventually opened up, it wouldn't take long to figure out what had happened. He went to the door and left the building. While locking the door with Tina's keys, he assured himself that he had at least three or four hours head start. And that was all he needed.

He hobbled back into the jet where the pilots were still preoccupied checking and double-checking instruments.

"See?" the pilot said to him, as they taxied to the runway. "That wasn't so bad, was it?"

Kharrazi smiled. "Not at all."

Chapter 25

By the time Nick and Matt arrived at the Baltimore Field Office, the press had already reported that President Merrick wouldn't be leaving the White House that night. It was a bold political move, even if Merrick was tucked safely into the bunker beneath the mansion. It only tightened the noose around the FBI's neck. Specifically, Walt Jackson's. If the White House was bombed after receiving advanced warning, everyone at the Bureau may as well dust off the old resume.

Nick and Matt made their way through the security locks and retina scans guarding the elevators down to the War Room. As they exited the elevator, Nick was startled at how cramped the otherwise large room looked. Matt was right, it bordered on computer geekdom. The walls were illuminated with huge, flat screen video monitors silently displaying satellite feeds from around the world. The room was packed with low partitions separating small, plain-looking metal desks. Each desk was occupied with an analyst wearing a headset, staring into a computer monitor. The hum of low voices and keyboard-tapping filled the air.

The biggest change Nick noticed was the lighting. The big overhead fluorescents were shut off, giving the wall monitors a sharper image. The room had a movie theatre feel to it. The bulk of the illumination came from the images flashing across all four walls. The only other lights were tiny goosenecks with a narrow beam that attached to each of the analyst's desks.

The front of the room contained a long narrow shelf with two fax machines, three computer terminals, and a series of devices that played cassettes, DVDs, and CDs.

Nick's attention was drawn to a round, wooden table in the corner of the room, next to the shelf. A makeshift ceiling light hung too low and the four men at the table had to lean forward slightly to make eye contact. Three of the men had rolled-up sleeves, ties that were pulled down to their sternum, and the wrinkled shirt look of an all-night poker game. They were Walt Jackson, FBI Director Louis Dutton, and the Director of the CIA, Kenneth Morris. The fourth man appeared fresh and neatly dressed.

"Shit," Nick said, when he saw who it was. "What's he doing here?"

Matt followed his gaze and shut his eyes tight for an instant. "Damn."

The guy Matt was referring to was Chief of Staff William Hatfield. Last summer, Matt caught the man slapping his wife with the back of his hand. Matt was staying at a resort up in the Blue Ridge Mountains of Virginia, when his girlfriend at the time suggested a romantic evening stroll along a tree-lined pathway around a small pond. The Chief of Staff was walking in front of them with his wife when Matt heard the unmistakable sound of skin on skin. It wasn't until Matt ran up to defend the woman that he discovered who the attacker was. Matt squeezed Hatfield's throat with one hand and simply said, "Don't." Nick understood there was more to the story, but Matt never revealed his inner thoughts on the matter. On the surface Matt appeared to be the epitome of a free spirit. He was single going well into his thirties, and never pretended that he was anything but on the prowl most all of the time. But ever since his indiscretion with a stripper the night before his wedding, Matt despised married men who cheated. He even hated married men who told stories about cheating, even if he knew they were lying. It contradicted everything that Matt appeared to be, but Nick knew him better than anyone. There was only one type of man Matt hated more than an adulterer. Wife-beaters.

Nick noticed that everyone at the large oak table but Hatfield had dark circles around their eyes. Hatfield had the uncanny ability to look as if he'd just gotten a full night of sleep. He sat with his suit still intact, and his hair sprayed into a permanent structure. His right hand played with the Presidential Seal cufflink on his left sleeve, in case there was someone left in the building who didn't know where he worked.

When Jackson saw Nick, he did a double take. "What are you doing here? I sent for Matt, not you."

"It's okay," Nick said, approaching the table. "Julie's going to recover. I'm much better off working."

"I didn't come all the way down here for small talk, gentlemen," Hatfield bristled.

Nick and Matt looked at him as if he spoke a foreign language, but the men sitting around the table with Hatfield didn't even act surprised. It looked like they'd been hearing a lot worse from the Chief of Staff. Although Hatfield held absolutely no authority at the table, everyone understood who he represented.

When Nick and Matt stood there unsure of their welcome status, Hatfield boomed. "Either sit down and help, or get the fuck out of here."

Nick saw Matt's face getting flush. He shot Matt a look and Matt tightened his lips, while he and Nick found seats opposite each other. Matt sat directly to Hatfield's left.

Nick wasn't sure how to introduce the subject of Sal's information. Hatfield's presence made it almost impossible to explain his source. Hatfield wasn't privy to any deals made with Sal's crew, and his proximity to the president precluded him from being briefed.

In a slow beaten voice, Jackson said, "Here's where we are." He said it in a reviewing tone, but Nick knew he was recapping for his and Matt's benefit. "We have Mustafa revealing Kharrazi's plan to attack the White House with an underwater missile. We have Kharrazi flying somewhere out west to detonate the missile. We also have every Naval vessel searching the coastline for anything suspicious, and we're scoping every body of water inside of five miles of the White House."

Jackson turned toward an electronic map of the United States on the near wall, pointed to Ohio, and clicked a button on his remote control. The city of Cleveland lit up with a small green light. "After interrogating a KSF soldier in Cleveland, we discovered that Kharrazi is still in America, and will remain here until his mission is accomplished." Another click and Las Vegas lit up, "Here is where Kharrazi kidnapped Phil Bracco. It took months for the KSF to prepare a safe house the way they did." Another click, and another light. "Henderson, Nevada. A tip at a local gun show nets us another three KSF soldiers. Yet we still have no big names. The way we see it, their headquarters is out west, probably in Nevada, more specifically, Las Vegas."

Jackson turned to Dutton and handed him the remote. Dutton clicked a button and a series of red lights sprung up in a circle surrounding the Washington, DC, area. "Here's where we have the Sentinel Radars stationed. If a missile is launched anywhere outside of this perimeter, we have anti-missile launchers in place."

"What if the missile is launched inside the perimeter?" Hatfield asked.

Dutton hesitated. "Well, we're fairly certain—"

"Fairly certain isn't going to cut it," Hatfield huffed. "If I wanted fairly certain I would have phoned you instead of coming to meet with you personally. The President—shit, the country can't afford for us to be fairly certain any more. We need certainty and effectiveness."

Hatfield seemed to compose himself for a moment. He clasped his hands in front of him and leaned forward, as if he were going to let everyone in on a secret. "I have a direct quote from the President. Would you like to hear it?" He didn't wait for their nods. "If the White House even gets egged tonight, his quote is, 'Tell them to find new careers, because theirs will be over.' Now, I don't have to tell you that President Merrick doesn't bluff, do I?"

It was a lie. Merrick was too polished to make such a crude threat, but Hatfield wasn't. In years past, Chiefs of Staff like Leon Panetta and Andrew Card would embrace their domain and stay perfectly happy within the walls of the White House. But Hatfield was of a different ilk. He spread his tentacles into places he had no business being, and as a consequence, he had few political allies. And in a place like Washington D.C., allies were a potent currency.

Regardless of the veracity of Hatfield's statement, everyone at the table commenced a slow squirm. Almost everyone. Matt McColm casually removed a stick of gum from its wrapper, and giving it his full attention, slid it into his mouth and began a leisurely chew. He was using the most powerful weapon he had to counteract an overbearing authority figure. Apathy. He wasn't about to give Hatfield the satisfaction.

Nick understood the move. Everyone knew the Chief of Staff had the President's ear, but he wasn't Matt's boss. Matt's boss sat directly across from him, and by the look on his face, Jackson was enjoying every minute of it.

Hatfield glared at Matt. "Do you understand me?"

Matt folded his gum wrapper with methodical precision.

"I'm talking to you, Mr. Sharpshooter."

Nick braced himself for the collision.

Matt took the empty wrapper, folded it, and carefully placed it in his breast pocket like it was a rare jewel. "Tell me something, Bill," he said. "When are you going to show us how to wipe our ass?"

The table smoldered with stifled laughter.

Hatfield's eyes tightened into penetrating beams of malevolence. He pointed a manicured finger at Matt. "Start reading the classifieds, asshole."

Matt leaned into Hatfield's finger. "What the fuck do you know about—"

"That's enough!" a voice boomed from behind them. Defense Secretary Martin Riggs loomed over the table. He still had on his suit jacket, but his tie was pulled down, and a portion of his collar was stuck on the outside of his jacket. Even though the ex-Marine looked as if he hadn't seen a bed in a week, his stature alone made you think twice before challenging him. Riggs dropped a large stack of manila files onto the table and strategically sandwiched himself in a seat between Matt and Hatfield. "After this is over they'll be plenty of blame to go around. Right now, we need to focus on the enemy."

Matt and Hatfield gave each other malicious glares, but nothing more.

Riggs thumbed through his stack of files. Without looking up, he said, "To answer your question, Mr. Chief of Staff," he glanced at Matt for effect, "there is no guarantee we can shoot this missile down whether it's inside or outside the perimeter."

Hatfield folded his arms. Riggs opened a file marked, "Classified" and continued. "We have twenty F-16's armed with the newest generation of Sidewinders dedicated to safeguard the White House. Even so, hitting a missile with a Sidewinder is tantamount to a bullet hitting a bullet. It's not easy."

Riggs placed the file on the table in front of him and addressed Hatfield. "There's also the issue of countermeasures. Our intelligence tells us that if Kharrazi does have missiles off of our shore, they'll almost definitely be Russian technology. If that's true, the missile will come supplied with decoys."

Hatfield had a confused look on his face, so Riggs took a deep breath. "Decoys, Mr. Hatfield. Sometime during its flight the missile will drop off large, aluminum-coated balloons. To our laser-guided radar system they will appear as metal objects, no different than the missile itself. It will give us too many targets to choose from. Mistakes will be made, I assure you."

"Still," Riggs said, turning back to his file, "with the amount of ground troops roaming the vicinity, and the Sentinels and fighters flanking the zone, I'd give a rogue missile one chance in three of making it through. And that's only if there's one missile deployed." He gave Hatfield a long look. "That good enough for you, Bill?"

Hatfield allowed a deep breath to convert itself into the tiniest of nods. "If that's the best we can do."

Matt looked away from Hatfield and shook his head, fighting to maintain control.

"You got those reports?" Jackson asked.

"Right here," Riggs said, sliding a large, folded piece of paper from the file and opening it all the way. He moved the stack of files to the side and laid the paper across the middle of the table. As Riggs leaned over the paper, Nick could see that it was a map of the United States.

Riggs removed a pencil from his breast pocket and hovered over the map. With millions of dollars worth of computer technology surrounding him, Riggs was going with his strength; a pencil and a piece of paper. He drew a straight line from Hoover Dam to Las Vegas. "Three-thirty this morning, an operative in Nevada made an ID on a KSF soldier traveling from Arizona to Las Vegas."

"What happened with him?" Hatfield asked.

Nick winced. Hatfield had obviously never been to a Riggs briefing before. Riggs didn't tolerate interruptions when he was disseminating intelligence. He would almost always answer your question at some point during the briefing, and the ones he didn't answer usually weren't pertinent enough to warrant an explanation.

Riggs simply gave Hatfield his game face. The Chief of Staff developed a sudden fascination with the diagram of Hoover Dam. Riggs returned his attention to the map.

"Now then," he continued. Drawing a line from Flagstaff, Arizona to Santa Fe, New Mexico, he added, "Four-fifteen this morning, an experienced trucker traveling east on Interstate 40 near Flagstaff noticed a truck pulling a trailer that didn't match the markings on the cab. He called DPS and they discovered two KSF soldiers transporting explosives." He looked up at Hatfield. "They made the arrest without incident."

Drawing another line from Yuma, Arizona, to San Diego, California, he said, "At five-twenty AM, a highway patrol officer discovered a car making a U-turn on a grass median, trying to avoid a road block on Interstate 8 West. He called for backup and they arrested two more KSF soldiers with a trunk full of explosives."

Riggs pointed to Jackson, "I assume you have the samples back."

Jackson nodded, taking his cue to finish the intelligence report. "Yes, we took soil samples from all of the captured soldier's shoes. There's trace of Pinyon Juniper present in each of their samples. This particular type of plant is most commonly found in higher elevation. In the four-to seven-thousand-foot range."

Jackson took the pencil from Riggs' hand and traced a serpentine oval around the northern Arizona portion of the map. "This puts them either up here in the Flagstaff, Prescott, Payson area, or down here around the outskirts of Tucson. It's a large region to cover in such a short time, but we should focus in or around the small towns. They need supplies, so we have to gamble a little here."

Riggs stood upright from his hunched position, as if to get a better perspective of the markings. He looked around the table, while pointing to the areas Jackson had just circled. "Gentlemen, the enemy is here somewhere. We just need good old-fashioned investigative skills to sniff them out."

Walt must have read Nick's face because he looked at him with raised eyebrows. "You have something to add, Nick?"

Nick looked up at Matt, but his partner's face was shut tight. This was Nick's call and he knew it.

"Nick?"

Nick looked at his watch, then back to Jackson. There wasn't time for the usual political dance. He either opened up and risked a scandal that made Watergate look like misdemeanor trespassing, or keep quiet and possibly watch the White House light up the night sky. He thought about Julie, and how desperate she looked when she pleaded for him to keep going. To find Kharrazi and kill him.

"Something wrong, Nick?" Ken Morris said.

Nick felt a drop of sweat tickle the back of his neck. "They're in Payson," he said.

"Is that a hunch?" Riggs asked.

Nick shook his head. "I have an informant."

"Who?"

Nick shrugged, but before he could pry open the can of worms, Matt stepped into the fire. "It's an operative we have working undercover," Matt said.

Hatfield glanced at Matt for a brief moment, then back to Nick. "Is that true, Nick?"

It was almost true, but not quite. He felt his stomach move ever so slightly upward. He was now in a corner. If he gave up Sal, then Hatfield would have questions. Questions that he couldn't be allowed to have the answers to. And if he contradicted his partner . . . well, he couldn't do that either. His brain swelled with frustration.

Suddenly, a commotion erupted in the back of the room.

"Get him!" someone shouted.

Nick looked up and saw a dozen analysts cheering in front of a big screen video monitor as if they were watching the Super Bowl.

On the screen, a dark-haired man in jeans and a long-sleeve shirt ran through a backyard, being chased by another man wearing an FBI windbreaker. The view was from overhead and it resembled video that reality cop shows would film from a helicopter. The clarity on the screen was remarkable. Nick could tell that the dark-haired man wore black, high-top sneakers. But they weren't watching a shot from a helicopter; they were watching an image projected from a spy satellite hundreds of miles in space. Nick had heard stories of its capabilities, but when he saw the picture himself, he was amazed.

Walt Jackson was having a conversation on his headset. "Bring it in closer," he said.

Nick thought if the image were any closer, he could tell which brand of hair gel the guy used.

Matt looked over his shoulder at Nick. "Recognize him?"

Nick squinted, trying to catch the face of the fleeing man. "Bali?"

"Uh huh."

"Who's Bali?" Riggs asked.

"Reyola Bali," Nick answered. "He's one of Kharrazi's top soldiers. They call him the 'Specialist.'"

"What's so special about him?"

"Well, it's common knowledge that everyone in Kharrazi's organization uses a knife as their weapon of choice. Bali is one of the few who prefers a gun. He's their premier sniper."

Riggs pointed at the screen. "Do you think this agent chasing him knows that?"

Nick watched the chase, anxiously tapping his fist to his lips. He saw the face of the young FBI agent and it reminded him of himself his first couple of years with the Baltimore P.D. — brash, aggressive, too aggressive. As if the aggression could somehow make up for his lack of experience. The agent was running recklessly toward Bali, practically stumbling on every third step. Nick could feel the agent's adrenal gland surging unnatural levels of hormones through his blood system.

Nick suddenly felt someone watching him. Riggs was staring at him, waiting for a response to his question. Nick considered how much an ordinary field agent would know about Bali. Finally, he looked away from the screen just long enough to make eye contact with Riggs and give him a grim shake of his head.

"Shit." Riggs turned back toward the screen.

Nick watched the action on the satellite feed with a new sense of dread. Now Bali was hopping a block fence and running down a dirt alleyway. The young agent was fifty feet behind him. He was a little sloppier with the fence and landed awkwardly, but he immediately jumped to his feet and started gaining on Bali. The angle of the screen was so close that it was hard to see the terrain, or what was ahead of the two men.

"Where is this? Nick asked.

"Gary, Indiana," Walt said, without removing his eyes from the screen.

"Where's his backup?"

"It's coming."

The cheering in the War Room grew louder as the FBI agent drew nearer, sending shivers up Nick's spine. Bali was quick, but he had to make decisions of direction that seemed to slow him up. The FBI agent appeared more familiar with the surroundings, and all he had to do was follow Bali.

Finally, a beam of swirling lights preceded the entrance of a local police car taking up the chase from the left portion of the screen. The buzz in the War Room grew intense with an ovation for the backup.

"Here comes the cavalry!" someone shouted.

Nick still tapped his lips with his fist, only his grip grew tighter.

The police car was spitting up dirt with its tires while fishtailing down a dirt alley, leaving a trail of sideswiped garbage cans in its wake. The driver slowed when he approached an intersection of alleys. As the car nosed its way into the intersection, Bali ran directly across the front bumper of the vehicle without even turning his head. The car backed up and attempted to turn down Bali's alley. The FBI agent banged the hood of the car with his credentials as he fled past the vehicle. The turn was too sharp for the police car so the cruiser had to make several back-and-forth maneuvers, costing precious seconds before finally returning to the chase.

Suddenly, Bali made a wide right turn around the corner of a block fence. The width of the turn made it appear as if he was picking up speed, but the moment Bali felt the agent was out of sight, he darted straight right and crouched up against the fence for cover. The agent couldn't see Bali double back, so he kept barreling forward. The entire War Room took a collective gasp. Someone yelled at the screen to look out. The agent couldn't hear the pleas from the War Room, nor could he see the man pulling a gun from his belt in the back of his jeans. Like watching a motorboat speeding toward a hidden waterfall, Nick cringed at the sight.

The agent slowed slightly as he turned the corner, but he obviously expected Bali to be in a full sprint. By the time his momentum took him past the fence line, it was too late. Bali was waiting for him, arms outstretched, gun trained on the agent. The soundless picture added a creepy element to the inevitable shooting. The agent tried desperately to get down, but Bali was too quick. When the agent hit the ground, he was already immobile. Bali moved closer. Someone shouted, "Let him be." But Bali was ruthless. Even with the police car approaching, and maybe because the cruiser approached, Bali edged to within three feet of the fallen agent. He pointed his gun down at the man's head.

Nick cupped his hand over his eyes. He heard the groans, first from the men around him, then from all four corners of the underground bunker.

Riggs slammed his fist onto the oak table and the War Room turned deathly still. The whir of the computers filled the silence as analysts found their way back to their desks, and their seemingly futile assignments.

Nick looked up in time to see Bali hopping over a fence. Eventually, Bali would be caught, or more likely, killed — but not until he took as many lives as possible; none more important to the agents in the War Room than the man who lay motionless on the ground. The police car finally reached the agent and the officer jumped from the vehicle and ran to him. The satellite camera focused back on Bali who jerked open a side entrance door to a large office complex. Screeching police cars suddenly surrounded the building. It was only a matter of time, but Nick knew that nothing good would happen inside of that building. Bali killed one of their own. He would never be allowed to leave the structure alive.

Nick waited for Riggs to resume his questioning about the identity of his informant. Instead, Riggs placed a hand over his mouth and slowly rubbed, as if he was measuring the precise amount of stubble his face could sprout after pulling an all-nighter. He appraised everyone at the table, eventually settling on Nick.

"Payson, huh?" Riggs said. He circled the small town on the map with his pencil, then looked at Jackson. "Now, we can go in heavy or go in silent. Which do you think would be more effective?"

To his credit, Jackson blew by the informant issue at light speed.

"With such a short window, I think silent might be more effective. If we go bullying our way into such a small arena, the KSF will hear us coming and dig in. Maybe even detonate the missiles early."

Riggs nodded his head. "That's right. If they think they're secure, they're more likely to make a mistake. Maybe even get a little careless."

Hatfield seemed unable to restrain himself. "What are you talking about? Are you saying that we don't send every available resource to that town immediately? That's insane."

Riggs did something that brought a huge grin to Matt's face. He turned to Jackson and continued the discussion unabated. "We send a small, tactical team of agents. Nick's team. Have them work with the local Sheriff's Department—with plainclothes." He looked at his watch. "If we hustle we can get the team on the ground in five hours. That puts them there by three o'clock Pacific time, and gives them six hours to find Kharrazi's headquarters." He made straight lines across every road that passed through Payson. "In the meantime, set up roadblocks here, here, and here. If we don't succeed in finding them tonight, then we can always have ground troops there by morning."

Jackson took the map and pushed a button on his transmitter. A minute later, he was speaking with a deputy in the Gila County Sheriff's Office in Payson, Arizona.

Hatfield shook a fist at Riggs. "Listen here, Martin, I'm not telling the president that we know where they are, but we're going to be clandestine about it. We should get the media involved, have them broadcast that reward money promo all over the networks. We'll get information, fast. Send in the damn military now for crying out loud."

Riggs glared at Hatfield's fist and it melted to the table like an ice cream cone on a hot summer day. Riggs scrolled his eyes right up into the Chief of Staff's face. "You can tell the president that we're doing our jobs to the best of our ability. With all of the years of experience putting our lives on the line defending our nation from domestic and foreign enemies, we feel that this tactic has the best chance to succeed. Unless you have some law enforcement training, or military service in your background that I'm not familiar with—we're not taking any requests."

Hatfield pursed his lips, but stopped there. Nick could see the frustration in Hatfield's face. Riggs knew that Hatfield was a former corporate attorney, who stepped in a pile of good fortune by marrying President Merrick's sister back when he was still a senator in Indiana. Still, Hatfield could make everyone's life miserable, adding pressure from the executive branch that no one wanted to deal with. He sat back in his seat with a childish frown on his face. With one final act of misguided authority, he said, "Proceed."

Riggs stood at attention. He pointed to Nick, then Matt. "You two need to get going. Gather the team and head down to Dulles. There will be a Defense Department plane waiting for you. My plane." He looked at Jackson almost as an afterthought. "That okay with you, Walt?"

Jackson nodded. "Of course. They're our best assets."

Riggs looked at Hatfield, who sat rigid, attempting to appear important. Riggs said, "Don't you have some shoes to shine or something?"

For a moment Nick thought Matt might stick his tongue out at Hatfield. Instead, Matt motioned to the door and said to Nick. "Let's go."

Chapter 26

Nihad Tansu entered the hospital wearing green surgical scrubs and a stethoscope draped around his neck. He strode into the lobby with a confident swagger and leaned over the half-circle reception desk, both hands on the white countertop. "I'm Doctor Marshall," he announced to the white-haired woman sitting behind the desk. He managed to transform his Kurdish accent into a Latin-flavored mixture of Italian and Greek. Just enough to add mystery without being mysterious. "I was called down to see a new patient—Julie Bracco. Could you please direct me to her room?"

The woman scrolled a finger down a laminated sheet of paper hanging from the upper portion of the countertop. "Dr. Marshall?" she said, curiously. "I'm sorry, I've never seen your name before. Do you have privileges here?"

Tansu smiled. "Of course, it's just that I only moved here a couple of days ago and the administrator hasn't gotten around to adding me to the roster yet."

The woman nodded her head, but continued to follow her finger up and down the sheet, even turning it over to scan names posted on the opposite side. "I see," she said.

"I'm a plastic surgeon," he said. "I'm only here to meet the patient and confer with Dr. Williams about her case."

With the introduction of Dr. Williams' name, the woman seemed to perk up. "Oh," she said, "well, yes. Dr. Williams just operated on her last night. Poor thing, got a bullet right in the back of the head." She pointed for effect.

Tansu cringed, but not for the same reason the woman thought it was for. He grimaced at the knowledge that Julie Bracco had somehow survived his gunshot. "Ouch," he said. "That's not good."

The woman looked at him. "But, you must know all about it already?"

He froze.

"I mean if you've spoken with Dr. Williams already."

"Actually," Tansu breathed relief, "I only received a voice mail from him. He just told me to meet him here at ten-thirty."

The woman appeared to be checking her computer screen for something. Tansu feared she was checking to see if Dr. Williams was even there. Tansu got the doctor's name from the newspaper that morning and hoped that would be enough of a password. He cupped his hand under her chin, holding it there as if he were framing her face for a portrait. "I hope you don't think me rude," he said, "but I only started seeing patients on Tuesday, and . . . um . . ."

This got her full attention—a plastic surgeon actually examining her face. "Yes?" she said, anxiously.

"Well, it's just that, being new and all . . . I could use some work to keep me fresh."

Her eyes widened as he moved around her, touching her cheek ever so softly. She sat perfectly still, as if the slightest movement could cause a miscalculation.

"If you are at all interested, uh—"

"Marie," she blurted.

"Yes, Marie," he said, gazing at her bone structure as if it was a fine diamond. "I'd be glad to do a little work on you, maybe a little around the eyes," he said, gently pulling her skin toward her ear, then using both thumbs to get the symmetrical effect. "It wouldn't take me more than a couple of hours. I could do it right across the street in my new office. And, of course, I would waive my fee. Like I said, I could use the work. At least until I develop my practice. You understand, don't you?"

"Of course," she said. What's to understand? He was offering her every American woman's dream come true. Free plastic surgery.

"That sounds great," she beamed.

Tansu looked at his watch. "Uh oh. I'd better get back there. Could you—" he pointed to the door that he hoped led to the patient rooms.

"Oh, yes, of course," she held her index finger up against the computer screen. "Mrs. Bracco is in room 406." She stood, then pointed down a long corridor. "Take the second set of elevators to the third floor."

Tansu was already walking away. "Thank you, Marie. I'll stop by on my way out and give you my office number."

She was smiling like a high school girl on her prom night. Tansu couldn't help but smile back at her. A very helpful woman, he thought. He was almost to the corridor when he heard her yell, "Dr. Marshall."

He turned.

"There's a police officer standing guard in front of that room," she said. They both stood there looking at each other. Tansu held up his hands, unsure what to say. He was prepared to kill a half a dozen people to get to Julie Bracco, one unsuspecting police officer didn't pose much of a threat.

Marie finally picked up a phone and said, "I'll call up there and tell him you're coming."

Tansu blew her a mock kiss. "Thank you, thank you."

He made his way down the corridor, searching for a storage room for medical supplies. He came unarmed in case he needed to pass through a metal detector. He knew that a hospital had more than enough weapons for him to choose from.

He wondered why Kharrazi had such a fixation for this Bracco person. It seemed that half of their time was spent attempting to put to death this FBI agent or some family member of his. Tansu tried not to doubt his leader, but sometimes personal reprisals seemed to get in the way of their ultimate goal: to force U.S. troops out of Turkey and allow his people to defend themselves properly. Tansu himself had a cousin who was shot by a Turkish soldier. His cousin was simply escorting his wife to the river for water, when a band of soldiers came driving by in an open jeep, waving their machine guns in the air. They were drunk with hatred and didn't stop to ask questions. If you were Kurdish and lived in Kurdistan, you had a target on your back at all times.

Now, all Tansu wanted to do was kill this woman as quickly as possible and get back to the business of pressuring the White House for a withdrawal. He saw the elevators he needed, but decided to find something sharp first. A nurse carrying a tray with glass tubes and packages of wrapped needles was walking toward him. He held up his hand to get her attention. "Pardon me, I'm new and a little lost here, could you direct me to the supply room?"

"Sure," the nurse said. She turned back where she had come from and pointed. "See that sign that says, 'Emergency Room?'"

"Yes."

"Follow that sign until you go past the cafeteria, then make your first right. About halfway down that hallway you'll find the supply room. Just tell Mitch what you need, he'll help you out."

"Thanks," Tansu said. These Americans were wonderful hosts, he thought. Very helpful.

He followed the directions and found the room he was looking for. Under a sign reading "Supply Room," was a wooden door split in half. The top portion was swung inward and open, while the bottom half was closed. Tansu leaned in and called, "Anybody here?"

A thin, elderly black man with a close-cropped, white beard slowly rose from behind a small, metal desk. The room appeared dim, but for the miniature gooseneck lamp illuminating the old man's desk. "Can I help you?" the man asked.

Tansu extended his hand and the man shook it. "Hi, I'm Dr. Marshall. You must be Mitch. I'm new here. I was told to come down and get some scalpels."

"Sure thing, Dr. Marshall. Do you have a requisition form?"

Tansu was perplexed. He shook his head. "I don't know. I was just up in the operating room, and they told me to come down and get some more scalpels."

"Who told you?"

"Well, uh, Dr. Williams."

The man broke into a soft, wide grin. "That rascal. He hasn't filled out one of those forms in twenty years. I guess that's what happens when you have his kind of clout."

"I guess," Tansu said. He was ready and willing to snap the old man's head like a stale pretzel if he resisted, but the man appeared ready to hand him the weapon he required.

"Which kind would you like, Dr. Marshall?" the man said, his shoulders already turning toward the shelves behind him.

"Oh, how about a big one?" Tansu said, casually.

The man stopped abruptly. He looked at Tansu with a leery expression. "Excuse me?"

Tansu shrugged. "They really didn't tell me which size. I just assumed they wanted a large one."

"A large one," the man repeated. He seemed to examine Tansu more closely. "Where did you do your residency, Dr. Marshall?"

That was Tansu's cue to take the man out. He looked up and down the corridor and noticed nobody in the immediate vicinity. He motioned for the man to come closer. And, as everyone else he'd met lately, the man cooperated. Tansu reached over the doorway and grabbed the man's throat with his right hand. With his left hand he gave a short, powerful jab directly into the man's nose. It was enough to cause the man's vision to blur with tears, and he fell straight backward, holding both hands over his broken nose. The man's head bounced on the cement floor hard and he appeared to lose consciousness.

Tansu reached over the ledge and twisted the doorknob, but it was locked. He hopped over the half door and jumped onto the man's chest. It took only a couple of seconds to snap the old man's frail neck, the bones clicking as they twisted sideways, unnaturally.

Tansu lifted the dead man's frame and dragged him into a nearby walk-in refrigerator. There were four rows of metal shelving with vials and bottles of medicine neatly organized on each shelf. Tansu dragged the corpse by his shirt collar and dropped him face down on the floor in the back corner of the refrigerator. Without some serious investigative work, the old man would appear to have fallen to his death. And that would buy Tansu plenty of time to accomplish his mission.

Once out of the refrigeration unit, Tansu explored the rest of the supply room. Tansu wondered why the large windowless room was so dim for a hospital. He was searching for a switch to illuminate the overhead fluorescent lights, when he found the shelf that contained the scalpels. He looked at the side of the boxes, which displayed an actual life-size illustration of the blade for the various scalpels. He now understood why the old man found it curious that Tansu simply asked for a big scalpel. Each scalpel had a numerical value for the type of blade that it contained. Tansu assumed that a physician would always request a specific numbered scalpel depending on their needs. The old man must have sensed something was wrong right away.

Tansu had spent countless hours over the past months practicing his English. He didn't, however, know very much about medicine. He pulled a scalpel from a box marked with a number 11 blade. He unwrapped the plastic sheath that kept the product sterile. He examined the blade, gently tracing it across the palm of his hand. It was sharp, but too pointed to cut long, deep lacerations. He put it back, then pulled one from a box marked with a number 15 blade. This was what he was looking for. The blade was sharp, but beveled. This was the kind of blade that could slice a neck right down to the bone. He put two of them into his pocket and smiled. I'm on my way, Mrs. Bracco. Enjoy your last few breaths.

Chapter 27

President Merrick sat on a sofa down in the bunker fifty feet below the White House. Even though it was only ten-thirty in the morning, his lead Secret Service agent began quoting statutes about his authority to protect the President of the United States. He had actually convinced Merrick that he could, and would, physically escort Merrick to the bunker himself if necessary. Merrick didn't see the need to dig in on that point, so he settled in at his new command post. Everything he needed to run the country was right there with him. Technology would allow him to be in constant contact with every branch of the military, FBI, NSA, and CIA.

The bunker had an unusual brightness to it, as if the windowless basement was trying to make up for its absence of sunlight. Overhead fluorescent lights flooded stark white walls and tan Berber carpet. Covering over five thousand square feet, the bunker consisted of three bedrooms, two bathrooms, a full kitchen, and a large multipurpose room that included five pullout sofas. The ventilation system assured that the inhabitants received the purest of oxygen, and the kitchen was stocked with enough dry goods and distilled water to support a dozen people for almost a year. Longer if rationed.

The bunker was initially constructed during the Cold War. Its initial purpose was to protect a sitting president, his family and a few choice aides throughout a nuclear attack. Other than a monthly maintenance check, the bunker had never been occupied, and rarely discussed.

Merrick's wife and two kids were away with his mother-in-law surrounded by Secret Service agents. If he was going to be a target, there was no reason to put his family in harm's way also.

Merrick sat on the sofa next to Bill Hatfield, who was hunched over a laptop computer with the Presidential Seal displayed on the back. The computer sat on a coffee table that competed for space with ten different newspapers layered between manila files marked 'Confidential', 'Secret' and 'Top Secret.' Bob Dylan's voice twanged sarcastically from the built-in speakers. Merrick had been stressed for so long that he was beginning to feel a bit numb.

Samuel Fisk sat in a leather chair across the coffee table from Merrick and Hatfield with folded arms. He listened while Bill Hatfield attempted to gain the President's attention for a briefing. The three of them were temporarily alone while the remainder of Merrick's staff noisily discovered the challenges of cooking powdered eggs and potatoes in the kitchen.

"They know where he is, John. Doesn't that bother you?" Hatfield bristled.

Merrick dug through files of the latest arrests stacked on the table in front of him. "Listen, Bill, I trust Marty to make the right moves. He's no dummy. If he thinks that surprising them is better than tipping them off, I'll buy it."

Hatfield looked at his watch. "We've barely more than thirteen hours to go. Why are we being coy here?"

Merrick understood Hatfield's tendency to panic, but he was tired and wanted to be certain of his judgment, so he glanced at Fisk for reassurance.

"He's right, Bill," Fisk said. "We've got to give Marty and Louis and Walt their opportunity to clean up this mess."

Hatfield looked back and forth between Merrick and Fisk. "I can't believe you two are taking this so calmly. Don't either of you understand the ramifications of the White House going up in flames? Even if it's abandoned, it will symbolize the extent of our vulnerability and encourage all kinds of terrorist attacks. Anyone with a slingshot will try picking off government employees going to their cars."

While Merrick reviewed his latest e-mail from the FBI War Room, he said, "I'm not real eager to make a mistake here, Bill. Let these guys do their job. I just spent the past three hours with that damn phone stuck to my ear and I'm getting briefed every thirty minutes. I believe Walt knows what's at stake."

Hatfield grimaced but said nothing.

Merrick read from his e-mail. "Walt's got a task force on its way to Payson already. Apparently, the Gila County Sheriff's Office has set up roadblocks disguised as sobriety checkpoints so they don't raise any suspicions, but they'll scrutinize everything they see. He feels confident that we're closing in."

"John, you're making a mistake," Hatfield said with a restrained voice. "This is a golden opportunity to—"

Merrick reached behind the sofa to a button on the wall. He turned the button to the right and Bob Dylan's nasally voice boomed over the ceiling speakers. Dylan was pining about some cryptic burden that Merrick was sure even the CIA couldn't decipher. It did, however, drown out Hatfield's ineffectual argument and that's all that mattered.

Hatfield stood, pointed to Merrick, and yelled over the dirge of harmonicas and steel guitars. "This is a flagrant miscalculation!"

Merrick held his hand to his ear and shrugged. A few aides poked their head into the doorway to see what the commotion was all about. They got there soon enough to see Hatfield throw up his arms and storm out of the room.

Fisk hopped up and took a seat on the sofa next to Merrick. He centered the laptop in front of him and continued opening e-mail messages in Hatfield's absence.

"Do you think I'm being too hard on him, Sam?" Merrick asked.

"You know how I feel about him. I plead the Fifth."

Fisk checked the final e-mail. It was forwarded from FBI Headquarters where Kharrazi had been sending his demands. "Look at this," Fisk elbowed Merrick.

The message was preceded with a note from the Assistant Special Agent in Charge. It read, "This seems legitimate. The trace came back with a dead end. A pre-paid server with a P.O. Box address, never been used before, like the others."

Merrick scrolled down to the body of the e-mail:

President Merrick,

We both know that your time is running out. You don't have the support of the American people any longer. I realize that you are hiding in your bunker like the coward you are. Tonight, when the White House explodes into a beautiful fireball, the United States will no longer be under your command. The media will disembowel you publicly and there will be nothing to prevent the impeachment process. Congress will not allow America to be destroyed over the tepid support for a country that means little to its citizens. It's only your ego that precludes you from doing the right thing and saving your presidency and the nation you swore to defend. Order your troops out of Turkey before midnight, and you will be safe. It is the only logical thing to do.

By now, you must be receiving intelligence suggesting that they cannot find the missiles that will destroy your home. They won't, Mr. President. And even if they do there is nothing they can do to prevent its launch. They can only expedite it.

I look forward to your press conference.

KK

Fisk shook his head. "Good old-fashioned Georgetown education. The asshole knows his politics."

Merrick looked at him. "He's right about one thing." He pointed up. "If this baby takes a hit tonight, I might not be impeached, but I could start packing my bags. It's six weeks until the election and I haven't left this damn building in three days. I could count on one hand the amount of votes I'd be certain of, and I'm including me and my wife."

Fisk scratched his ear. "If you withdraw troops from Turkey, you're fucked. You would forever be the President who cowered to terrorist demands."

Merrick nodded, still staring at the e-mail. The reward was nowhere near the risks, reputation or not. Didn't he have a responsibility to protect U.S. citizens?

"On the other hand," Fisk added, "if we're able to find these guys and put this issue to bed, you'd be the President who caught Kemel Kharrazi—the world's most notorious terrorist."

Merrick sat back in his chair and folded his arms, still regarding Kharrazi's words on the screen in front of him. "Missiles."

"What's that?"

Merrick pointed to the screen. "He said missiles. As in more than one."

Fisk patted his friend's back. "Don't worry, John, we'll get him."

Merrick turned toward him. "You know something that I don't?"

Fisk picked up a file and began reading, as if the question was never asked.

Merrick pulled a half-unrolled package of Tums from his pocket and with practiced agility popped one into his mouth and crunched down hard on the chalky tablet. "Boy, Sam, this better be good."

* * *

Nihad Tansu had taken a lab coat from the supply room and hid a couple of scalpels in his outside coat pocket for easy access. As he approached Julie Bracco's hospital room, he walked directly toward the stocky officer guarding the door. He made no pretense to avoid a confrontation. The man stared at him as he smiled a greeting. "Hello, Officer, I'm Dr. Marshall. I believe Marie called you about my visit."

Tansu had his hand in his coat pocket, ready for a quick nick of the carotid artery. To his credit, the officer did not appear comfortable with the last-minute addition. He kept a stoic expression, as if he was waiting for Tansu to crack; but Tansu stood his ground, a cheap forgery of a smile planted on his face.

The officer said, "Can I see some ID?"

Tansu pulled his fake identification from his pocket and handed it to the man. The officer looked at the photo, then Tansu. Finally, he handed the card back to Tansu and nodded toward the door. "Go ahead."

Tansu had altered his appearance slightly, dying his hair blonde and adding blue contact lenses. He knew that would be all he needed to get close enough to Julie Bracco to slit her throat.

Tansu abruptly entered the room, hoping that a quick confident entrance would seem more routine. He smiled at the woman sitting up in the bed, but the woman's head was slumped to the side. Was she dead already? He was actually disappointed that he hadn't had the chance to be the instrument of her death. Especially after she had the nerve to survive one of his best shots at a moving target.

"She's been asleep for almost an hour, Doc," a voice came from the corner of the room behind him. A man dressed in a white robe sat cross-legged in a shiny, padded chair scrutinizing the inside of a newspaper. The man had gauze dressing covering half of his face and a long cast on his left leg. A wooden cane leaned against the wall beside him. The man never took his attention away from the newspaper.

"I'm Dr. Marshall," Tansu said.

The man grunted something that sounded like, "'Nice seeing ya.'"

The newspaper had a full-length picture of a horse on the cover. The horse posed for the picture with a bouquet of flowers across his back where the saddle normally went. Next to the horse was a tiny midget of a man with a pink shirt.

"Nasty break you got there," Tansu said, looking at the man's leg, trying to decide who he should kill first.

"Snapped my metacarpal," the man said from behind the newspaper.

Tansu shook his head. The man was far too preoccupied to care what he was doing. He turned toward Julie Bracco and made sure the man's view was blocked. He removed the scalpel from his pocket and palmed it as he leaned over her limp frame. Her face was turned away from him leaving her neck exposed. Tansu felt like a vampire in an old black-and-white movie, approaching his victim with much the same passion for blood. He quickly glanced back at the man who was still buried deep behind the newspaper. He raised his right hand with the scalpel while his left hand held her head in place. "Mirdin, Mrs. Bracco," he whispered in her ear.

Suddenly, Tansu found himself lunging for the floor. His head bounced hard on the linoleum. He quickly turned to his side to see what happened. The man in the robe was wagging a finger at him. The straight part of his cane was in the palm of his hand. He had yanked the curved end around Tansu's ankles and pulled his feet from under him.

"What are you doing?" Tansu said.

"The metacarpal bone is in my hand," the man said, standing over him, holding up his free hand. "The metatarsal is in my foot. Capisce?"

Tansu saw the man favoring his good leg and realized that he could easily overtake him. The man reached down and picked up the scalpel from the floor.

The man looked at it with amusement. "Doing a little emergency surgery, Doc?"

Tansu slowly got his legs under him and remained in a crouch position, ready to strike. He was about to jump when he noticed that the man was now holding a gun. A gun with a silencer attached. Tansu was beginning to understand that this man was no ordinary patient. The man held a finger to his mouth. "Shhh, be real still. I'm not going to turn you in."

Tansu was listening. He knew the man wasn't a police officer, so maybe he could make a deal with him. In reality, all Tansu wanted was an opening. Just one little mishap or lax moment. He felt the outside of his pocket to make sure the other scalpel was still there. It was.

The man motioned Tansu to get to his feet. "You and I have a lot in common, Mohammed, or whatever your name is. By the way, if you're from Turkey, does that make you an Arab?"

Tansu didn't answer.

"Oh shit, you turds are all the same — talk, talk, talk. Can't shut you guys up."

Tansu had his hand in his coat pocket now and was removing the plastic sheath from the tip of the scalpel blade.

"Anyway," the man said, "all I want is a few answers to some simple questions and I'll have you back on the street in no time."

The man smiled at Tansu. He smiled like a fool without any knowledge of Tansu's physical abilities. Still, Tansu wished he knew who the man was.

* * *

Marie Clarendon sat at her reception desk facing the front door of Johns Hopkins Hospital. She was going back and forth between typing an admittance form for a new patient and sneaking glances at her pocket mirror. She kept pulling her skin back on the side of her face the way Dr. Marshall had done. She was imagining how many years her face could have back, when a man in a green sweatshirt walked through the automatic sliding glass door.

Marie snapped her compact shut and immediately returned to her paperwork. The man walked with a slight limp and went directly to the receptionist's desk.

"Marie?" the man said.

Marie had been told by the hospital's attorneys not to engage the man in conversation. He had filed a lawsuit against one of their doctors for negligence and was using discreet interviews with hospital personnel to incriminate the young internist. He'd already pilfered information from a couple of unsuspecting nurses while pretending to be waiting for a family member in the emergency room. He was a farmer from the south somewhere, and his good-old-boy accent lured them into believing he was harmless.

"Marie," the man said urgently.

Without looking up, Marie said, "I'm not talking to you, Charlie. You already got me in too much trouble."

"I'm sorry. I didn't mean to use you like that, it's just that—"

"Go away, Charlie. I'm not listening to you."

"You don't understand, one of your doctors is in real trouble."

Marie tapped away at her keyboard.

"It's not what you think," he explained.

Marie stopped and pointed at the man. "I'm telling you for the last time, if you have a complaint, take it up with the administrator. I'm not supposed to talk to you."

"I don't have any complaint. I'm talking about one of your employees being in trouble. Don't you care about him?"

"Who?"

"The doctor—that's who I'm talking about."

"Which doctor?"

"I don't know his name exactly."

"Then how do you know he's in trouble?"

"Because," he said, pointing toward the parking lot, "I just saw him jump out of one of your windows."

Chapter 28

At thirty-five thousand feet, the 747 ate up the sky in large chunks. Nick could hear the urgency in the four engines as clouds whipped by the windows.

"How fast you think we're going?" Nick asked Matt, who was scrolling through a Globe, Arizona, phone directory on his laptop.

"Huh?"

"How fast do you think we're going?" Nick repeated.

"Uh, six hundred miles an hour," Matt said, pointing at the screen with his finger.

"Hmm," Nick said, already forgetting the question. He was also on a laptop navigating through the FBI's private website. He'd just received a new level of security clearance and was now viewing information that had previously been unavailable to him. The most intriguing was the data pertaining to Kemel Kharrazi's renegade childhood. As he read the gruesome details of Kharrazi's upbringing, he actually found himself feeling sympathy for the man.

"I've got the Gila County Recorder's office," Matt said, scribbling down a phone number on a legal pad.

"Good. Get a listing of all houses bought in the Payson area over, say, the past twelve months. Have them fax it to the Sheriff's Office in Payson."

Matt pressed buttons on his cell phone and Nick could hear him getting right down to business. The seats in the 747 resembled a steakhouse restaurant; there were crescent-shaped, leather booths surrounding round, freshly-polished mahogany tables, all fastened to the floor. In the center of each table was the emblem of the Secretary of Defense—a bald eagle with its wings spread, proudly exposing red, white, and blue stripes on its chest.

Sitting at a similar setting behind them were agents Ed Tolliver, Carl Rutherford, Mel Downing and Dave Tanner. All four agents began the flight shuffling through files and writing notes. Now, they each seemed to be staring at the ceiling of the jet, until you noticed that their eyes were shut. They looked as if they had been the victims of chemical warfare instead of a simple deterioration of their sleep schedule over the past week. Behind them, sipping on a bottle of Diet Coke by himself, sat Silk. He was reading Forbes magazine with his feet propped up on the table.

Silk looked up and gave Nick a mock salute. Nick shook his head and smiled. He could use an army of Silks right about now.

Nick's phone rang and saw that it was Johns Hopkins Hospital. He pushed a button. "Julie?"

"No, it's me."

"Tommy?"

"Yeah, listen there's been something happening here."

"What are you talking about?"

"I'm talking about a visitor that came by to see your beautiful bride."

"Who?" Nick asked, not liking the sound of Tommy's voice.

"One of those fucking towel-heads stopped by dressed like a doctor. He wasn't here to bring flowers, if you know what I mean."

Nick squeezed the phone. "What happened? Is she okay?"

"Relax, Julie's unharmed. Fortunately old Tommy boy was here to put the kabosh on the whole thing."

"Tommy," Nick said, trying to control himself. "Let me speak with her."

"She's been sleeping. She slept through the whole thing. You want I should wake her up?"

Nick sighed. "No, let her sleep. Just have her call me when she's up."

"You got it, boss."

"What happened to the perp?"

"Perp?"

"The piece of crap who tried to kill my wife. Where is he now?"

There was a pause, then, "Well, uh, you see, the guy — he's in the parking lot right now."

"What's he doing there? Is he being arrested?"

"Actually, he's resting. As a matter of fact, he's going to be resting for a really long time."

Nick understood the term. "Tommy, by any chance did he stumble upon an open window?"

Tommy laughed. "Yeah, well, I told the guy to take a flying leap, and you know how these foreigners are, they take everything so literally."

Nick squeezed his eyes shut. His next call would be to Walt to add protection for Julie. There wasn't enough protection in the world for her.

"Nick?" Tommy said, "you still there?"

"I'm here. Are you in trouble with the police?"

"I just witnessed a KSF soldier attempt to murder an FBI agent's wife. He tried to escape out the window and lost his footing on the windowsill. They're bound to hand me a medal before they handcuff me."

"Who was it—do you know?"

"Nihad Tan-something."

"Nihad Tansu?"

"Yeah, that's it. Anyway, I got a hold of this guy's cell phone," Tommy said conspiratorially.

"You have his cell phone? How?"

"It must have fallen out of his pocket when he ran to the window."

"Tommy, that's important evidence. You have to give that to the police or the FBI right away."

"Yeah, yeah, anyway, I pushed a couple of buttons and discover only one phone number locked into the redial mode."

"You called it?"

"No. I figured I'd give you the pleasure. Want the number?"

Nick hesitated, but he wasn't sure why. "Yes."

Nick scribbled the number on his notepad. "Thanks, Tommy . . . for everything."

"No problem. I'll be here from now on. No one's gonna touch her. Just do me a favor and get this bastard, will ya?"

"Count on it."

Nick hung up and saw Matt point to the phone number Tommy had just given him.

"Whose number?"

"Don't know. I'm going to find out in a minute. Tommy caught Tansu trying to dust Julie in the hospital. He grabbed Tansu's cell phone and found this phone number in his call log."

"All this is because you busted Rashid? Kharrazi is still pissed over that?"

Nick shrugged. He called Walt Jackson and secured enough protection for Julie to rival that of a sitting president.

Matt hung up his cell phone at the same time. "I've got the house sales being faxed over to the Gila County Sheriff's Office in Payson."

"Good," Nick said, staring at his cell phone.

"What are you thinking?"

"I'm thinking it's time to find out whose number this is."

"Shouldn't you call Stevie and get a trace going first?"

Nick shook his head. "We're an hour from Phoenix, there's no time."

Nick dialed the number and let his thumb rest on the send button while he put his thoughts together. Who would be on the other end of this phone number? Kemel Kharrazi? What if it was Kharrazi? What information could he get from Kharrazi without him knowing about it? And if it wasn't Kharrazi, how could he parlay the call into information leading to the terrorist?

Nick felt Matt staring at him as he took in a deep breath.

"Oh, for crying out loud, do it already," Matt blasted.

Nick positioned his legal pad on the table in front of him and flipped to an empty page. As his thumb flexed to push the send button, he realized that his hand was shaking. He pushed the button. It rang once, then twice. "Yes," a man's voice said.

"Sarock?"

"Ye—" the man stopped. "Who is this?"

Nick scribbled the word 'Sarock' on his legal pad and circled it several times with nervous energy. Nick could feel Matt staring at him, knowing exactly whom he was talking to. Matt leaned up against Nick's ear and eavesdropped on the conversation. "I think you know," Nick said.

"Really?"

"It's the man who's chasing you. Now do you know who this is?"

"Yes, I think I do. How is your wife? I understand she had a terrible accident." Kharrazi's voice sounded guarded, but confident. It was as if a professor was asking a student to show his work.

Nick gritted his teeth. "You're not trying to weasel out of the country, are you?"

"Because you have to be careful these days," Kharrazi continued. "You never know when tragedy could strike."

"I doubt an incompetent crew such as yours will be able to pull off any White House bombing."

"That's where you're wrong," Kharrazi finally acknowledged Nick. "Do you know why I'm so confident of this?"

Nick didn't respond, so Kharrazi answered his own question. "Because the detonator was designed and created by the great Rashid Baser. The finest bomb expert the world's ever seen."

There it was, Nick thought. The Rashid factor.

Both men were silent. Two chess players thinking three moves ahead.

Finally, Kharrazi said, "Where are you?"

"I'm on my way to you. Can you see me?"

"How do you know where I am?"

"I'm good at my job."

"It sounds like you're in an airplane. Are you?"

"Yes," Nick admitted.

"It's too late," Kharrazi sneered arrogantly. "You can't stop the White House from exploding tonight."

"Don't bet on it."

"But I have, Mr. Bracco. I've wagered the lives of my family, and my friend's families, and every Kurd back in Kurdistan. If I fail, their lives are through. With America's support, the Turkish Security Force will perform the vilest form of genocide on my people."

Kharrazi let it sit there while Nick absorbed the message. "But I will not fail," he said resolutely. "Whether I am dead or alive, the White House will disintegrate at midnight tonight. That is not a threat, simply a fact. Even if you found the detonator in time, you couldn't do a thing about it. Rashid's legacy will endure. When you wake up tomorrow, you will be living in a very different country."

"Just like that, huh?"

"Just like that."

Nick considered what he had just read in Kharrazi's file. The sick, twisted mind of the world's leading terrorist had fertile ground to grow up in. It was time to find out who he was dealing with. "It must have been awful," Nick said softly.

"What?"

"When your own father raped you. The man you trusted more than anyone."

There was a stillness across the airwaves. Matt jerked away from the phone and looked at Nick with wide eyes.

"You weren't even ten years old," Nick prodded.

More silence.

"Now I understand why I'm the target. Everything you see in me, the honesty, the integrity—all things you wish your father was, but wasn't. By killing me, you erase his sins. Without me, you can continue to rationalize that everyone is the same all over the world, but I fly in the face of that theory."

A long pause hung there, then finally Kharrazi began a low, guttural laugh. "Are you trying to save me, Mr. Bracco?"

"It's a form of transference," Nick continued, "I'm seeing a specialist who helps me with certain issues. You could keep his schedule full all by yourself."

The laughter continued. "A specialist, eh?"

"And your mother was simply a tool."

The laughter abruptly ended.

Nick waited this time. He was trying to understand his adversary. Was Kharrazi a cold-blooded killer with demented motives, or was he a calculated leader without the restraints of morals or ethics to get in his way?

"You think you know something—what is it?" Kharrazi snapped.

Like a clever tactician, Kharrazi wasn't giving anything away. But it was too late. Nick had already struck the chord he was looking for.

"You held your mother at knifepoint in the middle of your village. As the crowd multiplied, you explained that she had given information about your combat plans to the Turkish government. You were going the make an example of her in front of hundreds of people. Kemel Kharrazi, the man who decapitated his own mother for squealing on him. The word spread throughout Kurdistan and you became an instant folklore legend. No one would ever cross the great Kemel Kharrazi. Only problem is, your mother never gave you up, did she?"

Nick could hear Kharrazi breathing.

"No, of course not," Nick churned forward. "You used her like a tool. Once your father died, you plotted for years, waiting for the perfect opportunity to get back at her. Your mother, the woman who stood there and watched as little Kemel was repeatedly molested by his father. Doing nothing to stop him. She was going to pay for her complicity."

Nick looked up and saw a stunned expression on his partner's face. Nick felt his heart racing while he fought the urge to go any further. He doodled furiously on the legal pad, making jagged lines around the word 'Sarock.'

"You never answered my question," Kharrazi finally said. "How is your wife?"

Nick strangled his pen with the palm of his hand. "She's fine."

"Are you sure?"

"When I tell you she's fine, you can trust that it's true. Now Nihad Tansu on the other hand isn't doing so well."

There was a pause. "Is that so?"

"He's dead, you twisted fuck. He couldn't even finish off my wife like you commanded. That's why I'm telling you, your plan won't work. Too many incompetents under your rule."

"I don't believe you."

"What don't you believe, that you're a twisted fuck or that Tansu's dead?"

"Tansu didn't die without completing his mission."

"Oh really? Then how do you think I got this phone number—directory assistance?"

There was silence while Kharrazi put it together. In a stern, but restrained voice, he said, "We should meet, you and I."

"I agree."

"Face to face."

"Absolutely. Tell me when."

"I will surprise you."

"I hate surprises. Tell me when and I'll have coffee made."

Kharrazi forced a laugh. "I must go, Mr. Bracco. I'd be walking with one eye over your shoulder if I were you."

Nick looked at Matt. "I have someone covering my back. Do you?"

"You would be surprised what protection I command. Why don't you give me your number and I'll phone you when it's time to meet."

Nick hesitated, then decided there was nothing Kharrazi could do with the number but call him.

"Please," Nick said, "call me when you're ready to surrender. I'll make sure you're protected." He gave Kharrazi his secure phone number. The second he finished the last digit, the connection went dead.

Nick pushed the end button and found Matt with a proud expression usually reserved for first-time fathers. "I didn't know you had it in you," Matt said.

Nick felt a trickle of moisture drop onto his wrist. He wiped his sideburns dry with clammy fingers. "It's hot in here."

Chapter 29

Miles Reese had been Washington Post's White House corre-
spondent for the past twelve years. Before that he was the
Post's Bureau Chief in Moscow. Somewhere between the Berlin Wall
crumbling and the impeachment of President Clinton, Moscow's
bud had lost its bloom and he came home to claim the paper's most
prestigious prize—covering the White House.

With the threat of an attack on the White House now just eight
hours away, Miles was hunkered down in his office, hammering
furiously on his computer's keyboard. A tap on his open office door
didn't deter him, and he said, "Go away," with his eyes glued to his
monitor.

"I know you don't want to be disturbed," his secretary's voice
said from behind him, "but you've got a call from someone saying
it's urgent."

"Who is it?"

"He wouldn't say, but he assured me that you would want the
exclusive. He says he knows where the terrorists are."

Reese stopped typing. He looked over his shoulder. "What line?"

"Four."

The reporter snapped up the receiver. "Reese," he said.

"Are you interested in knowing where the KSF are hiding?" a
man's voice said.

"Bill? Is that you?"

"You didn't answer my question."

Reese grabbed a pen from his penholder. "Of course I want to
know where they are."

"Good. Then I will tell you under one condition. This is going to
be an anonymous source—not an anonymous source from the White
House, or a high-ranking official, or even a government employee.
This is going to be an anonymous source—period. Understand?"

"Gotcha, boss. Let me have it."

There was a hesitation as Reese thought he heard the man murmuring to himself about whether it was the right thing to do.

"Look," Reese stoked the flame of free-flowing information, "I'm
not sure what your concern is, but I can not only guarantee your anonymity, I can assure you that—if the information is accurate—you'd

be doing the country a tremendous service. The more people who know where to look, the better chance we have of finding them."

Reese didn't hear anything for thirty seconds. The line was still open and he didn't want to hard-sell the guy, so he kept quiet. Finally, after a minute of silence, the man's voice said, "Payson, Arizona," then hung up.

Reese scribbled the name down, then pulled a map of Arizona from the bottom drawer of his desk. He groped through the state of Arizona with his finger until he found the tiny dot that was Payson. He circled it with a pencil. Tapping the pencil on his desk, he considered the call. Reese's suspicious nature kicked in. He'd received White House leaks all the time, but usually they came from an intern, or somebody completely expendable.

He looked up at his clock and picked up his phone. Regardless of President Merrick's motives, Reese had to move on the story.

"Fredrick Himes' office," a man's voice answered.

"This is Miles Reese with the Post. I'd like to have the Press Secretary comment on a story I'm about to put on our website. Is he available?"

"I'm sorry, he's not. I'm sure you understand that—"

"I'm publishing the location of the Kurdish terrorists' headquarters in the United States." Reese paused for effect. "Now is the Press Secretary available, or should I run with this story?"

There was a brief interval in the conversation. Although it was obvious that the man's hand was now covering the phone, Reese could hear his voice speaking urgently through the muted mouthpiece. A moment later, the man said, "I'll put you through to him now."

A clicking sound, then, "Himes."

"Fredrick, this is Miles. I've got a source telling me the general location of the KSF headquarters. Would you care to comment?" Reese always blurted out the leak quickly and listened carefully for the response. All too often the reply was practically scripted.

This time, however, the Press Secretary seemed genuinely dazed by the call. "Uh, are you saying that you know the actual state they're located?"

"And city."

"How certain are you?"

"I'm certain that my source is credible."

Himes hesitated, then sheepishly asked, "Who is your source?"

"Jeez, Fredrick, what's going on over there? Don't you guys even talk with each other? This is not something that's likely to miss your circle."

"Who is your source?"

"Come on, you know I'm not going to tell you."

Himes' voice got dark. "If you publish this information, you'd better know what you're doing. Otherwise, your career will be doing a tightrope act."

"My source is credible. So, what's your comment?"

"How can I respond without hearing where you think they are?"

Reese shook his head and leaned back into his chair. "You really don't know, do you?"

Silence.

"I'm told they're in Arizona. What's your comment?"

Reese could hear the man sigh. "No comment."

"That's all I needed to know. Thanks, Fredrick. Go introduce yourself to the President. He'll be the one with the herd of Secret Service around him."

Reese hung up. There was no sense trying to run down a second source to corroborate the story. After all, it came from the White House Chief of Staff. What more did he need?

* * *

As the helicopter breezed dangerously close to the ground, the treetops became larger and greener with every passing minute. They were heading from the desert of Phoenix, to the mountains of Payson. Nick had a death grip on one of the restraining straps while staring out of the front of the chopper.

"Isn't this thing flying a little low?" Nick asked anyone.

"Relax," Matt said. "Look at it this way—we're close enough to survive a crash landing. You can't say that about a commercial airliner."

"Gee, I feel better already," Nick said. He cupped his hand around his mouth and aimed at the pilot. "How much longer?" he yelled over the din of the rotor.

The pilot turned his head slightly, but kept his eyes on the landscape ahead. "Ten minutes."

"That's what you said ten minutes ago," Nick muttered to himself.

"What kind of assets do we have up here?" Matt asked.

"There's an R.A. They didn't give me a name."

"That's it—a resident agent?"

"We're supposed to be running a clandestine operation. It's up to us and whoever we can conjure up from the Sheriff's Department."

"Great," Matt said.

The helicopter circled an open patch of grass near a paved road. A red pickup truck sat next to the opening and someone stood beside the truck with his hand protecting his face from the gusty assault of the rotors.

When the chopper finally settled down, Nick was the first to jump out. He was followed by the rest of the team and Don Silkari. They'd gone from the desert to the mountains and the fall air had a crisp chill to it. Nick waved off the pilot and watched as the helicopter hovered out of the opening, then tilted forward and surged back to Sky Harbor Airport in Phoenix.

By the time Nick reached the local FBI agent, Matt was already shaking hands and exchanging pleasantries. He was surprised to find an attractive woman dressed in jeans and a dark nylon vest. She wore her long, brunette hair in a ponytail, which was pulled tight through the opening of the back of her baseball cap. It wasn't lost on Nick that Matt was the one who was doing the introductions, but with an awkward look on his face.

Nick shook her hand. "Nick Bracco."

"Jennifer Steele," she said.

"Jennifer Steele?" Nick squinted. He looked at Matt. Matt nodded. Yes, that Jennifer Steele.

Some women pull back their hair, throw on a flannel shirt and become Grizzly Adams. Steele didn't wear a speck of makeup, yet Nick could tell that underneath all the denim there was a body dying to be wrapped tight in an evening gown.

"I see," Nick said.

"Is there a problem?" Steele asked.

"Of course not," Nick said. "You've been briefed?"

"Well . . . actually, very little. The only thing I'm certain of is that you're searching for the KSF's home base. You have reason to suspect they're hiding somewhere in the vicinity of Payson. Is that true?"

"Yes."

She looked around at the group, all wearing casual clothes, no FBI windbreakers to be seen. "If you don't mind me asking, how much more backup are we getting?"

"None," Nick said. "You're looking at the task force."

"Oh," she said, regarding the team with a fresh set of eyes. "Well, I've been instructed to assist you any way I can. I've been the R.A. up here for five years, so I'm certain I'll be an asset." She raised her brow. "Of course the more I know, the more valuable I become."

Nick smiled. He knew how it felt to be in the lower echelon of the information chain. Most resident agents worked out of their homes in remote locations. For them, a bank robbery was about as exciting as it got. Terrorists harboring an operation center was way up the intrigue chart. And that's precisely what Jennifer Steele looked like to Nick. Intrigued. Almost as intrigued as his partner. Matt stood there listening to Steele as if she were reciting the Ten Commandments.

Nick lowered his voice conspiratorially. "I'll tell you what, Agent Steele, let's head toward our command post and I'll update you along with the local law enforcement."

Her eyes were bright with anticipation and the corner of her mouth always appeared to be on the verge of a grin, yet her demeanor was all business. She pointed to her truck. "It's your show. We'll be using the Sheriff's office as a command post, but don't expect a welcome wagon when we show up."

Nick smiled. "We never do."

"A couple of you can ride up front with me, the rest will have to rough it in the back."

Without a word everyone but Nick and Matt groped their way into the back of the truck. As they approached the passenger door, Nick gave Matt a wide berth and ushered him in.

The truck jostled back and forth as Agent Steele rolled the truck from the rough terrain onto the smooth surface of a paved road. Steele and Matt seemed eager to start a conversation, but neither of them appeared as if they could decide the proper way to begin. They rode in a stiff silence for a while until Matt ducked his head to look at the tops of the tall Ponderosa Pines waving in the autumn breeze. "Beautiful country up here."

"I think so," she said.

The silence lingered until the truck ascended the crest of a hill and downtown Payson came into view. Retail stores made out of logs and T-4 wood siding cohabitated with modern strip shopping centers and fast-food restaurants. Steele slowed the truck to match the lower speed limit. "I have to warn you about the sheriff," she confided. "He's a bit heavy-handed."

"You mean he's a bully," Matt said.

"I mean he's not exactly friendly toward us federal employees." Matt grinned. "He just hasn't met anyone as likable as us before."

Steele looked at him. "I know enough about you, Agent McColm."

Nick could feel Matt's body go rigid. He seemed prepared to defend himself, when Steele said, "I mean, what kind of agent would I be if I wasn't familiar with the FBI's two-time reigning sharp-shooting champion?"

A grin crept across Matt's face and he sat up a bit taller. "I guess you would be the uninformed kind."

This got her to display a smile that even happily-married Nick Bracco had to admire.

"Well, I happen to be a bit of a marksman myself," she said. "Maybe not as good as you with a handgun, but I'd give you trouble with a rifle."

"I'll bet you would," Matt said, looking her over as if he were appraising a fine diamond.

"Listen, kids," Nick interrupted.

"Yes, Dad," Matt said.

Steele let out the tiniest of a nervous laugh.

"First of all, we're pretty certain the KSF is tucked away up here somewhere. Do you have any ideas where we might start a search?"

"Well," Steele said," there are plenty of cabins scattered throughout the outskirts of town. If I wanted seclusion, that's where I'd hide. How did you discover their location?"

"Yeah," Matt said, turning toward his partner with a smirk. "Why don't you tell us that, Dad?"

Nick looked over his shoulder and saw the team appearing to be taking in the scenery from the back of the truck, but he knew better. Each set of eyes was rummaging the countryside, searching for anything suspicious. "It gets complicated."

Steele gave Nick a sideways glance. "Is that another way of saying get lost?"

"Not at all. It's just that some of the people involved aren't the type to . . . uh . . . be associating with law enforcement types."

She pointed a thumb over her shoulder. "You mean like the one with the purple toothpick?"

Nick looked back and rolled his eyes at the sight of Silk in his long, black, wool coat, and pointy black boots sticking out from the bottom of his perfectly creased jeans. He looked like he belonged on the sidelines of a college football game. "Yes, like him," Nick said.

"I see."

This seemed to satisfy her curiosity for the moment. She slowed even further and made a left hand turn at the first traffic light. After a few minutes they were rolling into the freshly asphalted parking area in front of the Gila County Sheriff's Office. Like most buildings in Payson, it was made of wood and topped with a shingled roof. Parked in front of the building was a sparkling new Ford pickup truck with temporary plates demonstrating its adolescence.

Nick pointed to the vehicle. "That's the Sheriff's?"

Steele nodded. "It's his baby. He's practically showing it off door-to-door."

The group unloaded duffle bags full of gear and followed Steele through the front door and into the administrative office. Three older women were busy behind the counter. Two were on the phone, and the third was heaving a cardboard box full of files across the room. The walls were lined with filing cabinets and the floor was an aging linoleum that curled slightly at the perimeter.

Steele removed her baseball cap and waved a thumb over her shoulder at the small crowd behind her. "Afternoon, Lorraine. This is the crew of agents from Baltimore that Sheriff's been waiting for. Is he in?"

The woman had the unimpressed look of someone who'd seen too much reality TV. She placed the box on her desk and picked up her phone. "They're here," she said.

After a moment she placed the phone down and pointed toward a hallway. "You know where to go."

Nick trailed the field, taking it all in. The agents all nodded at Lorraine as they passed and Silk pulled the toothpick from his mouth in a hat-tipping gesture.

Once inside the Sheriff's personal office, linoleum gave way to a brown, industrial-grade carpet. A giant picture of Geronimo loomed on the wall across from the Sheriff's desk, which was flanked by the United States flag and the state flag of Arizona. The Sheriff wore a tan uniform with a gold star on his sleeve. He sat with his legs crossed as if he were a guest on a talk show and his hands cradled a Styrofoam cup on his slight potbelly.

"Well, well," the Sheriff smiled, "look what the cat drug in.

The federal government has graced me with their finest men." He quickly nodded at Agent Steele, "And women."

"Sheriff Skrugs," Steele said, hat in hand, "This is Agent Bracco."

Nick made his way to the desk and reached over to shake the Sheriff's hand. "My name's Nick. This is Matt, Ed, Carl, Dave, Mel, and Don. I think you know why we're here."

"I have a pretty good idea," the Sheriff said.

Nick pointed and the men let the heavy bags drop to the floor in the back of the room. Carl Rutherford closed the door and assisted in unloading rifles, magazines full of rounds, video and audio equipment, and laptop computers.

The Sheriff squinted at the sight. "What's all that about?"

"Just setting up shop," Nick said.

"Now hold on. I told your boss I'd help you out, but I didn't think you were gonna take the place over."

No one paid any attention to the Sheriff. They kept to their task while Nick spread a map of Arizona across Skrugs' desk. Matt and Dave Tanner bent over the map with Nick and began the process of familiarizing themselves with the area. Agent Steele poked her head over Matt's shoulder and Nick encouraged her to participate.

"Please," Nick said, "could you mark the Sheriff's office for us?"

Steele pulled a pencil from a plastic cylinder on the desk and began examining the map.

"We'll need at least a half a dozen more men, Sheriff," Nick said.

"Just a doggone minute," Skrugs bellowed. "I never offered any manpower from my office, 'cause we just can't spare it right now."

"Sheriff," Nick said in a tight voice, "we're fairly certain that the headquarters for the Kurdish terrorists is in this area. We have until 9 PM to find them, or there's a good chance that the White House will be history. Does that help in the motivation department?"

The room became quiet while Sheriff Skrugs leaned sideways in his chair, looked down, and dropped a long, juicy, strip of chewing tobacco into the Styrofoam cup. When he sat up, he seemed to enjoy the awkward gap in the conversation. He smiled a brown smile. "I'm going to tell you something, Mr. Special Agent. There's an election in a few weeks and I'm going to be reelected to protect and serve the fine people of Gila County. Now your job and my responsibilities may not coincide, but that won't prevent me from assisting you. It's just that I have a manhunt going on at the moment and I'm not willing to spare my deputies for a wild goose chase."

"It's not a wild goose chase, Sheriff."

"No, huh? If this is so important to the President, then how come I see only a handful of FBI agents instead of a platoon of Marines?"

Nick folded his arms. He could see that logic wasn't going to play a big part in the proceeding, so he decided to lower himself down to the proper level. "That's a nice truck you have out there."

Skrugs turned his head suspiciously while boring a hole into Nick's eyes. "Thank you."

"It's a Special Edition, isn't it?"

"Yes."

"Must've been expensive."

"Thirty-thousand dollars," Skrugs said flatly.

"Thirty-one thousand, five-hundred and twelve, to be exact. And you paid cash."

Skrugs' eyes narrowed. "Why don't you come right out and tell me what you're getting at?"

Nick looked around at the office, sizing it up for potential. "If you can't spare any men, fine. At least allow us the liberty of using your office as a command post and stay out of our way."

Skrugs drooled another strip of tobacco into his cup. "Don't play games with me, Special Agent. What's the truck thing all about?"

"We'll need more detailed maps and I had a list of newly pur- chased homes faxed here from the county records department. Can you locate that for us?"

Now the Sheriff was on his feet and getting up into Nick's face. Matt and Dave Tanner each pulled an arm and wrestled Skrugs back into his chair. Nick stretched his arms out across the desk and leaned over. His tone was dead serious. "I don't need any more friends, Sheriff. Get the paperwork I requested, then you can get the fuck out of here and chase down your horse thief, or whoever you're protecting your citizens from."

"All right, all right," Skrugs shook off the two agents flanking him. "There's no reason to get all riled up about this."

Nick stood upright and nodded. "Good. I'm glad you see it our way."

Skrugs stood and reached for his belt hanging from a hook on a wall behind his desk, but he was blocked by Matt. The belt was abnormally wide and contained his holstered gun and radio. Matt gave Nick a look and Nick held up a hand signaling him to allow the Sheriff to get his belt. As Skrugs strapped it around his plump waist, he said, "There's no need for any lists."

"Why's that," Nick said, warily.

"Because," Skrugs said, adjusting his belt, "I already know where they are."

Chapter 30

Nick and Matt waited in the parking lot while Skrugs was inside drawing a map to the terrorist's hideout. Matt loaded a backup .38 snub and stood in the cold with his pant leg pulled up, exposing his ankle holster. Nick tore open a small aluminum pouch, then walked toward the Sheriff's truck and came back empty-handed.

"What are you doing?" Matt asked.

"I don't trust that guy."

"Why? He's giving us what we want."

"Exactly. One minute it's a wild goose chase, the next minute he knows where they are."

"You have something on him?"

"Not yet."

"Then what's with him paying cash for the truck?"

"I don't know. The records showed that he paid cash. I just threw it out there to see how he would react."

"And?"

"He acted a little defensive — didn't he?"

They returned to the Sheriff's inner office and Nick found Skrugs explaining the best angle of approach to Jennifer Steele. He was waving his arms while giving directions to the resident agent. Steele was in rapture, absorbing her function as the guide. Because of her knowledge of the area, she would be in the lead and therefore on the front line. The other three agents had their gear strapped over their shoulders and were in different stages of prepping their weapons.

Nick motioned the rest of the team to file out, but yanked Silk's arm as he passed. "Hang on, I need you for a minute."

Silk stood silently next to Matt and Steele as Nick approached the Sheriff. "You're not coming with us?"

"Sorry, Chief, but I've got a child-killer on the loose and I need to bang on some doors to get some information."

"How certain are you of this location?"

"I'm telling you," Skrugs huffed, "this is where they are. There's too much suspicious activity going on with that cabin. The phone company shut off the service to the new owner and I've never seen anyone leave the premises, yet there are fresh tire marks all over the backside of the property. I went fishing on a narrow strip of the river a couple of miles west of there and heard all kinds of engine noise. When I headed up the hill toward the cabin, the noises stopped. As I got closer I noticed a large tarp covering several vehicles and no sign of anyone living there. When I touched the hood of one of the vehicles, it was warm. Until you guys showed up, I just never put it all together."

Nick nodded. It sounded just a tad rehearsed for his taste. "That's fine. Just let us have the keys to a couple of cars and we'll—"

"No can do, Chief. I've got everyone available on this manhunt. You're going to have to get there the same way you got here."

Nick clenched his fists.

Matt said, "Are you telling us that you're not going with us and you can't even lend us one stinking vehicle?"

Skrugs looked at the two federal agents. His resolve seemed to temper. "Okay, okay." He removed a set of keys from a nail on the wall next to his desk. "I'll take my truck, you take my personal cruiser. It's the only vehicle we've got left. It needs some engine work, but it'll get you where you need to go." He looked at his watch. "I'm late, boys. Gotta find me a killer."

After Skrugs left, Steele said, "Now do you know what I mean?"

Nick stood there with his arms still folded, shaking his head in disgust.

Steele looked back and forth between Nick and Matt, then settled on the keys in Nick's hand. "How do you want to split us up?"

Nick handed the keys to Silk and pulled a device from his pocket that resembled a pocket calculator. "Here," he said, "take the cruiser and use this to track down the Sheriff."

Silk looked down at the device, puzzled.

"It's a GPS system. I planted a transmitter under the Sheriff's truck. Give him a five minute head start, then find out where he went."

"Hey wait a minute," Steele said. "You're going to waste a vehicle spying on the Sheriff?"

Matt nodded with understanding. "It's an insurance policy. We're better off using one vehicle anyway. It's less conspicuous."

"An insurance policy?"

Nick wrote something on the back of his business card and handed it to Silk. "This is my cell phone number. Call me as soon as you know where he is and what he's doing."

Silk frowned. "I didn't come all the way out here to play—"

"I know what you're here for," Nick said. "And you'll get your chance, I promise. But right now we need to find out who we can trust." Nick jabbed a finger into Silk's chest. "You, I trust. It's everyone else that I'm worried about."

Silk took the compliment to heart and grinned. "Whatever you say, Boss."

Nick showed Silk how to read the GPS system, then sent him on his way. Nick rounded up the team behind the building and had everyone test their headsets to assure communications were functioning properly. Since Steele didn't have a headset, she was instructed to stay close to Matt. This didn't seem to bother either agent.

Nick motioned Steele to brief them on their route.

With the professional look of a surgeon about to go into the operating room, Steele held up a map with a black line meandering through a densely wooded area. "Just past mile marker 78, we'll veer left onto a dirt road for about three or four miles." She looked at Rutherford, Downing, Tanner, and Tolliver. "Stay down in the back of the truck. The dirt road is a popular path for hunters, so three of us in the cab doesn't necessarily cause any suspicion." She pointed to a black line perpendicular to the truck's route. "At this juncture, we'll unload the gear and travel the rest of the way on foot. About another mile." She looked up and to the west. "The sun's going down in another hour and a half so that should give us enough time to position ourselves."

She looked at the group and said, "Any questions?"

"Yeah," Carl Rutherford said, "are you single?"

Matt momentarily glared at Rutherford.

"For you, Agent Rutherford," Steele deadpanned, "I'm happily married with twelve kids."

A few snickers followed Rutherford's put-down. It was a nervous laughter that Nick recognized as a release of tension. All eyes migrated his direction and he suddenly felt like a football coach needing a halftime speech. "All right," he said, "I don't want any heroics. We do our job and get out. When we get to the perimeter, Carl and Ed have the backside, Matt and Jennifer are the snipers."

Nick looked at Dave Tanner. "You have the Halothane mixture?"

Tanner tapped the duffle bag tugging on his shoulder. "Ready to go."

"When I give the cue, Dave will launch the gas through a window on the second floor. The gas is heavier than oxygen so it will settle all the way down to the basement. Thirty seconds later he and I will enter the building wearing the body suits. Our primary goal is to locate the detonator, then get Carl in there to disable the unit. Everyone know their roles?"

A cluster of nods.

"Good."

Matt seized the opportunity to inject some inspiration. He regarded each agent in turn, snapped shut the clip of his Glock and added, "Let's show them what a predator really is."

Hopped up on adrenalin, the team ran around the building. Rutherford and Tanner nearly banged heads jumping into the back of Steele's truck. Nick was in the cab again with Matt. Steele drove north with the setting sun sprinkling shadows of tall pines across the hood of the truck. She nodded ahead to a roadblock that caused a backup of several cars. "Do you want to wait?"

Nick saw that it was only three cars ahead of them. "Yes, wait."

When it was their turn, a DPS officer spied the foursome prone in the back of the truck. His right hand went for his gun, but he hesitated when he saw who was driving. "Jennifer? What's going on here?"

She pointed to her cab mates. "This is Matt McColm and Nick Bracco. All six of these guys are FBI Special Agents from Baltimore. They're on loan to us until we resolve this KSF issue."

The officer nudged his hat up a bit and looked at Matt and Nick. "You think they're in the area?"

"We suspect," Nick said. "Have you seen anything suspicious?"

The officer shrugged. "A few hunters without permits. Several DUIs. No one that could pass for a terrorist though."

Nick handed him a business card. "You come across anything, have dispatch put you through to me directly."

The officer nodded, then backed up and waved the vehicle through the roadblock.

"He's a good cop," Steele said.

"I'm jealous," Matt quipped. But by the look on his face, Nick could tell he immediately regretted saying it. Steele let it hang there unnoticed. The only refuge for Matt was the slight widening of her lips into the tiniest of smiles.

Nick's phone vibrated in his pocket. "Bracco."

Walt Jackson's voice had an upbeat tone. Nick thought he was either delirious from stress, or he actually had reason for hope. "Tell me something good," Jackson said.

Nicks gaze drifted west. An orange haze lingered over the mountainous peaks. "Well, the Arizona sunsets are beautiful."

A snort of laughter. "That's what I like about you, Nick. You never give up more than you have to. I have some good news for you, however. We found the missiles."

"You did?"

"Not me personally, of course," Jackson said. "Dolphins, actually. The Navy's got these dolphins trained to search for underwater mines, bombs, missiles. They're pretty darn good at it too. Apparently there's an offshore oil rig that was thought abandoned, but when they sent the dolphins in, they found silos disguised as drilling devices."

"That's great news, Walt. I guess we're just here to find Kharrazi then?"

"Not exactly."

"Why's that."

"I said they found the silos, I didn't say they disarmed the missiles in them."

"What are you talking about? Can't they just destroy the silos?"

"I guess not."

"Well, explain it to me like I'm a third-grader, because I'm not understanding."

"I don't understand it fully myself, but according to General Hitchcock there are seven silos spread out across an acre of ocean floor. All of them contain missiles that are less than two minutes airtime away from the White House. It appears that they're all wired together somehow and if one silo is destroyed, the other six automatically detonate. The entire area is booby-trapped. Navy Seals are down there right now working on it, but it's evening here and they're moving very cautiously. They think they can have it disabled in about twelve hours. And that's just one of them.

"Pretty remarkable technology at play here. I can't tell you now, but you'll be amazed when you hear who actually built these things."

"What about shooting them down once they're airborne?"

"That's what they intend to do. The problem is, the missiles will be armed with countermeasures. Hitchcock feels at least one or two will make it to its target."

"So we really don't have a handle on it."

"No, we don't. What's going on out there? Do you have any good leads?"

"We're on our way to check one out right now."

"How good is it?"

Nick could sense Matt and Steele listening in on the conversation and the last thing he wanted to do was dampen any enthusiasm for the mission. "I'll let you know in about forty-five minutes."

Steele swerved the truck onto a dirt road and Nick wasn't ready for the turn. He jerked up against the door and let out a low, "Umph."

"Are you all right?" Jackson asked.

"I'm fine." The truck was hopping furiously over the bumpy trail. Nick heard Steele comment on her desire to get away from the road as quickly as possible.

"Listen, Nick," Jackson's voice took on a fatherly tone. "I don't want you guys taking any unnecessary risks. I mean there's a faction of the administration that feels you're, well, sort of — "

"What?" Nick demanded.

"There's a sentiment growing that you're wound a little tight right now and maybe not thinking clearly. For one thing, Julie was just the object of an attempted murder and you're flying across the country the next day."

"Wait a minute. I thought Riggs was the one rubberstamping this thing?"

"Riggs will support you right up until the moment you're proven wrong. Then you will see him backpedal into the sweetest little softshoe of deniability you've ever seen. Besides, you've got to admit your information is more than a little tainted."

Nick sat quiet for a moment, allowing Jackson to finish his case. When he was satisfied the scrutiny had ended, he said, "And what about you?"

There was a pause. "After all is said and done, I trust you. That's why I'm telling you not to take any chances. I don't want you going off half-cocked trying to prove a point. If you get sight of a hot location, you call me and I'll get a SWAT team up there immediately. Otherwise . . ." Jackson let the thought play out tacitly.

"Otherwise, we're on our own," Nick finished.

The silence was as good as shouting, "Yes!"

"Walt?"

"Yeah."

"When I come home tomorrow with Kharrazi's head," Nick gripped the phone a little tighter. Several sarcastic thoughts ran through his mind, but he knew they would be misdirected if he hurled them at Jackson. Finally, he took a breath and finished, "I'll buy you a beer."

Chapter 31

Jennifer Steele found a low spot in the forest to park the truck and the team unloaded their gear. Nick threw his duffle bag over his shoulder and said, "Everyone wearing their Kevlar?"

The proper response was a fist pump to the chest. Nick heard five thumps and one, "Kevlar?"

Steele looked embarrassed. "I guess I didn't expect to—"

"Don't sweat it," Dave Tanner said, "I've got a spare." He threw her the lightweight body armor and Steele thanked him. Everyone else ignored the rookie mistake and allowed her a moment of privacy as she wrapped the Kevlar under her windbreaker.

While Nick waited for Steele, his phone vibrated in his pocket. He was hoping it was Silk, but it was Walt Jackson again.

"There's been a leak," Jackson said.

"What do you mean?"

"The Washington Post is about to print a story on their website claiming that the KSF headquarters is located in Payson, Arizona."

"Shit. Who did it?"

"We have our suspicions, but it hardly matters now. How far are you from the lead you're chasing?"

"Maybe ten minutes."

"I can hold off the story for another half hour, but that's it. Get in and get out. Call me as soon as you're done."

Nick dropped his phone back in his pocket and found his team with duffle bags over their shoulders, antsy to get going. Steele looked down at her compass and pointed to an area of gradually elevated terrain close to a mile away. "Over that rise. Once we cross that hill, the cabin sits in a bowl-like valley. It should be a perfect spot to gain a perimeter."

"All right," Nick said. His heart was pumping now. He tapped his headset. "Remember, no communications unless it's absolutely necessary. We go in silent. I'm not taking any chances." He pointed to Matt and Steele and motioned them to go wide right. He motioned Carl Rutherford and Ed Tolliver to go wide left. Nick, Mel Downing and Dave Tanner centered the lineup. They all walked at the same pace staying in line with each other. The trees were spread out so Nick could have clear sight of both groups thirty yards to each side of him. The ground was thick with brown pine needles. He had to move around pinecones every other step. His head was pounding so hard he was practically numb.

* * *

Matt crept between the trees carefully, as if someone could be hiding on the other side of each one. Steele was to his right. The only noise he heard was the pine needles crunching beneath their footsteps. It had been ten years since he'd last seen her, yet she looked exactly the same. The same smart eyes. The same dimples that framed her lips when she smiled. He wondered if she'd even given him a second thought. After what he'd done, he couldn't see how.

"Aren't there any birds around here?" he asked, quietly.

He could sense Steele rolling her eyes at the city slicker. "It's October," she said. "Besides, they know enough to stay quiet with a deadly sniper like you around."

Matt smiled. He met her eyes for an instant as he continually swept his surroundings. She seemed a little stiff. A fake smile was painted on her face. "You ever been involved with a maneuver like this before?" Matt asked.

"I've seen my share of maneuvers."

Matt looked at her. He wasn't sure which way she was going with the comment. They walked in silence and Matt nodded intermittently to Nick, signaling everything was clear. Matt was scanning the horizon when he heard Steele's voice come at him as a low sigh.

"You let me leave," she said.

Matt almost stumbled at the words. Suddenly, he couldn't remove his eyes from her. She moved through the twilight and brushed away branches as if she'd never said a thing. If Nick looked over, he would think Steele was deeply entrenched in the pursuit. But nothing could've been further from the truth.

Matt's heart swelled with regret. "You told me –"

"I know what I said," Steele snapped. "What did you expect me to say – 'Hey, Matt, would you be interested in stopping me from leaving you?' You had sex with a stripper the night before our wedding. What was I supposed to do?"

Matt didn't realize that he'd stopped walking until Steele was twenty feet ahead of him. "You mean you would have forgiven me?"

Steele didn't respond. Nick snapped a finger at Matt to get back into formation.

Steele motioned Matt to catch up. "We'll talk later," she said. "We're getting close."

Matt took syncopated steps to regain position. Looking straight ahead, he said, "I was only twenty-three, Jen."

"I know. You were a young twenty-three."

For some strange reason, it made him feel good that she seemed miffed. "Have you ever—"

"Not now," Steele said. "Later. We'll talk plenty. Right now we have a job to do."

And that's exactly where they were. The job. Something that was always more important to her than he ever expected.

"We'll talk plenty," Steele muttered under her breath.

They walked farther. Matt's head swam with questions for Steele, but he needed to concentrate on his surroundings and get back to sniper mode. It was too dangerous to lose focus now.

They passed a clearing to the right and Matt saw a log cabin a few hundred yards away surrounded by tree stumps. He gestured toward the cabin. "How come all the trees are cut down around that place down there?"

Steele glanced over. "A forest fire threatened the region six months back and the homeowners were advised to clear the area around their homes. Sort of a fire line. Most homes burn because embers drop onto the roof."

"How close did the fire get?"

She pointed to the left and Matt could barely make out a barren spot atop a mountain. "Two miles," she said.

As they kept pace with the other groups, Matt noticed she was swiveling her head in quick repetitions, as if trying to catch someone watching her.

"Relax," Matt said.

Steele nodded. Her voice lowered as they approached the crest of the hill. "Have you ever been shot before?"

"Shot at, but never hit. How about you?"

Steele shook her head. Matt sensed a little tension as her stride seemed to shorten.

The entire team slowed significantly while they crept toward the summit. Nick motioned everyone into an army crawl. As Matt peeked over the crown, he saw that the scene was exactly as Steele predicted. The cabin was about thirty feet below them in a tree-cut clearing, just like the cabin they had just passed. The sun was setting, but Matt could still see through the uncovered windows into each room of the place. There didn't seem to be any activity inside or around the building.

Since they weren't using communications, Nick motioned everyone to huddle up by him. Matt and Steele slid backwards until they were out of view from the cabin, then they hustled over and merged with the group.

Nick was on his knees and the team crouched down around him.

"All right," Nick whispered, anxiously rubbing his hand over the loose mixture of dirt and pine needles in front of him. "We have a slight problem. The clearing around the cabin is too deep to make a covert entry. I want to wait another fifteen minutes for night to give us more cover." Nick swept clean a patch of dirt and unfolded the drawing that Sheriff Skrugs had made them. "Here's the cabin." He put the cap of a felt pen in his mouth, quickly pulled the pen from the cap, then spit out the cap. He made two small circles on the diagram on opposite sides of the cabin. "These two boulders should give us the cover we need. Carl and Ed will take a wide path around the perimeter and belly down to this boulder here. It should be large enough to shield both of you. Dave and Mel will stay behind this boulder here and set up the Halothane launch."

Nick searched the perimeter of the tree line in the woods. He pointed to a spot between the two tree stumps. His voice seemed to get lower as darkness fell around them. "There," he said to Matt, "I want you and Steele tucked away up there. You'll have an open shot at both ports of entry. Get your night-vision gear ready, just in case." He looked at his watch. "It's five forty-five. At exactly six, we launch the gas. This gives everyone time to get into position. Remember, silence."

Matt grabbed his duffle bag and resisted the urge to carry Steele's bag. She remained quiet as they stealthily worked their way toward the firing zone. The wind died down giving the forest an eerie feel. Matt had the uncomfortable feeling that he was being watched, but he attributed that to darkness and the unfamiliar territory. Steele, on the other hand, seemed downright skittish. Her head pivoted from side to side in quick, jerky motions. She stopped suddenly and stared into the distance.

"I thought I saw something," she said.

Matt looked but saw nothing. "Calm down," he whispered. "Probably some animal looking for a meal."

They moved on, but Steele was still jumpy. Matt grabbed her arm. "Stop it," he said. "It's easier to pick up quick, irregular activity than slow, deliberate motion. If there is someone out there, you're a walking billboard."

She was panting too fast, so Matt dropped his duffle bag and held her shoulders. She looked up at him with soft Bambi eyes. "I'm sorry," she managed. "I guess I'm a little nervous."

He squeezed her shoulders. "Listen to me. We're going to get through this, okay?"

"Okay."

"When we're done . . ." he looked off, his head fogged with guilt. "When we're done, I'll explain everything. Everything I should have done, and everything I did instead. I've spent too much time living with regret. I'm going to say my peace, then live with the consequences."

She nodded. It seemed that she had something to add, but was afraid to give it up.

Matt looked over the perimeter, trying to get back to his task. "We're going to make a nest to crawl into, give the team some cover and finish this assignment. Just think about our job and what we should be doing. Stay low, and when we get situated, stay still. Okay?"

She smiled. The tranquil expression on her face gave him a chill. He'd had sex with women who didn't give him the thrill her smile had just delivered.

He let go of her and unzipped his duffle bag. He pulled out a stick of glue and told Steele to turn around. She did so warily and watched over her shoulder as he smeared the glue on her back, then took handfuls of pine needles and patted them on her shirt. When he was done, he handed her the stick of glue and said, "Here, you do me."

They patched each other up with camouflage and rubbed black wax on their faces. When Matt was satisfied with the results, he picked up his bag and said, "Now we're going to find a good spot to get invisible."

Matt motioned to a group of bushes that were thick and low to the ground. He dropped his bag and instructed Steele to set up next to him.

The sun was nearly set, but Matt knew there was still too much twilight for the night gear. He slid his rifle from its case and began working the scope into place. He was in his element now. Every move had been rehearsed over and over. Besides quarterly training, Matt had been on an average of twenty sniper assignments a year for the past eight years. It was the part of the job that made him the most comfortable. He could be invisible, yet strike the biggest blow for the good guys. He stopped to take a quick check of the location. He looked, listened, and smelled his surroundings, but found nothing that concerned him.

Matt went back to adjusting his scope when he heard Steele say, "There's something strange about this place."

Matt saw her gazing through a pair of field glasses at the cabin, then went back to examining his site. He was familiar with virgin nerves. On his first sniper job, he nearly peed in his pants as he fired the first shot. He didn't want to appear cocky, but he couldn't afford to waste time looking for ghosts either. "What don't you like?"

"Do you see all the cut down trees around the building?"

Matt turned his head just long enough to see the tree stumps surrounding the cabin. "What about them?"

"Well, like I told you, people cut down the trees to deprive a fire of fuel around their home."

"Yeah."

"If these people went through all the trouble of chain-sawing all of those trees . . .then why is there still a cord of wood leaning up against the house? And why is there still a pile of kindling next to the wood?"

It was a good question.

"And another thing," she continued. "Do you see the roof? It's not made of the shingle material you normally see up here. A few years back it became fashionable to pitch the roof with lightweight steel panels. They last forever and have no maintenance. Even though it looks like redwood, those panels are made out of metal. They can't burn."

Another good observation, Matt thought. He put down his rifle and reached for his binoculars. With the two of them gazing at the cabin through binoculars, Steele said, "Why would someone with a metal roof clear out all of the trees around their place?"

"You have an idea?" he said.

She ducked down next to Matt and whispered. "Yes." She turned and pointed toward the woods. "I think this is an ambush. I don't think there's anybody inside of the cabin. I think that the area was cleared out so we would be sitting ducks. Those two stones are in perfect position for a perimeter attack on the cabin, but if the enemy were behind us . . ." She looked at Matt as if she was going too fast for him. "Do you understand?

"Yes, of course." It was flimsy, but plausible. Oliver Stone would have loved it.

"You have to warn the others."

Matt had to look away. He was having trouble thinking straight and his feelings for Steele were damaging his focus. He gazed into the woods as if he was considering her theory, but he was really buying time. There was no way he was going to break the radio silence over her borderline premise.

"Hey, are you going to warn them or not?"

Matt brought his eyes up to meet hers. "Listen, what you bring up are good points, but maybe you're reading too much into it. It's possible that there's a simple explanation."

"Such as?"

"It's possible that the owners cut the trees down first, then later added the steel roof."

"What about the wood?"

"Again, it could have been placed there long after the forest fire."

Her eyes drifted toward the ground. "You think I'm just a nervous R.A. frightened by my own shadow."

Matt looked straight at her, but said nothing. She needed some kind of support and Matt groped for the right words without patronizing her. He looked at his watch. It was five fifty-five. Just five minutes before Nick would begin the assault on the cabin. He opened his palms. "All right, here's what we do," he handed her his rifle. "You know how to use one of these?"

She shot him a look.

"Okay, okay. You stay here, while I go back and tell Nick about your observations."

She smiled again and then it hit him. She could manipulate him with just a look. This both excited and frightened him.

"Stay low," he demanded. Then pointing toward the cabin, he said, "And keep your focus on the target. Don't move a muscle until I get back."

She glanced over her shoulder at the woods. "Okay, hurry back."

He grabbed his Glock and put the silencer in his pocket. As he turned to leave, he felt her gentle touch on his arm. She whispered, "Be careful."

Matt felt like he was back in high school again. His cheeks were flush and a smile lingered on his face as he crept back toward Nick's position.

A few minutes later he was making sure his footsteps could be heard as he walked into the clearing that surrounded the boulder where Nick and Dave Tanner hid behind. He held his hands up high while he approached the two agents who were training their pistols at his chest.

"It's Matt," he whispered.

Nick's face screwed up into a scowl. "What are you doing here?"

Matt lowered himself to his knees next to Nick. He told his partner about Steele's thoughts on the unusually large clearing around the cabin, the roof, and the pile of wood. Nick got to his feet and peered over the boulder at the silent cabin with Matt over his shoulder. They both returned to their knees.

"She seems to think that it's an ambush. She thinks they're behind us in the woods."

Nick appeared to be giving the idea some thought. He pressed his hand to the ground as if he was feeling for the warmth of a previous visitor. Before he could say anything, he reached for the cell phone in his pocket. Matt didn't hear it ring, but he knew it would be set on vibrate.

Nick put the phone to his ear and listened. His face dropped into a deep maddening glower. A minute later, he returned the phone to his pocket and looked past Matt's shoulder into the woods.

"Who was that?" Dave Tanner asked.

Nick was squinting now. "That was Silk."

Matt was beginning to feel anxious. He waited while Nick worked it out in his head.

Nick reached down and gripped the handle to his duffel bag. "Get your gear," he said. "We're going to the other side of this boulder."

They scurried around the large rock, leaving themselves completely exposed to an attack from the cabin.

"Are you going to tell us what's going on?" Tanner asked in a high voice.

Nick rummaged through his duffle bag. "Shit, where's the infrared scope? Do you have it, Dave?"

Even in the dark Matt could tell that Nick looked pale. A bead of sweat seeped down his temple. Nick growled, "The Sheriff couldn't be with us tonight because he was on a manhunt—remember? He had a killer to catch."

Matt didn't like the sound of it already.

"Well," Nick spat out the words, "he is currently sitting in a chair in a barber shop in downtown Payson getting a haircut. According to Silk he seemed to be yucking it up with the boys in the shop."

Matt was trying hard to piece it together. "You think he set us up?"

Nick found the infrared and slid the narrow tube over the edge of the rock like a periscope. The bottom of the tube fed into a hand-held device with a green screen. As he pushed some buttons on the device, he said, "We'll find out in a minute."

All three men watched the screen come to life. Nick slowly twisted the tube from right to left, all the while paying attention to the display in his hand. It remained a constant green field for a full minute. Suddenly, a tiny red blob came into view. Even though it appeared small on the screen, Matt knew it was too large to be a small animal. Nick wasn't ready to pronounce anything until they saw the appendage move in such a way that there was no mistake. It was a human. "Son of a bitch," Nick murmured.

Frantically, Nick pulled the arm to his headpiece directly over his mouth. He pushed a button and spoke with a low, urgent voice. "Carl, get to the other side of the rock. They're not in the cabin, they're behind us. Use the infrared scope to find them."

Matt couldn't hear Carl Rutherford's response, but Nick jammed it immediately. "I don't have time to explain. Do it now!"

"What if they're also in the cabin?" Tanner asked.

Nick shook his head. "No, they'd be catching each other in the cross fire. They probably have the building rigged to explode as soon as someone tries to enter."

Nick pushed the transmitting button on the headpiece again and said, "Do you see them? . . . Good."

Tanner kept working the infrared. "I've got two of them coming our way. Less than a hundred yards."

Matt had already strapped on his night visor and was ready to take out the two attackers in the woods when a thought suddenly jolted him. Jennifer. She was alone in his makeshift nest without any cover, or communication.

As if they had telepathy, Nick turned to Matt and said, "Steele. Where is she?"

Matt was sucking in deep breaths now.

"Seventy-five yards," Tanner announced.

Matt looked down at his watch. "Listen," he said, "give me three minutes before you start firing."

Nick looked at him with narrow eyes.

"Don't look at me like that," Matt snapped. "You know I'd do the same thing for any FBI agent left out there on an island like that."

Nick's face softened. He nodded. "Okay," he said, pointing a finger at Matt. "You've got three minutes. But you know how vital a first shot is. Understand?"

Matt knew all too well. If the squad were able to fire first, they would get fairly open shots at the unsuspecting goons. But if the soldiers fired the first shot they would be in a more defensive mode with better cover.

Matt nodded. He screwed his silencer onto his Glock and lowered himself. As he was leaving he heard a familiar line. "Be careful," Nick said from somewhere behind him.

Matt crawled at a smooth, rhythmic pace, keeping his limbs tucked in. Depending on the distance, he hoped to be mistaken for any number of animals, even under the scrutiny of night-vision glasses. He was moving lateral to the KSF soldiers, careful not to arouse any attention. He thought about Jennifer waiting for him to return, waiting for him to tell her she was safe, that there was no boogeyman out there trying to get her. But he couldn't. And when the first shot was fired, he knew he never would.

On his headset, Matt heard Nick berating Carl Rutherford for jumping the gun, but it was too late. A burst of gunfire came from Nick's position behind him and he realized that he had to run now. He was only thirty yards away from his nest when he stopped cold and hit the ground. In his haste, he'd forgotten the most basic rules of engagement: find the enemy before they find you.

He lowered his night-vision glasses and searched the woods surrounding his nest. Gunshots echoed off the mountain range all around him and he couldn't tell where they were coming from. None of the shots were coming his way, so he stayed perfectly still and found what he was looking for. Two soldiers were tucked behind trees with rifles and Matt could see the flash of their muzzles firing directly into Jennifer Steele's position. He quickly unscrewed the silencer from his Glock. He needed accuracy more than stealth. As he lined up his shot, he noticed something he'd never encountered before — his hands were clammy with sweat. His breathing became sporadic as he lined up for a shot. With a shaky hand, he caught the soldier off guard and clipped him in the shoulder. Matt's second shot was a kill to the head, finishing off the first soldier.

He suddenly lost all control of his training. Instead of concentrating on the enemy, he followed the direction of the second attacker's muzzle flash. It was a semi-automatic rifle and the rounds came blasting out with such rapid force that he was compelled to see what damage they had caused. It took just a second to find Jennifer Steele. She was on her stomach with her back to the attacker. She was facing the cabin with Matt's rifle tucked under her arm, diligently following his instructions. He was close enough to see her torso jerk spastically with every round that peppered her body. She never even had a chance to turn and defend herself. Now her head shuddered so violently that Matt could see her ponytail bounce with each fatal headshot. His stomach fell like a free-falling elevator.

Matt turned back toward the soldier and aimed his Glock for the kill. As he tried to locate the target, his vision suddenly became blurry. At first he thought he'd been shot and blood was seeping into his eyes. He wiped his eyes clear and looked down at his hand. To his amazement he found something he'd never experienced on the job before. Tears.

Unable to stop the flow of moisture to his eyes, he managed the best shot he could. It was good enough to knock the rifle from the soldier's hands. The attacker left the weapon and ran, using trees to cover his trail. Matt tried futilely to get another shot off, but he was seeing double now and didn't waste the ammo.

He scrambled toward Steele, his gun flying from his hand as he hit a tree stump. He approached her body with a morbid sense of loss. Jennifer Steele lay in a crumpled heap. The lower half of her body was hidden under thick undergrowth and her arms were contorted like a discarded rag doll. Her head was tucked between two fallen logs that had served as perfect cover for an attack from the cabin. Through the dim moonlight, he could see her ponytail dangling lifelessly from the back of her cap. His rifle was just under her armpit, the front end lifted on its tripod. She never saw it coming.

Matt noticed that the gunfire had ceased and heard Nick's voice in his headset.

"Matt, Dave's been hit. I've got to get him out of here—you okay?"

Matt rubbed his eyes dry. "Yeah."

"What about Steele?"

Matt swallowed. He choked on the words. "She's . . . um . . . down."

The way he said it Nick must've known what he meant. There was a moment of silence while Nick gave Matt privacy to deal with the loss. "I'm sorry."

Matt felt a sense of betrayal. Steele wasn't the frightened greenhorn he made her out to be. She was simply aware of her surroundings. He had the strange desire to say goodbye, to apologize for his blunder.

Suddenly, he heard a click behind him and realized that he had made more than one mistake that night. He turned and faced his destiny. The KSF soldier he thought had run away simply doubled back on him. The rifle was wedged into the terrorist's shoulder and from ten feet away, he already had pressure on the trigger.

At that moment, the thought that flashed through Matt's mind was that he would finally be reunited with Jennifer Steele. He squeezed his eyes shut and braced himself for death. When the shot was fired he was surprised how painlessly the end came. He felt his entire body floating weightlessly as if he were being lifted from all of his anguish. The gunshot still rang in his ears as an aftereffect of his previous life. It became dead still and the only sound he heard was a nearby thud. When he was brave enough to open his eyes and discover his fate, he saw an angel. The angel was smiling at him warmly, as if she knew him all of his life and was simply waiting for him to return to her. The angel was Jennifer Steele.

The only difference he noted in her appearance was the short hair that sprouted recklessly from her head like a porcupine. Matt looked down and saw the KSF soldier lying dead in front of him. He blinked hard, then twisted around to see Steele's body still lying next to him. He did a double take back to the angel, then to the crumpled remains of Steele. He tugged on Steele's ponytail and came up with a capful of pinecones. He felt her shirtsleeve and pushed down on the leaves and pine needles that had replaced her arms. A crooked smile crept across his face.

"There are two kinds of FBI agents," Steele said. "The ones who follow their instincts, and the dead ones."

Chapter 32

President Merrick stood facing a map of Arizona in an office fifty feet below the Oval Office. Turning, he searched for a window out of habit, like opening the refrigerator without an appetite. There weren't any windows in the bunker, so he chose a map to let his mind wander. He sipped from a mug of coffee with the presidential seal attached, examined the dot on the map that was Payson, and shook his head.

Behind him, his phone line blinked with an open extension to a domestic event conference currently convened at the Pentagon. He was so overwhelmed with information and suggestions that his brain was beginning to freeze up. He needed a moment to reflect and allow his head to clear. He had countless decisions to make and time was dwindling.

There was a knock on the door; Samuel Fisk poked his head through the narrow opening. "He's here," Fisk announced.

"Great," Merrick said. "Send him in."

Merrick heard the man enter his office and decided to let him sweat for a moment. His thoughts remained thousands of miles away while he stood with his back to the man and listened to his erratic breathing.

At the sound of an anxious cough, Merrick squeezed a hand over his eyes. "Sit down, Bill."

Bill Hatfield dropped into the leather chair with the dead-legged thump of a boxer trying to go the distance.

Merrick finally turned and saw his Chief of Staff cowering like a dog who had just peed on the carpet. Hatfield refused to make eye contact and that just fueled Merrick's anger.

"Look at me, Bill," Merrick demanded. "I want you to look me in the eyes and tell me the truth. You're only getting one chance at this, so don't blow it." Merrick placed his mug on the desk and pushed up his already rolled-up sleeves even further. "Did you leak the Payson location to Miles Reese?"

Hatfield was already beginning to shake his head when Merrick pointed an accusing finger at him. "Don't even think about lying to me, Bill."

Hatfield retreated into a blank stare.

Merrick sat down at his desk and leaned on his elbows, hands clasped. "What you did jeopardized the lives of seven FBI agents who were on a dicey assignment to begin with. When you shot off your mouth to Miles, you put all of them at risk. One of them is in the hospital in serious condition."

Merrick picked up the mug, then quickly put it back down. "I'm giving you two weeks to get your affairs in order. Give whatever projects you have working to Sarah. At that time I'll announce that you're resigning due to personal reasons, you want to spend more time with your family—" he waved his hand in the air, "whatever bullshit I can have written for me. Either way, you're gone. The only reason I'm allowing you to leave with even a shred of dignity is because you're married to my sister. Otherwise, I'd throw you out in the street tonight and declare you an incompetent. You wouldn't be able to get a job as a dogcatcher."

Hatfield attempted a nod.

Merrick dismissed him with the back of his hand. "Get out of here before you make me sick to my stomach."

Hatfield left so quickly that Merrick never saw him go. The next thing he knew, Sam Fisk was standing over him, dropping a thick manila file on his desk with a thud. Merrick ran his hands through his hair and heard Fisk replace Hatfield in the chair.

After a long minute of silence, Fisk said, "Aren't you going to read the file?"

Merrick had his head in his hands trying to recover whichever neurons were still firing after the longest week of his life. "Why?" he said softly.

Fisk laughed. "You need to get some sleep."

Merrick scanned his desk. His computer was receiving so many e-mails that he was having ninety percent of them screened and deleted before anything popped up on his monitor. It was information overload. He looked up at the clock. "I've only got three hours to go. After that, I'll either get plenty of sleep, or I'll pass out and have no choice."

"Do you want me to tell you what's in the file?" Fisk asked. "Please."

"Kharrazi's uncle owned an offshore oil company up until a couple of years ago. The silos were built during the construction of one of the rigs. This is going back maybe three or four years."

"So Kharrazi had been planning an attack long before we ever sent troops into Turkey?"

Fisk nodded. "We gave him the perfect justification. However, he lured us in by moving so aggressively against the Turkish government. He knew we wouldn't stand by and watch thousands of civilians get slaughtered without trying to help."

"Should we have seen this coming?"

Fisk shook his head. "No, absolutely not. Kharrazi's uncle, Tariq, was an honest businessman without a shred of unlawful activity in his career. Unless we used an overt form of racial profiling, we would have never discovered the silos."

Merrick pinched the bridge of his nose and sighed. "It's getting to the point where anyone with an accent will endure a form of scrutiny they'd never seen before. This is not the country I grew up in."

"Yes, but it's the country you've been voted to lead. Your decisions will have a profound effect on the future. You can make changes necessary to promote a safer, less suspicious environment."

Merrick looked at his friend with a guarded glare. "I've instructed Fredrick to schedule an eleven thirty press conference."

Fisk gave him a stony look, but didn't speak.

"I'm sorry, Sam," Merrick said, looking at his desktop. "If we don't find Kharrazi by then . . ."

"You're going to pull the troops from Turkey?"

Merrick nodded. "A U.N. peacekeeping force will remain, but we will no longer participate in the effort. I won't risk any more American lives. I refuse to wake up tomorrow morning with a smoldering White House on the cover of every newspaper in the world."

Fisk stared at Merrick and kneaded his hands. "I don't believe you."

Merrick kept his head down. After a couple of awkward minutes passed, he sensed Fisk get up and leave his office.

* * *

They sat in the reception area of the Sheriff's office in the stunned silence that often followed a shooting. Especially an ambush. Especially an ambush set up by another law enforcement official.

It was after 5 PM and, except for a dispatcher buried behind the reception area, they were alone. They sat in old, cloth-covered chairs with lumpy padding and worn arm rests. Jennifer Steele was in the bathroom with a pair of scissors, trying to repair the damage she'd inflicted on her hair with her Swiss army knife. Ed Tolliver, Carl Rutherford and Matt were devouring fast-food burritos, looking drained, as if they had just run a marathon.

Nick paced, stopping only occasionally to feed the ancient vending machine for a Diet Pepsi. His head felt like the hull of a submarine diving too quickly toward the ocean floor. Another fringe benefit of stress-induced trauma. He could practically see Dr. Morgan rolling his eyes from two thousand miles away.

They weren't any closer to the KSF hideout and now the news was interrupting programs on every station, including the cartoon channel, identifying Payson as the headquarters for Kemel Kharrazi and his crew of terrorists.

"What did Walt have to say?" Matt asked, wiping his mouth with the back of his hand.

"He said that everyone was proud of us. Riggs wanted to congratulate me for finding the KSF hideout."

"But we haven't found the hideout."

"That's what I told Walt, but I guess they're finally convinced that Kharrazi has his crew up here somewhere. DPS has quarantined Payson. No one comes in or goes out without inspection. They're sending us a SWAT team and Special Ops from Phoenix."

"How long before they get here?"

Nick looked at his watch. It was seven-fifteen, nine-fifteen in D.C. "The first chopper should get here in about twenty minutes." Nick took a gulp of Diet Pepsi, then looked at Matt. "He said something else."

Matt cocked his head.

"He said the President has scheduled a press conference for eleven thirty p.m. Eastern Standard Time.

A frown curled Matt's lips. "Don't tell me."

Nick nodded. "If we don't find Kharrazi by then, he's announcing a withdrawal."

"You tell Walt that it wouldn't be the last time terrorists threaten the White House?"

"I told him."

"He have anything to say about it?"

"He said we should get Kharrazi and make this all moot."

Matt walked away shaking his head. He shoved open the door to the men's room and disappeared inside.

Nick knew that every minute counted, but he had to let the crew catch its breath while reinforcements made their way to Payson. He dialed his cell phone and when he heard his wife's feeble voice, he nearly wept. "Hi, Baby," he whispered. "How are you feeling?"

"I miss you," Julie said. "Are you almost done?"

"Almost."

"You know, Nick, what I said about . . . you know, killing him . . . I was kind of juiced up on painkillers at the time. I really want you to come home and be here with me."

Nick cupped a hand over his eyes. "Jule, I'm not coming home to spend the rest of my life looking over my shoulder."

There was a pause. "Is that how you would feel if you stopped right now — like danger will follow you home?"

He didn't want to frighten her, yet he couldn't allow her to be caged by FBI protection twenty-four hours a day. Not long term.

"Yes," he admitted.

"But Sweetie, that puts us back to square one. There will always be someone out there," her voice cracked. "It's never going to stop."

Nick paced into a dark hallway that led to the prison cells. The only thing on the wall was an ancient payphone jutting out into the narrow corridor. Atop the phone was an abandoned Styrofoam cup. Nick increased speed as he spoke. "Listen, Jule, this time it's different. It's personal. I promise I will not be an FBI agent thirty days from now. One way or another, I will be done."

"I don't know if I like how you said that, Nick. What do you mean 'one way or another you'll be done'?"

"I mean . . ." Nick thought about what he meant. He wasn't sure. He didn't plot out his goals on a chart and check them off as he went. How could he possibly resolve the KSF threat in such a short period? "I mean . . . I mean I'm going to get Kharrazi."

"Will you ever be able to let go?"

Nick didn't have the details yet, just disconnected ideas floating around in his head like tiny bits of hydrogen and oxygen looking for a way to merge into something significant. He was distracted by a pair of headlights that lit up the inside of the reception room. He heard Carl Rutherford murmur something about sticking a bullet between the Sheriff's eyes.

"Listen, Jule, I've got to go." Tell her, he thought. Tell her what she needs to hear. But the moment passed, and once again, Nick grappled for something resembling appropriate. "I'll be home tomorrow — I promise. We'll talk then."

"I love you." She hung up, giving him the out he needed.

"Now listen up," Matt was instructing Rutherford and Tolliver. "We go straight by the book. We read him his rights and take him into custody. End of story. We don't want any well-paid attorneys getting him off on a police brutality charge. Understand?"

The two agents were more interested in their burritos than some corrupt Sheriff. They both nodded with mouths full of beans. The front door creaked open and Sheriff Skrugs marched in with his airy smile intact. He stopped cold when he saw the audience waiting for him. He tried, but he couldn't hide his astonishment. He continued through the doorway tentatively while his eyes darted from agent to agent as if he was trying to discover how much they knew.

"Evening, Sheriff," Matt twanged.

"Well . . . how did it go?" Skrugs' voice was shaky.

Matt approached the sheriff with a sinister grin. "Bet you didn't think you'd ever see us again."

Skrugs assumed his trademark pompous smirk. "Now why in the world would you go and say a thing like that?"

Matt hesitated for just a moment, then squeezed his fist shut and flew an uppercut into Skrugs' chin. The Sheriff's teeth snapped together like castanets as he fell back and hit the floor flush, the full weight of his body causing the room to shake.

Nick jumped to Matt's side. He looked sideways at his partner. "By the book, eh?"

For the first time in their tenure together, Matt was speechless. He just stood with his fist clenched as if he were waiting for Skrugs to get to his feet and take another blow.

But Skrugs was phlegmatic. He slowly rose to one elbow and rubbed his chin with an air of superiority, as if his acquired knowledge would sustain him. Nick wasn't sure if it was the grin or the residual tension left behind from the ambush, but he suddenly found himself with his hand grasping the Sheriff's throat. His grip was so tight that Skrugs' skin oozed from between Nick's fingers like Play-Doh. Skrugs' face turned red while appearing anxious to hear Nick's demands.

Nick simply squeezed harder and harder until he was fairly certain he would suffocate Skrugs in a matter of seconds. The Sheriff desperately pulled on Nick's arms and searched the room for support from anywhere he might find it. He found nothing but steady glares from the observing agents.

With the wall of blood rushing to his head, Nick didn't hear the door open.

"What the fuck is going on here?"

Silk stood in the doorway with the confused expression of a child who had just found his little brother opening up all of his Christmas presents. He froze open-mouthed, while a green toothpick defied gravity on his lower lip. He looked at Nick for an explanation.

Nick released Skrugs and the big man's head bounced on the linoleum floor like a bowling ball. A strained surge of air fought its way through the Sheriff's collapsed trachea.

Silk looked down at the Sheriff gasping for air. He pointed his toothpick. "That's supposed to be my job."

"Silk," Nick stopped him before he went any further. "This is not who you're after."

Silk looked pensively at Skrugs, as if any revenge might curb his appetite.

Nick kicked Skrugs. "How much did they pay you?"

Skrugs was on his side. His chest heaved as he gasped for breath. Nick couldn't tell if one of the heaves was a shrug. He pulled out his 9mm and pointed the barrel at Skrugs' head. "Where are they?"

The Sheriff's eyes widened.

The bathroom door opened and even before Nick saw Jennifer Steele working a towel over her wet hair, he heard her gasp. "What are you doing?"

Almost embarrassed, Nick holstered his gun.

Silk leaned into Nick and whispered, "You want I should take him out back and get some answers?"

Nick sighed. He stared at Skrugs, who had resumed his eternally smug grin.

"What do you need to know?" Silk asked.

Matt answered for his partner. "We need to know where the KSF are hiding."

Silk nodded and seemed to turn this information over in his head. He pointed to Nick, "I think I know someone who could maybe help us."

Nick was still looking at Skrugs and noticed his face fall.

"Who?" Nick asked.

"Let me make a call."

Silk flipped open his cell phone and stepped outside. Nick

tapped Skrugs with his foot and said to Matt, "Cuff him and throw him into a cell."

Matt ripped the Sheriff's shirt when he yanked him upright, then slapped cuffs on him. As Skrugs was led toward the back detention area, he sneered, "You ain't got squat on me, Mr. Federal Agent."

Nick ignored the comment and looked at his watch. His head was one gigantic pulse.

Chapter 33

Kemel Kharrazi sat back in his chair and picked at a plate of grapes and cheese. He pointed at the television monitor. "Truly they are idiots, no Hasan?"

Hasan Bozlak nodded, sitting upright at the edge of his chair. The two men watched the small television monitor in the basement of the safe house, in Kharrazi's private quarters. The walls were bare but for a detailed map of Arizona and a map of the United States littered with colored thumbtacks. The low ceiling gave the room a closed-in feeling. It bolstered the stillness that thrived in the basement. Thirty soldiers patrolled the grounds, protected the perimeter and secured the interior of the cabin with the professional quiet of jewel thieves. Kharrazi could barely hear their footsteps overhead as he enjoyed the scene on the monitor.

A lamp sat alone on an end table between the two men. Kharrazi twisted off the light, causing the TV to become the only source of illumination. The room became eerily dim.

On the screen, Matt McColm, Ed Tolliver, and Carl Rutherford attacked tortilla-wrapped food, while Nick Bracco spoke with his wife on his cell phone. From the angle of the camera hidden in the ceiling panels of the Sheriff's office, Kharrazi could hear Bracco speaking with his back to the group. Even from behind it was obvious that the FBI agent was wiping his eyes.

Kharrazi mocked. "His entire world is about to explode and he's worried about his female partner. What emotional weaklings these Americans are."

Kharrazi had fiber optics installed inside of the Sheriff's station weeks ago. He knew that once Payson became a focal point, the Sheriff's station was the most likely place to set up a command center. His foresight was now paying huge dividends.

Like people waiting for the ball to drop in Times Square on New Years Eve, Kharrazi and Hasan were counting down the minutes until the White House exploded into rubble.

"One hundred and forty-two minutes, Sarock," Hasan said. They both found the digital display atop the detonator irresistible. The detonator beamed the countdown from an open-doored wall safe. At the first sign of trouble, Kharrazi would lock the safe, but he knew it was irrelevant. The detonator was foolproof and could withstand scrutiny from the world's best bomb experts without deactivating. Any tampering would merely cause the missiles to deploy earlier than scheduled. A true Rashid Baser masterpiece.

Kharrazi noticed his number one soldier fidgeting in his chair. "Relax, Hasan. You worry too much."

"Yes, Sarock," Hasan replied, twirling his thumbs.

"What is your concern?" Kharrazi asked.

Hasan pointed to the detonator. "We should push the button now. It makes no sense to wait." The second Hasan finished his statement he immediately appeared to regret it. He searched Kharrazi's face for a reaction and squirmed with anticipation.

Kharrazi smiled. "Hasan, you are a warrior. I can't expect you to understand the finer points of using political pressure to maximize our assets." He patted his soldier on the knee. "You have a bulldog mentality, but sometimes all a bulldog need do is bare his teeth."

This only added to the confusion on Hasan's face. Kharrazi offered his plate of grapes and cheese to the young man and Hasan nodded, placing it on his lap. He picked a couple of grapes and flung them into his mouth.

Kharrazi rose to his feet. This caused Hasan to gulp down his partially chewed grapes.

Kharrazi's stiletto was leaning up against the wall in the corner of the room. He reached down and retrieved his favorite blade. "You see, the American people do not have the backbone for a war on their turf. They will do anything necessary to avoid it, including impeaching their own President."

With his stiletto behind his back, Kharrazi paced in the darkness. Hasan watched Kharrazi with hawk's eyes.

"If we explode the White House early," Kharrazi explained, "it could make the President a victim, which would draw sympathy from U.S. citizens. But if we give him the full opportunity, every possible chance, every minute we offered, and still he refused to remove his troops from Turkey, well, then he got what he deserved. And we did precisely what we said we would. And any threat that followed —" he swiftly dove his dagger into Hasan's lap, stabbing a large chunk of cheese and drawing it to his mouth. Hasan nearly fainted at the maneuver.

"Would be treated with respect," Kharrazi finished with a cheek full of cheese.

Hasan nodded enthusiastically, appearing grateful to be alive. "Yes, Sarock. You speak the truth."

"Of course I do." Kharrazi returned his attention to the TV screen. The FBI had no clue where he was. Even if they found him and overcame his squad of soldiers protecting the safe house, they couldn't stop the missiles from deploying. In just over two hours, Kemel Kharrazi would harvest the fruits of his labor.

He watched as Nick Bracco turned toward the camera. He yawned and rubbed his eyes. Bracco looked to be a beaten man. Kharrazi remembered his failed attempts at eradicating Bracco's family. Bracco himself would not be so lucky. He had to be done away with. Kharrazi was going to put him out of his misery very soon.

Kharrazi thought about his own wife and his children back home, counting on him to rid their country of the pestilent American soldiers. Soon he would be able to return to a hero's welcome and rally his soldiers to victory over the Turkish Security Force. Statues would be erected in his image. Kemel Kharrazi was going to be a legend for all of eternity.

He found it hard to remove the smile from his face.

* * *

Headlights flashed across the front window of the Gila County Sheriff's Office. Nick knew it was too soon for the SWAT team from Phoenix. A short, burly man eased out of a Cadillac wearing a dark suit. Nick realized who he was. Silk went out to greet the man with a bear hug. Both of them pecked each other's cheek. They exchanged pleasantries for a few minutes, then Silk pointed inside. He stood gesticulating this way and that. The squat man nodded repeatedly. The conversation ended with the two smiling and slapping one another on the back.

Silk led the man into the building and the man strode in patting his generous stomach. "The veal scaloppini is to die for, Silk. They have—" the man looked up and noticed the group of short-haired FBI agents sitting behind the receptionist's desk shuffling papers and banging on laptop keyboards.

"Jeesh," the man said, "some fancy deputies you got up here."

Silk found Nick working a highlighter over a list of newly purchased homes in the area. "This is a friend of mine," Silk motioned to the man. "Gasper Continelli, this is Nick Bracco."

Nick shook the man's hand, almost expecting to come away with a couple of hundred dollar bills. "Good to meet you."

"The pleasure is all mine," Gasper said affably.

Silk gave Nick a conspiratorial nod toward the Sheriff's personal office. Nick glanced at his watch wondering when reinforcements were coming. He waved the two men into Skrugs' office.

The Sheriff's private sanctuary seemed of keen interest to Gasper. His head circled the place as if admiring the decor. He gestured toward the tall portrait of Geronimo, "Hey, I know that guy. He used to play second base for the Indians."

Nick pretended not to hear the remark as he took up a chair behind Skrugs' desk. Silk laughed hard enough for the both of them.

Gasper sat down across from the desk and leaned back and crossed his legs.

Nick rocked anxiously in his chair, his hands folded to his chest. "You have something for me?" he asked.

Silk stood behind the plump man and patted his shoulders. "Gasper here knows something that you might find interesting."

Nick lowered his head toward Gasper and raised his eyebrows.

Gasper looked about the room with wide-eyed innocence. "I'm a big fan of the police," he announced loudly.

Nick glanced at Silk, then back to Gasper. "Excuse me?"

"I donate a couple of dimes each year to the Police Athletic League." Gasper was nodding as if to verify his own declaration.

Nick bit his lower lip. "Listen, Gasper, I'm not an IRS agent looking for dinner receipts. I'm kind of tied up with—"

"Tell me about it," Gasper said. "I've been watching it on TV all day. They've evacuated a square mile around the White House."

"Look," Nick said, "speaking for all law enforcement officials nationwide, I truly appreciate your financial support, but if you don't get to—"

"I ain't saying a thing until we're alone," declared Gasper.

Nick tilted his head. "You want Silk to leave the room, or Geronimo?"

Gasper pointed to a silver sprinkler hanging from the ceiling above them. "That thing ain't just loaded with water up there. If you look close enough, you'll notice that the part where the water is supposed to come out, well, it's filled in with a wire. Probably fiber optic if my eyesight ain't failing me."

Nick stared at the man. He thought about Skrugs and his deception. Had Nick underestimated the depth of the man's betrayal? Had he actually allowed Kharrazi to wire his own office? Nick finally looked up and saw exactly what Gasper saw. The head of the sprinkler was covered with a tiny glass bulb. Behind it, a faint red light beamed its narrow beam of absorption. It never occurred to him to debug the Sheriff's office, but someone like Gasper probably never entered a room without scanning for bugs.

Nick almost put his finger to his lips, then remembered who he was dealing with. He pulled his duffle bag onto the sheriff's desk, unzipped a side pouch and produced a narrow metal cylinder topped off with a clear plastic ball. The ball was a gauge with the needle leaning up against the left side of the dial in the green zone. Nick crawled up on the desk and got to his feet. Before he moved the device even halfway toward the sprinkler, the needle was already buried deep into the red side of the gauge. Nick grabbed the sprinkler with his free hand and tugged hard. It came loose, but not completely unattached. He reached into his bag again and retrieved a Phillips screwdriver. A minute later, he had loosened the casing that held the sprinkler in place and yanked down on the device. The sprinkler came free and Nick cursed as he unfurled the black cable that came rushing out of the ceiling behind the sprinkler head.

From below him he heard, "Am I good, or am I good?"

Nick looked into the tip of the cable and said, "You don't know how much I learned from this little game, Kharrazi. Is this what your daddy used to do to you when you were a kid? Did he spy on you and watch you get undressed, you piece of shit?" He quickly clipped the cable with a wire cutter and rendered it useless. "You were right, Gasper. Fiber optics. State of the art video monitoring." He waived his wire-tapping detector around the room and found no other devices. He would sweep the reception area as soon as he finished with Gasper.

Gasper's chest heaved with pride while Silk maintained a steady grin.

"It's a gift, really," Gasper said. "Like when people can sense when they're being watched. I can always tell where the wires are. Actually, I'm pretty good at both."

Nick hopped down from the desk and returned his tools to his duffle bag. "All right, Gasper, we're all clear. Tell me what you know."

Gasper folded his arms across his chest. "So you're Tommy Bracco's cousin, huh?"

"That's right," Nick said.

"From whose side of the family?"

"Tommy's dad is my father's brother." All male connections. Nick knew this would make Gasper happy.

Gasper nodded toward the ceiling. "Smart guy like you, how'd you let something like that get by you? Aren't you supposed to be in charge here?"

"Listen," Nick said with a tight, searing look of impatience. "I didn't know about the wire because the Bureau didn't put it there, someone who was trying to spy on us had it installed before we got here. Secondly, Tommy is my cousin, like a brother really. As kids we spent every summer day playing the ponies at Pimlico. I even lived at his house after my folks died."

Nick gestured toward Silk. "Don must've told you that much already. He and Tommy have been best friends since grade school. The three of us were inseparable throughout high school." Nick leaned forward, his arms flat on the desk in front of him. "I wear a size ten-and-a-half shoe and a forty-two long suit jacket. What else can I tell you before we get down to business?"

Gasper nodded. "Of course. I got just one other thing."

"What's that?"

"I need to know what's in it for me?"

Nick blinked a couple of times. "Tell me, Gasper. What do you want?"

Gasper shrugged. "Actually, nothing now that I'm thinking about it. I'm just in the habit of asking—wait a second, I know. I got a speeding ticket a couple of weeks back and I have to go to one of those safety-driving classes next month. You ever been to one of those things? Like going to a wake, only without the alcohol. Anyway, I'd like to get out of it without getting points on my driver's license."

"That's it?" Nick asked.

"Believe me, that's plenty."

"Consider it done," Nick pronounced. "Now can we get on with it?"

Gasper turned and gave Silk a hesitant glance. Silk nodded.

"Silk here says you can be trusted. He says that anything I tell you will stay inside of this room."

Nick grimaced. "Are you going to be telling me anything about dead bodies that you may have contributed to?"

Gasper seemed appalled. "Of course not. I don't even like the way you said that."

Silk gave Gasper a reassuring pat on the shoulder. "Gaspers runs book down in Scottsdale. Once a week he makes a trip up here to Payson. He simply brings Las Vegas to Arizona for people who don't have the time to drive back and forth."

"Sort of a public service," Nick commented.

"Exactly," Gasper said, appreciating Nick's insight.

"The answer is yes," Nick said. "Anything you tell me will be confidential and won't go any further than this room."

"Good," Gasper said, settling back in his chair and pulling his white cuffs out from the sleeves of his double-breasted jacket. "So this customer of mine up here is the guy who got his head cut off. His name is Fred something," Gasper snapped his finger a couple of times searching for the name.

"Fred Wilson," Nick said.

"That's it," Gasper exclaimed. "Well, he makes an unusually large play on the Cowboys a few weeks back. He was bragging about some shady blasting-cap deal he'd made with some foreigners. I'm guessing these are the type that could be used to blow up houses, if you get my drift. Anyway, a friend of his tells me that he suspected something fishy and warned Fred not to make the deal, but the money blinds Fred to the danger and he goes and does it anyway. So one day this friend is in the parking lot of Fred's business when this one particular Arab-type walks out the front door in a hurry. This guy don't like the way the Arab is acting, so he waits in his car until he's gone before he goes in and finds the mess that he was afraid he'd find."

"He's the one who found Fred?"

Gasper nodded. "Headless. Like that horseman guy."

Nick rubbed his temple. "And how does this help me?"

Gasper flashed a knowing smile. "Because he recognized the Arab. This guy is an aluminum siding salesman and he drove up to the Arab's cabin once to try to sell him some siding. He remembers that the Arab chased him away. Very rudely, I might add."

Now Nick was interested. Since Rashid Baser killed Fred Wilson, he had to be the Arab this guy was speaking of. There's no question Rashid would have been staying at the headquarters before he took a revenge bullet from one of Sal's crew. "So he knows where the Arab lives?"

"Yeah."

"And this is the same guy who killed Fred?"

"Yeah."

"What's his name?"

Gasper spread his arms with his palms up. "See, I'm not real good with names. Faces and numbers are really my strong suit."

"You don't know his name?" Nick asked.

"I think it was something religious, like Moses, or Peter, or Paul."

"Paul? Religious?"

"What, you don't know the Apostles?"

"Oh, for crying out loud, Gasper. All this and no name?"

"Well, I can tell you where he hangs out."

"Where?"

"The Winchester. A bar over on Main Street. He's some kind of a pool shark. I do a lot of business down there."

Nick went to the door and called Jennifer Steele into the office, then closed the door behind her. She wore a borrowed FBI windbreaker and had on her black baseball cap minus the ponytail. If she were bald and wore a lavender sports jacket, it wouldn't have detracted from her looks.

Gasper jumped to his feet and offered his hand. "Pleased to meet you. I'm Gasper Continelli."

Steele had one eye on Nick while she exchanged pleasantries with the character.

"He's a big fan of the police," Nick deadpanned.

"What's up?" she asked, shaking off Gasper's groping handshake.

"Are you familiar with a place called the Winchester?" Nick asked.

"Sure."

"You've been there?"

"Yes."

"Are you familiar with anyone who might be hustling pool down there?"

"Well, hustling might be a strong word considering the amount of money—"

Nick held up his hand. "No, you misunderstand me. I'm not accusing you of anything. I'm just looking for a name. Anyone in particular you might remember shooting pool and," Nick chose his words carefully, "winning fairly often?"

Steele looked down in deep thought. Gasper dropped back down into his chair and waited for her to come up with someone.

Finally, Steele looked up at Nick. "The only person in this town that could even be considered a pool shark is a guy by the name of Angel."

Gasper snapped his fingers. "That's it! Angel. I knew it was religious. I'm good at association."

"And numbers and faces," Nick quipped. "What's his last name?"

"I don't know," she said. "I'm not even sure Angel is his real name. Nicknames are real common up here."

"She's right about that," Gasper chimed agreeably. "Something about small towns and nicknames. I never quite understood it."

"Great." Nick looked down at his watch. Less than two hours to go and he was discussing nicknames with a bookie whose major concern in life was having to attend a driver's education class.

"Tell you what," Gasper said. "It's a little early, but there's a chance he's down at the Winchester shooting pool right now. I'll go down there and check it out. If he's there, I'll bring him to you."

Nick couldn't afford to augment his band of mercenaries any more than he already had. He looked at Steele. "You know what he looks like?"

She nodded.

Nick walked around the desk and offered Gasper his hand. The bottom-heavy man lifted himself from his seat and vigorously shook Nick's hand. "Thanks for the offer," Nick said, "but we can take it from here."

"It's been my pleasure." Gasper smiled. "That's all you need?"

"That's plenty," Nick said.

"Give Tommy my regards."

Nick clasped his free hand over their handshake in a sign of respect. "I'll take care of the speeding ticket." He paused and eyed Gasper intently. "You did your country proud on this one. You know that." Nick struck the proper chord to send the man off with a smile on his face.

Once Gasper was gone, he looked at Steele and Silk. "I want both of you to head down to the Winchester and find this Angel character. I don't care what it takes, find him."

Steele looked at Silk. "No offense, but I don't need an escort."

"None taken," Silk said.

"I want Silk with you," Nick said. "In case Angel isn't there and no one wants to cooperate with an FBI agent."

Steele's eyes narrowed. "What are you suggesting?"

Nick spoke deliberately, trying to reason out his response with the slower tempo. "I'm simply suggesting that Silk can do certain things that go beyond the scope of your capabilities."

She frowned. "You mean things like intimidation and brute force?"

Silk stood silently, allowing Nick to do all the work for him.

"Yes, I mean intimidation, brute force and animal husbandry if it's called for. If this guy knows where the KSF headquarters is, then he's our best chance to save the White House, and maybe even our country."

Steele looked as if she was ready to walk out, but didn't want to be insubordinate. "Don't you think this is going over the line?"

"Probably," Nick said. "The line's getting blurrier and blurrier all the time. But I don't have time to debate protocol with you, Agent Steele. If you don't want to go, tell me, and I'll send someone else."

Steele looked over at Silk who appeared to be suppressing a grin. "Are you at least going to give me a chance to do this legally?" she asked him.

Silk looked offended. "Of course. What do I look like, a monster?"

She looked back at Nick and seemed ready to agree, when Nick said, "Whatever Silk needs to do, he does. No questions asked."

"And he receives a get-out-of-jail-free card?" she asked.

Nick walked behind Skrugs' desk, sat down, and placed his hands flat on the desktop. "Look," he said, "you saved my partner's life. I owe you. Please work with me here. We're dealing with someone who will kill women and children just for something to do. He tried to kill my wife. I need you to give me some room to maneuver."

Steele's look softened. She nodded.

Nick didn't say any more. He'd taken on more responsibility than he could handle and it didn't hold up to the scrutiny of a fellow FBI agent. It seemed the faster he acted, the more palatable his commands became.

Steele left with Silk trailing her. He was on his toes. A lion on the prowl. Nick wondered exactly what he had just unleashed.

He looked up at the cable dangling from the ceiling. "Fuck you, Kharrazi," Nick spat. "Fuck you and everything I've become to get you."

Chapter 34

Jennifer Steele's house was less than a mile from the Winchester, so she decided to stop for a quick change of clothes. Walking into a cowboy bar wearing an FBI windbreaker wasn't the most effective way to extract information. She had decided to use another tactic and by the time she and Silk reached the bar, the transformation was complete.

"You're one talented FBI agent," Silk said, leering at her spaghetti-strapped top and tight-fitting jeans.

Steele was uncomfortable using her body as a tool, but she despised the alternative that Silk represented.

They were outside of the Winchester. Steele applied lipstick while looking into a compact mirror. "You are going to give me a decent shot at this, aren't you?" she asked.

"Hey, a guy takes one look at you and he's spilling all of his secrets including some stuff about his mom."

"Thanks. I think." She put the finishing touches on her face, then snapped her compact shut and slipped it into her tiny purse, next to her gun. "Give me a couple of minutes head start," she said, leaving Silk to pace on the creaking wooden floorboards that fronted the bar.

The Winchester had been a large barn that was converted into a cowboy bar over twenty years ago. The Berlin Wall had crumbled and private citizens were planning space travel, yet time seemed to stand still inside of the Winchester. Other than a few obvious tourists, the standard attire included jeans, cowboy boots, Stetson hat, and the occasional bandanna. There were piles of hay bound up in strategic spots, giving the place more authenticity than it really needed. On the overhead speaker system, Willie Nelson pleaded for mommas not to allow their babies to grow up to be cowboys. It was already too late for most of the clientele.

Steele scanned the room. The bar itself was a square-shaped, wooden frame with shelves of whiskey covering up a full-length mirror. A bartender rang a cowbell, then dropped a few dollar bills into the silver bucket tip jar that hung from a nail.

She wasn't inside more than a minute before someone took the bait.

"Buy you a drink, Ma'am?" Steele turned to see a thin, young man wearing a large Stetson hat that might have weighed half his body weight. The hat was supposed to make him look older, but his baby face worked against him. He pushed the brim of his hat up with the tip of his longneck bottle of beer. "Be my pleasure," he added.

"Sure," she said. "That would be nice. I'll have a draft."

The man smiled. He hurried over to the bar as if Steele's acceptance might have a short shelf life. It gave Steele just enough time to adjust to the darkness and by the time he returned she was certain that Angel wasn't there.

"Here you go," the man carefully handed her the overfilled glass of beer. "They don't cheat ya here."

"No, they don't," Steele said, sipping the foam off the glass of beer. They were standing dangerously close to the dance floor and several slow-dancing couples moved them back a couple of steps. "I've never been here before, how about you?" she asked.

"A few times," he said, in an overly innocent tone that made Steele think he slept in a room out back. "I didn't catch your name," he said.

"Jennifer. What's yours?"

"Zeke," he said with a straight face.

"Hi, Zeke."

Steele waited a brief moment, then acted like she was trying to fill the awkward pause with conversation. "Have you ever heard of a guy named Angel? I understand he hangs out here sometimes."

Zeke looked up at the high ceiling in deep thought. Probably considering which answer would benefit him the most. "I think I do remember a guy by the name of Angel. Why? Is he a friend of yours?"

She rubbed her index finger around the rim of her glass and offered a crooked smile. "He's not my boyfriend, if that's what you mean. I don't have one of those right now."

Zeke's eye's widened. "Um, well, why are you looking for him?"

"My brother lost some money playing pool with him and I was looking to pay him off. It's a big sister kind of thing."

Zeke nodded, as if the story rung true. He'd probably lost money to Angel himself. "Yeah, I can see that happening."

Steele lowered her head and whispered into Zeke's ear. "I was hoping you might know where I could find him, so I can free myself up for the rest of the evening." She lingered a little before backing up and for that brief moment she allowed herself to imagine it was Matt McColm's cheek she was brushing against. It surprised her how quickly his image had popped into her head. They hadn't had a chance to talk privately since the shootout. Was that the cause for the butterflies now swirling in her stomach? She needed to focus on her assignment, but for some reason she felt compelled to permit the small fantasy to creep into the fray. If even for a brief moment.

She must've been glowing when she stood upright because Zeke's blush deepened. He appeared willing to help her, but his face told her that he didn't have the information she wanted. He shrugged slightly and looked at his boots. "I really don't know him all that well," he admitted.

Steele smiled. "It's okay." She rubbed his arm. "Do you know his last name?"

He shook his head. He looked deflated.

"Is there anyone here that might know something about him?"

Zeke brightened. He nodded toward the stand of pool tables on the opposite side of the bar. "Rocky over there is his playing partner. The one in the white shirt. They play in a lot of pool tournaments together. I'm sure he knows stuff."

Steele saw a solid-looking man with a white tee-shirt tucked tightly into faded jeans. He was holding a pool cue in front of him with both hands and was tapping it against the floor in time to the music. The man he was playing with was a tall, thick Native American Indian with a braid running down his back.

Steele leaned toward Zeke and gave him a peck on the cheek. "Thanks, Sweetie. I owe you one."

Zeke's face held eternal hope as she turned to go.

It was still early, yet the bar was more than half full. Steele meandered between single men trawling for young girls and couples holding hands on their way to the dance floor. She found the man in the tee-shirt hanging over one of the four pool tables, lining up a long shot. She casually leaned over the pocket where he was aiming. She wasn't wearing a bra, so he got the full treatment. He had one eye shut and was sliding the tapered pool cue through his curled index finger when he noticed her smiling at him. He came up for a moment and ran his eyes up and down her body. Then he returned to his crouch and smacked the cue ball into the 5-ball, which slammed into the back of the corner pocket right below Steele. She jumped back.

The Indian smiled at her reaction.

The man picked up a cube of blue chalk, twisted the tip of his stick into the cube, then placed it back onto the ledge of the table. He moved around Steele and as he crouched down for another shot, he bumped her aside with his hip.

Steele crossed her arms. "Am I in your way?" she asked.

"Yup," he said without looking at her.

The Indian seemed to enjoy the free entertainment.

Steele saw Silk playing at a pool table next to them. He was gliding around the table, on the prowl for a good shot. When their eyes met, he winked at her.

Another ball slammed into a pocket and the man continued lining up his shots as if she weren't there. She noticed he was wearing a silver belt buckle with the Confederate flag flying in the center of it.

Steele began to lose her patience. "Is your name Rocky?"

The man ignored her.

Steele looked at her watch. She suddenly felt like Cinderella at the stroke of midnight.

"Are you Rocky?" she repeated, a little louder.

He made no attempt to respond. It was obvious she had found the right man.

Steele reached into her purse and flipped open her credentials. She grabbed the man's pool stick and shoved her creds in his face. "I'm an FBI agent. Tell me your damn name."

The Indian stopped smiling.

Rocky yanked the stick free. "I don't give a shit who you are, lady. This is a free country and I don't have to talk to nobody I don't want to."

Steele stood with her hands on her hips. Randy Travis was now pining about missing an old flame. The music was loud enough to cover up most of the commotion, but the few patrons who were watching made Steele nervous. Or maybe it was the fact that she suddenly felt extremely vulnerable. She wasn't dressed for an altercation.

Silk was lining up a shot at the table next to them. He drew his stick back with a short jerky motion and jabbed Rocky in the ribcage with the back of his pool cue. Silk turned and brushed off the man's shirt.

"Sorry about that," Silk said. "Hey, you're kinda cute."

Rocky squared up on him and his shoulders seemed to swell.

Silk was a couple of inches shorter, but he looked up at the man with the practiced stare of a professional assassin. Rocky tried to keep up, but the best he could do was look menacing. Nobody spoke as the two men stared each other down.

Finally, Silk glimpsed down at the man's belt buckle. "The fuck is that?" he said, pointing at the Confederate flag.

Rocky maintained his stare. He was trying out his best scowl, but Silk seemed immune.

"Didn't anyone tell you?" Silk asked. "The South lost. What happened, you drop your subscription to the Redneck Daily News?"

Rocky's eyes flared with fury. He gripped his pool stick with both hands and roundhoused a swing at Silk.

Silk ducked.

When Rocky came back with it, Silk deflected the shot with his right arm and grabbed the stick with his left. He pulled down with both hands, snapped the stick over his raised thigh and came up with two splintered pieces. Rocky stood startled at Silk's agility. Silk wheeled and clocked the Indian who was now reaching for Silk from behind.

The Indian went to his knees. Blood trickled down the side of his face. Silk barked, "Stay down, Chief, I got no gripe with you."

Rocky had grabbed another pool stick and was about to swing when Steele fumbled her gun out of her purse and pointed it at him. "Stop, or I'll shoot."

Silk looked at Steele as if she'd ruined his birthday party. "Aw, leave him be," Silk said, with open palms. "He ain't gonna hurt nothing."

Steele held the gun steady and wondered what else could go wrong that night.

"Put it down, lady," a man's voice boomed from behind her. When Steele turned, she saw a large man with a dirty, white apron tied around his bowling-ball gut. He was holding a shotgun and leveling it at Steele. "Get out of my bar . . . now."

Steele held up her credentials. "I'm an FBI agent here on official business."

"I don't' give a shit who you are."

"You don't understand —"

The shot reverberated throughout the spacious room, followed by screams and a frantic rush for the exit. People nearby lunged to the floor and began scrambling for the door on their hands and knees.

Steele flinched for a moment, but when she regained her focus, she saw the bar owner on the floor clutching his leg. Silk holstered his revolver, kicked aside the shotgun that lay next to the bar owner, and crouched over the fallen man. "Sorry, pal. You just don't know how serious all this stuff is."

Silk unfastened the bar owner's apron and tied it snug around his upper thigh as a tourniquet. He motioned to the Indian, who was getting to his feet, holding his hand up against his bloody ear. "Hey, Chief, get him to the hospital. Pronto. It looks like you could use a stitch or two yourself."

The Indian stood expressionless.

Silk casually steered his revolver in the Indian's direction. "What? I gotta shoot you too?"

The Indian moved toward the injured man.

The bar owner's face was screwed up into a knot. He appeared to be fighting off the effects of shock.

"You didn't have to do that," Steele said, still breathing heavy from relief.

"You're welcome," Silk said, helping the bar owner to his feet and placing the man's arm around the large Indian's shoulder. The two of them shuffled off and Rocky started to follow them. Silk grabbed the back of Rocky's shirt and pulled. "Where do you think you're going, Sport?"

Rocky unleashed an elbow into Silk's ribs and caught him by surprise. Silk took a step back, then regrouped and kicked Rocky in the crotch, like he was punting a football. Rocky curled over in pain.

Silk scowled. "What's the matter with you, you don't see me shoot that fat fuck with the apron? You think I'm like one of your cowfolk friends that carry around a six-shooter just to impress his girlfriend?"

The room was empty, but for the three of them now. Johnny Cash was singing about shooting a man in Reno just to watch him die; his voice resonated throughout the rafters of the elevated ceiling.

Silk lifted his foot and shoved Rocky to the ground. He landed on his back in between two pool tables and looked up at Silk. "Are you the law?" he asked in a breathy voice.

Silk opened the chamber of his revolver and dropped all five bullets into the palm of his hand. "More like an outlaw," he grinned.

"What are you doing?" Steele asked.

"I'm not sure," Silk said. "I think I'm trying to save the free world."

Rocky squinted incredulously at what he was watching.

Silk slipped all but one of the bullets into his pants pocket. He waved the single bullet in front of the man, gently holding it between the index finger and thumb of his right hand. He eased the bullet into one of the six chambers, then flicked it shut with his wrist. He spun the cylinder. It clicked around like a roulette wheel. Rocky's mouth opened.

"What are you doing?" Steele asked. Louder this time.

Silk spun the chamber again. He knelt next to Rocky and cocked the hammer. "You know what I'm doing, don't you? I might have to put you to sleep, if ya know what I mean."

Rocky sat frozen. He looked at Steele. His eyes pleaded for help, but his mouth only quivered.

"Silk, you're not doing this," Steele ordered.

"You see," Silk said to the man, "I need to know something." He stopped, then looked back at Steele. "He does know where this Angel guy lives, doesn't he?"

Steele didn't want it like this. Not her first big assignment. Not in the town she lived in. When everyone else had packed and gone home, she would still be there representing the Bureau. "This is not how we do things," she said.

"Uh huh," Silk said. "I'll take that for a yes."

He returned his attention to Rocky. He pressed the gun to the man's temple and said, "I need to know where Angel lives. Can you tell me? Or do we start gambling with your life?"

"I don't—"

Click.

Rocky screamed.

Steele aimed her pistol at Silk. "Stop it!"

Rocky's face was drained white. He screamed incoherent words.

Silk cocked the hammer again and cupped his ear. "What did you say, I can't hear you?"

Click. Silk pulled the trigger for the second time.

Rocky was convulsing. His eyes were saturated with tears.

Steele fired a shot over Silk's head. The blast startled Rocky. It startled her. Silk didn't flinch. "Stop it, or I'm going take you down," she ordered.

Silk kept his hand cupped around his ear. "What?' he said in Rocky's face. "I can't hear with all this racket."

Click.

Steele blasted a second shot, closer this time. Wood splintered off of the side of a pool table and splashed Silk on his cheek.

Silk brushed his hand down the side of his face and glared at Steele. "You're starting to piss me off here."

"I'll tell you!" Rocky screamed. "I'll tell you!"

"See," Silk said. "His memory came back to him."

"He lives over on Sycamore," the words rushed out of the man's mouth. "Take 260 east toward Heber. About two miles past the Ranger Station on the right hand side is Sycamore. That's the road he lives on. Second house on the left."

Silk patted Rocky's face. "Good boy." Then Silk's face turned dark. "You wouldn't lie to me, would you?"

Rocky shook his head furiously, his eyes fixed on Silk's revolver. "N-n-n-o."

Silk reached into the man's back pocket and yanked out his wallet. He opened the billfold and pulled out some plastic cards. His forehead wrinkled. "Your name is Arthur? I thought she was asking you if your name was Rocky."

The man was still trembling. "That's what my friends call me."

"Oh. You wanna know what my friends call me?"

The man's eyes rose in anticipation, like he was extremely eager to hear something so important.

"Well, the ones that don't lie to me call me Silk. Wanna hear what the ones who lie to me call me?"

Rocky's tremble segued into a nod.

Silk smiled. "Well, let's just say, graveyards don't have any telephone booths. So they don't get to call me so much." Silk stood and held up the man's wallet. "And I know where you live."

Steele wiped her forehead with the back of her gun hand. "You're crazy," she muttered.

Silk dismissed Rocky. "Go home, Arthur," he said. "And change those pants, will ya?"

Rocky got to his feet and shuffled backward toward the door, dubiously staring at Silk, never showing him his back.

Silk walked up to Steele, opened his cell phone and began pushing buttons.

"What are you doing?" Steele said.

"I'm calling Nick with the info. That's why we came, right?"

"We need to discuss what just happened."

"What is it with you broads, always gotta talk?"

Steele ignored the comment. "There's been a shooting. I have to write a report. You almost killed an innocent man."

"What, the bartender?" Silk asked. "I shot him in the leg on purpose. If I wanted, I'd of nailed him between the eyes."

"I'm not talking about him, I'm talking about your other victim."

"What, Arthur?" Silk looked bewildered.

"Yes, Arthur. You could have killed him playing your little game of Russian roulette."

Silk let a breath out and shook his head. "Listen," he glanced over his shoulder at the empty bar. "I'll tell you something that I never told nobody. Ever. You understand what I'm saying?"

Steele nodded, without a clue as to what he was talking about.

"I make my living through intimidation and fear. I make both of these things do a lot of my work for me. Capisce?"

Silk raised his revolver and slid open the cylinder. He rotated the cylinder exposing six empty chambers. Like a smooth magician, he opened the palm of his left hand and showed Steele the missing bullet. "You know how much I practice that move? Maybe two, three hours a month. Every month." He pointed a finger at her. "But if word ever got out that I use this move, I might as well open up a deli in Topeka, Kansas. Sensitive guy like me would get eaten alive."

Steele pursed her lips. "Why didn't you tell me ahead of time? I could have shot you."

Silk stifled a laugh. "What, and ruin a perfectly good performance? Besides, when we left the Sheriff's office, Nick said to let me do whatever I needed to do. I know you didn't forget that."

Silk continued to push the buttons on his cell phone, hovered his index finger over the send button and looked up at Steele. "Are we done talking here? Or do you wanna know about my feelings?"

Steele shook her head. The KSF could learn a lot about terrorism from a guy like Silk.

Chapter 35

Angel Herrera sat hunched over a grilled cheese sandwich with his hand on a cool longneck bottle of beer when he heard the noise. He picked up the remote control from his TV tray and lowered the volume on Jeopardy. Alex Trebek mouthed the question to an answer that Angel didn't know. Angel hadn't known the question to any of the answers Alex was giving. He was on his fifth longneck, but probably wouldn't have known any of the questions even if he'd been sober. Ever since he found Fred Wilson decapitated, Angel couldn't get enough alcohol in his system. The foreign bastards were sneaking into America and killing innocent citizens—including a harmless businessman like Fred.

Angel had heard the rumors about terrorists hiding out in the Payson area and it spooked him. His name was in the paper as the person who found Fred and he wondered if the terrorists knew that he had seen the killer. In fact, he knew exactly where the killer lived. It was the reason why he never said anything to the Sheriff. What kind of protection would he get? A patrol car might drive by a couple of times a day, but what good would that do him? He figured he had a better chance of staying alive by keeping his mouth shut and letting it go.

It seemed like a good plan until now. He heard the noise outside of his cabin sounding like something moving. Angel's wife, Mabel, was in the basement doing laundry, so he knew it wasn't her. He waited to hear more. Nothing. Maybe a branch scraping up against the siding, like it always did whenever the wind picked up. He glanced out of his living room window and saw there was no wind. Not a breath.

He turned back toward the TV and saw, "Breaking News," at the bottom of the screen. He raised the volume and took a pull on his bottle of beer. The screen went blank for a moment, then a local newswoman was standing in front of a familiar landmark.

"Theresa Sanchez reporting for Channel 3 News. I'm live at the Winchester Bar and Grill, where a shooting took place just minutes ago."

Angel almost choked on his half-swallowed beer. He'd planned to head down to the Winchester after dinner. The woman held her hand to her ear as if someone was talking to her through an ear-phone, maybe even telling her what to say. "Eyewitnesses have told Channel 3 News that Max Gordon, owner of the Winchester, was shot and rushed to the hospital. We also have reports that a dark-haired man in a white tee-shirt was seen running from the scene shortly after the shots. It is yet to be confirmed whether this event is related to the terrorist organization reportedly hiding somewhere in the Payson vicinity. We will keep you informed with any breaking news as it happens. Theresa Sanchez, Channel 3 News."

Another sound, this time from the backyard. Angel shut off the TV. He crept to the kitchen and turned off the overhead lights. He peeked past the curtain hanging over the sink. It was dead still. Angel squinted into the tree line behind his cabin. He thought he saw something. He squinted harder and his peripheral vision became hyperactive with movement. If he stared straight at some-thing it wouldn't budge, but everything around it seemed to come alive with motion. Someone was out there.

He pulled open a kitchen drawer and grabbed a long carving knife. His senses swirled with suspicion. He thought he heard a man's voice. He picked up the telephone hanging on the wall. The line was dead.

Shit. His gun was in the glove box of his truck out front like always. Just great.

He thought about hiding down in the basement. Maybe buy him-self some time. But he couldn't get rid of the vision of Fred Wilson's headless body, spurting blood like a dropped bottle of red wine. He wasn't dealing with any local punks, that was for sure. These guys were the real deal. Hiding would only delay the inevitable. Better to face them head on.

The doorbell rang. Angel felt his legs tense with fear. He strug-gled to the basement door and saw his wife's feet at the bottom of the stairs, sorting laundry, her purple robe almost dragging the floor. "Mabel," he said in a forced hush. "Stay down there until I tell you to come up."

"Why?" Mabel asked over the hum of the dryer.

"Just do as I say," Angel said.

The doorbell rang again, only this time it was followed by a cou-ple of urgent thumps on the front door.

"Damn," Angel said. He crept to the door. He placed his hand on the doorknob and became paralyzed with fear. A pounding fist shook the door. He thought the frame was going to give out. He tightened his grip on the knife, tucked it behind his thigh and threw open the door as quickly as possible, trying to startle whoever was on the other side.

He froze.

A bright spotlight engulfed his entire doorway. Angel squinted and held up his arm to shade his eyes. Two men in navy windbreakers stood on his porch. Behind them, he could see the silhouettes of men wearing military fatigues crouched into an attack mode. A couple of dozen. Maybe more. Each had a machine gun pointed at him. He heard a helicopter approaching, then glanced up, blinded by another spotlight shining down on him. When his vision adjusted, he saw two military men leaned over the open door of the chopper with their eyes tucked behind the scopes of a couple of powerful looking rifles.

He was overwhelmed with the scene and was trying to make sense of it when the dark-haired man on his porch said, "Are you Angel?"

They had to be from the government, he thought, or he'd be dead already. There was no advantage to lying. They wouldn't be the gullible type like those Angel swindled out of a couple of hundred bucks every weekend at the Winchester. They wouldn't send this much force just to be deterred by some creative storytelling. He suddenly became aware of the knife he was still gripping tightly by his side. "That's what my friends call me," he said, in a voice too scared to speak slowly.

The two men at his doorstep were the only ones not pointing a weapon at him. They appeared unconcerned about any danger Angel might pose. The dark-haired man turned to his partner and gave him a look. The man nodded. He looked at Angel and held up a gold shield. Then, with the coldest stare he'd ever seen, the man said, "We're not your friends, Angel."

Angel dropped the carving knife to the floor.

* * *

Kemel Kharrazi fought fatigue as he ascended the wooden staircase and left the basement of the safe house for the first time that day. A mild autumn breeze greeted him at the door to the living room and he took in a breath of fresh air. He'd spent the entire day monitoring communications and preparing for his departure. As front man for the KSF, he understood how important it was for him to escape capture. As long as he remained at large, his threats would carry the weight of the number one terrorist in the world. A distinction he neither relished nor cared about. But he knew enough to use its credentials to get what he needed.

Conversations dissolved into quiet as Kharrazi strode toward the kitchen with a sense of purpose. The kitchen was a large room with a high ceiling, but it was overmatched by the throng of soldiers who were crammed into the area. The gathering of warriors parted seamlessly as Kharrazi walked unencumbered to a stepstool in the corner of the room. The kitchen was a mere shell of what it had been before the KSF inhabitation. Cabinet doors had been removed, allowing easy access to twelve-gauge shotgun shells and cartridges for Magnum autoloader rifles. Handheld rocket launchers were stacked on the countertops next to cases of heavy caliber ammunition.

Kharrazi uncorked a bottle of Turkish Merlot sitting next to a canister of .44 Magnum magazines and poured a glass of wine. As he drew the wine to his lips, he heard the murmur from his dedicated force behind him. He turned and stood on the stepstool and appraised his soldiers. They spilled into the living room of the A-frame and craned their necks for a glimpse of their leader. They were excited to be the chosen ones. Thirty of them in camouflage gear and blackface who Kharrazi had taken from their families, smuggled into a foreign country, and convinced to take the fight to the Americans on their own turf. Some of them he'd known since they were teenagers. Most had grown up idolizing him the way American kids would idolize a rock star.

"It is a glorious day to be a Kurd." Kemel Kharrazi raised his wine glass and brought smiles to the faces of the usually scowling soldiers.

Kharrazi peered down into his wine glass and focused on the vortex his swirls had created. The lives of his men teetered in his hands with the same vulnerability. He knew the minute Nick Bracco had discovered the wire in the sheriff's office that the FBI would come after them hard. Overwhelmingly hard. His soldiers would inevitably fight to their deaths, but the outcome was of little consequence. The detonator was unsolvable, rendering it impossible to disassemble. His ferocious fighting force had been reduced to a simple distraction for his getaway.

Now, he searched their faces and considered the words he would choose to notify their loved ones of their demise. The bravery they had displayed. The hopes for their children to live in a Kurdish country of their own. His words would of course be manipulated into a verse that supported his agenda. Kemel Kharrazi, the first dictator of a newly born Kurdish country. The father of all Kurds. The George Washington of his nation. A chance for immortality.

Kharrazi took it all in. He suppressed a telling grin and spoke to his men with great self-importance, "The President of the United States has scheduled a press conference to take place in less than an hour from now," he proclaimed. He slowly covered the room with his eyes, making eye contact with as many soldiers as possible, men who would gladly take a bullet for him. They listened eagerly, with a glint of hope in their eyes. Kharrazi would not disappoint them. "It has been leaked to the news media that he will be announcing the withdrawal of troops from Turkey."

The room exploded with cheers. The butts of machine guns pounded the floor with the rapid beat of anticipation. Kharrazi finally let loose a smile and joined in with his men who began chanting an old Kurdish victory song. Hands clapped to the rhythm of the chant while Kharrazi raised his glass in a celebratory gesture.

Kharrazi let the cheering continue for a few minutes, then held up his hand and watched the room become still. "We have some work left before we can go home and see our families again. We must remain vigilant. We must wait to hear the President address his country. Then we will know if the withdrawal is a fact. As I have told you, the Americans are willing to trade their souls for the safety of the White House."

There was a sudden lull as the rotors of an approaching helicopter whumped overhead. Everyone stopped and stared at the ceiling as it breezed past the cabin at a rapid pace. When the sound of the rotors dissipated, they looked at Kharrazi.

A leader like Kharrazi would never appear concerned. Not now. Not when they were so close. "Heading toward town," he said, unimpressed. "As usual, they are too late."

The cheers sprang up and Kharrazi raised his glass once again. The climax was coming fast. Kharrazi was heading home and he strained to keep from laughing out loud.

* * *

A half mile from their target, the troops assembled in the forest for operational instructions. Included were a squad of Marines and a dozen field agents, all rushed up from Phoenix on transport helicopters. They'd arrived just in time to intimidate Angel Herrera into disclosing the KSF's headquarters in record time. The man was ready to drive them there if necessary.

The Marines wore fatigues and shifted their weight anxiously, ready to run through walls, tear down buildings, and initiate a stockpile of terrorist corpses. Nick instructed the team commander that he needed a surgical approach to the attack. They couldn't afford to go in loud and heavy. It might trigger an early detonation of the White House missiles and would defeat their purpose altogether.

Sergeant Hal McKenna was the Marines' team commander. He was in his sixties and looked more like someone's grandfather than team leader of an elite group of sharpshooters and soldiers. Until you got close enough to notice the scar. A six-inch gouge from the corner of his right eye to the middle of his jutted chin. One look and you immediately tendered respect. Nick could tell it was job related without asking. The knife must have been serrated. It devoured too much healthy tissue to allow a clean repair. Some poor surgeon must have worked desperately just to keep his face intact.

McKenna squatted low while the Marines and others gathered around him. The blueprint of the cabin was stretched out on a bed of pine needles that scratched at its underside. McKenna was at the middle of an inner circle, which spread into the murky wilderness behind them. The stand of trees where they gathered wasn't very dense and it allowed for virtually everyone to get a clean look at him. A large streak of moonlight filtered between the canopies of pine trees and illuminated the opening where they assembled.

"Here," McKenna said, pointing to a spot on the diagram. "This is where they're most vulnerable."

Nick nodded, half listening to the briefing and half studying the latest satellite images that McKenna had brought from Phoenix. Matt was beside him with a magnifying glass, examining the same photos. They were taken a couple of hours earlier, right at dusk. Nick was steering a penlight across the images without really knowing what he was searching for. But something bothered him. Kharrazi was too sharp to allow himself to be cornered without an escape plan. Somewhere in the photos there was a clue. He just needed to recognize it.

McKenna was elbow to elbow with a Marine Sergeant and focused everyone's attention to a specific target. "So we launch the 720 in this window and — "

"No," Nick said.

Seven or eight heads turned toward Nick, including McKenna whose scar created a scowl on its own. "Excuse me?" McKenna said.

Nick opened his palms and tried the soft approach first. "The reason I directed you to formulate a plan was because of your hostage rescue skills. We need to be surgical. Quick and stealthy."

McKenna's face appeared to be fighting two or more emotions. "You have a hostage inside I don't know about?"

"Yes, I do. The detonator. If we start a firefight, they could detonate the missiles early and make this entire mission a moot point."

"What about Kharrazi?" McKenna said. "Isn't he inside?"

Nick glanced down at the satellite photos. "I don't know."

"That's great," McKenna said. He looked down at his watch. "We've got sixty-eight minutes until a missile takes out the White House. Even if we get inside the building in less than thirty minutes, that gives my bomb guys a half an hour to deactivate the detonator. If they can. And on top of that, we have to be stealthy. Any other requests, Agent?"

"That's enough," Matt said, locking eyes with McKenna.

An awkward silence hung in the night air. Nick considered the restraints those sixty-eight minutes put on them. He thought about Julie lying in her hospital bed ordering him to kill Kharrazi. Her bruised face looking up at him, her eyes pleading with him for retribution. He wiped his temple and was surprised to find it moist with sweat in the cool, autumn night. He needed to stay focused on the White House, though. He couldn't afford to let Kharrazi force him into a mistake. Not now.

"You're right," Nick said.

McKenna raised his brow. The scowl deteriorated and the grandfather face returned.

"Yes," Nick continued. "We don't have time to do this my way. But we must get to that detonator first."

McKenna nodded. "Okay. Where do you suspect it is?"

"Well," Nick looked over McKenna's shoulder and added his own penlight to the blueprint. "Something that important would be protected fairly well. I would have to say it's in the basement."

"Agreed," McKenna said. He moved his finger around the perimeter of the diagram. "Here. This is the outside entrance to the basement. It's in the back of the cabin below two second-story windows. We could get in there without entering the cabin. We secure the basement and gain control of the detonator before they can react."

Nick asked, "How, um . . ."

"Stealthily?" McKenna finished for him. A slight grin tugged at the corner of his lip. He looked over at a young man who sat next to the group with his legs crossed. A small digital device sat on the ground in front of him. A pair of wires extended from the device to his ears where he covered them with his hands. He was concentrating so hard, his face looked as if he had an upset stomach.

McKenna waved a hand and snapped a finger to attract his attention. "What have you got, Kelly?"

Kelly made eye contact with McKenna for a moment, then returned to his trance. Ten minutes earlier an Apache helicopter had flown directly over the KSF cabin and dropped a transmitter on the roof of the cabin. A sticky malleable device that would fasten itself to the A-frame with little noise. Kelly's palms pressed even harder to his ears. "Singing, Sir."

"Singing?"

"Yes, Sir. If I'm not mistaken, it's an old Kurdish anthem. Apparently they've heard about the President's press conference and sense victory."

McKenna looked at Nick. "Let's get over there before the party breaks up."

"Sir." A soldier stood under the dipping branch of a mature pine tree. His face was painted so dark that his eyes seemed luminescent. "We have a problem."

"What's that soldier?"

"The place is land-mined with motion detectors, Sir. A quarter mile around the entire complex. There'll be no sneaking up on them."

McKenna scooped up a handful of dirt and slammed it down. "This is getting better all the time."

Nick reached into his duffle bag and came out with a green handle and flipped it a couple of times like a baton.

"What's that?" McKenna asked.

Nick pulled up on the expandable antenna and admired the instrument. "Electronic jamming device. It'll jam any frequencies within a mile radius. We cut off their power, destroy any generators, and jam any other signals. They won't be able to see or hear us coming. Plus, the sentries outside won't be able to communicate with the cabin, or each other." Nick pushed a button on the plastic handle and a green light began to blink. "Let's see if there's still any singing going on over there."

Chapter 36

Nick crouched low in a thicket of woods outside of the KSF cabin. He looked at his watch. They had forty-nine minutes to get inside and disable the detonator. Adrenalin pumped through his veins. Beside him, Matt worked his Glock with his hands while examining the terrain with hawk-like eyes.

Nick looked up at the night sky and felt the stillness of the night. A hundred federal employees surrounded the cabin, yet Nick couldn't hear a twig snap. They'd set off the jamming device and had made easy work of the twenty KSF soldiers patrolling the exterior of the cabin. With silencers and superior night vision, they'd taken their positions and readied to encounter the strength of Kharrazi's force who would certainly be waiting for them inside the building.

But Kharrazi had months, maybe even longer to prepare for this battle. Nick had thrown together a crew of Marines and FBI agents in just a couple of hours. Kharrazi would leave little to chance.

Nick smelled drifting smoke from a distant fireplace. A mile or so away, a father was probably reading bedtime stories to his children, blissfully unaware of the danger that lurked just over the ridge. Nick wondered what it would be like to be so insulated from the harsh realities of the world. While parents tucked in their fragile youngsters, people like Nick were chewing Rolaids by the handful, acutely aware of the threats that awaited them.

Now, Matt was to his left and Jennifer Steele to his right. Both had rifles tight against their cheeks aiming at the two upstairs windows, the only openings on their side of the cabin. Flanking them were a team of Marines. Agents Rutherford and Tolliver were tucked in behind the Marines with Silk. The night covered them like a blanket of moss.

McKenna tapped Nick's elbow and gave a silent thumbs up. Then he nodded toward a Marine Sergeant twenty yards away in the brush and got a nod back. McKenna raised his right hand. He let it hang there while the chain of command responded with their appropriate signals. It seemed he was about to drop his hand when something peculiar occurred.

The upstairs window opened abruptly and a balloon slipped out. Just as quickly the window was shut. Nick heard the flutter of night-vision visors flapping up and down. Unlike the forest they hid in, the cabin stood in a clearing and the moon bathed the walls of the cabin with significant light. That made night vision somewhat superfluous, yet some soldiers still tried both ways.

Matt looked over at McKenna awaiting instructions. He seemed frustrated. McKenna had given orders not to shoot until he gave the signal, but he couldn't have anticipated this. Matt twisted his attention back and forth between McKenna and the window, then to Nick. McKenna appeared unsure, his hand still frozen over his head. Nick saw the balloon moved downward in a gradual angle toward the tree line where they hid.

Nick saw Steele aim her rifle at the balloon.

"Don't," Nick said, louder than he should. He knew that it didn't matter now. Kharrazi obviously knew where they were.

"Call off the attack," Nick said to McKenna.

"What?"

"No time to argue. Call it off."

McKenna waved his hand, signaling a stand down. The balloon slowly drifted toward them. Only it didn't quite drift. It seemed to move in a straight line. The wind was having no effect on the balloon's direction. Nick's stomach twisted into a tight cramp. With the time constraints given them, they had frantically planned for a sudden offensive with little regard for a defense.

"Do you have gas masks?" Nick asked McKenna.

"Sure," McKenna answered, with paralyzed confusion on his face.

It was too late. The balloon only had another twenty feet to go. Maybe ten seconds before it hit the tree line. But where was it headed? Nick calculated the spot where the balloon would first contact the pine trees. He aimed his binoculars to the contact point, scrambling to see something. Anything.

Then, he saw it. A razor sharp spike fastened to the first pine tree it would contact. Maybe fifteen feet up the trunk of the tree. The balloon was now ten feet away from the needle. Nick only imagined what kind of gas the balloon contained. He crouched next to Matt, handed him the binoculars and pointed to the spike. "See that? A spike sticking out of from tree."

Matt squinted through the lenses and said, in a surprised voice, "Yeah."

"See the line going from the spike to the cabin? Thin, like a fishing line."

"Yeah," Matt said, seeming to get it now.

The balloon was five feet from the spike. Ready to burst open with an array of poisonous gas.

Matt didn't wait for Nick to say anything. They tuned into each other's rhythm like a lead and bass guitarist. He aimed his rifle at the narrow gap between the balloon and spike. "You going to catch this thing?"

"I'd better," Nick said, scrambling out from the thicket and into the open field.

"Where are you going?" McKenna said.

But he was ignored. Matt tightened his finger around trigger and yelled, "Cover Nick."

Matt squeezed the trigger and the bullet pierced the night sky with a thunderous scream. It was the only shot he would need. He clipped the wire perfectly. The balloon didn't drop straight down, however. It swung back in an arc away from Nick. He was caught off guard and slipped on pine needles as he shifted his weight from his back foot to his front. From his knees, he could see the balloon angling toward the ground thirty feet away from him. He wasn't going to make it.

Nick was working off adrenalin rather than intellect; he rushed toward the balloon. It was merely five feet from the ground when it came completely free of the fishing line and became vulnerable to the laws of inertia. The external force that maneuvered the balloon was a favorable gust of wind. Nick managed to leap at the ground and cup his hand under the balloon as it gently bounced into his fingertips. He held it above his chest, just inches from his face while he tried to control his erratic breathing.

Nick sensed the clumsiness of the balloon in his fingers. He carefully rolled it and felt dense molecules shifting its mass to the bottom of the balloon while his fingers twitched involuntarily. He sat up and cradled the balloon like an infant. His feet wanted to run for cover, while his hands fought to keep the stretched latex in one piece. He was up on a knee when he heard the creak of a window opening.

Nick stiffened. He could barely hear the muffled cough of a silenced rifle, but he felt the bullet buzz past his face. One second he was staring at the balloon between his hands, the next second he was staring at his open hands. The balloon had burst.

Time stood still. His vision blurred and his feet were planted to the ground like cement posts. He saw Matt screaming at him while firing his rifle over Nick's head. A thousand muzzle flashes sparkled from the tree line as he stood in front of them like a firing squad.

With his eyes almost swollen shut, he ran. He dove through a thin bush and landed on a jagged rock that stabbed his ribcage with the pressure of a barehanded uppercut. He groaned as he rolled behind a wide tree trunk. He couldn't see anything now, but the cacophony of gunfire raged around him like he was in the center of a fireworks display.

Nick wasn't sure if he'd lost consciousness, or if he'd become incapacitated. He reached for his eyes and his hand came back wet. He forced an eye open and saw that his hand was bright red. Blood. Was he hit? He felt something powdery sticking to his fingers.

"Nick." Jennifer Steele's voice sounded muffled. He thought his hearing had been damaged until he saw that Steele wore a gas mask. She quickly wiped his face with a wet towel, gently blotting up whatever was there. McKenna shouted orders over the barrage of bullets splintering up the cabin.

Nick found it hard to breath. His chest heaved up but little air was getting to his lungs. This was how it happened. Depending on the chemical, or germ, Nick had a dwindling amount of time left. "I can't see," he said.

"Hang on." Steele forced his left eyelid open and ran a cotton-tipped applicator around the inside of his left eye. Then she blinded him with a blast from her penlight. She moved his head back and poured a sterile saline solution into his eyes, then poured the remainder on his left hand and exposed an open laceration.

"We're on top of it," a male voice said. Nick wiped his face and peered through a slit of his blinded eye to see the silhouette of a young soldier. He sensed it was the same one who eavesdropped on the KSF cabin just a while earlier. Nick squinted and was able to focus on the young man. He wore a black baseball cap over his buzz cut and an emerald stud on his left earlobe. He had his head down and was working with a black probe that resembled a miniature umbrella. The wide tip had a blue glow to it. He moved with precise little movements back and forth from the probe to his black medical bag. Nick noticed that he worked without a gas mask.

"What are you doing?" Nick blinked constantly trying to improve on the shadows he was coming up with. "I need atropine. Do you have any?"

"Yeah, in my bag."

"Then what are you waiting for?"

The man didn't say anything.

"What's your name?" Nick asked.

"Kelly."

"Kelly," Nick blinked, "are you listening to me, or have the biological weapons impaired your hearing?"

Kelly pushed a button on the probe and the blue light grew more intense in the darkness. Nick sensed soldiers advancing on the cabin behind him.

Kelly smiled. "No, Agent Bracco, my hearing is just fine. And there is no chance that we've been exposed to any biological weapons."

"What are you talking about?" Nick gasped, sucking up thimble-sized pockets of air.

Kelly smiled at his handheld device. "This here is the TIMS 2000. It's the latest in fiber-optic biosensors." He pointed to the tip of the umbrella-shaped tool like a proud father. "You see this probe is covered with antibodies that bind to specific bacteria — anthrax and the like — then the system pipes light from a laser diode through the fiber probe. It turns orange, we're in a heap of trouble." He held the probe closer to Nick. It glowed with a deep purple mist. "You can see that we have a strong negative result. Virtually no chance for a false negative. If there were any biological agents within a hundred yards of this spot, this thing would be a sparkling shade of orange."

Nick tried to get to his elbows, but a jolt of pain ripped through his chest. His ribcage pinched every time he took a breath. Steele was tightening a thin butterfly bandage around his index finger to close up the laceration. "What about chemicals?" Nick asked.

Kelly nodded. He reached over to his right and returned with a flat plastic tray that had ridges symmetrically etched into the face. An LED display beamed a numerical value across the screen. It read zero. He showed it to Nick. "Primary Ion Detector," he said, as if he were handing him something as simple as a screwdriver.

Nick looked up at him. He was confused and Kelly seemed to sense it. He traced a penlight over Nick's eyes and said, casually. "It hasn't detected anything pernicious. Plus, if you were exposed to any nerve agents, you'd have tiny, little pupils. Your pupils are quite large, despite constant attacks from our penlights. If it were a blister agent, you'd have obvious lesions. And if it were a choking agent, you'd be, well . . . choking."

The more Nick listened to Kelly, the more confused he got. He could hear McKenna ordering his troops to teargas the windows and moments later the whoosh of the propelled canisters flung upward.

"Then what the fuck was in that balloon?" Nick asked.

"That's the question, isn't it?" Kelly grinned.

Nick's breathing had slowed considerably. His anxiety lowered itself to a level he could control.

Kelly took the tip of his pinkie, licked it, then dabbed it into the inner part of the busted balloon. He stuck his tongue out and, with sharp precision, lightly touched his pinkie. He methodically moved his tongue around the inside of his mouth, then looked skyward and appeared in deep thought.

Steele removed her mask and she and Nick took time to look at each other.

"Well?" Nick asked, after he waited almost a full minute for Kelly to contemplate his taste test.

"If I were to guess," Kelly said, then took a swig of water from his canteen and wiped his mouth with his sleeve. "I would say mustard."

"Mustard gas?" Nick said, appalled at the cavalier manner the man investigated an unknown substance.

"No. More like dry mustard."

"Dry mustard?" Jennifer Steele asked. "Why in the world would they put dry mustard in a balloon, send it down a wire, then shoot it with a rifle? It's a complete waste of time."

Nick looked at his watch. Thirty-nine minutes before the White House missiles ignited. They'd wasted ten minutes dealing with the damn balloon. Nick knew exactly what Kharrazi was doing with those precious minutes.

He pulled out the satellite photos taken of the cabin just before sunset. He forced himself to sit up and the grimace he made seemed to startle Steele.

"Please," she said, holding him upright to prevent him from toppling over. "You need to stay still. You could have broken some ribs."

In between short, well-paced breaths, Nick said, "There's not much that could be done for that anyway." He worked his way to his knees and his peripheral vision began to clear up. Matt was only a few yards away, crouched down, providing cover for the assault on the cabin. It didn't seem as if there was much resistance left. Matt was close enough to hear everything that Nick and Kelly had discussed. He looked at Nick and said, "You got lucky, partner."

Nick spit powder from his mouth. He realized that it tasted like mustard. "Are they inside yet?"

Matt peered into the magnified scope of his rifle. With his cheek clenched up against the butt of his rifle, he said, "Yes."

"You know Kharrazi's gone already, don't you?" Nick said.

In the corner of his eye, Nick saw Kelly swivel his head and take in the muzzle flashes from the wooded terrain surrounding the cabin. Nearby, McKenna barked orders like a born leader. McKenna was behind him now and Nick suspected he was close to the cabin.

"I think that dry mustard is affecting your judgment, Agent Bracco," Kelly said. "There's nobody escaping from that cabin. Not tonight."

Nick looked at Matt and saw his partner make a scooping gesture with his left hand without removing his right eye from the scope. Both of them thought the same thing. They'd seen the tunnel that Kharrazi had built in the basement of the safe house back in Las Vegas.

Nick returned his attention to the satellite photos. Steele handed him a miniature single-lens microscope with an illuminator tip. He smoothed out a patch of dirt and lay the photo on the ground. He pressed his eye into the lens and searched a particular distance around the perimeter of the cabin. It took a couple of passes, but he found what he was looking for. It was just a glint. Normally it wouldn't be enough to warrant a second glance. But under the scrutiny of the powerful lens, Nick had discovered the unmistakable reflection of a mirror. It winked out from the middle of a large bush. Once Nick examined the shrub itself, he realized that it didn't have the symmetrical canopy that nature would provide a mountain bush of its type. It seemed to be a manmade covering.

Surmising how Kharrazi was going to escape only complicated matters. The next thirty minutes had to be dedicated to finding and disarming the detonator. Nick's vendetta with Kharrazi had to be put aside for now. They didn't have the resources to mess with him.

Nick tried to get to his knees and stopped for a quick breath.

"You know," Steele said, "you could puncture a lung if you aren't careful."

With every intake of air, Nick worked to increase his capacity. He got greedy with one breath and his lungs rejected it immediately. His entire chest stung as he coughed a short, staccato cough.

Matt grabbed his arm. "Are you okay? McKenna's inside. They've got the basement secure. He's asking for you."

The shooting subsided. Nick muscled his way to his feet, careful to stay behind a wide tree trunk. "What's the status?" he asked.

"There's a few tough ones inside, digging in, a handful maybe. The basement is clear, however, and they need our help."

"Kharrazi?"

Matt shook his head.

Nick dusted himself off and saw Rutherford, Tolliver, Downing, Steele and Silk gather around them. Smoke billowed from the two upstairs windows, illuminated by the moonlight. A half-dozen Marines were blending in with the forest, their machine guns impatiently waiting for any sign of enemy activity. There was a clear path to the basement doors, which yawned open like a bible on a priest's lectern. Nick caught the eye of one of the Marines and gestured for cover. The Marine nodded.

Nick led the way to the edge of the tree line. When he pulled the 9mm from his holster, his ribcage felt like he'd just taken an injection from a long hypodermic needle. He doubled over for a moment causing Steele to ask him if he should stay put. Nick thought about how close he was to Kharrazi's headquarters, how much information they would eventually garner from this raid. With his hands on his knees he looked across the open pathway to the basement doors just thirty feet away. He knew it was the portal to his destiny. There was still time to stop the missiles. They could still find Kharrazi. He came up to force a quick breath and said, "Let's go."

Chapter 37

Nick and Matt ran down the cement stairs to the cellar, followed by the rest of the team. Silk was a few steps behind them, his revolver by his side. Gunfire on the opposite side of the cabin caused them all to duck as they hit the basement floor.

The room was musty from lack of circulation. Nick, on all fours, looked up to see McKenna standing in a darkened corner with Kelly chiseling something on the wall. They were the only two in the room besides Nick's crew. A solitary wooden desk and fabric sofa were the only pieces of furniture in the unfinished basement. When Nick saw the stacks of newsmagazines behind the desk, he knew it was Kharrazi's lair. The chair behind the desk was pushed in. It didn't appear that Kharrazi was in any rush to leave.

McKenna pointed to the adjacent room with his machine gun. "Their communications room," he said. "Probably the nerve center of the entire operation."

Nick peered into the next room where Marines patrolled the area. He could see TV screens and sophisticated radio equipment layered on top of each other. Shelves were stacked with spools of wire and canisters of what Nick assumed were explosives.

Nick nodded at McKenna, who watched Kelly creating sparks against the cement wall.

"What are you doing?" Nick asked.

"You said the detonator would be down here. We've gone through most of the basement. My guess is that baby's inside this wall safe."

Nick rushed over and grabbed the chisel from Kelly's hand. Kelly looked to McKenna for instructions.

"What are you doing, Bracco?" McKenna asked.

Nick stared at Kelly, looking straight through him and thinking like a chess player, four moves ahead. There was a long silence and just when McKenna was about to speak, Nick said, "There's no time for this."

"If you're suggesting we use explosives," Kelly said, "I think there's a good chance that will set off the detonator."

"I know," Nick said.

McKenna looked at his watch and bristled, "Listen, Agent

Bracco, we have exactly thirty-five minutes to get inside this safe and try to diffuse this thing. You're wasting valuable time."

Nick made eye contact with Silk and nodded. Everyone watched as Silk smiled and rolled up his sleeves. "I thought you'd never ask," Silk said.

Kelly backed away as Silk cracked his knuckles and wiggled his fingers like a concert pianist about to begin his sonata. He leaned close to the safe door and let out a mock laugh, "Shit, a Haussman 8000. It's older than my grandfather. I used to wind these suckers open when I was just a—" he stopped when he realized everyone was staring at him. He looked at Nick. "Should be less than two minutes."

McKenna said, "What the—"

Nick put his finger to his lips and everyone watched quietly as Silk gleefully twisted the knob back and forth with practiced skill. After a minute, there was a click and Silk broke into an all out smile. He pulled down on the handle and opened the safe door.

McKenna shook his head in disgust. "Not exactly by the book."

When the door of the safe swung open, Nick's mouth went dry. In the tunnel-like opening, a red digital timer beamed its fatal number. The time read 33:18 and diligently worked its way toward zero. The timer was attached to a band of multicolored wires that wound its way to a small metal box, then to something that looked like a miniature car battery.

"Shit," McKenna murmured.

Kelly bent over and spread open his black bag. Everyone gave him room as he pulled out a high-beam flashlight to illuminate the interior of the safe.

Nick motioned to Carl Rutherford to take a look. Rutherford was the team's bomb expert and was the only one in the room who knew more about bombs than Nick. Kelly sensed his presence and moved slightly, allowing Rutherford to inspect the device with him. Everyone in the room jumped when Rutherford clicked open the metal box. It squeaked as it swung up and Kelly and Rutherford seemed to generate a mutual concern over the discovery inside.

"I don't see the transmitter," Kelly said. "How is this thing sending its signal across the continent?"

Rutherford beamed the flashlight into the back of the safe. He pointed to a clear plastic line that seemed to disappear through a narrow opening in the back corner. "I'm guessing it's a wireless system."

Nick felt his phone vibrate in his pocket. He looked down and saw that it was Walt Jackson. He looked at his watch and realized that the President was due for his press conference in less than two minutes.

"I've got the President on conference call with us, Nick. What have you got?"

Nick searched for the proper words. He knew Merrick would be making a colossal mistake if he gave in to Kharrazi's demands. Nick also knew that in the next thirty minutes, he was the only person on the planet who could prevent that from happening.

"Mr. President, Sir," Nick said.

His crew stood up straight and circled around him. He felt the weight of their stares. Matt stood next to Steele, holding her hand. All of them seemed anxious to hear Nick's exchange.

"I don't like the sound of that greeting, Nick," President Merrick spoke with tension thick in his voice.

Nick saw a Marine enter Kharrazi's private quarters from the communications room and brief McKenna on the status of the cabin. Nick pulled his ear from the phone to overhear the Marine tell McKenna the cabin was completely secure. All KSF soldiers were either dead or captured. No Kharrazi.

"Nick," Walt said. "Are you there? We're holding up this press conference for your report. The President feels the only option is the withdrawal of troops from Turkey."

Kelly and Rutherford seemed to be in complete agreement on the assessment of the detonator. They turned to Nick and waited for him to get off the phone.

"Hold on," Nick said, and covered the tiny mouthpiece with his thumb. He looked at Rutherford, who was shaking his head.

"We're screwed," Rutherford said, in exactly the language Nick expected from him. "It's a Rashid special." He turned and pointed to the metal box between the battery and the timer. "There's a surge monitor. If we disconnect any of the wires from the battery that support the detonator—" Rutherford flipped open his fingers in an explosive manner. "Auto destruct. The missiles fire immediately."

"Then Kharrazi had no way of ever stopping the detonation, even if the President acquiesced?" Nick said.

Rutherford shrugged and reached into the safe to show Nick something. Nick heard Walt's voice booming from the earpiece of his phone, "Nick! Answer me!"

Rutherford held up a square plastic board with at least twenty pegs that appeared to look like switches of some sort. It was connected to the other three devices with the same wires, but was hidden behind them. Kelly handed him a small forceps allowing Rutherford to hold the board with his hand aside, giving Nick a better view.

"What is it?" Nick asked.

"Twenty-four dummy switches and one kill button," Rutherford said. "I'm sure only Kharrazi knows which button would shut the device off. The other twenty-four simply detonate it early."

"Nick!" Walt's voice gained in volume and pitch.

Nick stared at Rutherford and put the phone to his ear. "I'm here, Sir."

"Damn it, Nick, what the hell's going on over there? The President has a nation waiting for him."

"Hold on, Sir," Nick put the phone down again and looked at Rutherford. "But Kharrazi's not here, so he can't disarm it."

Rutherford nodded. "Like I said, we're screwed."

Nick brought the phone to his ear just in time to hear Walt muttering his name.

"Yes, Sir. I understand, Sir. I have the information you're looking for." Nick stamped his thumb over the mouthpiece again and pulled the phone down. "What about draining the battery?" Nick asked Rutherford. "Can't you drain its power slowly without creating any surge in energy loss?"

Rutherford turned to Kelly to discuss the possibility. As they exchanged headshakes and discouraging murmurs, Nick returned the phone to his ear. He interrupted a barrage of cursing so harsh that Nick could actually see Walt Jackson's face twisted with aggravation. "I'm here, Sir. I was just getting a last minute brief."

"You leave this phone again and I swear I'll—"

"Sir," Nick interrupted. "There's no need for any news conference. At least not one that announces any withdrawal."

There was a pause. Nick found it hard not to stare at the timer. Thirty-two minutes.

Finally, Nick heard the dejected voice of President Merrick. "Why do you say that, Nick?"

"Because, Sir . . ." Nick thought carefully about his words. Rutherford made eye contact with Nick and shook his head with disheartened expression. "I'm looking at the detonator right now—"

"You found the detonator!" Jackson's and Merrick's voices collided across the airwaves.

"Yes," Nick said. "We're working on it right now."

"So, you'll be able to disarm the thing then?" Merrick sounded desperate.

Nick watched Rutherford's grim face grow increasingly bleaker. Rutherford shook his head as if he could hear their question from across the room. Nick's stomach tightened and his jaw clenched shut. He tried to open his mouth, but it locked up on him.

"Nick?" Walt said.

Nick couldn't understand what was happening, but he became nauseous without an opening to vomit through. He thought he might have to vomit through his nose, when he turned from the group and slowly shuffled into the communications room. Matt trailed him with a suspicious look in his eye. Nick settled onto a round stool next to a tall wooden cabinet. Matt paced in a semicircle in front of Nick, half the time scrutinizing his partner's physical appearance, the other half making sure no one approached them.

Nick heard Walt's faint voice through the receiver, like background music in an elevator. He grasped the phone in a claw grip and felt the words tumble out of his mouth before he could realize their gravity. "Yes, Sir. We can disarm the detonator."

There was silence. On the phone, and all around him, Nick heard nothing. Matt stared at him, expressionless.

"Nick," Walt said tentatively. "Are you certain?"

A pause while Nick reasoned with his struggling psyche. If the President gave in to Kharrazi, it would only be a matter of time before every terrorist on the globe was taking pot shots at America. Nick couldn't afford to see that happen. His thoughts seemed to meander into a dim future, then surprisingly they resurfaced on the image of the small battery powering the detonator.

"Yes, Sir, I'm certain," Nick said, feeling empowered somehow with the deceit. "The missiles will not be firing tonight, Mr. President, or any night for that matter. Tell the nation, we're on the verge of capturing Kemel Kharrazi and putting an end to all of this madness."

More silence. Nick saw astonishment sweep over Matt's face.

"Nick?" Walt said. "Are you serious? You have Kharrazi?"

Nick wiped his brow and came back with moisture. At first he thought it was nerves, but it was more than that. It was as if he'd broken a fever; a ball and chain had been lifted from his subconscious. He was blurting fabrications like a politician. "He's within our grasp. He won't make it until morning."

Merrick's voice seemed to raise an excited octave. "Agent Bracco, I'm trusting you. I'm basing my decision solely on your report. Are you certain you can disarm the detonator?"

"Yes, Sir."

"And you're positive you'll have Kharrazi in custody tonight?"

Nick realized he'd passed the point of no return. He may end up doing prison time or spend the rest of his life bagging groceries, but he'd be damned if he was going to allow Kemel Kharrazi to terrorize America into submission.

"Yes, Sir," Nick said.

"When you get back to Washington, I want to see you personally. We'll set up a dinner for you and your wife up here at the White House. That sound all right with you?"

Nick's hands trembled. "That'll be just fine, Sir."

Nick clicked off the phone and found Matt looking incredulous. "You just lied to the President of the United States?"

Nick looked down at the cell phone in his hand like it was a fired pistol.

Matt stared.

Nick wiped his clammy hands on his pants. "Um, it seems that we have work to do."

Matt turned toward Kharrazi's private quarters where Kelly and Rutherford were using nervous energy to appear productive. He gazed up the stairs that led to the main cabin where Kharrazi had certainly escaped.

"That's great, Nick," Matt said. "But in less than thirty minutes the White House is going to explode and Kemel Kharrazi will still be on the loose. Have you considered your future thirty-one minutes from now? Or have you thought that far ahead?"

Nick shook his head. "If I didn't know you so well I'd almost believe you didn't trust me anymore."

Matt didn't say anything, but his expression changed. He looked at Nick with a shrewd smile. "You know where Kharrazi is?"

"I have an idea."

"You're going to find him and convince him to tell you which is the kill switch?"

Nick shrugged. "I don't think there's time for that."

Over Matt's shoulder, Nick saw Silk lurking nonchalantly.

Matt nodded toward the adjacent room. "Then how are you going to stop that thing from detonating?"

Nick pointed to a roll of thick black wire that curled around an enormous spool the size of a golf cart tire sitting on the shelf next to them. "Take that into the other room and start cutting it up into forty-foot sections."

Matt only hesitated for a second, then he hefted the spool onto his shoulder and dutifully headed toward the room. He looked over his shoulder as he went. "You'll tell me why eventually, right?"

With that started, Nick found McKenna at the base of the stairs exchanging words with another Marine. He gave Nick a steely glare when he approached.

"We have three KSF prisoners upstairs," McKenna said. "You want to speak with any of them? Maybe get some ideas about that switchboard in there?"

Nick held up his hand. "Not right now. I need you to radio DPS and have them divert all vehicles down this private driveway. Have a couple of your men waiting outside the basement and instruct the cars to park facing the basement doors. As close as possible."

McKenna started to ask a question, but Nick quickly cut him off. "Please, Sergeant, we don't have time to discuss this. I promise a full explanation."

McKenna paused. Staring at Nick, he pushed the button on the radio clipped to his shirt pocket and gave the orders Nick requested. When he was done, he said, "Does Kelly know about this?"

Before Nick could respond he heard Kelly's voice from over his shoulder. "Do I know about what? And what's going on with all those wires in there?"

Nick took a frustrated breath and addressed both of them, "DPS is diverting traffic to the basement doors. We'll attach one end of the wires to the headlights of the cars and the other end to the detonator's battery. One by one so we don't cause a sudden voltage surge. The battery was never meant to do anything but power that small detonator, so it's undersized and vulnerable. If we hustle we could drain it before the deadline and render it powerless to detonate those missiles."

McKenna looked to Kelly for his reaction. Kelly stood motionless for a moment, seeming to let the idea run around in his head. Finally, he arched an eyebrow. "It might work."

Kelly hurried to the back room and Nick followed. When they got there, Kelly took over the operation, explaining to Rutherford and the others as he went.

Silk grabbed Nick by the elbow and pulled him aside. "I overheard your conversation with Matt. You think you know where Kharrazi is?"

"This isn't the time."

"What are you talking about? This is exactly the time. You think I'm here for the scenery?" Silk glanced over his shoulder, then back to Nick. "We're the ones who got you here. Without our information none of this is even happening." He placed a fist over his heart. "You promised me a crack at this guy, Nicky. Don't back away from that."

Nick looked at his childhood friend and thought of the consequences. He wasn't worried about himself, this was his last mission as a special agent. His career with the FBI was certain to end that night. Silk took the silence as a sign of agreement.

"Nicky?" Silk said. "You don't trust me?"

Nick stared at Silk. "He's too dangerous. I can't let you do it."

Silk narrowed his eyes. "I'm not exactly chopped liver over here."

Nick looked at his watch and thought about the ability to stop the detonator and get Kharrazi at the same time. Silk was an unbelievable asset to leave on the sidelines. He brought Silk into a corner of the communications room and smoothed out a copy of the satellite photos on a wooden end table. He looked at the man he had grown up with in the streets of Baltimore and sighed. "He's crafty, Silk, and without the usual thug mentality. He'll surprise you."

"Enough already."

Nick nodded. "Just do me a favor. Don't play with him. Put him down hard and fast. Capisce?"

Silk smiled at Nick's perfect Sicilian dialect.

Nick showed Silk where he would find Kharrazi on the photo. He pointed out the glint from the mirror that he suspected was from a car or truck covered by branches. Nick gave him a compass and one last warning. "Be careful. He's probably waiting until he's certain he's alone before he approaches the area."

Silk patted Nick's cheek. "Don't worry, Boobala. Old Silk has a few tricks of his own. Besides, he started this whole thing by having the Capellis killed. Not to mention what he done to your family." He turned to leave, then stopped. "Listen, Nicky, you gotta promise me one thing."

"Anything."

"I screw up, you gotta track this guy down and finish him off for me."

Nick didn't say anything. He'd never heard Silk be anything but cocky.

Silk gently punched Nick's shoulder, then left with a strut in his step.

But something gnawed at Nick deep inside. For the first time since he'd known Silk, he was actually concerned for his safety.

Chapter 38

Kemel Kharrazi was seething. His greatest moment as the KSF leader and he would be forced to hear about President Merrick's withdrawal speech after the fact. He had hoped to be in his private quarters enjoying cheese and grapes while Merrick bowed to his political prowess in front of a worldwide audience.

Nick Bracco had been clever and was probably the best the FBI had to offer, but he was always one step behind. It didn't prevent Kharrazi from grasping a handful of dirt and slowly grinding it around in his fist.

Kharrazi threw the dirt to the ground and pushed a button on his watch, which illuminated the dial in the dark. In twenty minutes the White House would explode. Merrick wouldn't dare change his mind about the troops, because the next threat Kharrazi made would be so severe, the American public wouldn't even allow the words to leave their lips. Nuclear bomb. Those two words were all he need use and America would hand over the deed to their nation.

Kharrazi sat up, his back against the base of a hill, surrounded by a thicket of bushes. He scrutinized the landscape under the nearly full moon. Patience. Time was on his side now. The vehicle he'd hidden was in perfect position to escape, yet he would take no chances. He could afford to wait until he was certain of his solitude.

Kharrazi had spent many hours familiarizing himself with the countryside. He'd walked every inch of the landscape and even spent time maneuvering with a blindfold. He was ready for anything and had no less than three escape plans prepared for the occasion.

Kharrazi thought he saw movement in the shadows. He used his field glasses to sweep the area, then kept his focus trained on a specific point in the woods and hoped he had guessed the spot correctly. His patience paid off.

Through his field glasses he saw a figure glide from behind a tree and disappear behind a larger tree trunk. He came from the west so Kharrazi could hear him much easier than if he'd traveled from downwind. The man had also crept through the low spots of the terrain assuring himself of trekking through water, mud and debris. A city dweller, Kharrazi thought, not considering the advantage of higher ground. Still, the man carried himself with a self-assured swagger as he meandered through the trees.

Kharrazi silently trained his Beretta on the man as he crept left to right across Kharrazi's position. It took a few minutes, but Kharrazi could see the man's face now; he was disappointed that it wasn't Bracco. This man was tall and athletic and his head moved smoothly from side to side. Kharrazi slowly screwed the silencer onto his Beretta. He'd lose accuracy with the silencer, but the man was heading close enough where it wouldn't matter.

The man snapped a twig with his foot and he instinctually froze. Kharrazi used the opportunity to fire a shot into his leg. The bullet spit from the Beretta and immediately the man dropped to the ground. Kharrazi leapt from the bush like a leopard and quickly seized the man's fallen gun before he could retrieve it from a bed of pine needles. He stood over his prey and watched with great pleasure as the man writhed in pain from the gunshot wound to his thigh.

The moon was over Kharrazi's shoulder and he could see the man's face clearly, fighting to maintain his composure.

"How did you find me?" Kharrazi said.

The man either didn't want to give Kharrazi the satisfaction of seeing him squirm or he was a tough foe. He ignored his leg and struggled to get to his feet. Kharrazi shoved him back down with his foot and heard the thud as the man was obviously caught off guard. This didn't deter the man and he made another attempt to get to his feet. This time Kharrazi allowed him.

When he reached his full height, the man brushed himself off and said, "You're a short little fuck, aren't you?"

The comment baffled Kharrazi. This man was certainly not an FBI agent.

"Who are you?" Kharrazi asked.

The man smiled through the pain of his gunshot wound. "I'm Silk. I'm here to kill you."

"Who sent you?"

The man gestured with his hands as he spoke. "A fella by the name of Nick Bracco. Apparently you two have some history."

"Are you alone?"

"What, I look like I need help here?"

Kharrazi looked around to see if there was anyone else. "You are friends with Mr. Bracco?"

"Since we was thirteen. I run around with his cousin, Tommy."

Kharrazi put the names together in his head. Suddenly, he recognized the man from the camera he'd used to spy on the sheriff's office. This man was truly a friend of Nick Bracco. "Good," Kharrazi smiled. He was finally going to exact revenge for Rashid's death.

"But I got other reasons to be here."

"You do?"

"Yeah. Apparently, some of your thugs whacked a family that I was very close to."

"That's too bad," Kharrazi said flatly.

"Yeah, well I could tell it really chokes you up."

"They deserved to die."

"How you figure that?"

"According to the polls, seventy-eight percent of Americans supported the use of troops in Turkey. I am going to have to assume they fit into this category."

The man's eyes narrowed, "The fuck's that got to do with the price of tea in China?"

"I only wish I had the time to explain," Kharrazi said, lifting his Beretta.

The man shrugged, "So, how do you want to do this? You're gonna put the gun down, aren't you? You know, fight like a man."

Kharrazi wondered what kind of idiot he was dealing with. "You came out here by yourself to try and kill me?"

"That was the plan. You think I should have thought things through a little better? I mean you being so difficult about the gun and all."

Kharrazi's patience wore thin. "You are a very stupid man."

"Yeah, I know. So how do you want me to kill you?"

Kharrazi pointed the Beretta at Silk's chest, "You are already beginning to bore me to death."

The man laughed. "Hey, that's a good one, Shorty." Then, he seemed to turn serious. "Of course someone your height, I guess a gun is mandatory, isn't it?"

Kharrazi hesitated at the insult and was startled to see the man use the moment to rush toward him with a look of determination on his face. Kharrazi actually backpedaled as he quickly fired shots with his automatic, including one in the neck and one to the head. Still the man kept coming into the onslaught until his bullet-ridden body limply wrapped itself around Kharrazi's frame like a drowning man.

As his life rapidly slipped away, the man seemed to be frisking Kharrazi's body; he groped Kharrazi's torso until one hand weakly found the knife tucked inside his ankle holster. Fighting until the bitter end, Kharrazi thought.

Kharrazi held the Beretta inches above the man's head, but didn't feel the need to waste another bullet.

It sounded like the man said, "See you soon," as he slipped down Kharrazi's legs and crumpled to the ground by his feet.

Kharrazi stood there in the still night air amazed at the man's tenacity. He checked the man's hands to find them empty. He felt for a pulse and found none. Kharrazi grinned at the corpse. "You were a brave soldier, Mr. Silk. Almost as brave as Rashid Baser."

* * *

The tension inside of the four cement walls was palpable. The timer ruthlessly beamed its diminishing red numbers, unfazed by the frenzy of Marines and FBI agents running up and down the cracked stairs with wires dangling from every appendage.

Kelly stripped the insulation from the tip of the wires and handed them individually to Rutherford at a rate of two a minute. Carl Rutherford was drenched with sweat even though the cool night air fed steady breezes through the open basement doors. He quivered slightly as he wrapped each wire around the positive pole protruding from the top of the small battery. A chorus of headlights poured into the basement from the parked cars just outside of Kharrazi's private quarters. Each time Rutherford attached a wire, a new set of headlights came to life along with a hesitant flicker from the rest of the group.

Nick and Matt found themselves splitting their attention between Rutherford and the small TV set atop a shaky wooden table against the wall. The monitor showed an empty podium with the Presidential Seal attached. Newscasters interviewed supposed terrorist experts and retired generals as the nation impatiently awaited President Merrick's press conference.

"Why is it," one female newscaster asked, "that there isn't a consensus on the subject of this speech?"

An unseen political pundit replied, "Well, this is still Washington, Susan, and at this late hour, so close to the White House missile deadline . . . I'm sure the President is making certain that every option is explored before making any decisions. There's even some speculation that he is negotiating right now with Kemel Kharrazi himself trying to find a way out of this catastrophic event. Although that has not been confirmed."

Nick rolled his eyes. "Good thing they have specialists available, otherwise we could be misinformed."

A bead of sweat dripped from Carl Rutherford's nose as the timer passed the five-minute mark. Nick wondered if the brightness of the LED display should be fading while the battery drained. Since the display didn't seem to lose any intensity, he didn't ask. He was afraid of the answer.

"Hey, Carl," Matt said, reading Nick's mind. "Maybe you should speed it up a little. Those headlights still seem pretty strong."

Rutherford gave him a dirty look, then nodded to Kelly to quicken the pace.

McKenna came in with a stranglehold on a thin man, his arm twisted behind his back causing a painful expression. The man wore khaki fatigues and made no eye contact as McKenna shoved him into the room toward Nick.

"You know this asshole?" McKenna said, pulling up on the man's contorted arm.

"Hasan Bozlak," Matt said. "Yeah, we know him."

McKenna grasped a handful of hair and snapped Hasan's head back. "Why don't you see if he knows anything? He doesn't seem to understand English."

In plain English, Nick said, "Where is it, Hasan?"

Hasan stared up at the ceiling. McKenna looked confused.

"The tunnel," Matt said. "Where?"

This got Hasan to shoot a glance at the wall behind Kharrazi's desk. It was ephemeral, and if Nick weren't looking for it, it would have easily gone unnoticed. It was the only wall in the room with any covering. Nick slammed his hand up against the wood paneling and banged around until he found the dead spot. He motioned to a Marine who hammered the butt of his M-4 into the composite panel and quickly broke through. Matt peeled back the flimsy section exposing the dark opening of a tunnel. A couple of Marines looked at Nick expectantly.

"Don't," he said. "It'll be full of traps and probably explosives." Nick faced Hasan. "How long has he been gone?"

Hasan grimaced as McKenna continued the pressure on his arm. Nick could hear the ligaments pop in the soldier's elbow.

"Maybe he knows about the traps in the tunnel," McKenna said. "No," Matt said. "He wouldn't know. The traps were set for him more than they were us."

McKenna looked at the two FBI agents with disdain. Information was the FBI's main currency and McKenna seemed uncomfortable converting his military energy into reconnaissance. He tightened his hold on Hasan and said, "So what do you want with this guy?"

"Leave him with the others," Nick said. "He's already given us more information than we could ask for."

"Under a minute," someone said. And the room became still.

Rutherford and Kelly were the only ones moving. Everyone else just stared at the timer, their peripheral vision taking in the presidential podium. Still vacant.

Suddenly the camera switched to an outside shot of the White House. In the bottom right of the screen a timer counted down to midnight. Nick could practically see network executives rubbing their hands together with glee over the impending disaster. He felt like a spectator at a NASCAR race just after a severe oil spill. He found it hard to believe anything less than a catastrophe could occur.

Outside, the car lights flickered.

"Hey, Carl," Matt said. "How much voltage does it take to set off that detonator?"

Rutherford furiously worked the wires with a renewed sense of urgency. "A volt, maybe two."

Kelly stood next to Rutherford with a handful of primed wires; his neck craned toward the open basement doors, exasperation etched on his face.

"Thirty seconds," the same voice said.

"Don't you have a voltage meter, Kelly?" Matt asked.

"Huh? Oh, yeah," Kelly said, stammering to gather his thoughts. He reached into his black bag, then turned up to Matt. "You really want to know?"

Matt looked at Nick.

Nick shook his head. "No point."

"Fifteen seconds."

Matt snapped, "Shut the fuck up. We can see the timer."

The last ten seconds seemed to pass in slow motion. The intensity of the car headlights seemed worn down, but the timer appeared unfazed by the effort.

With five seconds remaining, Rutherford grabbed a handful of wires and desperately jammed the entire mess up against the battery pole.

Jennifer Steele found her way next to Matt and clutched his hand.

McKenna still had a stranglehold on Hasan Bozlak, yet Hasan's face was now serene.

In the stillness of the basement, Nick noticed the TV journalists had learned something from sports announcers when an astonishing event was about to occur. They were completely silent. This gave the room a muted feel. It seemed as if the entire world was now holding its breath.

Kelly dropped his head in anguish.

Nick fixated on the red numbers tumbling toward the inevitable.

When the number three flashed it appeared to stutter. Nick couldn't be certain, but it seemed to take a moment before the number two hiccupped to life.

Steele gasped as the number two hung there, suspended in time. Three seconds had passed, four seconds, five seconds, and yet the number two remained frozen. Its neon edges crackled with an ominous foreshadow. Rutherford seemed paralyzed. He held the handful of wires against the batteries pole, his mouth pursed shut, his nostrils sucking in air.

Then, an eerie darkness fell over the room. The TV and the lamp on the desk became the only sources of light. The stream of headlights had extinguished in unison, leaving everyone in shadows. Nick stared at the dim number two for an exhaustive minute of pure agony until it too finally surrendered to the darkness, its neon tracing forever etched into Nick's brain like a phantom pain.

"Two seconds," someone mocked.

A nervous chuckle.

A stifled snicker.

Jennifer Steele giggled.

Nick would always remember Matt's face still staring down at the impotent timer, not ready to pronounce it dead. When their eyes finally met, Matt had Steele tucked into his shoulder for a relief cry. He winked at Nick.

A smattering of applause began to bubble into a cheer. Starting as a whisper the Marines began to chant, "USA . . . USA." In only seconds the entire basement swelled into a cry that would make an Olympic Stadium jealous. "USA! USA!"

Carl Rutherford was a statue. His hand was still frozen to the battery like he had his finger in the hole of a dike.

Nick waved at Rutherford. "It's okay, Carl," he yelled over the din. "It's over."

Rutherford slid to the floor. His entire body sagged from the release of tension.

Suddenly, Nick felt his phone vibrate in his pocket. He stepped into the adjacent room to escape the noise. A smile broadened his face as he anticipated President Merrick calling to congratulate him.

He pushed the button and put the phone to his ear, "Bracco."

The voice that came back at him seared a hole in his gut as if he'd swallowed a capful of pure acid.

"Remember me?" Kemel Kharrazi said.

Chapter 39

The cheering and excitement of the night spilled into the communications room where Nick stood alone, his right hand pressed to his ear, straining to hear the phone. Kharrazi must have heard the commotion.

"There is some reason for enthusiasm?" Kharrazi said.

There was a pause while Nick considered where Kharrazi was calling from. He heard the sound of a car engine, something large, like a pickup truck. Kharrazi was on the move as he spoke. He hadn't heard the news about the detonator though and this little piece of knowledge gave Nick the slightest advantage.

"The guys are throwing a little party," Nick said. "Why don't you stop by and I'll buy you a drink?"

"What is there to celebrate?"

"It's Friday night."

Kharrazi didn't seem to appreciate the coyness. There was silence while they played cat and mouse. Nick relished the quiet, but every minute that passed put more distance between him and Kharrazi. He shut his eyes tight and listened carefully, using all of his skills to garner any clue as to the terrorist's location. He could hear the suspension of the vehicle jostle continuously, suggesting that Kharrazi was not driving on a paved road.

Kharrazi must have seen little benefit with the one-sided discussion. "I just called to say goodbye. I'm sorry I missed your little invasion."

"The White House is still standing," Nick said, trying to prolong the conversation.

There was a pause while Kharrazi dealt with the blow. "That is the reason for all the noise?"

"Yes."

Kharrazi was quiet. He was probably calculating exactly how overdue the missiles were.

"We disarmed the detonater," Nick informed him. "There will be no fireworks tonight."

"Do not confuse this fact with success, Mr. Bracco. Americans will still die tonight. The attacks are not finished. And neither am I."

"Uh huh."

"We are still very much alive and well."

"Who are you kidding, Kemel? Our count has your little group of terrorists down to sixteen. Tansu is dead and we have Hasan. What's left are bottom-of-the barrel flunkies. Without you to guide them, their biggest accomplishment will include letting air out of tires and pouring sugar in gas tanks."

"What makes you think I won't be there to guide them?"

"Because I'm going to find you first."

"Mr. Bracco, such bravado for a desperate man. You sound like another gentleman I met tonight. His name was Silk."

Nick's eyes popped open. With everything that had happened, he'd lost track of Silk. If Kharrazi was still alive, that only meant one thing.

"He cried for mercy like a little baby," Kharrazi beamed. "Groveled right up until his last breath. Of course, I made certain he suffered greatly."

Nick felt bile surge from his stomach. He swallowed several times to maintain control.

"I thought you would come yourself," Kharrazi said, "but perhaps you don't have the constitution for such a confrontation."

Nick had sent Silk on a suicide mission and Kharrazi was going to layer the guilt like a third coat of paint. He'd exposed a nerve that Nick knew would always remain raw. Nick strangled the phone so tight, his fingers were cramping. "I'm going to kill you, you son of a bitch." Nick said. "I'm going to find you and rip your heart out of your chest."

"There, there, Mr Bracco. I think you're losing your temper."

Nick's throat was tightening up so much it was hard for him to take a normal breath.

Kharrazi's voice came smiling over the airwaves, "This is just the beginning, Mr. Bracco. You and your family will never be safe again. I'll make it my eternal quest."

And right there Nick knew he was right. Nick would either have to find him, or have Julie wrapped up in a safe house the rest of her life. His clenched jaw began to ache.

Suddenly, Matt was beside him holding the GPS monitor and pointing to the screen. Nick saw a green dot slowly blinking right to left across the LED display.

Nick tried to remember where he'd left the locater. The last time he'd seen it, Silk had planted it on the Sheriff's truck. He'd told Silk to remove the miniature locater, but he didn't remember Silk giving it back to him.

"Are you there?" Kharrazi asked.

Nick barely heard him. His mind raced. He remembered Silk's last comment. "I screw up, you gotta track this guy down and finish him off for me." Silk must have kept the device so Nick could track him. Silk had known he wouldn't come back, and in the deep recesses of his mind, so did Nick. He chewed on his lip and forced himself to keep it together. He needed to draw information from Kharrazi.

"Where is Silk now?" Nick forced out.

Nick sensed Matt go rigid with the question. Nick held up a hand to calm him.

"Precisely where I encountered him. His body is spread out a bit, though, a finger here, an ear there. I would not look with both eyes open unless you had to."

Nick cringed. His stomach went through acute spasms. He learned something, however. Kharrazi didn't have Silk with him, so it wasn't Silk who was moving across the display. Nick examined the GPS screen again and suddenly realized who he was looking at. Somehow, Silk had managed to plant the device on Kharrazi. And Kharrazi wasn't aware.

"Where are you going?" Nick asked, trembling with a mixture of fear and excitement.

"I believe I'll go visit another relative of yours. See how many pieces I can make with that corpse."

Why was Kharrazi goading him? What was Kharrazi doing wasting time like this? It was just like the balloon filled with harmless powder. Kharrazi was utilizing every minute, stalling Nick for even the tiniest delay. He was close to his escape and if Nick didn't leave soon, Kharrazi would disappear into the night like he'd done countless times before.

"By the way, how is your wife?" Kharrazi jabbed.

"Fuck you!" Nick exploded and threw the cell phone against the cement wall, shattering it into pieces as if it were glass. Matt watched. The celebration in the next room didn't skip a beat.

Nick found himself panting. He sucked in small doses of air and wiped moisture from his brow.

Matt held up the GPS device. "Who is this?"

Over Matt's shoulder, Nick saw Jennifer Steele peeking out of the doorway. Matt turned and waved for her to go back.

"No," Nick said. He gestured to Steele. "Come here."

Steele approached warily. "What's going on?"

"How familiar are you with the surrounding area?" Nick asked.

"Very," Steele said. "There's a path I take to run every morning that goes right through here."

"Good," Nick said, spreading out the satellite photos on the same end table he'd used with Silk. He opened his hand and Matt gave him the GPS device. Nick pushed a button and activated the longitude-latitude grid which sprang to life around the border of the screen. He put his finger on the photo that matched the exact plotting on the GPS screen.

"Do you know where this is, compared to where we are?" Nick asked Steele.

"Yes. It's approximately five miles from here."

"What's over there?"

Steele thought about it for a moment. "Not much. There's a dirt road that meanders through that way, but other than that—"

"Where does the road go?" Nick said, urgency in his voice.

"Who is it, Nick?" Matt said. "Who is the GPS tracking?"

Nick couldn't do what he wanted without Matt and Steele. He either came clean or spent too much time fighting their inquisitions. He looked at his partner. "Silk is dead."

"What?"

"Kharrazi killed him. Somehow Silk slipped the tracking chip on Kharrazi before he died."

Matt stared at the device. "That son of a bitch." Then a surprised smile came across his face. "We've got him. We've got the bastard. Let's get McKenna and—"

"No," Nick said. "I've got him. I'm going after him. Alone."

"The fuck you are," Matt said. "We've got an entire squad of Marines, helicopters, and FBI agents. We've got him cold."

"I sent Silk after Kharrazi and got him killed. Kharrazi is my responsibility. I need to finish this."

"You're not talking rational, partner. I'm not letting you go after Kharrazi alone. It's suicide."

Nick clenched his fists. "If you don't let me go, I might as well eat a bullet right now."

Matt grabbed Nick's shoulders and shook him. "Nick."

Nick stood firm. Every muscle flexed into a taut bulge.

Matt studied the intensity in his partner's face and sighed. "All right. I'll give you five minutes head start, then I'm sending the dogs after him. You understand? Five minutes."

Steele said nothing. She seemed grateful that Matt wasn't going with him.

Nick let out a breath, then murmured, "Thanks."

Steele placed her finger on the photo, just below a narrow streak of brown. "This is where he's going."

"What is it?" Nick asked.

"It's an old dirt airfield. Firefighters use it to fly up their gear from Phoenix. It's strategically positioned close to some danger zones this side of the mountain."

Matt looked at Nick. "He makes it there before you do, we'll lose him for sure. That GPS will only work if we're close."

Nick nodded. "I know."

"There's an unmarked road not a half mile from here," Steele said. "The trees are thick and there's barely enough room for one vehicle, but I can show you how to get ahead of him. It'll get you to the southern part of that strip. He'll be coming from the east." Steele fished the keys from her jeans pocket. "Here, take my truck. You leave right now and you'll have a chance."

"Show me," Nick said.

Nick dug out the compass from his duffle bag and hustled out to Steele's truck with her and Matt. Steele pointed to a narrow opening in the woods and gave Nick the direction he would find the unmarked trail. Nick gave Matt a quick nod, then started the truck and pulled out before anyone could change their mind. Behind him, he heard Matt say, "Five minutes."

Chapter 40

The GPS device jumped on the bench seat next to Nick as he traversed the side of the mountain in Steele's truck. He could still see Kharrazi's green dot blinking steady on the screen. Nick's headlights barely kept up as he navigated between tree trunks and heavy undergrowth. He had the nagging feeling that he was forgetting something.

Nick tore open an aluminum pouch with his teeth and slapped an adhesive microchip on the dashboard. He pushed a button on the GPS system and a second dot came to life on the display. This one was red. It allowed him to see where he was in comparison to Kharrazi. He was driving too far to the west and he steered more toward an intersecting route to the east.

The terrain seemed to leap out in front Nick, forcing him to make split-second decisions with the steering wheel in his left hand. His right hand steadied the GPS device and at one point he stuck it between his legs in order to strap on his seat belt. He looked again and realized that Kharrazi was forced to take a circuitous route because of the direction of the dirt road. Nick was literally scaling the side of the mountain with Steele's four-wheel drive. It was a riskier method, but it dramatically cut the distance to the runway.

Within a couple of miles of Kharrazi, Nick realized what he had forgotten. A plan. He was so incensed with the idea of rushing after Kharrazi that he failed to come up with a course of action.

He kept flinching at tree branches that scraped the windshield as they brushed past until he spotted the clearing for the makeshift runway. He darted the truck into the clearing and without obstructions was able to step down hard on the accelerator. He glanced down at the screen. Kharrazi was still on the road, but less then a mile away.

In the dark, Nick barely made out the silhouette of a prop plane idling at the far end of the dirt strip. He prayed Kharrazi wasn't in contact with the pilot. He was completely conspicuous with his tires spitting up loose rocks just a couple of hundred yards away.

Nick headed for the mouth of the dirt road hoping to reach it before Kharrazi emptied into the clearing. When he barreled onto the road, Nick glanced at the GPS screen. He was headed directly at Kemel Kharrazi at fifty miles an hour without the slightest idea what to do.

Nick flirted with the notion of turning off his headlights, but that would force him to slow down to a crawl. He glanced at the screen again. Kharrazi was closing fast. When he looked up, he knew he wouldn't need the device any longer. Kharrazi's headlights bounced up ahead. A large pickup truck. The lights disappeared below a ridge, then popped up a moment later with renewed intensity. No retreat in their demeanor. Even Kharrazi's headlights seemed evil.

Kharrazi had to see Nick coming and it had no affect on his velocity. He bore down on Nick like a heat-seeking missile. Suddenly, the plan became inevitable. In the game of chess you gladly lost a pawn to capture the opponent's King.

With less than fifty yards separating them, Nick's heart pumped furiously. He licked his lips and searched for an opening, but found none. They were on a collision course. Two bulls charging down a bowling lane lined with tall trees, nowhere to turn.

Kharrazi's truck flew up over a rise and seemed to gather speed. Now it was a game of chicken. Kemel Kharrazi was a shrewd, conniving terrorist with sinister desires and malevolent aspirations.

But Nick Bracco was prepared to die. He was drained and weary and welcomed the repose that death offered. He was ready to go to the other side and apologize to Silk in person.

Nick slammed his foot down on the pedal and the truck lurched forward. Kharrazi also appeared committed. The front end of his truck jerked upward from acceleration.

They were twenty yards apart, both engines screaming into the night sky. As the intensity of Kharrazi's lights blinded Nick, Julie's face flashed in front of him. She was smiling. Nick had finally put a long-awaited smile on her face.

Just before impact, Nick clutched the steering wheel with both hands, closed his eyes and pressed forward. It took a beat longer than he anticipated, then the devastating explosion of the head-on crash jolted him forward. And then there was nothing.

Nick could've been unconscious only moments, but when he came to, he was disoriented. His mouth tasted of dust and his head throbbed unmercifully. A horn was blaring relentlessly. He had trouble focusing. He was sitting upright, strapped in by his seat belt and his hands felt pinned to his lap.

It took a moment to realize that the air bag had deployed. He could taste something powdery in his teeth and shards of glass blanketed the cab, including the dashboard, which was much closer than it should have been. His side-view mirror lay cracked in his lap along with a couple of branches. That horn. He tried to move his left arm and found that to be a useless chore. With his right hand, he pushed up and moved the bag from his face.

When he tried to turn his head, he yelped involuntarily and grabbed his neck. He looked down to inspect his body, but his world went spinning and he lay his head back and shut his eyes. The horn was coming from behind him. He was confused. How did Kharrazi get behind him?

Nick opened his eyes, twisted his entire torso around to the right, and followed the sound of the horn. Where the back window used to be, a clear opening existed. Shards of remaining glass clung to the border of the aperture. Through the opening, Nick could see a truck facing into the woods, its back end still sticking out into the road. The front end encircled a massive pine, which had stood its ground against the speeding mass of the truck. Nick couldn't see anyone in the cab of the truck. He instinctively reached for his gun, even before his brain had the time to understand why.

Just before contact, Nick had shut his eyes, so he didn't see it happen, but Kharrazi must have turned at the last possible moment. Nick had continued into a large tree. He hadn't even thought about the air bag, but it certainly had saved his life. At least until Kharrazi found him.

Nick saw steam wafting upward from under the hood of Kharrazi's truck. The horn still pierced the air. He was able to unholster his gun with his right hand. His left arm and shoulder were useless. Liquid dripped down the side of his neck and when he touched it with the back of his gun hand, he came back with blood. He looked up to see himself in the rearview mirror, but it was gone. He pulled the side-view mirror from his lap and saw lacerations streaking the left side of his face. They were already beginning to coagulate down to a slow ooze.

The truck's engine was still running, but when he stepped on the accelerator, nothing happened. Everything looked real promising.

He was a sitting duck if he didn't force himself out of the truck. First he unsnapped his seat belt harness and rolled to his right onto the bench seat. His legs seemed to be working properly, so he boosted himself up and, using only his right hand, he opened the passenger side door and hobbled outside of the truck.

Nick scoured the perimeter. He didn't see or hear anything, but the truck's horn dominated the sounds of the night. He wondered if Kharrazi had purposely managed to leave the horn blaring. It would cover up any peripheral noise he might make from the woods. It was precisely the kind of thing Kharrazi would do.

Nick found himself favoring his right leg as he limped toward Kharrazi's truck. He worked his way there from a wide semicircle. Keeping his attention on the cab of the truck, he slithered between trees and undergrowth. It was an older model truck and didn't appear to have air bags. When he was even with the driver's side door, he saw something move inside the cab. An arm, or maybe a branch, moved from the other side of the cab. He stood motionless and saw it again. An arm seemed to be banging against the dashboard. No, not the dashboard, the steering column. Kharrazi was pounding his fist against the horn, trying to get it to stop. Nick watched cautiously, trying to evaluate Kharrazi's condition before approaching him.

A moment later, the horn stopped.

It left a sudden void, which was filled with an eerie silence, like just before a hurricane was about to hit. Only the hiss of the torn water hose remained. Kharrazi simply sat there, his left hand pressed up against the side of his neck. Nick thought he heard moaning, and noticed the windshield was smashed. Kharrazi didn't appear to be wearing a seat belt and there was no air bag. He must have catapulted through the windshield, then rebounded back into his seat.

Nick thought about firing a couple of rounds at Kharrazi. He was close enough. The man didn't deserve a warning. Not Kemel Kharrazi. Finish it.

Hesitation, doubt, indecision: these were all things that got FBI agents killed. Nick had to decide, then commit to the decision. Slowly, he stepped out of the woods and approached the truck. His right arm was fully extended, his left arm was limp by his side. His gun seemed yards ahead of him.

"How did you find me?" Kharrazi said, without turning his head.

"You even scratch your nose, I'll blow your head off," Nick said through clenched teeth.

Kharrazi finally turned his head and Nick got a good look at his damaged face. His right eye was swollen. Streaks of blood ran down his face like a map full of rivers marked in red. Kharrazi's left hand kept constant pressure against the side of his neck, yet blood still seeped between his fingers.

"Get your right hand up on the steering wheel," Nick closed in. When Kharrazi didn't move, Nick fired a shot directly across his face and through the broken windows of the cab of the truck. Kharrazi quickly placed his hand on the steering wheel.

"I am going to kill you, Mr. Bracco," Kharrazi's voice was raspy.

Nick had a million questions, but he was so relieved to be alive, he shivered. His teeth were actually chattering. He noticed the blood saturating Kharrazi's left shoulder. Kharrazi must have nicked his carotid artery when he went through the windshield. He needed attention soon, or he would bleed out.

Kharrazi gave Nick a deadly stare. "You have just condemned your wife to a life of fear and ultimately a painful death."

"You're going to prison for the rest of your life, Kemel."

Kharrazi seemed appalled at the accusation. "You think for one minute that I don't have the funds to acquire the best team of attorneys money can buy? You think I left fingerprints or any trails that lead back to me?"

Nick considered this for a moment. What evidence did they actually have that Kharrazi was the one who was giving the orders. Everyone in the Bureau knew it was him, but how much physical evidence did they actually have? Who in the KSF would ever turn on their leader?

Kharrazi sneered, "You don't think I can get to you from prison?"

That was the clincher. Yes, Kharrazi could reach Nick from prison. Unmistakably, unequivocally, and with little effort.

Nick wasn't about to live the rest of his life with that hanging over his head. Before he knew it, he was leaning into the cab of the truck and pressing the tip of his 9mm against Kharrazi's head.

Kharrazi didn't flinch. "You don't expect me to believe you will shoot me?"

Nick pressed hard enough to force Kharrazi's head back. "You don't think I can?"

Kharrazi's face was cool, but his eyes had difficulty leaving Nick's gun. "I have to give you credit," Kharrazi said. "You surprised me back there with the head-on move. It took a lot of courage to do what you did. But that was a spontaneous act. This is different. Now, you have a prisoner under custody. I am no longer a danger to you. You are too honest, Mr. Special Agent. You are not me. You play by the rules. Rules that I have no need to abide by. But you're not about to lower yourself because of me or anyone else."

Nick actually smiled. His face hurt when he did, so he stopped. He lowered his gun and watched Kharrazi's expression grow smug.

"That is better," Kharrazi said.

"What I'm wondering," Nick said, casual, non-threatening, an inquisitive tone.

"Why you?" Kharrazi finished for him.

"Yeah."

"Because of Rashid."

"So, revenge."

"Oh no, it is much deeper than that. Rashid was much closer than a brother. When you were able to chase him down and arrest him, I took notice. The FBI is a large, sluggish, political system that moves at a snail's pace. There is always one person that finds their way around the obstacles in a massive entity like the Bureau. You were that person. And I knew if you were clever enough to capture Rashid, you were clever enough to thwart our operation."

Nick waved his hand at the crumpled truck that enclosed Kharrazi. "Your logic was obviously flawless."

"Don't be so arrogant, Mr. Bracco," Kharrazi scoffed. "You have not even begun to see the extent of my control. There are people I can contact who would gladly finish my chores for me. Your beautiful wife will not put up with the restrictions you'll require in order to protect her. She will be more of a prisoner than I will ever be."

Nick didn't need to hear any more. He pulled his handcuffs from his belt and quickly snapped one around Kharrazi's right wrist, on the hand that was gripping the steering wheel. It took Kharrazi by surprise.

"You have a Constitutional right to remain silent," Nick said.

This seemed to relax Kharrazi. He was being arrested and it didn't appear to faze him.

Nick pulled Kharrazi's left hand from his neck and tugged it through the opening in the steering wheel, under the left side of the steering column. He then snapped it together with the handcuff on Kharrazi's right wrist before Kharrazi knew what was happening.

"What are you doing?" Kharrazi said.

Nick continued. "Anything you say may be used against you in a court of law."

Kharrazi tugged on the handcuffs. He found himself hunched over the steering wheel. Both hands were on the opposite side of the steering column, which was bent upward from the collision and tight against the dashboard. He desperately tried to get his left hand to his neck, but couldn't manage. When left exposed, the carotid artery in his neck began flowing freely. Each pulse of his heart sent a surge of blood squirting from the gash like a fireman's hose.

"You cannot do this," Kharrazi searched for a threat, a command, a plea. When he realized there was nothing left to draw from, he repeated, "You cannot."

Nick stood back and wiped his brow with his sleeve. "You're right about me, Kemel. I always go by the book. So before I call for backup, I want to make sure you understand your rights."

"I need medical attention," Kharrazi demanded.

"Did I mention your right to an attorney?"

"This is not the way you treat a prisoner," Kharrazi's voice was cracking. He tilted his head down against his left shoulder, futilely trying to slow the blood loss.

Nick folded his arms. "You asked how I found you. Do you still want to know?"

Kharrazi looked like a circus animal, hunched over, squirming. "What do you want from me?"

"I found you because a very brave man by the name of Don Silkari gave his life to plant a tracking chip on you. He was courageous. Not the type of man who would bail out in a game of chicken."

"All right," Kharrazi's voice was diminishing. "You made your point. This Silk guy was gutsy. He went down fighting. Is that what you want from me? Now get me help, like we both know you will."

Kharrazi's eyes met Nick's and right then he knew his fate. Kharrazi lifted his head and tried to look dignified, but he was fading. His mouth moved to speak, but nothing came out. In just a few seconds, Kharrazi's face was bleach white. The blood leaving the artery was down to a gurgle. His eyes lost clarity and became distant.

Nick came close and leaned into Kharrazi's ear. "You picked the wrong guy to fuck with, Kemel," he whispered.

Kharrazi turned toward Nick's voice, but couldn't possibly have seen him. His head collapsed onto the steering wheel and the horn began to blare again.

In the distance, Nick heard the thump of a helicopter's rotor. He reached into the cab, unlocked the handcuffs from Kharrazi's wrists and returned them to his belt clip. He stared at Kharrazi; a crumpled heap of flesh and bones and nothing else. Nothing that could ever threaten him or his family again. He could almost see the malevolence dissipate from Kharrazi's corpse.

"You have the right to remain silent," Nick said. "Forever."

Chapter 41

The line of parked limos stretched over the horizon down Pinewood Lane adjacent to the cemetery. In a black-clad semicircle, three hundred friends and family members stood around the casket that held Don Silkari. The casket was draped with an American flag. A priest in a dark silk robe recited nuances of distinction fit for a war hero. A distinction Silk had earned. Behind the priest were enough flowers to fill an Olympic swimming pool.

Nick stood front and center, Julie clutching his left hand, his cousin Tommy to his right. Tommy still wore a large, flesh-tone bandage across his cheek, while just a trace of gauze wrap could be detected under Julie's black hat. The remainder of the front row consisted of stern-looking men with practiced steely glares. Occasionally one of them would glance over at Sal Demenci, who stood to the right of Tommy Bracco. Sal was holding it together, but as the ceremony progressed, so did his temper. He kept looking at the priest as if he were speaking a foreign language. He'd shake his head and stare out over the casket, seeming to be searching for an answer.

As the casket was lowered into the ground, the men formed a line and one by one they dropped playing cards, dice, and other paraphernalia into the grave. The most common item dropped was a single bullet that was palmed just before it left the donor's hand to remain with Silk for eternity. Apparently, Silk's sleight of hand act was more popular than he suspected.

Matt and Jennifer Steele dropped flowers into the opening, while Julie passed by the coffin and broke down. She caught up with Silk's mother and the two of them shared a convulsive hug.

When it was his turn, Nick looked down at the box and tried to come to terms with his judgment. He felt the need to pray and purge his soul, full of remorse. It seemed like just last week they were teenagers and Silk was showing Nick and Tommy how to sneak into Pimlico Race Track from the backside stables. The three of them risking capture so they could save two bucks for the daily double. He whispered, "Forgive me, Silk."

Nick reached into his back pocket and slid out a folded copy of that day's Racing Form. He held it over the grave and was about to drop it when he felt an arm drape around his shoulder and a second

Racing Form appeared next to his. He looked up to see Tommy duplicating Nick's ritual. Tommy winked at him. They both looked down and let go of the Forms at the same time.

Tommy probably sensed Nick's composure about to get away from him, so he patted his cousin's back and encouraged him to move on and allow the line of mourners to progress.

As the ceremony wound down, the crowd spread out in different directions, heading toward their cars or limos, shaking their heads.

Matt took Julie's arm and directed her toward an open limo door where Jennifer Steele waited for her. He looked over at Nick and gave a silent nod.

Nick then nodded to Sal Demenci and the two men headed for a separate limo. A group of Sal's men fell into step behind them. As they approached the limo, a large man pulled open the back door and Sal offered Nick the honors. Nick slid down the long bench seat and watched Sal do the same directly across from him. Tommy sat next to Sal and chewed on a red toothpick. It only took a few seconds for the rest of the seats to fill up. The door closed and the silence began. Nick hadn't smoked a cigarette in fifteen years, yet he craved one right now.

Sal broke the silence. "So, how was dinner at the White House?"

"Yeah," Nick said, "it was good. Julie's still buzzing over it."

"Good, good," Sal said, his hands clasped over his stomach.

More silence.

Finally, Tommy said, "Look, Nicky, you gonna tell us what happened?"

Nick knew he should tell them the story. So he did. Everything. Even the part about him sending Silk into an ambush. When he was done, his elbows were on his knees and his head was down. He could hear Sal sigh.

"Of all people," Sal said. "You're the one."

Nick stared at his shoes.

"You're the one who insults Silk," Sal said.

Nick looked up.

Sal sat upright with his arms folded. He turned to Tommy next to him. "You buying it?"

Tommy shook his head. "Nah."

"What are you talking about?" Nick said. "Those are the facts."

Sal flipped his index finger back and forth between Tommy and Nick. "You two grew up the Three Musketeers with Silk. Was there ever a time one of you pulled the wool over Silk's eyes? Ever?"

Nick made eye contact with his cousin. Without either of them saying a word, Sal had made his point.

Sal leaned forward now and was only inches from Nick's face. "I'm gonna tell you something, Silk not only knew it was an ambush, he walked into the damn thing just awkward enough to be taken lightly. If he didn't, that Kharrazi character would've picked him off with a night scope and Silk wouldn't be able to plant that chip thing. He knew exactly what the fuck he was doing."

Sal leaned back to murmurs of support from his crew.

"C'mon, Nicky," Tommy said, disappointed. "You know better than that, huh?"

Nick was beginning to understand it now. If Silk was simply ambushed, it makes him look slow, which is not exactly how these guys want him remembered. Neither did Nick.

"There is one other thing," Nick said, and he went on to tell them Silk's last words, that Nick should track Kharrazi down if he screwed up.

This opened up a chorus of, "See that?" and "Exactly what Sal's trying to say."

Nick was actually beginning to feel better. This was worth twenty sessions with Dr. Morgan. He was at Silk's funeral and was finding himself almost happy. Talking with Sal was practically cathartic. Why did he suddenly feel so blissful? Maybe it was the relief of confessing his sins. Maybe it was the document he had tucked in his jacket pocket. Maybe it was the fact that they were right. Silk could be many things, but slow wasn't one of them.

"Does your boss know you're telling us all of this?" Tommy said.

"I don't have a boss right now," Nick said. "I resigned from the Bureau yesterday."

"You shittin' me?" Tommy said.

"Nope."

"What're you gonna do?"

"I'm looking for a place up in the mountains. I think Julie and I are going to take it easy for a while. Get rid of some stress."

"Good for you," Sal said. "I always thought you were wound up a little tight. You're doing the right thing." He paused and thought for a moment. "So, we all square with the Feds?" He looked out the window at Silk's grave, "I mean, we pay enough of a price for them?"

Nick glanced at each man, one by one. When he got to Sal, he said, "You overpaid."

"Ain't that the truth," Sal grunted.

Nick reached into his inside jacket pocket and came out with a black leather case. It was a document holder the size of a large checkbook. The case gleamed in his hand and Nick could smell the fresh leather.

"What ya got there?" Tommy pointed his toothpick.

Nick handed the leather case to Sal, then watched.

Sal's face brightened as he reviewed the document inside.

Nick waited to let the concept sink in before he hit him with it. Finally, after a minute, Sal looked up at Nick. "What does this mean exactly?"

"It means you've been selected to be an Honorary Consulate of the United States of America."

Sal smiled and held up the shiny leather case to give everyone a good look. When they were all done gawking at the official document inside, Sal looked back at Nick, "Okay? What exactly does a, uh, Consulate do?"

"Well, technically, he would look after American commercial interests in foreign countries."

"American commercial interests? What the fuck's that mean?"

"Well, Sal," Nick said, "you're a successful businessman. We need someone with your talent to help grow your industry throughout the world."

Sal's eyebrows furrowed. "But I run an exterminating business."

"That's right," Nick said. "It's precisely the type of business we need to export. We need a good exterminator."

Sal tapped the case against his leg and gave Nick a skeptical glare. "You need an exterminator?"

Nick nodded, giving nothing away.

Sal looked like the tumblers were falling into place as understanding crossed his face. "You said, technically I look after these interests? What about untechnically?"

Nick grinned. Silk wasn't the only one who could smell an ambush. "Well, untechnically, you would report to a Victor Pedroza in the U.S. Embassy in Amman, Jordan."

"Jordan? What the fuck—"

Nick held up his hand. "Hold on, Sal. Before you get all bent out of shape, let me explain."

Sal leaned back and folded his arms across his chest.

"Only if you're willing," Nick continued, "Victor Pedroza will be your contact at the embassy. Pedroza is a twenty-year veteran of the CIA. He will furnish you with classified papers and photos of the world's most powerful terrorists and their current whereabouts. Leaders of Hamas, al-Qaeda, Hezbollah. Your expertise will help eradicate these leaders."

Sal lifted an eyebrow. "I see." He studied Nick for a moment and said. "If they know where these guys are, how come they need us? And how come it took so long to find . . . uh, what's his name?"

"We always know where they are, Sal. Sometimes it benefits us to watch who comes and goes more than it does to take the guy out. Then there are times when we don't have enough evidence to arrest, yet we know what they're up to. We use wiretaps, satellite photos, stuff that sometimes doesn't hold up too well in court. We need someone to, well, let's say, we need someone to take care of certain projects behind the scenes."

Sal nodded, thinking about the idea. "If we always know what they're up to, then what happened on September 11th?"

Nick sighed. "Yeah, well, that's when the gloves came off and all of this satellite communications stuff became routine. We've been infiltrating their networks ever since. And as far as Kharrazi goes, the CIA had the goods on him, but egos got in the way."

"Ain't that always the case," Tommy said.

Nick rubbed the side of his face. "Look, there's going to be mistakes made. That can't be avoided. But we can diminish their abilities dramatically. You only have to go over there a couple of times a year." Nick looked around at the rest of Sal's crew. "You'll need to find some staff members to take with you."

Sal sat still a moment, then unfolded his arms and slapped his knees. "Damn. So the government actually wants us to go whack these assholes?"

Nick winced. "Let's just say, the United States Government doesn't mourn the loss of terrorists. And they're willing to pay handsomely to expedite their demise."

"What happens if we get caught?"

Nick nodded again, ready for the question. "When a terrorist is killed, the CIA becomes the lead investigator. They will work with the local authorities and confiscate any evidence left behind. This evidence has a way of getting buried. As long as the incident isn't filmed by the media, it's a safe bet that the killer will never be caught. The CIA will guarantee that."

"They can do all that?"

Nick grinned. "Sal, if the CIA wants to, they can always find a way to gain jurisdiction. Once they have jurisdiction, they control every- thing. And I mean everything."

Sal seemed satisfied with that.

Nick thought about something Kharrazi told him just before he bled out. "The United States has been forced to play by the rules when it came to terrorism, yet the terrorists don't have those restrictions. Up until now it hasn't been a fair fight." Nick pointed to the document in Sal's hand. "We've just evened up the odds."

Sal lifted a brown cigar from his jacket pocket and played with it. "I don't know." He pointed the cigar at Nick, "How do you figure in all of this?"

"I'm simply the liaison for the State Department. Just an ex-FBI agent making decisions on my own. There'll be no footprints to follow back to the White House." Nick hunched over and looked up at the crew as if he were a quarterback in the middle of a huddle. "Everyone in this car is an American. It's time we show these assholes how to play the game. We've always had the technology, now we have the muscle to back it."

Nick could feel the testosterone level elevate around him as he spoke. He pressed down a bandage that was coming loose from his sweating forehead. He spoke, not as an ex-FBI agent, or Tommy Brac- co's cousin, but as a salesman trying to close the deal. He'd spent too many sleepless nights worried about the things he couldn't do because of the law, or because of his moral obligation to follow the Constitu- tion. Nick had turned the corner and he wasn't ever going back.

He noticed Sal absently finger his cigar as he concentrated fully on Nick.

Nick said, "It's time we go after the leaders of these groups. We sort of take all the fun out of being the boss. It disrupts their plans and lowers the quality of leader they choose. After a while, they're doing more fighting among themselves than anything else."

Sal stopped playing with the cigar. He put it back in his jacket pocket, leaned over and rubbed his hands together. "What kind of protection we get?"

"The best," Nick said. He looked straight at Sal and said. "Look at me, Sal. What do you see?"

Sal appeared leery of the question and didn't say anything. "I'll tell you what you see," Nick said. "You see a man who's just lost a close friend, and who isn't about to take unnecessary chances with any more of his friends. You also see a man of Sicilian heritage who's proud to be an American and who's not afraid to make right some injustices that have been inflicted upon us. Now, does that remind you of anyone else in this car?"

It started slowly, but the corners of Sal's lips quivered upward and kept going until it was a full-grown smile. This, of course, became contagious and a few moments later every man in the limo was smiling. Sal began to chuckle and the background chucklers filled in behind him. Now the whole car was a symphony of laughter, with Sal gently slapping Nick's cheek. "You're good, Nicky. You are really good."

* * *

Nick slid into the limo next to Julie and across from Matt and Steele. The four of them rode in silence as the vehicle pulled away from the gravesite. Nick glanced at Matt and gave him an imperceptible nod.

Steele had a tissue up against her nose as she gazed out the window. Julie focused on the ball of tissues in her hands. Nick couldn't remove the smile from his face. Matt ignored it, but Steele sat cross-legged in a knee length black dress and took notice of Nick's behavior.

"Something funny?" she said.

Julie turned and saw a straight-faced Nick say, "What?"

Matt covered for him as he always would. He looked out at the opening in the overcast sky. "Looks like it might be clearing up out there."

Julie must have seen the contentment return to Nick's expression. She touched his face. "You okay?" she whispered.

Nick nuzzled her ear. "I'm fine." He turned her chin to face him, their foreheads pressed together. "We're fine."

Julie smiled, then dug her face into Nick's shoulder and let it all come out until Nick could feel the moisture make it through his jacket to his shirt. From the corner of his eye he saw Matt put his arm around Steele and watched her fall perfectly into Matt's hold, like two pieces of a puzzle reuniting for the first time since leaving the box.

Nick met Matt's eyes. A partnership that needed no words.

Nick's smile lingered. He looked out the window. "It does look like it's clearing up, doesn't it?"

Epilogue

Six months later

A couple of puffy white clouds looked lonely crossing the expansive Arizona sky. Beneath them, a spring breeze tickled the tops of the Ponderosa pines that surrounded a small fishing lake. At the east end of the lake, Nick and Julie gently rocked on the porch swing. From their wooden deck they could take in the entire scene. Nick was reading the Sunday edition of the Arizona Republic while Julie worked a pair of knitting needles around a spread of yarn on her lap.

"Here come the neighbors," Julie said.

Nick looked up from the paper and had to squint from the reflection of sunlight glaring off the lake. He saw two figures emerge from a path in the woods just north of the lake. Matt McColm and Jennifer Steele furiously pumped the pedals of their lightweight bicycles toward the Bracco's A-frame. Their momentum guided them up the slope of grass that separated the Bracco's home from the lake itself. They stopped in front of the porch, straddled their bikes, and took long swigs from their bottled water. They both wore shorts and tee-shirts, which were marked with small patches of sweat. Matt slid his water bottle into the carrier below his seat and peered over the wooden railing that surrounded the deck, "Howdy, Sheriff."

Nick rolled his eyes. "You'd be Sheriff too if the President flew into Payson to campaign for you a week before the election."

Matt shook his head and smiled. "Sheriff Bracco."

"He never gets tired of saying that," Steele said, wiping her forehead with the back of her hand.

"I never do," Matt agreed.

"Well, I love it," Julie said. "It sure beats, 'We were shot at today, Jule, but don't worry, they missed us again.'"

Steele laughed. Nick and Matt shrugged, as if they hadn't a clue what she was talking about.

"You guys staying for coffee?" Nick said.

"Naw," Matt said. "I've got to get back and shower. I'm on call today."

"On call?" Nick scoffed. "Exactly what does 'on call' mean to a resident agent in Payson—on a Sunday? You waiting for someone to pull a gun on an ATM machine?"

"Very funny, Sheriff." Matt pointed to a couple of teenagers in an aluminum rowboat fishing the far end of the lake. "I suppose you're spying on the Chandler boys, waiting for them to exceed their limit. That would be a big catch for you, wouldn't it?"

"Listen to you two," Steele said. "Both of you bellyaching over the lack of stress in your jobs. Do you really miss the action that much?"

"A little machismo never hurt anyone," Matt said.

Now it was Julie's turn to roll her eyes. She looked at Steele who was still breathing heavy from the bike ride. "How far did you go?"

"Forty miles." She gestured to Julie, "You should come with us sometime."

Julie smiled. "I think I will."

Matt pointed to the newspaper in Nick's lap. "Too bad about Mustafa, huh?"

Julie gave Nick a suspicious glance. "Mustafa?"

Nick handed a section of the paper to Julie and tapped a particular article listed under 'World Events.' Julie scanned the story. "Small caliber shot to the back of the head," she said. "Almost sounds like a Mafia hit."

Nick and Matt were quiet.

Steele cocked her head. "What do you two characters know about it?"

"Just what I read in the paper," Matt said.

"Ditto," Nick said, opening the comics. "There's too much violence in the world."

While still reading the article, Julie added, "It says that Mustafa was the fifth member of the FBI's top-ten list to be murdered in the past five months."

Matt leaned over and felt the pressure in his tires.

Nick held up the comics and laughed. "That Dilbert just kills me."

Julie finished the story and put the paper down. She looked over at Nick who was pretending to be fascinated with the entire section of animated cartoons. She shook her head. "You can take the boy out of the FBI, but you can't take the FBI out of the boy."

"Amen," Steele said, watching Matt hop on his bike seat and begin pedaling down the hill.

"We'll see you guys later," he said.

"Yeah, thanks," Nick said sardonically.

Steele glanced over her shoulder as she pulled away. "Was he always this helpful when he was your partner?"

"Worse," Nick said, waving her off.

As they watched the two resident agents ride away, Julie said, "I like her."

"So do I."

Julie picked up Nick's coffee mug and headed inside. "Another cup?"

"Why not?"

A few minutes later Julie returned and placed Nick's coffee mug on the railing. She sat down next to him, picked up her knitting needles and regained a familiar rhythm. Nick reached over and grabbed the business section of the paper.

Julie gazed at the majestic setting before them and sighed. "It's so pretty up here, isn't it?"

"It sure is."

"A beautiful place to raise children."

"You bet."

"Do you remember telling me that you would build a swing set in the yard when we had kids?"

"I do," Nick said, turning a page.

"How long does it take for you to build something like that?"

Nick snapped the paper shut and turned to see Julie working her knitting needles with a sly grin.

"Why?" he asked.

"Because," she reached into her pocket and held up a square, white cuvette. In the center of the cuvette was the universal plus sign for positive. "You've got approximately seven months to finish the job."

Nick's smile was instant and genuine. He pulled Julie into a warm hug and the two of them melted into each other's arms. Their dreams mingled together like the sheets and blanket of an infant's crib.

Nick took in a deep breath as they rocked back and forth. All those years of silence built up inside of him. He whispered, "I lov—"

"I know," Julie said, clutching Nick with all of her might. "I've always known."

The End

Gary Ponzo's sequel to *A Touch of Deceit* is now available. Read the first chapter of *A Touch of Revenge* on the next page.

A TOUCH OF REVENGE

The bullet left the sniper's rifle at 3,000 feet per second. Unfortunately, Nick Bracco didn't hear the shot until it was too late. He was sitting on his back porch, staring at a pregnancy test his wife had just handed him. It was positive. After eight long years their dream of raising a child was about to come true.

Those plans were made long before the sniper's bullet made it halfway across the small, calm lake sitting in their backyard. It was the same lake that lured them into buying the mature cabin. After years of city living they'd decided to move to northern Arizona and breathe the mountain air.

As the bullet cleared the lake, Nick was focusing on the positive line of the pregnancy test and imagining what it would be like to be a father. Until recently he'd never allowed himself the luxury of relishing the concept. As the head of the FBI's terrorist task force he wasn't sure he'd even survive long enough. Now, though, he beamed with pride. Nick had complied with his wife's desires to get out of harm's way. He left the Bureau to become a small town sheriff and raise a family. The happy couple had reached the pinnacle of their dreams.

That's when the bullet hit him in the chest.

* * *

FBI Agent Matt McColm heard the gunshot from a mile away. Before his new partner and girlfriend, Jennifer Steele, knew which direction it came from, Matt knew it was a Remington 700 sniper rifle. He also knew the target.

"Hunters?" Steele asked.

"That's no hunter," Matt said. They were heading down a dirt path on mountain bikes. He twisted his bike around and hustled down the narrow trail toward the source of the shot.

"How do you know?" Steele pumped her legs hard to keep up.

Matt wanted to say, "Because I've been dreading this day." Instead, he pointed to an opening to the right while he veered left. "Go back to the Bracco's cabin," he said. "And call for an ambulance."

Her tires spewed dirt as she sped away.

Matt pulled up on the handlebars and forced his torso down into a rhythm with the stride of his long legs. As he passed the lake to his right, Julie Bracco's wail carried over the water like a wounded animal. There were no trees to buffer the helplessness of her howl. Matt knew Steele was qualified to handle the situation at the cabin. Nick Bracco was probably dead and the thought made him pump even harder. His job now was pure revenge.

Matt realized he could be heading into a sniper's lair, but he banked on the sniper retreating. Adrenalin surged through his bloodstream as he dodged low-hanging limbs and made hairpin turns on the sliver of dirt between the pines. He put the shot at five-hundred yards to Nick's cabin. There was very little wind. Good shooting weather. From that distance, a sniper should get within five inches. The average human head is ten inches. Matt prayed it wasn't a head shot.

As he flew over a rise in the path, gunshots exploded all around him. He dove from the bike and slammed headfirst into a pine tree. When he opened his eyes, he was staring straight up into a fuzzy group of treetops. As his vision cleared, he touched his forehead and felt a knot growing already. His fingers came back gooey red. That's when his Special Forces training kicked in. He took deep breaths and tried to sort things out. There were three shots. Four including the shot at Nick. The full magazine of a Remington 700. The sniper had to be reloading.

The sniper had been impetuous and it was the only reason Matt was still breathing. You don't unload your weapon on a moving target unless it's moving out of range. If the sniper were experienced, he would have used one shot to immobilize Matt, then the other two to finish him off.

Matt rolled to his side and crawled behind a tree. He knew more about a Remington 700 than anyone on the planet. After all, he was the FBI's current sharp-shooting champion. The sniper was using the 7mm Magnum bullet instead of the .308 caliber. There was a distinct difference in the sound, which is how he knew the sniper had only four bullets. The .308 caliber held five. The sniper didn't know about his expertise and Matt was prepared to take full advantage of his ignorance.

Matt pulled his Slimline Glock from the holster under his tee-shirt. Fully loaded, it held twenty rounds. "I'm all in," he whispered.

A shot blasted just under his right foot and ricocheted over his shoe. Matt quickly tucked in his thin frame and moved farther left with his back to the tree. He ripped off his bright orange shirt. It was worn to stand out for hunters, not snipers.

A second shot blew away the side of the tree spraying shards of wood across his face. Matt spit out wood fragments and readjusted his position. The shooter was close, inside a hundred yards. The sound of the bullets breaking the sound barrier echoed throughout the forest and brought a creepy urban feel to an otherwise serene mountainside.

Matt knew more than just the weapon the sniper was using, he knew the organization he belonged to as well. Matt and Nick had chased terrorists for a decade with the Bureau. During their final mission together, Nick had finished off the leader of the Kurdish Security Force. Matt had always feared someone from the KSF would go after Nick, even after he'd resigned and became sheriff of the Arizona mountain community.

Now, Matt waited behind a pine tree and counted bullets. He needed to use the sniper's impatience against him. He grabbed his shirt and quickly stuffed it with loose leaves and pine needles, then tied the bottom into a knot.

A third shot whizzed past. Close. The one vulnerability of a sniper was the need to be somewhat exposed. The barrel of the rifle needed a clear path to its target. This meant the sniper wouldn't be behind a tree or a rock. He would be flat on his stomach with camouflage as the main source of cover.

The fourth shot came dangerously close. It cracked off a large branch above Matt's head that swung down into his face. Matt deflected the limb, then snapped off a thin piece of the branch and jabbed it into the sleeve opening of his stuffed shirt. He worked on his breathing while he waited for the sniper to reload. He actually heard the bullets clip into the bolt-action rifle.

Matt gripped his Glock with his right hand and swung the stuffed shirt out into the open, quickly, before a trained eye could determine the dupe. It worked. Four quick shots blew apart the shirt full of leaves. He saw the muzzle flashes under a canopy of bushes just fifty yards away. For someone with Matt's skills, the shooter might as well have hung a neon sign around his neck.

Matt jumped up, pointed the Glock at his target and fired once. That's all he needed. The barrel of the rifle flipped upward on its bipod and remained still. Matt charged up the hill toward the sniper's den. He was sweaty and shirtless and anxious to see the son-of-a-bitch who murdered his ex-partner. Julie's cries still haunted the forest as he scrambled the last few steps, his Glock out in front of him. Matt kicked away the brush and pulled off the layers of branches that covered the sniper. He tugged on the shooter's shirtsleeve and rolled over his limp frame. Then he froze.

"Rami," he gasped.

Afran Rami moaned and squeezed both of his hands over the entrance wound just below his heart. His shirt was already saturated with blood. He didn't have long.

Matt's mouth went dry. "Where is he, Rami?"

"He'll find you first." Rami tried to grin, but failed.

"Where?" Matt asked again, but it was too late. A pair of dead eyes stared up at him while an ambulance siren wailed in the distance. Matt turned and saw the open view the kid had of the Bracco's front porch. Nick was down behind the wooden railing and Julie was hunched over him, moving with frantic urgency.

It was starting all over again. Nick had thought the move to Payson was the answer, but he was wrong. Terrorism doesn't have a neighborhood. You can't just move away. There are simply hot targets and cold targets. And Nick and Matt were hot targets.

The ambulance screeched to a stop next to the cabin. Two men flew out the doors and ran to the porch with their black bags. The flashing red and white lights seemed out of place at the edge of the lake. They belonged back in Baltimore, swirling against row houses and illuminating darkened alleys.

Matt took a long look down at Rami's corpse. For the first time in his career he'd lamented his marksmanship. He wanted to keep the terrorist alive, just so the warrior could see Matt capture his new leader.

The familiar squeak of a mountain bike's suspension came rushing up the path behind him. Jennifer Steele jumped off her bike and wrapped her arms around his bare torso.

"Are you okay?" Steele asked.

Matt gave her a gentle squeeze. "I'm all right."

Steele pulled away and examined his banged-up face. "That's a relative term."

Matt wiped his forehead and came back with bloody fingers. He'd been going so hard, the adrenalin had disguised the pain.

She looked past him at the corpse. "Who is he?"

Matt looked down. "Afran Rami."

"He's with the KSF?"

"Yeah," Matt said. "Temir Barzani's nephew. Barzani probably offered him the opportunity to kill Nick."

"You mean try to kill Nick."

Matt snapped his head to face her. Steele's wobbly smile said it all. She pointed to a spot between her left shoulder and her left breast. A spot where no major organs resided. A survivable spot, even from a 7mm Magnum.

"He's alive?" Matt said.

Steele shrugged. "You don't want to see the exit wound, but he's going to make it."

Matt thought for a moment. "I need to see him."

"I'm sure he's on his way to the hospital by now."

Matt nodded absently, trying to figure out the best way to proceed. Without Nick by his side, he was at a momentary standstill.

Steele tilted her head. "What are you thinking?"

"Did Nick say anything?"

"Yes," she said. "He was in shock, but he urged me to get to you. He wanted you to know that it wasn't a pro. Otherwise, he said, he'd be dead already."

"What else?"

Steele shook her head. "He's lying there practically bleeding out and he's telling me to go back and help you. Like I need incentive."

She turned sad and Matt gathered her in his arms. "It's all right," he said.

She dug her face into his neck and sighed. They stood there embracing for a moment, letting their heartbeats settle into a steady rhythm.

Then Steele said, "It's just starting, isn't it?"

Matt smoothed her hair and never even considered lying. "Yes."

"How well do you know Barzani?"

"Well."

"Are you better than him?"

"Yes."

They clung to each other, sorting things out in their heads. Finally, Steele pulled back and said, "You can't kill every terrorist in the world, you know."

Matt smiled. He leaned down and kissed her on the forehead. "I'll try to remember that."

Made in the USA
Lexington, KY
28 May 2017